THE WORLD THAT WAS

JAY PELCHEN

Make history !!!

THE WORLD THAT WAS

ISBN 978-0-6458509-0-1 (Paperback)

ISBN 978-0-6458509-1-8 (Hardcover)

ISBN 978-0-6458509-2-5 (eBook)

ISBN 978-0-6458509-3-2 (Early Adopter's Edition)

First Edition, published by StoryPlot Studios in 2024

Printed by Book Printing UK in Great Britain

Cover designed using Midjourney, DALL-E and Canva

www.the-world-that-was.com

THE WORLD THAT WAS

JAY PELCHEN

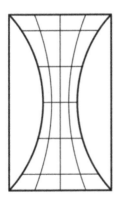

For my grandparents

*You instilled in me a love for reading and history,
technology and learning.*

You kindled a thirst to improve and a yearning to create.

For these gifts, I am forever thankful.

This book explores the realities of a journey back in time.

We live in an age where issues of gender, race and sexuality are increasingly understood but there is always room to improve.

Please be aware that this book contains scenes that may be distressing for some readers, including **sexual assault** and **domestic violence**.

These scenes show that the lessons we could teach to the past go far beyond fancy technology or advanced medicine.

We have come a long way as a society too.

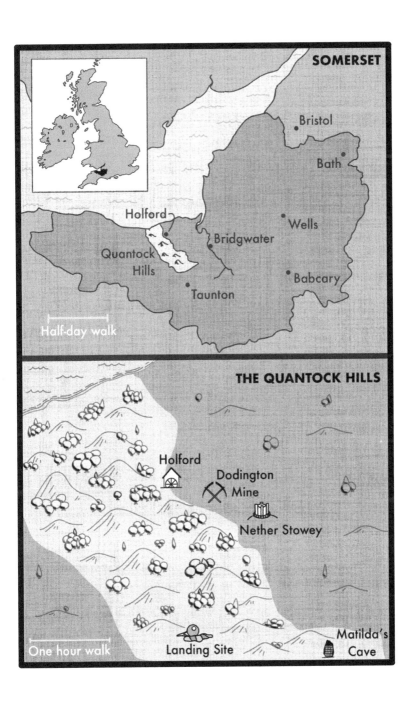

SOMERSET

Bristol

Bath

Holford

Wells

Quantock
Hills

Bridgwater

Babcary

Taunton

Half-day walk

THE QUANTOCK HILLS

Holford

Dodington
Mine

Nether Stowey

Landing Site

Matilda's
Cave

One hour walk

Sam's T-Mach

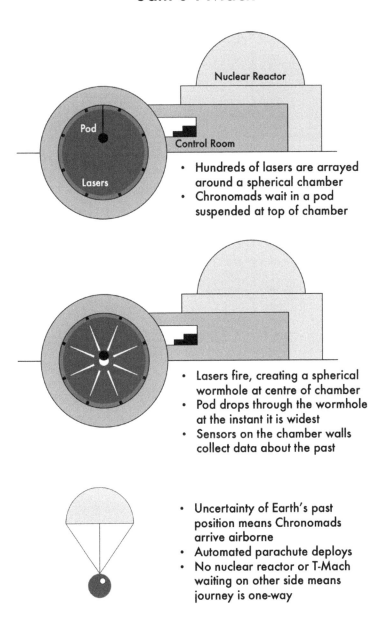

- Hundreds of lasers are arrayed around a spherical chamber
- Chronomads wait in a pod suspended at top of chamber

- Lasers fire, creating a spherical wormhole at centre of chamber
- Pod drops through the wormhole at the instant it is widest
- Sensors on the chamber walls collect data about the past

- Uncertainty of Earth's past position means Chronomads arrive airborne
- Automated parachute deploys
- No nuclear reactor or T-Mach waiting on other side means journey is one-way

PROLOGUE
3 July 2025

The Sun blazed bright against the black emptiness of space.

Charged particles raged deep beneath its surface to fuel the celestial furnace, just as they had for millennia. But something unnatural disrupted their age-old procession and the particles felt the tug of an outside force. It was slight, but enough to disturb paths that had been predetermined for aeons. Ever obedient to Nature's laws, the particles surged along their new trajectory and began a long journey.

Towards Earth.

Few knew that anything was awry until their phones stopped working. Freed from technology's tight grip, people looked up from their devices and craned their necks to marvel as ribbons of light streamed across the sky.

The Sun had spewed large flares before but this one was on another scale. And cast directly into Earth's orbit. It far surpassed the Carrington Event, an 1859 solar flare so strong that disconnected telegraph lines powered up and goldminers resumed their toil in the middle of the night, thinking it was morning.

What came to be known as the Long Day was just as intense, but longer. Auroras streaked across the sky for fourteen hours. Night became day and nowhere on the planet was untouched.

Although initially alluring, the solar flare devastated the delicate web of silicon chips around which humanity had built its civilisation. Cars and phones. Power grids and pacemakers. In mere hours, the entire intricate web was fried by electrical currents induced by the storm raging in the magnetosphere above.

An unnerving silence descended across the planet.

The full impact only became apparent when the auroras faded. Families tried in vain to contact their loved ones and immobilised vehicles clogged arterial roads, obstructing the endless stream of food required to feed cities' bulging populations.

Anarchy erupted as overwhelmed governments struggled to coordinate relief efforts, battling against others who sought to leverage the calamity for their own selfish ends. Food and medicines ran out in days. Within weeks, all was chaos.

Hundreds of millions died across the globe.

Yet it was at the start of this period of pandemonium that a lone physicist – working with pencil and paper during a cross-country journey back home – made the biggest scientific breakthrough of all time.

Time travel.

CHAPTER ONE
10 April 2037

"This is it! Today we'll make history. By remaking it!"

The control room burst into a flurry of crisp white lab coats and military uniforms as Institute scientists enthusiastically broke from the huddle around their dear leader and rushed to finish preparations for their historic undertaking. The air was electric, buzzing with the business-like babble of engineers and the hum of charging capacitors.

It was all too much for David, a simple history teacher in a sea of brilliant technical minds. He extracted himself from the fray and slunk into the comfort of the background.

He was drawn to the yellow-tinted window at the front of the control room and stared down into the Time Machine's enormous spherical cavern, watching as a crane lowered a large steel ball into position.

The final precious piece.

A pair of David's students sat cramped within the reinforced pod. Harry and Matilda. Teaching them had been the highlight of David's career and each was wise beyond their twenty-two years. They were the bravest people David had ever met, for they were about to leave. Forever.

They were Chronomad One and Two. Humanity's first time-travellers.

History's greatest scientific achievement – a technologically plausible theory of time travel – had been discovered in the ashes of its most devastating calamity.

The Long Day.

Memories of the carnage flashed through David's mind. Brilliantly colourful auroras streaming across the sky. Blank phone screens. Empty plates. Long forgotten illnesses. Violent gangs roaming the suddenly lawless land. The death toll was catastrophic, easily orders of magnitude greater than any famine or plague.

But a decade later, civilisation was mostly restored. And if his students' journey to the past succeeded, some parallel version of humanity would never need to experience its greatest tragedy.

David recognised a distinct voice amongst the control room chaos and turned to watch his childhood friend, the most brilliant physicist of the age, darting around to confirm that everything remained in place. The Institute's tireless leader caught David's gaze and angled towards the yellow window.

"The capacitors are almost charged and the vacuum is nearly ready," Sam updated upon arrival. "Let's see if this was all worth it."

"You're sure you got your calculations right?" David jibed.

Sam elbowed David in the ribs. "Of course they're correct! The military wouldn't fund all this if everything wasn't up to scratch. I just wish they'd given us a little more time. Ironic really. But for the real question, are you certain these two are the right ones for my inaugural Drop?"

Sam's playful riposte hit a nerve. David had grappled with the question for years.

Matilda and Harry were just one team from an entire cohort of budding time travellers. Chronomads as Sam had taken to calling them.

As headmaster of the Institute for Temporal Relocation, David had identified fertile periods of history – times of social or scientific growth that preceded great upheaval – and trained his students in everything they might need to journey back to their allocated period. Science and medicine. Economics and politics. Even ancient languages and music.

The Chronomads became Jacks and Jills of all trades and each was tasked with imparting their knowledge on the past to kickstart an early Renaissance in their new timeline. With technological understanding growing exponentially, the early introduction of modern scientific concepts meant that a future civilisation could be much better equipped when the Long Day's solar storm inevitably struck.

Chronomads were initially planned to be sent into the past alone as the fledgling wormhole technology meant space was the key limitation for each mission. However, by restricting their possessions and reducing safety margins, David had eventually succeeded in postponing the departures until two-person teams could be sent.

The Institute's military sponsors hadn't been happy with the delay – some unnamed bogeyman state was perpetually 'just about to catch up' – but they begrudgingly agreed when David pointed out that pairs of Chronomads would provide redundancy and greatly increase the chance of success.

The Chronomad candidates were hastily reorganised into pairs that best matched in period and region. The pairs were gender-mixed to maximise potential societal engagement in the past and, while remaining amicable, Matilda and Harry appeared to have avoided the…romantic entanglements that had plagued other pairs. But while Harry remained the Chronomad program's posterchild, equal parts charismatic and knowledgeable, Matilda's brilliance had paled in comparison and she wilted in his shadow.

Even so, they were David's leading pair and the Institute scientists had lobbied for Matilda and Harry to be Chronomads One and Two, arguing that the relative spatial and temporal proximity of their planned destination – medieval England – would be the simplest to tune with their fledgling Time Machine.

The machine was still in development and could only open a small portal. For a split second. Just long enough to send Matilda and Harry back to the past. And without another enormous Time Machine and its accompanying nuclear reactor waiting for them in the past, there could be no contact when the portal closed. Return was impossible.

David had performed the ethical gymnastics required to justify exiling someone from existence but still had his reservations. The Institute scientists told him that they couldn't send multiple teams back to the same destination, something about space-time ripples jeopardising an already successful Drop. So he had campaigned to postpone again, until Sam's wormhole technology matured enough to send larger teams to the same location, but a Headmaster's authority wasn't enough. His concerns had been overruled and the scientists got their way.

"They'll do just fine," David eventually replied to Sam, also reassuring himself. "Harry's my most accomplished student and they've both beaten all of our tests. Matilda's brilliant, in her own way. Provided she's got her textbook."

Sam shrugged. "Give me nuts and bolts any day. There's a right and wrong answer with this technical stuff. It's black and white. There are just too many shades of grey when you throw in the human element. It's impossible to predict. You can keep that."

The control room's productive atmosphere shattered as the door burst open and the Institute's flamboyant spokesman entered, inanely nattering away. Harry's gruff father and Matilda's distraught family trailed behind him, fresh from their final farewell. Matilda's mother clasped her young son's hand, her eyes red and puffy.

"This man is an utter idiot," David hissed to Sam as he left to intercept the spokesman. "No tact at all. These people are about to lose their children!"

David marched over to the families and gave a consoling smile. "Welcome, everyone. I trust that Harry and Matilda appreciated your company as they loaded the pod?"

Harry's father grunted and Matilda's mother wiped her eyes. David had longed to say his own final farewell but respected the need for privacy in those precious final minutes.

He brusquely dismissed the spokesman, noting the families' visible relief as the man left to prepare for the post-Drop press conference.

An engineer announced that the capacitors were fully charged.

Not long now.

David withdrew an analogue radio from his pocket, a rare piece of technology since the Long Day. "We've got enough time for one final farewell."

Phone conversations always felt impersonal, never as good as the real thing, but Matilda's mother beamed with unbridled excitement as David switched on the radio.

"Hello? Are you there? It's David. Can you hear us?"

The line went to static before the first distorted words crackled through the speaker.

"David?" came Matilda's distorted voice. "Can you hear me?"

"We sure can," David replied with a grin as Matilda's family lit up with joy. "I've got your families here and they'd love to speak with you both. Who wants to go first?"

There was a brief silence before Harry's voice chimed. "This isn't really a time for ladies first, is it? Dad and I should go first so Til can have the last goodbye."

"So chivalrous," Matilda said with a choked laugh. "Looks like you're ready for medieval life. Sounds good."

Harry's father took the radio from David and slouched over to a private corner, leaving Matilda's family looking forlorn.

Hoping to provide a distraction, David crouched to the level of Matilda's younger brother.

"Hi Richie. Have they shown you how this all works?"

The boy nodded.

"Tell me," David nudged, gesturing at the giant machine.

The boy led David to the viewing pane and pointed out the Time Machine's key features, leaving Matilda's parents to their mournful embrace.

"Tilly's going back to help the King," Richie said matter-of-factly, "to teach him medicine. And science. Those lasers in the walls will make a door to the past, right there in the middle. But after it closes, it can't open again."

Richie continued, impressing David with the level of technical detail he understood about the process. Only eight or nine, he was well advanced for his age. Just like his sister.

"And that ball just above the centre is…where Tilly is," Richie said finally with an involuntary sob.

David gave the boy's shoulder a consoling pat and returned him to his mother.

Harry was just finishing up. "…love you Faj."

"Love you too son. I never said it enough. Your mum was always better at that, bless her. You take care now."

Harry's father handed the radio to David and briskly left the room.

Making a mental note to send someone to collect him before the Drop, David handed the radio to Matilda's mother and showed her how to use the archaic device.

"Tilly? Tilly? How are you doing in there? How are you feeling?"

Static.

"I'm alright Mum. I didn't know if David's surprise would work."

Matilda's mother fought to hold back tears and savoured her daughter's final words.

Sensing her mother's mood, Matilda continued. "It's so surreal. I'm torn between excitement at doing the thing we've worked so hard for and the impossible sadness of saying goodbye to all of you.

It feels like only yesterday that I was bouncing around home in my Institute uniform, begging to leave for the new school."

Matilda's mother nodded furiously but silently broke down and handed the receiver to her husband.

"Always the excited one, Til. I've never seen a twelve-year-old so eager for homework. Channel that enthusiasm when you reach the other side. You've put in a decade of hard work and we're all so proud. Words can't describe how much we'll all miss you but it's reassuring to know you'll be out there saving the world. I'm still hoping your colleagues might work some of their sciencey magic to find you again."

Matilda started to reply but gave a sob, followed by a long static. David sometimes forgot, with all Matilda's brilliance, that she was still just a young girl forced to say farewell to her family forever.

"Thanks Dad," she eventually croaked. "I love you all so much! And hey, the Institute has some really clever people so who knows? Perhaps Richie could figure it out, he's smarter than me by far."

Little Richie's chest swelled at his sister's words and he snatched the radio from his father. "I'll do it for you Tilly! Maybe if I can get the photoms to travel faster...?"

Static, as Richie dropped the receiver in his excitement.

Matilda's strained laugh carried through the radio. "Faster photons would definitely do it. We'll be talking again in no time."

Short static.

"Hey Richie?"

"Yeah?"

"Can you promise to look after Mum and Dad for me? You're the only fun one still at home so make sure they don't get too boring. And try to eat all your vegetables. But mostly just look after Mum and Dad."

"I promise Tilly," Richie replied solemnly. "Even the mushrooms."

An engineer at the back of the room announced that ideal vacuum had been achieved. It was time.

"Sorry," David interjected as gently as possible. "We need to start the final stage of the process. Can you please say your goodbyes?"

David stepped away to give the family some semblance of privacy for their final moments, holding back until Sam shot a particularly stern look. He moved in to take the receiver offered by Matilda's grateful but distraught father.

"Hey, Matilda? Harry? It's David."

"Hi David," they replied in unison, understandably flat.

"I know you're both tired of hearing it but we really are so proud of you. You're doing something truly amazing today. You'll be in every history book and spoken of in every household. I promise."

"I'll totally hold you to that," Matilda replied sarcastically, prompting an amused scoff from Harry.

Static.

"You both go and change the world," David said. "We'll all be thinking of you."

Static.

"David?" Matilda added. "I know it's not your job. But. Could you please look after my family for me? You know, just check in on them every now and then?"

David smiled. "That was always a given Matilda. You have my word."

"Thanks, so much," Matilda choked. "For everything. You've been so much more than a teacher. For all of us."

"It's been an honour." David paused. "Matilda, we really have to say goodbye now. The vein on Sam's head is about to burst."

"Ok. Thanks again David."

"Goodbye Matilda. Good luck."

There was a final click as David turned off the radio. He gave the all clear but Sam was already barking orders. There was a final flurry of activity and then, all of a sudden, the room was silent. Tense.

David heard his heartbeat in his ears.

An engineer started the countdown. "Portal in 30."

David ran outside to collect Harry's father before hurrying back towards the yellow-tinted viewing pane.

"Ten."

A red light began to flash in the control room.

"Nine."

Matilda's mother wept silently into her husband's shoulder.

"Eight."

The cavern lights went out. A single spotlight illuminated the Chronomads' pod.

"Seven."

Sam joined David by the window.

"Six."

David looked out at the pod, hoping that Matilda and Harry could see them all watching.

"Five."

A photographer's camera let off a flash, recording the historic moment.

"Four."

Richie's head bumped against the glass.

"Three."

David's stomach churned.

"Two. Avert gaze!"

Everyone looked away from the centre of the chamber.

"One."

The room froze.

Suddenly, there was a brilliant flash of light.

David managed to look back just in time to glimpse a small sphere of bright blue sky in the centre of the cavern and the shiny pod falling into it. The sphere of sunlight vanished, leaving the Time Machine a dark and empty shell once more.

It worked!

David was struck by a conflicting mix of elation and loss.

The tense silence of the control room evaporated and there was a frenzy of activity as scientists and engineers ran their various diagnostics. Machines emitted alarms and scientists yelled out numbers.

Matilda's poor family crouched by the window in a tight huddle. An island of grief, weeping at the loss of their child and sister. Harry's father was already gone.

The cries of the scientists continued.

"O_2 and atmosphere normal."

"Capacitor temperature well within safe margins."

"Unexpected debris on the cavern floor!"

"Wormhole stability greater than anticipated."

And then Sam called out.

"Lat-long confirmed! Quantock forest. Somerset, England. Elevation two hundred and twenty-four meters."

There was a cheer from the control room.

Silence descended again before another scientist bellowed out the information they were all waiting for.

"Pulsar triangulation complete. Date confirmed. September 24, 1123."

CHAPTER TWO

24 September 1123

"Goodbye Matilda. Good luck."

Matilda switched off the radio as the finality of David's words echoed around the pod. Ever the gentleman, Harry gave a consoling smile and patted her knee. He looked ridiculous crammed into their tiny spherical pod, his head at an awkward angle against a curved strut. Wiping away tears, Matilda forced a smile and tightened her harness before staring through the pod's porthole to savour her family's silhouettes. One last time.

A light started to flash in the control room, signalling their imminent departure. Already thundering, Matilda's heart leapt into overdrive. Her sweaty palms clutched the radio to her chest. Stilling herself, she took a deep breath and waited.

Suddenly, there was a brilliant flash of light.

And then they were falling.

There was a strange feeling of being squeezed all over and a slight change in trajectory as the pod dropped through the wormhole but within several rapid heartbeats the dark interior of the time machine swapped to a sunny blue sky. Matilda looked through the porthole and glimpsed a pristine vista of golden fields and verdant mountains.

She jolted as the pod's automatic parachute deployed…only to watch in dismay as the gravity-defying fabric tangled up an instant later, flailing uselessly behind the pod.

Harry peered out the porthole then shot Matilda a panicked look. "Too fast! Come on secondary!"

The earth loomed as they continued to plummet but the pod finally lurched again as the backup parachute took hold. The floor surged upwards as they decelerated.

Matilda's stomach had only just settled back into place when the crashes started, small at first but quickly growing in intensity as the pod pinballed through the branches of a large tree. The Chronomads and their carefully packed belongings were flung around the cramped metallic ball. Matilda heard something snap.

The pod glanced off the tree's roots with a final jarring impact, sending a searing flash of pain from Matilda's left ankle. They rolled a short distance downhill before coming to a surprisingly gentle stop. Matilda felt jostled and disoriented, hanging upside down at an awkward angle. Even through the pain of her ankle, the strange feeling of compression from the wormhole lingered.

Matilda clutched at her boot but took a moment to just hang in sheer disbelief as her heart-rate finally settled.

"We did it Harry! We made it!"

Harry didn't reply. He never would again.

Unblinking eyes stared up at Matilda from a head bent at an impossible angle.

A wave of icy terror washed over Matilda and settled in the pit of her stomach.

"Harry!?" Matilda screeched.

She clawed at her harness and pried her way free, dropping amongst their jumbled belongings and rushing towards her partner.

Harry's unfocussed eyes stared upward, unmoving. Matilda checked his pulse. No sign of life.

"No," Matilda muttered in disbelief. "No way!"

She clambered over to the pod's hatch, inconveniently angled towards the ground, and wrestled it open.

Matilda emerged from the pod with all the grace of a new-born bird, a tangle of long limbs and curly red hair. She crawled awkwardly from the obstructed opening and out into Twelfth Century England, scrambling on her stomach through the mess of parachute cords.

Not wasting a second, she fought the pod into a more workable position before diving inside to clear space around Harry. Ignoring the pain from her ankle, Matilda tossed their precious possessions out onto the leafy forest floor.

When the pod was mostly empty, she leapt back inside and performed a proper medical examination.

C vertebrae fracture, probable severed phrenic nerve. He was gone.

Matilda sobbed as she closed Harry's lifeless eyes. A thought struck her a heartbeat later.

She was alone.

A fresh wave of terror hit and Matilda threw up.

She was alone. Stuck in the Past with no way to get back.

Matilda tried to gather herself but hopelessness eroded her resolve. Harry and Matilda had trained together for years, like partners in a buddy cop movie. Him the charming lead, her the scrappy problem solver. They'd prepared for scenarios where they got separated or hurt. Even situations where one of them died.

But never so soon.

Matilda allowed herself a moment to grieve, crying into Harry's chest.

It wasn't fair. He never experienced the world they'd fought so hard to visit. He never even left the pod.

The world outside the pod didn't exist. Inside, with Harry, Matilda was safe. She lay with her dead partner in mournful silence, curled up amongst their possessions until her universe stopped spinning. One final farewell embrace.

Wiping her eyes, Matilda backed outside and, as gently as possible, began to extract Harry's limp corpse. His muscular frame was heavy, easily double her weight. Each heave felt disrespectful. Excessively rough.

Harry's head lolled freely as Matilda lay him down upon a bed of decaying leaves. She stepped back and looked down at his peaceful form, almost expecting him to wake up, rub his eyes and crack some clever joke.

Matilda felt a tide of hopelessness rising once again so set about keeping busy. In a daze, she set off in search for the shovel amongst the scattered possessions. But with her first solid step, a flash of pain burst from her busted ankle.

Matilda screamed in frustration and hobbled away. From Harry's lifeless body. From the pod. From everything.

The dense forest quickly obscured the landing site and Matilda dropped to the ground. Her mind raced with implications and anxieties but it was sheer pain that eventually cut through her turmoil. With difficulty, she carefully removed her boot and examined the ankle with an expert eye. It didn't look broken but was definitely sprained.

Her loud expletive prompted several nearby birds to flee from their perches.

A solitary tear of pain and frustration rolled down Matilda's cheek as she calculated the consequences.

Harry was gone, there was nothing she could do to change that. Her ankle was injured. But their mission could still succeed.

She'd worked with Institute planners to craft a meticulous schedule for the journey to see King Henry in London, including a little extra time for potential setbacks. But Matilda couldn't travel to London with a busted ankle. It would be dangerous embarking out into the strange new world without the most basic means of escape. Without her partner. Yet waiting to recover would consume her entire buffer.

Matilda's mind was lost amidst a fog of despair. She was absentmindedly brushing herself off when suddenly, she heard it.

Nothing. Absolute silence. Complete stillness.

There had always been some form of commotion in Matilda's busy life. Her mother crashing around the kitchen, a roommate snoring, engineers arguing or teachers droning. Construction works on the T-Mach – Sam's precious Time Machine.

But now there was just silence.

Matilda strained her ears and slowly started to make out the sounds of birds and other creatures rustling in the undergrowth. The forest teemed with life.

Despite everything, Matilda took in a deep breath of the fresh forest air and soaked in the unspoilt Twelfth Century landscape around her. Undulating hills sloped down to a riverbed and trees were yellowing in the autumn sun. A tapestry of yellows, reds and greens. Dappled morning sunlight filtered through the canopy and a slight breeze made the scene shimmer.

It was glorious.

Matilda wiped her eyes and set her resolve. The Institute's psychologists had warned that the transition would be the most emotionally charged period of her journey – *little had they known* – but they'd prepared her for it.

Time to save the world…

The Chronomad picked herself up and hobbled back towards the pod. She needed a shovel.

Coming up to her waist, the giant metallic sphere was much easier to move when mostly empty. A scent of bile emanated from within.

Matilda reached inside and removed the final contents, carefully inspecting each item before arraying them on the forest floor for a final inventory. Her ankle flared with each step but she soldiered on, carefully retrieving the belongings she had tossed outside and adding them to the collection.

Harry's motionless frame loomed in the corner of her vision but the purposeful task calmed her mind.

When she was finished, Matilda's entire eclectic collection of worldly possessions was sprawled out before her. The final remnants of a now-lost world.

There was a jumble of cooking equipment, a tent, a comprehensive first aid kit, the radio, her bow and some arrows. The shovel. A change of clothes, a flint, a box of plant seeds, a hatchet. A pair of magnets, Harry's spare knife and torch, a telescope, some warm blankets, a small pack of rations, winter cloaks and a case of bottled chemicals. A cracked bottle of acetone leaked an acrid chemical scent but Matilda was relieved that the spill was mostly contained within the case and fortunately hadn't mingled with any of the more reactive reagents.

Most prized of all was Matilda's satchel, a simple leather bag stuffed with her most valuable items. Precious metals and spices, but also several sentimental personal objects. A small bottle of champagne from David. One of Richie's poorly painted toy soldiers. Her grandmother's engagement ring and a family photo.

It also contained her most priceless possession, a well-worn copy of the Institute's standard-issue Chronomad textbook. Rebound with her own embossed leather cover and filled with a decade of annotations, Matilda called it her bible. The Chronomads had been required to learn its contents by heart but its physical presence evoked a strong feeling of safety. It was rarely out of her sight.

Matilda had worked with Institute planners for months to plan and procure everything she and Harry might need for their mission and yet she remained baffled at how much could fit within the metallic sphere.

Notably absent among their possessions was a firearm. Institute planners had wanted them to bring one for self-defence but Harry had strongly declined, insisting that he and Matilda hoped to create a timeline that skipped combustible technologies wherever possible. It was only after Harry highlighted the difficulties of producing additional ammunition and Matilda demonstrated her proficiency with a bow that their Institute supervisors finally surrendered.

Matilda smiled at the memory. David had often joked about what a wilful young woman she had become, so different to the meek twelve-year-old that arrived at the Institute a decade earlier. He'd asked, only semi-rhetorically, where his teachings had gone wrong.

Matilda also had the clothes on her back. She had worked with local historians for months to design attire for Harry and herself, struggling to strike an appropriate balance between the tighter fitting finery that would convey status in King Henry's court and more conservative rural clothes that would attract less unwanted attention as they trekked to London. Each piece had been expertly crafted by the Institute's busy seamstress, from the warm fur-lined cloak down to her wonderfully supple calf-length leather boots.

Her fancy clothes hid an additional treasure, one that even the King would lust after. The Institute's parting gift was a vest of titanium chainmail, 3D-printed to her exact measurements using a remarkably fine mesh. Sam promised that it was sufficiently strong to stop an arrow while still remaining light enough to wear every day. It was an extra security in an unfamiliar world and Matilda had no intention of ever taking it off.

The thought jerked her back to the present, reminding her of the morbid task yet to be done.

Delicately shuffling amongst her possessions, Matilda collected the small shovel and pondered where to bury her companion. The enormous oak that had broken their fall was majestic but burying Harry beneath the tree that killed him would be a cruel irony.

Matilda instead spied a thicket of blackberries nestled amongst a distinctive outcrop of mossy rocks. She hobbled over to it and sunk her shovel into the decaying forest floor.

Matilda worked tirelessly, determined to create a suitable resting place for Harry. Her ankle throbbed and sweat dripped from her brow despite the frigid autumn morning. Each thrust of her shovel was an act of prayer for the partner she had lost. Her companion and confidant. Never anything more.

Hours later, the sun started to fall but Matilda pushed on through rocks and roots, refusing to stop until she had carved out a hole as deep as she was high. She hauled herself from the earthy trench and solemnly approached Harry's corpse.

The body had its own strange gravity, bending the dappled light of the landing site such that it was the only object in focus. Matilda savoured the view of Harry's peaceful form one last time. Then, with a sigh, she bent down to move him.

Matilda dragged the body as reverently as possible, lowering it down the narrow steps she had carved into the grave. She held back tears as she arranged the corpse into its final resting pose. Even amongst the bare earth, Harry looked as mighty as ever. Externally unscathed.

A fog of grief hung over Matilda as she clambered up to the landing site to gather items to adorn Harry's burial site. She placed the radio in his hands and, in lieu of a coffin, used his winter cloak as a shroud. The radio had been fried by the Drop's electromagnetic pulse but it would forever show that Harry was of another time. That he'd had things to say and people to talk to.

Matilda climbed back out and looked down into her partner's grave.

"You didn't deserve this," she choked. "You were always the best of us. Stronger, more diplomatic. But I won't fail you. Our mission will succeed. I promise."

Matilda couldn't watch as she threw the first shovels of soil into the grave. She sang Harry's favourite song as she toiled and the hole gradually filled, each shovelful smothering the reality of his demise.

Matilda's arms burned and sweat rolled down her back, making her tunic cling to her chainmail. The grave was already half full when she recalled Harry's own armoured vest, prompting another loud profanity. The chainmail was worth a fortune but she lacked both the physical and mental energy required to exhume her partner.

Images flashed through her mind. Carefully digging to avoid damaging his corpse. Delicately scraping the soil from his shroud before revealing a face already stiff with rigor mortis. Avoiding his closed eyes as she undressed him. Pulling the mail over his broken neck.

It was all too much.

After some final soul-searching, Matilda elected to leave the chainmail with Harry. The titanium vest wouldn't rust so could always be extracted later, if *truly* needed. The luxury made Harry's burial worthy of a king.

Exactly as he deserved.

Matilda worked until only a neat mound of dirt remained to give any indication of Harry's final resting place. Matilda vowed to someday erect a headstone but forced her mind onto her next task – finding out exactly when and where she had landed.

She couldn't calculate the precise date until the stars emerged but the nearby hill would provide a vantage point to survey the surrounding lands. Matilda knew that keeping busy would stop her mind from dwelling on the enormity of the past hours.

She looked back at the landing site and considered the safety of her belongings but laughed at the absurdity. The forest was pristine, entirely untouched by humans. Excluding the grave, the giant metal sphere and the broken branches hanging from a nearby tree, of course. Matilda judged it was safe to leave her belongings scattered across the forest floor. It was unlikely that anyone would stumble across them in the short time she was gone and forest critters would find them an unsatisfying snack.

Away from the mournful landing site, Matilda marvelled at the sheer beauty of the forest and its lack of human contact as she struggled uphill. Despite being almost a thousand years younger, this forest felt much older than any she'd explored during her adolescence. Thick gnarled trees stood where they had for centuries. By Matilda's time, anything that ancient had been harvested for timber or firewood.

A particularly large oak awaited Matilda at the crest of the hill. It looked perfect for climbing, if her ankle weren't busted. Still, the hill provided a decent vantage point for inspecting the surrounding landscape and Matilda circled the tree in awe. She could see for miles and marvelled at the pristine Somerset landscape. The only indications of human occupation were a patchwork of cultivated fields and wispy pillars of smoke rising from scattered villages.

The T-Mach and its giant reactor buildings were conspicuously absent as she scanned the horizon, providing the clearest evidence that she had actually travelled back in time. Matilda's father had been a doctor at the Hinkley nuclear reactor so Matilda had grown up nearby, allowing her to learn more about the region and its history than even her Institute teachers.

Matilda was relieved to recognise several landmarks from her own time: mountains, rivers and even a hint of coastline off in the distance. When she'd found her bearings, even the pillars of smoke corresponded with familiar villages.

Matilda suddenly longed to get moving. She needed somewhere more permanent to store her pod and bulkier belongings. The Institute had recommended burying them – hence the shovel – but Matilda's family had explored a nearby cave during hikes back in the future which could double as a base camp while her ankle recovered. She plotted a mental course from the landing site and hobbled back downhill, collecting wildflowers for Harry as she went.

After laying the flowers upon Harry's grave, Matilda quickly assessed which belongings she could carry to her new camp before neatly stacking the rest back into the sphere. She struggled to conceal the giant metal pod with forest debris but, realising the futility of the activity, vowed to instead collect her remaining belongings when she returned with Harry's headstone.

Matilda fashioned herself a makeshift crutch and set off towards the cave, limping along animal trails and river banks. Grief prickled at the back of her mind yet she still managed to appreciate simple joys like dipping her feet into a crystal-clear stream or stopping to watch a herd of deer grazing in a glade.

Familiar landmarks occasionally came into view, though the differences from her own time were jarring. The colony of ancient trees was boundless, rock formations showed reduced signs of weathering and wildlife was much more abundant. Matilda didn't relish the idea of hunting her own food with a damaged ankle but the forest inhabitants seemed much more appetising than the basic rations the Institute had provided for the initial nights in the past.

The sun had already started to set when Matilda finally arrived at the entrance to a familiar gully. She stared into the gentle depression into the landscape and saw the cave opening at its end, overgrown with ivy but undoubtedly the same cave she'd once explored with Richie. Matilda shambled inside and dumped her belongings on the ground before hurrying to gather firewood while there was still light.

Upon returning, Matilda hastily kindled a small fire to boil water for one of her unappetising ration packs. Her stomach rumbled and she realised that she hadn't eaten since being loaded into the pod.

Matilda felt another wave of overwhelming loss begin to rise but pushed the feelings down once more. She decided to enjoy the remaining sunlight, hoping it might make her nutritious gruel slightly more bearable. She collected her satchel, telescope and David's champagne before exiting the cave and hobbling to the crest of a nearby hill where she seated herself among the roots of yet another ancient tree.

A glorious pink sky signalled the end of Matilda's first day in the past and she devoured her food while the setting sun cast long shadows across the untouched landscape. She popped David's champagne as the stars emerged and gave a toast.

"To Harry. My family. And a momentous day."

She took a deep swig. Coming from a world where her every minute had been accounted for by others, Matilda appreciated the chance to finally enjoy things on her own time.

She got back to work when the sun had fully set, withdrawing her telescope and expertly measuring the position of several key stars. She performed familiar calculations in her notebook, working by the light of her hand-cranked torch. After some brief consultations with her bible, she drew a square around a date.

24 September 1123.

The Institute scientists had been confident that Matilda would arrive exactly when and where they had planned but she was relieved to verify it herself.

The date had been deliberately chosen to maximise the impact of Harry and Matilda's journey. England had been on the verge of a renaissance when King Henry's only heir died in a tragic shipping accident in 1120. The ensuing power struggle sparked a period of civil war known as The Anarchy, briefly teasing the possibility of female empowerment through the widespread backing of Empress Maud but ultimately extinguishing the flame of progress.

Matilda's mission was clear. She had several weeks to journey to London and meet King Henry before he departed for a year of campaigning against rebels in Normandy. She would use her knowledge and limited equipment from the future to win his trust and join his campaign, allowing her to rub shoulders with royalty and senior clergy across Europe. This would maximise the number of people exposed to the Institute's teachings, fuelling the budding renaissance and kickstarting society's progress to save this timeline from the calamity that awaited their future.

The Long Day.

Matilda shuddered at the memory. She was only ten when she'd witnessed a star's sheer power, marvelling with her parents as beautiful ribbons of light danced across the night sky. Her memories had faded but fragments of the aftermath lingered. Months without electricity. Missing favourite foods and television shows. Her father tending to an elderly neighbour, savagely beaten for protecting his backyard orchard.

At only twelve, Matilda had volunteered to help the Institute undo the stellar carnage, understanding even then that it would require great personal sacrifice. She'd never really been ready to leave home and her father's parting words of encouragement had reminded her of what she'd lost. While she had cherished her Institute friendships, they were never quite family.

Matilda was pensive as she lay at the base of the ancient tree staring up at the night sky. The Milky Way was a beautiful band of shimmering stars, unobscured by light pollution and more beautiful than she'd seen since the aftermath of the Long Day.

So beautiful. So powerful. So dangerous.

Matilda's mission was clear and she knew what needed to be done. But her ankle throbbed, a painful reminder of her own fragility. It would need weeks to recover.

Matilda rankled at the need to stay put but a part of her breathed a sigh of relief. The final weeks of preparation for her journey had been a rollercoaster of stress, anticipation and loss. As her departure loomed, she had increasingly fretted at how much she still didn't know. She worked to the very end, struggling to cram more into either her head or jotted in the margins of her bible. Only a week earlier, her frustrated Institute classmates had even resorted to hosting her a combined farewell and birthday celebration in the Institute library.

Matilda knew she was on the verge of burnout, even before Harry's death. Taking time for her ankle to recover meant slightly less time to influence the King, but it also gave her time to grieve. Time to plan. The resulting mental clarity could prove valuable.

Her mind instantly leapt to planning crafts and activities to fill the time. But no, she needed to relax and unwind. To ease into her new life and mourn the one she'd left behind.

Convinced that her revised approach made sense, Matilda pushed back the niggling feelings of loss and loneliness once and for all. She placed down her tools and reclined against the tree, settling in to admire the starry night. A weight lifted from her shoulders, knowing as she swigged her champagne that she could just enjoy herself for the first time since childhood.

The knowledge made it easier to process the enormity of her achievements. In a single day she had gone from a scared young woman afraid to leave her family to the most educated person on the planet.

She was Chronomad One. The first time traveller.

CHAPTER THREE

4 October 1123

William bristled with frustration as he watched his family working in the fields. His father cleaved wide paths through the wheat with sweeping cuts of his scythe, while William's two eldest sisters followed in his wake and baled the cuttings to dry. William's mother and youngest sister sifted the dried grain in the shade of the field's giant oak. William had his own mindless role in the process, bashing bales of dried wheat with a flail. It had been the exact same routine for almost a month and William was sick of it.

Judging by the sun, Pa was still a long way off laying down his scythe and ordering the family back home to rest. William looked down at his pile of unsifted grain and guessed there would be enough to keep Ma and Elizabeth busy for the afternoon. He glanced around the field once more and saw that his family were all absorbed in their tasks. No one paid any attention to him.

A devilish thought crossed William's mind. He stole the opportunity and slunk away from the field like a sly fox, nabbing an apple from Ma's basket before dashing into the woods to find his friend.

Ralph's family farmed a nearby field that also backed onto the forest. William was pleased to find Ralph's family similarly distracted with the harvest. Ralph worked alone, stacking sacks of grain into a hand cart.

William tossed his apple core into the trees and snuck closer to the boy.

"Oi, Ralph!" William called in a hushed voice. "Get over here!"

The large boy jumped at the unexpected sound and looked up, spotting William hiding behind a boulder.

"Why are you hiding?" he asked, casually strolling towards the rock.

"Shh. Get. Over. Here. Your brothers will see you." William dragged Ralph behind the boulder. "How's your family almost finished already?"

"Father says it's going to be a bad year so we shortened the drying time so we'd finish in the fields before the rain sets in."

"Yeah, yeah," William dismissed. "All I'm hearing is you have time to get away for a bit."

Ralph started to protest but William withdrew a messy bundle from his pocket. "I made another sling. Come on, let's give it a try."

Ralph was torn, staring at the unstacked sacks next to the cart. "Mother will scold me if I leave the others to return the cart. Again."

"Not if you bring back a pair of juicy rabbits," William said in his most enticing voice. "Quick, let's go!"

William dashed off, trusting that his friend would follow. The boys were soon running through the woods on one of their usual adventures, imagining bandits waiting in ambush behind every tree. William used a curved stick as a pretend bow and Ralph fashioned himself a wooden broadsword.

They ventured deep into the forest to increase their chances of finding small game. Some mischievous village elders had thought it fun to bait the boys into making a sling, knowing that their strict parents wouldn't approve. For William, the risk of getting caught by Pa – a village juror – only added to the illicit excitement.

They found a clearing and selected an unlucky tree to use as a target for their practice. The tree had little to worry about.

William was already proficient with the sling when Ralph scored his first hit.

"Good job," William praised impatiently. "Now let's find some real prey."

"Not fair," Ralph complained. "You got way more throws."

"We'll return home emptyhanded if we don't go after some real animals soon. You want upset parents, again?"

Concern dawned on Ralph's face.

"Here," William said with his most convincing smile, "you start with the sling and I'll herd game towards you. Ten shots and then we'll swap."

Ralph reluctantly agreed. "But what if the Baron's men find us hunting his lands? Did you hear about the old man from Dodington? They cut off his hand and that was just for *having* deer antlers."

"Pa said the codger was also underpaying his taxes," William dismissed. "Anyway, we'd need to actually catch something before worrying about the Baron."

The pair began their hunt, spreading out to search for prey but keeping within yelling distance. Ralph loosed his stones at a squirrel and some small birds, whooping with excitement after each attempt but managing no hits. He grudgingly handed William the sling and set off in search of game.

Armed with the sling, William felt like David as he stalked through the forest. The towering trees were an army of Goliaths.

William was so focused on the hunt that he eventually realised that he couldn't hear Ralph. He called out several times but there was no response. William grew concerned. Pa had always warned that outlaws lived in the deepest parts of the forest. He forgot about the hunt and instead scoured the undergrowth for any sign of his friend.

Hoping for a better vantage point to search for Ralph, William started to climb a hill when a clump of bushes rustled. Too big to be an animal, William applied tension to his sling.

With a sudden flurry of movement, a large form lunged out and raced across the clearing towards William. But William was quicker and loosed a projectile at his oncoming attacker.

The hardened clump of dirt hit his friend directly on the forehead, shattering upon impact.

"Ow!" Ralph complained, rubbing his head and tossing his mock sword to the ground.

William burst out laughing, impressed at his shot. "Sorry Ralph, you startled me. I'm still getting used to this sling."

Truth be told, William had exceeded his supply of stones and had just hoped for the best if it had been a real outlaw. Not that he could admit that to Ralph.

William's friend continued rubbing his head and looked up to the sun.

"We should head back Will. We've been gone long enough and I really should help bring the cart home."

William objected. "But if we cross that stream we'll be further from home than ever...!"

"No Will, my head hurts! I'm going home. Seriously, your family cuts you a lot of slack but you're almost sixteen. We need to start dealing with extra responsibility before it just gets dumped on us."

William started another rebuttal but Ralph was already returning to the fields.

"Come on Ralph!" William called. "Let's keep exploring. There's a whole lifetime of responsibility ahead of us!"

But Ralph was gone.

William kicked at a small bush and trudged down to the stream to collect more stones for his sling. He crossed the water and defiantly delved even deeper into the forest, well past any familiar landmarks. William saw many unfamiliar plants on his journey and wished his younger sister was with him. Elizabeth enjoyed gathering flowers but William knew she would never venture so far into the unknown.

Elizabeth was William's favourite sister. Only a year older than William, she was a kind soul and the least likely to berate his frequent skiving from the family's work. William's older sisters were prone to constant sniping at his poor work ethic and Ma and Pa's coddling.

Ralph was right. William's parents did give him special treatment, allowing him to run off on adventures and requiring fewer chores of him than the girls. Pa had always wanted a son and, after four girls, William was their pride and joy. He understood why his sisters felt hard done by, though it didn't stop him enjoying his time off.

William came upon another stream and stopped for a drink. Spying some stepping stones upstream, he quickly crossed the water but slipped on the rocks, soaking his foot up to the knee. His soggy shoe made walking unpleasant but William was determined not to let some minor discomfort force him back to the harvest.

William was squelching through the unfamiliar forest when he noticed a strange object hanging from the branches of a distant tree. Even from afar, he knew it was unnatural and had to be the work of a human.

But why would anyone live so deep in the forest?

William's curiosity got the better of him and he edged towards the hanging object. He pulled his most jagged stone taut in the sling.

As he drew nearer, William was mortified to see that the hanging object was a small red doe. The poor beast hung from a rope around its hind legs. Its throat had been slashed. A slow patter of blood dripped into a pool on the forest floor, raising William's tension with each drip.

The doe's lifeless eyes stared up at him. He'd never seen a sadder sight and the memory of the majestic creature seared into his soul.

The beast had been gutted before being hung. William poked the animal and it slowly swung around, revealing the most unusual arrow he had ever seen. A perfect black rod jutted from the animal's chest, its fletching unnaturally colourful and made of an odd material that was definitely not feather.

William noticed a quiver of similar arrows propped against the base of nearby tree, beside the most bizarre bow he had ever seen. It looked to be constructed from three different parts and was barely half the size of Pa's yew longbow.

The strange weapon struck William with a terrifying thought. Someone had used it to hunt the Baron's deer. Only an outlaw would be so brazen. William found the reality of an encounter with outlaws much less exciting than it had been in his games. His mind screamed danger but he found himself frozen in place.

William tried to take stock of his surroundings. The tree stood near the entrance to a small gully, a sloping gouge in the land that ended with a cliff face and the jagged mouth of a cave. The gully was surrounded by trees and thick undergrowth but the entrance to the cave had been recently cleared. There were other signs of human activity around the cave entrance. A neat pile of firewood was stacked against the cliff wall and the remains of a small campfire lay near the entrance. Looking closer, William saw a roughly hewn door inside the cave entrance.

A noise from within the cave startled William back to his senses and he darted away from the gully to crouch behind a nearby bush.

The door opened and a strange young woman emerged from the cave. Her head was a mass of curly red hair and her clothes hugged her body. William found her very attractive.

The woman sang an otherworldly song as she worked, more erratic than parish hymns but more graceful than popular drinking songs. William didn't understand the lyrics but some words sounded familiar.

William enjoyed watching the woman move purposefully around the camp, kindling a fire and placing a pot of water to boil. She re-entered the cave and emerged with a long knife. William was wondering what she planned to do with it when she hobbled up from the gully and straight to the doe, only a stone's throw from where William crouched frozen in place.

The tall woman lowered the doe and tenderly lay it on the ground before using her knife to extract the arrow from the beasts' chest. She cleaned the arrow with a handful of leaves and placed it into her quiver before starting to butcher the beast. She cut with expert precision, each slice of her blade removing a specific chunk of meat. Looking satisfied with her harvest, she hauled the carcass back up the tree and out of reach of forest scavengers. William wished he had a knife to portion a chunk for his family.

The strange woman returned to her fire and threaded the meat on a makeshift spit to hang over the flames. The aroma of roasting meat filled the gully and William's stomach grumbled at the rich smell. He'd only tried venison a handful of times but knew exactly what he was missing. The woman retrieved the meat as the outer edges began to char and bit into it, crying out as the hot juices ran down her chin. She looked to be enjoying herself and showed no signs of remorse at killing the Baron's deer.

William skirted around the gully to sit behind her, eager to learn more about the Stranger but anxious not to be caught. The woman packed away her food and started carving an ornate piece of timber. She didn't match William's expectations of an outlaw, not nearly half as deranged as Pa had described of his own outlaw encounters.

Hoping to get a better view of the campsite, William edged closer to the cliff. As he crawled, his elbow dislodged a rock which tumbled down the cliff face. William threw himself flat on the ground and felt the Stranger's gaze pass over him. Down below, he heard her set down her carving and rise from her spot next to the fire.

William didn't wait to see if she was approaching. He ran.

William skirted around the gully and dashed back across the stream. He ignored the stepping stones altogether and ploughed straight through the water. William didn't stop running until he began to notice familiar landmarks. Exhausted, he paused to listen for any sign that the Stranger had pursued him but the only sounds were the calls of distant birds and the wind rustling through the canopy. Even then, he walked cautiously.

It was twilight by the time William slouched back to his family's field, only to find that they had already packed up for the day and returned home. William trudged back to the village as darkness fell and saw Ralph chopping firewood in penance for their day's adventures. Noting the purple lump that had formed above Ralph's eye, William gave an apologetic wave. Ralph waved back and all was forgiven.

William arrived at his family's cottage and went to stash his sling in his favourite hiding place. Reaching into his pocket, he was surprised to find only a couple of smooth river rocks. The sling was nowhere to be found. He prayed that the outlaw woman wouldn't find the evidence of his visit.

William entered the cottage and sat down for the evening meal. He ignored his sister's taunts and let Ma's scolding flow over him while his mind raced over what he had seen that day. Surviving his first encounter with an outlaw filled him with confidence and William vowed to return to the cave.

Soon.

CHAPTER FOUR
14 October 1123

Matilda thoroughly enjoyed owning her own schedule for the first time in her life. Postponing her journey to London while her ankle recovered had done wonders for her mental state. She was coming to terms with Harry's passing, extending the Institute's grieving strategies to include him as well as her family, friends and entire world she had left behind. She focussed on the good in her new life rather than the injustice of his premature death or the implications for their mission.

Matilda had established a comfortable routine in the weeks since her arrival. She woke around sunrise each morning and hobbled around the hills near her cave, determined to exercise her foot and explore the new world. Matilda loved watching as it came alive. Birds sang their morning songs, animals grazed in the meadows and the warmth of the rising sun cut through the autumn fog. It was pristine. Untouched.

On her return to the cave, Matilda gathered wild plants for a basic breakfast and a warm tisane. Her food situation was neither comfortable nor dire. The limited rations from the future were only intended to last several short days before Harry and Matilda embarked on their mission to London. Even with Harry's supplies, the rations had been quickly exhausted.

Although her ankle caused great difficulty, Matilda had succeeded in hunting a small doe but only managed to consume or preserve half of it before the meat had perished. Matilda felt guilty at the memory of dragging the rotting corpse away from her camp and strategically dumping it in the hope that scavengers might salvage one last meal. She'd vowed to kill no more of the elegant creatures and her meals became much less decadent, though she occasionally treated herself with a strip of dried venison.

Leisure activities started after breakfast. Leaning against a tree, Matilda read her Institute bible for the thousandth time and pondered obscure philosophy or physics. She missed the banter with her classmates and found herself longing for human interaction as the days passed. She journeyed to Harry's grave every other day but the conversation remained one-sided.

When the afternoon sun had removed the bite from the autumn air, Matilda limped to a nearby stream to swim. The icy water numbed her swollen ankle and she relished the freedom of floating on her back as the dappled sunlight shone through the canopy above.

More than anything, Matilda's favourite activity was making her cave feel homey. She'd explored the cave with her little brother when it was almost a thousand years older, a special getaway for the siblings to bond during her rare weekends away from the Institute. The cave was already full of memories but, missing her family, Matilda sought to recreate a feeling of home.

She cleared away the larger rocks and swept the bare dirt floor with a hastily crafted broom. Matilda had always enjoyed making things but lessons at the Institute had focused on framing a house, plumbing sinks or wiring a light fitting. She suddenly found herself free to create for aesthetics rather than just utility or learning. After carving a headstone – 'Harry Carroll, gone before his time' – she had started with simple practical items, crafting a door and a stone wall to stem the flow of bats that visited the cave each evening. More domestic items came next, first a cot so she didn't need to sleep on the floor and then a shelf to hold her most precious belongings.

With her leg almost fully mended, Matilda promised herself one last project before departing for London and started on a table and chair to introduce some civility to her cave dwelling. She took particular care in crafting the chair and her attempts at carving leaves and flowers made it a truly luxurious item. Crude but a rare work of art nonetheless.

Matilda was excited to be around people again and longed to see Twelfth Century civilisation firsthand. She was surprised at how few signs of humanity she'd seen since her arrival. She'd deliberately avoided roads and dwellings but had spotted the occasional person working in a distant field. After years of studying the period through books and paintings, it felt like being in a zoo where the animals refused to play.

Though she hadn't seen any people up close, Matilda began to suspect that the area surrounding her cave wasn't completely abandoned. She frequently had the unnerving feeling of being watched and she'd discovered a rudimentary sling while returning from the stream. It was still supple and hadn't been hardened by the elements, suggesting it was only recently discarded.

The feeling of being watched increased after discovering the sling and Matilda started to find her belongings in odd places when she returned from trips away from the cave. She initially attributed this to absentmindedness but was convinced that something strange was afoot when Harry's utility knife went missing altogether. Matilda vowed to solve the mystery and planned an ambush to catch her unwanted visitor the following day.

She left for her afternoon swim as normal but upon reaching the stream, quickly looped back to her cave to lie in wait for the intruder. She crouched behind a bush near the gully entrance, peering through its branches.

It wasn't long before Matilda saw signs of movement and a lanky, shaggy-haired adolescent dashed into the gully, peering around to ensure he'd not been seen. Matilda was intrigued when the Boy filled one of her pots with water and placed it over the still-warm embers of her fire.

Showing no interest in waiting for it to boil, the Boy strode to the cave and expertly shimmied the latch that kept the door closed. It was clear he'd visited the cave before. Matilda had hidden her most important belongings and wasn't overly concerned by the Boy's intrusion but felt slightly violated by the invasion of privacy nonetheless.

The Boy eventually emerged from the cave carrying Matilda's dismantled recurve bow and a handful of her carbon fibre arrows. He inspected the arrows before tinkering with the bow, assembling it through trial and error. Matilda was impressed by the care he applied to the task, carefully bending the arms with his body rather than risking the whole contraption exploding in his face.

With the bow constructed, the Boy tested its draw and propped a piece of firewood on the opposite side of the gully to use as a target. Matilda quickly learned that he knew his way around a bow and three of her arrows plunged deep into the wood in quick succession. The Boy seemed equally impressed with the performance of the otherworldly bow. He retrieved the arrows and repeated the process several more times.

There was a sudden hiss and a cloud of steam as the Boy's pot of water boiled over. Admiring his inventiveness, Matilda realised it was a makeshift alarm clock. He calmly finished his remaining shot before collecting the arrows, restacking the firewood and emptying the boiling water. He methodically dismantled the bow and returned it to the cave. Wisps of steam from the emptied water was the only sign that he'd ever visited.

Matilda decided she was ready for some human interaction. It was time to introduce herself. She darted into the gully and sat on a log by the fire, legs crossed. She donned her most bored expression, hoping that casualness might unnerve the Boy.

He emerged from the cave much quicker than before, looking content with his successful expedition. Then he noticed Matilda, startled and stopped in his tracks. His satisfied expression evaporated, replaced in an instant by one of sheer terror.

"What are you doing in my camp?" Matilda asked nonchalantly, picking at her fingernails.

The Boy's eyes darted over Matilda's shoulder as his fight or flight reflex kicked in. Determining that the path out of the gully was blocked, his hand hovered towards a familiar knife hanging from his belt.

"I wouldn't do that," Matilda suggested firmly. "Nice knife, where'd you get it?"

The Boy paused again, confused by Matilda's lack of threat. "Your accent is strange," he answered defiantly.

Matilda laughed in spite of herself, shattering the tension. "You're spirited, kid. Don't get cocky, I'm not here for a fight. Come, take a seat. And give me back the knife." Her last point was dead serious.

The Boy didn't seem to fully understand but begrudgingly occupied a log opposite Matilda, tossing Harry's knife irreverently at her feet.

"What's your name?" Matilda asked.

"William. Who are you?"

Matilda ignored his question. "And what are you doing in my camp William?"

The Boy stared at her, weighing his options.

"I was curious," William replied defensively. "You're not what I expected of an outlaw."

"Outlaw!?" Matilda asked with feigned outrage. "What gave you that idea?"

"You. Living alone, in the Baron's woods. Your weapons! I've never seen a bow like yours before."

"You're quite a good shot," Matilda conceded, making William look uneasy. "Yes, I watched the whole time. You're not the only one who can spy from the bushes."

"Oh." William said stupidly. A silence fell over the camp.

"Who taught you to shoot?" Matilda asked.

"My Pa," William answered. "He was an archer. Served with the King and won our family's plot of land."

"He taught you well. How long have you been visiting my camp?"

"A couple of weeks perhaps? I saw the deer in the tree."

Yes, Matilda thought, *that lined up with the feeling of being watched.*

"You shouldn't do that you know," William berated. "Killing the Baron's deer. He's hanged people for less."

Matilda gave an appreciative nod. "I'll remember that. Not that I'll be killing any more, I need to depart soon."

"Already?" William asked, his curiosity returning. "You can't have been here long, your cave is so bare. Where are you going?"

Matilda weighed whether she should share her true plans but saw no harm. "I'm heading to London, to visit the King."

The Boy blinked at her, unimpressed. "Why would he want to see you?"

The bluntness of his question made Matilda stumble.

"You've been snooping through my stuff," Matilda replied defensively. "What do you think?"

William pondered her question. "If you're not an outlaw…I'd guess you are some sort of tinker. But you don't have much to sell."

"Sometimes it's more about the quality of what you're trading than the sheer amount of merchandise. Plus," Matilda said patting her satchel, "I don't leave my best items where just any rabble might find them."

William stared greedily at her bag. "What's in there?"

Matilda considered the Boy. He'd had many chances to steal her things and she couldn't blame him for succumbing to the temptation of the knife. Judging it was safe to show him, she withdrew some of the satchel's contents. He was very impressed with her bible but was disappointed when Matilda refused to let him hold it.

Next she withdrew the discarded sling. "This wouldn't be yours by any chance?"

William nodded and she tossed the sling back to its owner.

Matilda continued to show him her possessions, enjoying the company and answering his questions about what each was for. He gawped – a little too hungrily – when Matilda showed him her spools of gold, silver and tungsten wire. As a distraction, she quickly withdrew her torch and showed him how to use it.

"What is this sorcery?" William exclaimed as he flicked the light on and off. "Ok, perhaps the King would want to meet you. Forget tinker, are you some kind of witch?"

"I'm not doing anything," Matilda insisted. "You're the one turning it on and off."

William put down the torch and stared at Matilda seriously. "Where do you come from? What place can create such treasures?"

"That'll do, for today" Matilda interrupted abruptly, realising that she'd probably shown too much. "I've got much to prepare and can't afford any interruptions. So please, run along. And stay away from my things."

William looked crestfallen, his curiosity unsated. "Can I at least keep the knife? You've got others, surely you don't need them all?"

Matilda couldn't believe his nerve but found it endearing. "You're an unusual boy, young William. Wilful, yes, but curious. And brave. I like that."

The Boy waited impatiently for an answer to his request.

"I can't just give you a knife," Matilda said. "That's bad luck. Perhaps you could buy it from me, I'm supposedly a tinker after all. But it's a fine piece, so the price will be high."

William was frozen in place, stuck deep in thought.

"Run along William. I feel that we'll meet again, though tell another soul that I'm here and today will be the last you ever see of me. Or the knife. Understand?"

He nodded.

"Goodbye William," she said firmly. "I'm Matilda, by the way."

William rose without a word and left. Matilda sat back by the fire and picked up her carving, craning her neck to watch the Boy scamper out of the gully. *What an intriguing young man.*

CHAPTER FIVE
19 October 1123

William could make the return journey to the cave in half a day, if he marched. His treasure burned in his hand as he headed along the now-familiar path.

Surely Matilda would accept his trade this time.

He'd returned to the Stranger's camp several times since their first meeting but she had rejected each of his previous offers for the knife. An assortment of vegetables swiped from Ma's garden. A handful of Pa's best arrowheads. His grandmother's precious silk. William had even tried sneaking an iron ingot from the blacksmith, only to be chased through the village square. Yet still his offers were rejected.

It was frustrating but William welcomed the chance to continue seeing Matilda and used the opportunities to ingratiate himself. Their conversations became easier as he taught her proper phrases and corrected her pronunciation, though she still often reverted to her strange new language. She was undoubtedly odd but her eccentricities intrigued William, compelling him to keep his discovery to himself.

He still knew so little about her. She had slowly opened up to him, even letting him look at the remarkably lifelike pictures within her Book. Yet she remained coy about her past and their conversations remained one-way exchanges where William bombarded her with questions only to receive answers for one in ten. He'd tried to learn more by watching from a distance as in the early days but Matilda quickly detected his presence.

She was cooking when William arrived.

"Come down from there William. If you must watch, please do it where I can see you."

The Boy scurried out from his bush and took his regular log by the fire. Matilda fished some meat from the boiling pot and carved him a piece.

"You don't seem to have any qualms eating the Baron's deer," she mused in her bizarre accent as he savoured the meaty treat.

"The beast is already dead," William replied matter-of-factly. "It'd be a bigger crime to let it go to waste. I rarely get to eat venison."

Matilda smiled and the pair chewed the tough meat in a companionable silence until William judged she was sufficiently relaxed for him to begin his questions. How was the meat still fresh? How long did it take to prepare? How did she know he was up there?

She was in a pleasant mood and humoured him with some scattered answers before asking a question of her own.

"What's clutched in that hand of yours?"

"Payment, for your knife," William replied simply, handing it over. Matilda's face lit up immediately.

"William, this is incredible! It's…Roman! Where'd you get it?" she asked.

William beamed. Ma's father had found the lucky coin years ago, while building an extension for his granary. Mama kept it squirrelled away with the rest of her dead husband's belongings, saying it was too painful to look at. William doubted she would notice it missing.

"Pa says Holford was originally a Roman settlement," William replied with disinterest.

"Is that your village?" Matilda asked absentmindedly, still entranced by the coin in her palm. "Holford?"

"Yeah, it's not far from here. Where are you from?" William asked opportunistically, not really expecting an answer.

Matilda went silent, considering William and then the coin.

"Having an independent confirmation of my arrival *could* prove useful," she whispered, as if to the coin. "And I'll be long gone before any blabbing could cause trouble." She looked at William with a twinkle in her eye. "Very well. I'm from the future."

"The future?" William asked, confused. "What does that even mean?"

"Another time," Matilda said, as though he was simple. "Like tomorrow or next week, but much further away. You are as old to me as this coin is to you."

William considered this new information. "How?"

"I fell from the sky in a metal egg."

"Now you're just poking fun," William complained.

"I'm not!" Matilda said earnestly. "I can show you."

William weighed the risks of venturing into the woods with a potential witch. "Only if you give me the knife. To keep."

Matilda judged him once again before handing over both the knife and coin. "This treasure belongs with your family. Put it back where you found it. And promise to take care of that knife. It belonged to a dear friend, though I'm sure he would approve of one as annoyingly inquisitive as you becoming its new owner."

William excitedly strapped the knife back onto his belt and the pair set off into the forest. Their path seemed random but Matilda walked with purpose, her limp all but gone. He was puzzled when she stopped at a mass of dead branches piled at the base of a random tree but excitement swelled as Matilda removed branches to reveal a giant metallic egg.

"You weren't lying!" William cried. "You really are from the future!?"

Matilda simply smiled as William clambered over the branches to inspect the egg. He ran his hands along its smooth surface and yelped when he discovered how to open it. He quickly manoeuvred it upright and clambered inside before thrusting his head out of the opening. "So you're *really* from the future?"

"I'm afraid so. The year 2037."

William sat back in the pod as he considered the absurdity of her claim. *And yet it seemed to make sense.*

"Good lord! You really are going to see the King!"

"Yep. I'll teach him everything from my Book and make gadgets much more exciting than the torch or my bow."

"But how? You can't just stroll into London and demand to see the King."

Matilda shrugged. "True. I haven't worked out the specifics but I'll make my way to London and then find a way into his court. I'd hoped to meet a baron on my way and request a letter of recommendation."

"Pa has to go to the castle to deliver our taxes this week!" William interjected excitedly. "And our new bishop was in town only a couple days back. There was a special Mass and everything. He's a foreigner too, Pa said he travelled to England with the new Queen. Surely he could help you meet the King."

"That makes sense. Bishop John would've died what, last year? His successor would probably tour the parishes." Matilda pondered William's proposal. "An introduction from a bishop *could* be even better than a baron," she whispered to herself before giving a big sigh. "I guess my chair carving will have to wait."

William's mind raced. He'd prayed for more excitement in his dull life but never dreamed that something so amazing could happen. To him! He was so full of questions that he struggled not to blurt them all out at once.

"So you'll come back to my home and Pa can take you to see the Bishop?" he asked with absolute restraint.

Matilda thought again before responding. "Ok," she agreed. "I'd better go pack my things."

Matilda walked across the clearing to what William realised was a fresh grave. The soil had not fully settled and an unweathered stone sat at its head. A fresh bunch of flowers lay atop the earthy mound.

"Well, it looks like I'm off dear Harry," Matilda murmured. "It's time to finally get started. I won't let you down."

She turned back to her cave after finishing her quiet farewell, not even bothering to cover her egg with branches.

Doesn't she know how valuable that much metal is?

"Wait!" William called out. "What about the egg?"

Matilda looked around with an impatient look. "What about it? I can come back for it later, if I ever need it."

William was baffled. "Surely you jest?"

Matilda shrugged, her mind no doubt already planning her trip. But William refused to abandon such an amazing object to the forest. Holford's blacksmith would pay a fortune for it, provided he didn't attack William first. He grabbed the open rim and started dragging to test its weight.

"Can I have it?" he asked sheepishly.

Matilda looked surprised but nodded.

William hooted in triumph. It was surprisingly easy to move once it was rolling. William struggled to push it up a hill but hollered with glee when the ball rolled away down the other side, bouncing off trees before coming to a rest in the valley below. Matilda smiled as he bounded down after it and even helped push it up the last few hills. The pair made a more controlled descent into the gully and left the egg by the cave door. Matilda headed inside while William piled rocks around the base.

When it was secure, he walked freely into the cave, noting how strange it was to be invited and not need to sneak in. Matilda sat cross legged on the dirt floor, surrounded by a pile of her belongings which she sorted for her journey to London.

"There's too much," she moaned, shuffling piles back and forward. She muttered to herself before throwing her hands up in defeat. "Forget it! Can I trust you to make sure no one *else* breaks in while I am away?" Her emphasis on the word else cut like a knife.

William nodded guiltily.

"Good." Matilda said. "It'll be much easier to travel without all of this. And it will be nice to know that someone is looking after it for me."

She bundled clothes into a sack and added some extra items to her satchel before piling her remaining belongings on the bed and gently shooing William out of the cave. She fastened the latch behind her, taking time to ensure that it was extra secure.

"Come on William. Let the journey begin."

William trotted after Matilda as she marched out of the gully and guided her to the familiar trail back to Holford. Matilda spent much of the trip lost deep in thought but William couldn't hold his tongue.

"What is it like, in the future?" he asked as casually as possible. "Do the Norman's rule the world or did us English manage to break free?"

Matilda was jolted back to the present but laughed. "Oh no, the English broke free. We actually ended up colonising much of the globe at one stage, unfortunately. It's no fluke that you and I are speaking English."

William still found her language puzzling. He didn't know what a globe was but she definitely spoke English. Something close to it anyway.

"There's a lot more freedom in England's future. Many people own their own land and even commoners can buy whatever food they want. We've cured many illnesses and use machines to either swim underwater like fish or fly like birds."

Questions came to William faster than he could mentally register them. He blurted out the first one that solidified into a complete thought.

"Fly!? Up in the sky? How? How high!?"

Matilda laughed again. "As high as you can imagine! We've flown to the moon. The sun. To other planets."

William was mesmerised. He stared through the canopy and up at the sky where the sunset created brilliant shades of purple and red. A crescent moon was shining and the first stars had come into view. *People could go there? Surely not.* William was so enthralled that he failed to notice an exposed root and went tumbling to the ground.

"Careful!" Matilda dashed forward and helped him up. William's ego was battered more than his knees.

"Tell me about your family," she said gently.

"Well, there's Pa. His family have always farmed for the Baron but he got his own plot of land after serving the King. He's on the town jury now too. Ma runs our home, always juggling at least three things at once and making sure us children do our share. And then there's Mama, Ma's Ma. She's ancient and grumpy, always yelling and saying us children are in the way."

"So you have siblings?"

"Three sisters, all older than me. Rachel's the oldest. She's…difficult." William paused, trying to think what to say without sounding too whiny. "We don't really get along. She's never really liked me."

"That's disappointing," Matilda said, her tone understanding.

William shrugged. "She spends most of her time with her friends or Mama. There's also Margery. She keeps to herself most of the time but helps Ma run the house. And then there's Elizabeth. She's my favourite. She's only a little older than me and sometimes joins me in the woods, collecting flowers or singing with the birds."

"She sounds nice," Matilda replied with a warm smile.

"What about you?" William asked. "Do you have a family?"

"Yeah, I do…I did." Sadness fell across Matilda's face. "My Dad was a doctor. Helped heal sick people. And Mum was a librarian. She looked after a building full of books."

Matilda's Book had been the first William had ever touched. He struggled to imagine more than two books in one place at once, let alone an entire building full of them.

"Then there was my little brother Richie," Matilda continued. "He was much younger than me. Younger than you even. But it was fun having a younger brother."

She sounded sad. William gave her a consoling smile but let her walk on in silence.

The pair eventually reached the familiar fields at the outskirts of Holford. People had long since retired for the evening and William only crossed paths with a handful of villagers as they walked to his family's cottage.

Each person they passed looked intrigued by the Stranger's mass of red hair and unusual clothes. They eyed her up and down before throwing William either reproachful or bemused expressions. It was only then that William realised the rashness of his decision to invite a complete stranger to stay with his family overnight. A strange *woman* no less.

"We're almost here," William told Matilda whose spirits lifted as Holford came in view. "It's not much, but its home," William added, feeling a need to defend his simple village to someone who had travelled through time.

"Not at all," Matilda replied enthusiastically. "This is one of the most amazing places I've ever seen."

William didn't believe it but she sounded surprisingly genuine. Matilda commented on mundane things like the thatched roofs or the glow of rush lights cutting through the twilight haze.

The silhouette of the family's cottage came into view. Light flickered through gaps under the shutters and door, promising a warm fire within.

William and Matilda passed through the vegetable garden and stopped at the door. William didn't know how he would explain the Stranger to his family, with her bizarre accent and unusual clothes. Bringing unannounced company after dark was rude. A stranger even more so, no one trusted outlanders. A female stranger was even ruder again, and one as unconventional as Matilda…William knew he'd be hearing about it for a while.

Matilda gave him a quizzical look, wondering why they had stopped. With a big sigh, William pushed the door open.

The family were scattered around the cottage's single room, eating their evening meal by the light of the central fire pit while Elizabeth's cats begged for scraps. Their conversations continued uninterrupted when William entered but abruptly stopped as a second figure ducked under the doorway after him.

Ma's back was turned to the door and she called out joyfully as she ladled a scoop of stew into a bowl, "Look who's finally back, late as usual. Honestly Willy, how often must I ask that you at least return before dark? Oh..."

Pa gave a cough and Ma froze when she saw Matilda, William's meal still held outstretched in her hand. She was momentarily speechless and William's sisters stared at Matilda disapprovingly. Even Pa shot William a raised eyebrow.

William grabbed his food and tried to make light of the situation. "Thanks Ma, I'm starving. Family, this is Matilda. She's a, uh, foreigner. She's travelling to London and thought she would try catching the Bishop in Stowey town. Can you take her with you tomorrow Pa?"

William knew it was a stretch. The family had endured many of his eccentric appeals for assistance, most recently with an injured hare that eventually ended up in their stew. But requesting assistance for an unknown woman was probably a plea too far.

Never one to miss a jab, Mama leapt in with a snide remark. "You'd have to be foreign to dress like that, walking around with your hair out and no doubt as loose as your morals! Where'd you come from?"

Matilda glanced down at her clothes but ignored Mama's rudeness and replied politely. "From Exeter, dear lady. I was seeking word about rare herbs from a local apothecary."

"Not more herb nonse..." Mama began but Pa interrupted.

"So you're an herbalist? A useful skill, very practical. Our Elizabeth loves plants, don't you Beth? You should show *our guest* your garden in the morning."

Elizabeth gave a meek nod, uncomfortable at being dragged into the tense conversation.

Ma also sought to defuse the situation, though her own disapproval was thinly masked. "I'm sure she's much too busy for that. And you'll need to depart early if you've any hope of avoiding additional penalties from the Baron." She swatted Pa before turning to Matilda. "So you're just passing through Holford on your way to London?" Ma's inflection made it clear she wasn't really asking a question.

William was impressed by his parent's quick composure. He'd never seen them act as such a fluid but synchronised team.

"I hope you're planning to change into something modest before you see the Bishop," Rachel squawked from her perch on the bench next to Mama.

"Be nice Rachel," Pa said. "I'm sure the Bishop would be more interested in her herb lore than her clothing."

Mama grew further agitated. "I don't care what she knows about weeds! What is this whore doing in our house?"

"Come now Agnes," Pa interjected firmly, shocking Mama into silence. "That's no way to talk to a guest, no matter how they might be dressed. It is our Christian duty to provide hospitality to a traveller, and perhaps some gentle encouragement should we find their morals…lacking."

Mama huffed and abruptly crossed her arms but remained silent.

"Now, Matilda was it? Please join us for a meal. Emma, another serving please." Pa passed Ma his own bowl to fill and stood from his stool. "I'll happily accompany you to the castle in the morning, though my dear wife is correct as ever. We'll need to leave early to deliver our family's tithe on time." Vacating his seat, Pa left the hut to collect firewood.

William sat at his normal place at the hearth and Matilda accepted the bowl from Ma before sitting on Pa's stool, oblivious to the blatant violation of the family's normal hierarchy. The family watched in silence as the pair ate, their own food abandoned. Mama and Rachel seethed quietly in the corner, Elizabeth fed her cats and Ma shot puzzled looks at Margery, both wondering what exactly had just happened. The sound of Pa chopping firewood echoed from outside.

Ma collected the family's empty dishes, taking William's before he had even finished. He mentally thanked Matilda for their venison lunch.

Pa returned with an armful of wood and threw some larger pieces on the fire. "Time for sleep. It'll be an early morning for Matilda and I, and I need you all working in the field while I'm away if we're ever going to finish the harvest."

The family didn't need to be told twice and no one complained at the unprecedented omission of their bedtime bible tale. There was a rush of activity as everyone prepared for sleep. William settled into his regular corner while Ma set Matilda up next to his sisters on the opposite side of the room.

Everyone said their goodnights, though their breathing betrayed that all remained awake and on edge. Mama and Rachel whispered rapidly to each other, matching the sounds of Ma and Pa's own back and forth. True to form, Margery was the first asleep and her snores reverberated around the small room. One by one, the others eventually drifted off as well.

But not William. After all the excitement, his mind could finally process the day's incredible experiences. A beautiful woman from the future lay in his family's simple hut. A woman about to meet the King! William hoped that Matilda would remember him and his family. That they'd been the first people she met before journeying to London.

William tossed and turned late into the night, stressed that he would sleep through Matilda and Pa's departure and miss his final opportunity to make an impression before she departed. When sleep eventually claimed William, his dreams were filled with futuristic visions of magnificent birds that flew beyond the moon to lay their giant metallic eggs.

CHAPTER SIX
20 October 1123

Matilda woke before the sun had risen but lay completely still, not wanting to wake the family and feeling her stomach gurgle from the previous night's unfamiliar medieval food. The frostiness of her reception still hung over the single-room hut and Matilda berated herself for thinking that William's family might be as welcoming as the Boy. She should've known that a strange woman accompanying their son, at night, would be confronting in a conservative medieval community. Her clothes had been the final straw, too different for villagers more accustomed to frumpy tunics and loose skirts.

On the plus side, her journey had finally started for real and she would soon be headed to London. With just a little more momentum, there would be no stopping the message she brought from the future. William's suggestion to meet the bishop was an unexpected win and could save Matilda weeks of climbing the rungs of London's social ladder.

Matilda was impressed with the Boy. There was a widespread misconception that medieval rural peasantry would be mostly devoid of intellect and, while appreciating that was untrue, Matilda was still surprised to find anyone with William's open-mindedness. He gave her hope for the mission. David had always said that an Institute student's ability to test and accept new ideas mattered much more than how much they knew when they arrived at the Institute gate.

The brilliant boy woke and shuffled towards the door. He wearily rubbed his eyes, another person suffering from a poor night's sleep. Matilda heard him relieve himself outside but he didn't return indoors. She pushed herself up and self-consciously wrapped her cloak over her shoulders to show at least some attempt at modesty.

Matilda left the hut and stepped out into the cool morning air. William sat on the dry-stone wall at the front of his parent's property, whittling a stick with his new knife. Matilda dropped her bags at the base of the wall and boosted herself up to sit beside him.

"You made it look easy back at the cave," William complained. "Those leaves on your chair looked real."

"Give it some practice," Matilda reassured. "I'd been making things for years before I attempted anything that intricate. Be patient, the best results come with time."

William resumed his whittling, a little slower and more deliberate. Matilda enjoyed the silence and just watched as the sun rose over the village. It looked completely different in the light of day. More spread out. Alive. She soaked in a scene that she had dreamt of for years. Simple mud-walled homes with thatched roofs were haphazardly scattered around the valley, each with their own vegetable garden and livestock tethered nearby. Goats bleated and roosters crowed. The smell of manure mingled with smoke. Books had told Matilda what she would see but hadn't prepared her for the smells and sounds. It was magical.

"Your village is wonderful!" Matilda gushed. "What did you say it was called?"

"Holford," William replied, not looking up from his whittling. "It's home but it's small and boring. Just wait until you get to the town though. There's so much more to do. They have stores. And a market. And the castle! I long to live someplace more exciting like that."

"No way William, your family is here. You crave the excitement now but you'd yearn for the peace of the country life before long. To be back in the forest."

"Of course you'd say that! You don't need excitement, you're from another time! Any more excitement in your life and you would probably explode."

Matilda laughed. "I can't argue with that."

William stopped his carving and looked up at Matilda seriously. "Please don't forget us, when you're surrounded by all the excitement of London. When you're meeting the King. Remember that it was boring little Holford that first welcomed you into our world."

"Never, William." Matilda was genuinely touched. "How could I forget that it was a boy from Holford..." She touched a hand to her heart. "...who broke into my cave and messed with all my stuff!"

Matilda playfully nudged the Boy's shoulder, pushing him off balance. Still holding his knife and stick, William's arms windmilled comically before he finally tipped backwards and fell from the wall. William quickly picked himself up and the pair burst out laughing.

Their commotion prompted movement within the hut and a bleary-eyed Pa emerged. He was a blur of activity and quickly had three large sacks stacked by the door. The noise of his preparations woke the other family members and they too emerged from the hut. Elizabeth showed Matilda her vegetables while Ma and Margery toasted the previous evening's bread. Pa returned inside to herd out Rachel and Mama who begrudgingly joined the family for a morning meal.

"What's the plan for today?" Ma asked her husband as she handed around the toast.

"Matilda and I will deliver the tithe at the market. I'll collect some things from town then meet you all in the field. It'll be nice to have an extra pair of hands, it means Will can stay here and help you get started on the lower half. We're racing against winter so anything we harvest now will mean more plentiful days when the weather turns."

"Plentiful?" Rachel scoffed, earning a look of approval from Mama.

"Pa!" William protested. "I wanted to come with you to Stowey. To see the market. To bid farewell to Matilda."

Pa considered his son's request before shaking his head. "Not today Will, we need you on the scythe so that we don't lose more time. It's that or go hungry. We're weeks behind."

Rachel muttered under her breath to Mama. "We wouldn't be late if his royal highness didn't run off every other day." William threw his crust at her.

"Stop it you two," Ma scolded. "Willy, you can follow them as far as the old mill but I need you by the time we've set up. It's going to be stormy today."

Ma was right. The blue sky from the previous day was rapidly disappearing and the grey clouds were gathering.

"That reminds me, dear," Ma said before running inside and returning with an armful of discoloured rags. "They're a bit old but they're warm and should draw less attention than your current…attire."

Matilda graciously accepted Ma's clothes and ran back into the hut to put them on. She left her Institute chainmail on underneath but admittedly looked less conspicuous with the new clothes. She stuffed her clothes into her bag and exited the hut to thank Ma profusely.

"Now people will think she's a pauper rather than a whore," Mama chimed. "A slight improvement I guess." Rachel snickered along with her.

Matilda had tired of the horrible old woman and her minion. Looking them in the eye, she reached into her satchel withdrew a vial of sugar which she gave to Ma. It was the entirety of Matilda's stocks and worth a small fortune but she happily parted with it just to see Mama and Rachel's faces drop in an instant. Ma was stunned at the generous gift and tried to refuse.

"I insist Emma,' Matilda reassured her. "Consider it payment for the bed, breakfast and clothes. And for your husband guiding me to the town." Matilda deliberately stared at Mama. "Thanks for your hospitality."

"Ok then, let's go," Pa said impatiently, hoisting a sack over each shoulder and motioning for Matilda to pick up the third. She tied her hair back and struggled to lift the heavy bag. William kindly offered to carry her bag of clothes and Matilda eventually found an almost comfortable position before the trio said a final farewell and departed.

William was a ball of energy, literally walking rings around Matilda and Pa as they left Holford and talking a mile a minute. He threw an endless barrage of questions, though Matilda appreciated that he avoided any allusions to her being from the future. Pa listened without comment. His face was stony but his eyes occasionally betrayed his own intrigue. They discussed medicinal plants, techniques for building fences, how birds were able to fly. Each answer inspired another three questions. They soon reached the ivy-covered ruins of an old mill which signalled the village boundary.

"This is it Will, you've talked the poor girl's ear off. Time for you to help your Ma."

It was clear that William didn't want to go but he swallowed his discontent and acknowledged his father's command with a gracious nod. He unlooped Matilda's bag and handed it back, helping Matilda with the awkward juggle to settle it into a comfortable position.

"Well, I guess this is goodbye," William said formally.

"It is, for now," Matilda said. She was surprisingly upset to say goodbye to her little fan, despite having only just met. "Come say hello if you ever escape and make it to London. Just ask for the eccentric redhead with the strange accent, you shouldn't have too much trouble finding me."

William smiled. "You promise you won't forget us?"

"Never," Matilda said before dropping her voice. "Plus, you're taking care of my belongings until I come back. I'll feel a lot better knowing you're keeping an eye on them. Try not to break too much during your experiments. And, avoid anything with red writing if you want to keep your fingers."

William laughed but Matilda gave a small shake of her head to show she was serious. Only when his smile evaporated was she satisfied that he'd grasped the severity of her warning.

"Shall we?" Pa asked impatiently.

"Please, lead the way." Matilda gestured forward, smoothly transitioning the gesture into a salute to the Boy. "Farewell young William. May our paths cross again." She followed after Pa before yelling over her shoulder, "Keep asking questions!"

The trees grew thicker as the travellers entered the forest and Matilda looked over her shoulder one last time. The Boy stood by the old mill's rotting waterwheel, watching until he could barely see them. Matilda gave a final wave and settled into the walk.

Pa was a much more reserved travel companion. Matilda tried to make some polite small talk, asking questions about Holford and Pa's plans at the market but she only received short gruff responses. She eventually gave up and the pair walked on in a stiff silence. It was a welcome break from William's endless questions and Matilda was glad to return to the unspoiled medieval forest.

The walk would've been much nicer without the bag of grain which seemingly grew heavier as they climbed an endless hill. Matilda had always seen herself as fit but was puffing like a smoker by the time they reached the summit and her shoulders burned from the weight.

Matilda got a strange vibe from Pa as they walked. He seemed on edge, frequently staring at her when he thought she wasn't looking and quickly shifting his gaze when she spotted him. Matilda couldn't tell whether he was merely judging a newcomer with the eyes of a law enforcer, or if something more sinister was afoot.

She became very aware that she was physically exhausted and alone with an unknown man who had the home ground advantage in a desolate and unfamiliar forest. It made for an uncomfortable walk and Matilda longed for it to be over. She kept a distance and tried to pick up the pace without being obvious.

The town eventually came into view and they began their descent from the forested hills. Matilda felt safer as the trees thinned and other people came into view, a mix of practically-dressed farmers and stuffier townsfolk.

Matilda marvelled as they approached her first medieval town. The monolithic stone castle towered above the surrounding timber structures. They had only reached the outskirts of the town when Matilda decided that she much preferred Holford's earthy smells to the town's fetid streets which were strewn with stagnating muck. The smell worsened as the buildings grew denser and eventually became interconnected.

Pa finally broke his silence as they neared the centre of town.

"My apologies for the cool reception you received last night. We aren't accustomed to receiving strangers after dark. It is quite rare in our little village."

"It was rude of me to show up unannounced," Matilda conceded.

Pa gave an appreciative nod and the pair concluded their walk in a more comfortable silence. They stopped at the town's single major intersection, where a straight road led up a hill to the castle.

Matilda threw down her sack of grain at the first opportunity.

Pa pointed out the town's various landmarks. "Welcome to Nether Stowey. You should find the Bishop up at the castle and I need to go to the market down here." He hesitated. "Look. You're intelligent, judging by your discussion with Will back at the village. It was all well over my head. But please know that people around here won't take kindly to outlandish behaviour. My family's reaction to your clothing was but a tame example. You'd do well to hide your eccentricities. Just fit in, it's easier."

While she disagreed with the principle of his message, Matilda sensed Pa's genuine concern for her and felt guilty for doubting his character in the woods.

"Thanks...Pa. I'll get myself a more appropriate wardrobe and watch my tongue. Thanks for your hospitality and for being my guide. I'm lucky to have stumbled across your family."

Pa grunted. "Feel free to visit if you're ever near Holford. I promise we'll be much more welcoming next time." With a simple nod of farewell, he scooped up the third sack of grain with ease and set off toward the market.

Matilda stood alone in the street and loosened her shoulder as she wondered what to do next. It was mid-morning and she wanted something extra to eat but remembered that she had no money and little to barter. The castle loomed on the hilltop above.

"Might as well get started," Matilda said to herself as she picked up her bags.

She made her way uphill but was underwhelmed when she reached the castle. Its outer walls were made of timber and scalable with only a running jump. The outer gate was manned by a scrawny guard who was much more interested in a hole in his sleeve than watching the entrance. Matilda crossed the dry moat and, using William's tinker story, explained that she was a merchant visiting to see the baron. The guard stared at her blankly and shrugged before waving her in. *Much easier than expected.*

Inside the castle was exactly as Matilda had imagined. A stableboy brushed a brown stallion in front of a small stable, a blacksmith hammered at his anvil and a gaggle of women chatted away as they washed clothes by the well.

The keep was much more imposing than the castle walls. Its architecture was brutally practical, a solid rectangle of stone with only a handful of narrow arrow slits dotted around the wall. A wooden staircase wound around the structure to a door halfway up the monolith. Matilda climbed the stairs, only to have the entrance barred by a surly looking guard.

"No entry today," he said bluntly.

"I'm a merchant and have travelled from Exeter to see the baron."

"A merchant? In those rags? Fallen on hard times have we?" the guard scoffed. "I don't care who you are, the Baron is unavailable today. Possibly for the week."

Matilda swore internally and retreated, letting the guard's laughter wash over her as she returned to the castle courtyard. She'd exhausted her luck with the first guard.

Matilda was pacing around the courtyard trying to concoct an alternate plan when she heard screams echo from the upper floors of the keep. She resumed her pacing but stopped again when the screams repeated. A kind-looking old priest noticed the shock on her face.

"Something's wrong with the Baron," he told Matilda. "He returned early from yesterday's hunt and has been bellowing ever since. Made for a wretched night's sleep for the castle dwellers. Baron Walter is lucky the Bishop happens to be visiting, he studied medicine with an order of monks in Europe."

Matilda cringed as she imagined the so-called medicine being inflicted upon the Baron. *No wonder he's screaming* Matilda had an idea and hastily thanked the priest before dashing back up the keep stairs.

"I need to see the Baron," she told the guard.

"I've already told you, he's not available."

"He's in tremendous pain. I know medicine, I can help him!"

"You're a medicine woman now? What happened to being a merchant? No! Now leave the castle before I have you thrown in the stocks."

Matilda was about to launch another volley of her argument when a well-dressed knight limped over from inside the keep, his hand resting on the hilt of his sword.

"What's the problem here?" he asked, swiping a strand of grey hair from his face.

"She's making up all manner of excuses to see the Baron. First she claimed to be a merchant and now she suddenly knows medicine."

"You know how to heal people?"

"I do, sir. I am an herbalist from abroad, returning to London after an expedition to Exeter. I've procured a number of rare plant extracts on my journey, which I planned to sell, but came to offer my assistance to the baron as soon as I learned that he was unwell."

"I see," the old knight replied thoughtfully. "And you believe these plants have medicinal properties?"

"I do. I've spent years understanding their effects on the human body and I know without doubt that my herbs will reduce pain or fever. Some can even cure illness."

The man looked intrigued but not convinced. Matilda took a risk.

"If I may, my lord. Your limp, is it an old battle wound?"

"Yes, though it has gotten much worse with age."

"And you have tried willow bark to ease the pain?"

The knight nodded.

"This will sound strange," Matilda said, "but try eating more fish."

The knight raised an eyebrow.

"It won't work immediately but after several moons it should lessen swelling around the joints, which will help reduce the pain."

The knight considered Matilda with a piercing gaze.

"Stand aside Alfred. I'm going to introduce this woman to the Baron."

"But sir…"

"No lad, that's an order."

"But the Bishop said…"

The knight glared and Alfred stood aside to allow Matilda through.

"Being constable awards some privileges," the knight said with a smile. "You seem to know what you're talking about so I'll give you an introduction and see what my lord says. Only an introduction, mind you. I want you straight out of there if he objects. No arguing."

Matilda smiled in agreement and the Constable led her into the depths of the keep. They climbed up a spiral staircase and walked along a dimly lit corridor before stopping in front of a heavy oak door.

"A word of warning. The Bishop is administering his own treatments. While they might sound painful, it would be unwise to claim stronger healing powers than a man of God."

With that, the Constable gave Matilda an encouraging smile and knocked.

CHAPTER SEVEN

20 October 1123

Baron Walter groaned in bed as Bishop Godfrey completed a third bloodletting. Godfrey had been tending to the Baron since their hunt the previous day – organised in the Bishop's honour – had gone awry. Walter had proven to be a boorish host, keeping Godfrey awake throughout the night. The Baron spent his time locked away in his quarters bellowing in pain rather than entertaining his high-profile guest. Typical of an Isle-dweller to lack true European sophistication.

The Baron's accident was yet another misfortune on Godfrey's dreary tour around his newly acquired parishes. He had arrived from the European continent only months earlier, escorting the King's second wife to her new home. Godfrey's appointment as the Bishop of Bath and Wells was a reward for years of faithful service as Her Majesty's chaplain.

Being on the wrong side of sixty, he was eager to receive the promotion. And the improved standard of living that came with it. But his welcome tour had revealed that, even for a bishop, life on the road was still an endless repetition of the same boring service in overcrowded chapels for unengaged congregations.

The Baron's injury didn't even make for an impressive story that Godfrey could recount to future guests. Rather than something gallant, like being gored by a cornered boar or falling from his horse at full gallop, Walter had managed to be stung by a humble bumble bee. All children were familiar with the sharp pain and hours of throbbing that followed a bee sting but for some unknown reason the Baron's entire finger had swollen and turned a worrying shade of blue. The hunting expedition was cancelled before they had spotted a single animal.

Godfrey was a progressive man and had used his limited spare time to experiment with treatments beyond those accepted amongst his fellow clergy. His experiments had mixed success for his usually compliant patients but he'd learned several tricks while helping those in his care. For Walter, Godfrey created a pure environment before cleaning the wound. The Bishop tried to remove all of the Baron's jewellery but he wouldn't hear of cutting the gold ring from his stung finger. Godfrey was certain it was the source of his host's pain but Walter was adamant so the Bishop was forced to consider alternative options.

Next he tried bloodletting. Godfrey reasoned that extraction of blood would reduce the volume of the swollen digit but was displeased when the finger remained enlarged despite several extractions. It appeared to be turning a deeper shade of blue too. Godfrey was unsure what more he could do but, unless something changed soon, would need to amputate the finger to prevent the corruption from spreading beyond the ring.

Walter glared at the Bishop as he applied a cork stopper to the latest vial of blood, despite the generous efforts to help. There was a knock at the door and Godfrey growled in annoyance. He'd been abundantly clear that he didn't wish to be disturbed.

The door opened and Walter's old Constable limped in, bowing to Godfrey before ushering a girl into the room. She had brilliant red curls and was unusually tall. Godfrey's annoyance rose when he noticed that the woman wore the rags of a peasant, strange to see within a keep but not entirely unexpected from the English rabble. As if the interruption weren't bad enough, Godfrey felt dirty just looking at her and he resented the woman for ruining the pure healing environment he'd worked so hard to create.

Godfrey was pleased when his assistant – a dour and businesslike priest – moved to quickly intercept the newcomers.

"What is the meaning of this? His Excellency explicitly asked for no interruptions while he is tending to your lord. Healing is a delicate process."

"My lord," the Constable said to the Baron, ignoring the Assistant. "You have most fortuitous timing. We've been visited by a healer woman travelling from Exeter. She has an excellent knowledge of herb-lore and might alleviate your pain while we wait for the Bishop's efforts to take effect."

The Constable turned on his heel and limped from the room before anyone could respond. The four remaining occupants awkwardly tried to size up the room. The Baron propped himself up in bed and appraised the newcomer, also viewing her ragged appearance with open distaste. Godfrey's assistant moved to shoo her away but in the same instant she spoke directly to the Bishop and the Baron.

"My lord. Your Excellency. I am indeed a healer. What is it that ails the Baron? I would be honoured to do what I can to assist."

Godfrey was shocked on two counts. First, that a lowly peasant had the gall to directly address nobility, without being asked to speak. More surprisingly, he registered that she spoke to them in French. The language of nobility. It was a strange dialect but unmistakably French.

Who was this woman?

Walter responded first. "My damned finger is about to fall off!" He brandished his bloody hand at the woman, splattering droplets across his quilt.

The peasant made to move towards the bed.

"Your services won't be needed," Godfrey told the woman firmly in French, testing her understanding. "Walter's humours are in balance and I have already administered appropriate treatment. You can do nothing more but pray for his speedy recovery."

The peasant's steely eyes revealed complete comprehension and a hint of disapproval.

"Your treatments haven't worked Bishop," Walter told him acidly. "If anything, they've made it worse. Let the girl take a look."

Godfrey was stunned by the Baron's insolence. He was only minor nobility, well beneath a bishop in rank, and surely knew when to defer to authority. The Bishop's blood began to boil.

"She wouldn't even know where to begin," Godfrey scoffed. "If she thinks she knows more than the Lord's highest representative to these lands, then by all means."

"I'll try anything at this stage," the Baron groaned. "Let her have a look."

With Walter's permission, the woman placed her bags by the door and delicately walked around the Baron's bed. As she passed, Godfrey noticed that beneath her ragged clothing she wore the most beautifully crafted boots he had ever seen. They looked better than any boots Godfrey had ever owned, an unusual design and precisely cut from the finest leather. The blatant display of wealth by one so far below his station stoked Godfrey's rage even further.

"Greetings lord Baron, I'm Matilda. What happened?" She spoke to the Baron in an insultingly casual tone.

"I got stung by a wretched bee out in the woods," he grunted. "Now my finger is the size of a carrot."

Matilda inspected the finger before turning to Godfrey.

"What treatments have you administered to remedy the situation?" she asked in an accusatory tone.

"I have released blood from the finger to reduce its size. Three times." Godfrey replied, though he was unsure why he defended his actions to a mere peasant.

"Has anyone tried to cut the ring off?" the woman asked.

"No!" Walter commanded. "This is my family's heirloom, a gift from the Conqueror himself."

The girl nodded and continued her examination of Walter's hand. Propped on the edge of the Baron's bed, she paused in thought before suddenly reaching up to her head and removing the ribbon from her hair. Her red curls fell down over her face, completely inappropriate for a woman in the company of clergy.

She pushed the ribbon under the Baron's ring using a hairpin which caused Walter to bellow in pain once more.

"Hush," she reassured him, like a mother calming a babe. "That was the worst part. I'll be able to remove the ring now, then the swelling should start to reduce."

She spoke in English, saying something about miniature suffering and extended reward. Godfrey didn't understand but the Baron gave a forced laugh and allowed her to continue.

Matilda pulled the ribbon so there was a length on either side of the ring and began to wrap it tightly around Walter's finger, causing him to wince with each loop. She wound the ribbon with deft hands and before long had wrapped the entire finger.

Matilda caught Godfrey's eye before gently pulling the length of the ribbon closest to Walter's knuckle. Like magic, the ring slid along the coiled ribbon with ease, leaving only a puffy red finger in its wake. With a final tug that made Walter cry out in pain, the ring suddenly fell into Matilda's outstretched hand. The bloody ribbon hung from her other. She beamed at the Baron as she held up both prizes.

The Baron's face flooded with relief and Godfrey saw colour already seeping back into the finger.

"How does it feel?" Matilda asked, handing Walter his heirloom.

"Better. So much better." He hollered in glee. "Where did you learn a nifty trick like that?"

"Just here and there," Matilda said with a smile. "My father was once asked to help a man in a similar situation, though his hand had been struck with a hammer and lost the finger before they could remove the ring."

"But I didn't lose the finger! I'd have sworn it were magic if I hadn't seen you do it with my own eyes. A ribbon!" He shook his head in disbelief and accepted the bloody ribbon from the girl. "A reward! You name it, I will see that you are handsomely compensated. What do you want? Silks? A horse?"

"That is very kind my lord," she said absentmindedly as she removed some small white stones from her bag. "But for now, let's focus on your recovery. Swallow these. It'll take time for your finger to return to a normal size and the pain from the sting will remain for a few days, though those cuts look like they might be more painful."

"They are," Walter said, glaring at Godfrey again. He waved his uninjured hand. "Bishop, leave me to recover. You've done enough."

The rude dismissal was Godfrey's final straw. Determined not to let his inferior see him crack, the Bishop managed to maintain his composure just long enough to collect his instruments. His diligent assistant received them on a tray and the pair strode from the room without a word. As they left, Godfrey heard the Baron tell Matilda to return later that afternoon to discuss her reward. It was galling to think that a peasant would be rewarded for a bishop's hard work.

Godfrey marched up the hallway to the guest quarters with both his jaw and his fists tightly clenched. His assistant trotted to keep up, making Godfrey's tools jingle on the tray.

Godfrey exploded into his room and slammed the door behind his assistant.

"Put those on the table and leave me. I've never been so humiliated!"

His assistant obediently placed the tray on the table and made to leave.

"Actually," Godfrey called, "on second thoughts. Prepare our things, we're leaving. I'll not be stuck in this hellhole of a town for a moment longer."

"But Your Excellence, we postponed our arrival at the next town for another two days. And we wouldn't arrive before nightfall. Surely you would be more comfortable here."

"I don't care Peter, just make it happen. Let's get this trip back on schedule. Perhaps even return to the cathedral early. I am growing weary of these rural paupers and their self-righteousness."

"I'll send a rider ahead to warn our next host to expect us this evening," Peter replied diligently. "But it will take time to pack your things and prepare your carriage before we can depart. Will you be staying here in your room?"

Godfrey strode over to the narrow arrow slit in the wall. Pulling back the heavy drape he looked down into the castle courtyard just in time to see the Redhead depart the keep and walk back into town.

"That's fine Peter, do what you must. I'll go stretch my legs before the ride."

Peter closed the door softly behind him and Godfrey continued to peer outside, watching as the mass of curly red hair disappeared beyond the castle walls.

Godfrey walked back to the table and inspected his collection of medical instruments. Forced to relive his humiliation, he snapped and launched a vial of blood across the room. It shattered against the keep's thick stone wall, the blood seeping down along the mortar.

Without a backwards look, Godfrey marched from the room.

With purpose.

CHAPTER EIGHT
20 October 1123

With a spring in her step, Matilda strode away from the keep and back towards Nether Stowey. There was a slight drizzle but she didn't mind. She was elated to have helped the Baron. As a child, she'd often played doctor with her father who had taught her the ribbon technique using his wedding ring. Matilda never dreamed that she would need to use it but her brain had dredged the technique from the depths of her memory and she'd operated by instinct.

Baron Walter's relief had been instant and he repeatedly insisted that Matilda be rewarded. Her mind ran wild with possibilities. Some were practical and in aid of her mission while others – like asking for formal ownership of her cave – were much more fanciful.

Walter had insisted on solitude to catch up on rest after his painful ordeal. He summoned Sir Phillip back into the room and explained the situation before ordering that the Constable take care of Matilda's belongings and grant a small allowance to enjoy the market. Matilda graciously accepted, though she took her satchel with her despite Phillip's continued offers to mind it. It was much too precious.

Matilda found she had an entire afternoon to explore the town and experience medieval life. She enjoyed every step of the journey back into Stowey, admiring the architecture and craftsmanship of the town's simple buildings. Ignoring the smells, it was actually quite quaint and Matilda happily foresaw frequent returns if Baron Walter became her patron.

The only dampener on Matilda's day was the Bishop. She'd tried to be diplomatic but knew that her medically necessary intervention had destroyed any chance that he would help with her quest to meet the King.

It had been a calculated decision. Matilda had quickly judged that the elderly Bishop was a thoroughly unpleasant man, from his arrogant attitude to his sagging face. His approach to medicine was barbaric and Matilda couldn't bring herself to let a patient suffer through his primitive ministrations. Plus, approaching a baron had always been the Institute's plan and Walter could still provide the introduction needed for her mission.

There was a slim chance that Pa would still be at the market so Matilda headed there first. He could relay the good news back to William. Matilda longed to see Rachel and Mama's faces when they learnt of her success.

Matilda passed a small stone chapel as she exited the castle. It looked newly constructed, the mortar still unweathered. The friendly priest from the castle stood outside, sweeping the front steps with a well-worn broom. He stopped and waved at Matilda so she detoured to say hello.

"You managed to help the Baron?" the Priest asked.

"I did, thanks to your tip-off. How did you know?"

"The screams from the keep finally stopped. Shortly after you ran off. And the Bishop's assistant just informed me that they would leave town today. He seemed quite agitated."

The Priest's brilliant blue eyes bored into Matilda, evoking a feeling of guilt.

"My methods may have differed from the Bishop's," Matilda admitted sheepishly. "You're right, he wasn't pleased."

"Not to worry. Bishop Godfrey will soon be gone, no doubt wanting to return to a life of luxury in his palace. He will quickly forget little old Stowey."

Matilda raised an eyebrow. "Careful Father, you wouldn't want people to think you're slandering your superiors."

He laughed. "Let them think what they will. I'm much too small a fish for anyone higher up to waste time with me. No ambition, you see. I'm content to sweep my little chapel and tend to my flock of parishioners. Leave the politics to the thrusters, they can keep the palaces."

"Well said," Matilda agreed. "Though I've definitely seen shabbier chapels. And in worse locations."

"True. I see most of the traffic passing into the castle, perfect for keeping watch over my flock...and keeping up with town gossip." The Priest patted the stone building. "It was a gift from the Baron for tending to his mother during her final days. Poor Isabel, and so soon after her husband's death. Walter is often a real pig, risk averse and primarily concerned with protecting his status quo. But he's also fiercely loyal and can be generous when he wants."

"That's nice to know," Matilda said. "He asked that I return to the castle to discuss a reward for my services. You have pretty good friends for a little fish."

"I'm blessed. And what of you? The town is already abuzz with news of the mysterious redhead with the strange accent. Where have you come from?"

"I'm travelling to London and only arrived in Nether Stowey today. I trekked from a tiny village in the hills, not far from here. Speaking of which, I need to see if my travelling companion is still at the market."

The Priest looked disappointed at the abrupt end to their conversation but recommended merchants to avoid and told Matilda to return to him for directions to London.

Pa was nowhere to be seen when Matilda arrived at the market but many stalls remained open so she purchased an apple and inspected their wares. She took great joy in examining the simple tools and trinkets on offer, asking perplexed sellers in great detail how they were made. Even the produce was fascinating, many items differing in size or colour to those she knew from the future. Harry, ever the budding botanist, would've loved it.

Matilda eventually exhausted the market's offerings but, being too early to return to the Baron, decided to explore the town. She combed the interconnected buildings of the inner streets before following a random road to the town's outer limits. She was surprised how quickly the town's population melted away, the buildings replaced with recently ploughed fields.

Matilda enjoyed seeing the rural area in action. She watched the rudimentary farming techniques until the clouds parted and revealed that the sun was well into its descent. Ready to see the Baron, Matilda turned around and happily strolled back toward the castle.

Fields transitioned to houses and she had just passed a particularly derelict hut when there was a sudden flurry of movement, followed by a sharp crack over her head.

Stars burst before her eyes and she dropped to a knee. Two pairs of hands were upon her in an instant. She was dragged behind the shack and pinned against a wall before she could put up a fight.

It took Matilda a moment to come to her senses and take stock of the situation. A bulky ox of a man held her upper arms tightly against the wall while another weedy man stood nearby with a club.

Feeling groggy, Matilda channelled her Institute combat training and lashed out with her legs while simultaneously trying to headbutt or bite the larger man. He dodged her flailing feet with ease and pinned her even tighter against the wall. Looking entertained, the smaller man sauntered over and struck her across the face with the back of his hand. A fresh wave of stars obscured Matilda's vision.

The hut's rickety door swung open and the Bishop emerged, his face livid and eyes ablaze.

"Who the hell do you think you are?" he spat. "A peasant girl thinking she could outsmart a bishop? A peasant girl that speaks French? A peasant girl with fancy boots and knowledge of medicine? It's preposterous! Who in damnation are you?"

Matilda stayed silent, glaring at him but clutching for a way out of her predicament.

"Do you know who I am? How powerful I am? And yet you try to undermine me. Do you think yourself smarter than a bishop?"

When Matilda failed to reply, he pointed to the smaller assailant.

"Bring me her bag. If she won't talk then I'll find out myself."

The smaller man dropped his club and moved to unloop the satchel from over Matilda's head. He dodged Matilda's kicks but her head surged forward as he reached for the strap and she sank her teeth into his arm. She bit with all her might and managed to draw blood before he wrenched his arm away with a yelp. Yet still the bigger man held her steady, squeezing her arms with immense force.

The smaller man inspected his arm before punching Matilda in the face and taking the bag. "She's a fighter," he noted with forced nonchalance as he handed over the satchel.

The Bishop scowled at him before opening the flap and emptying its contents onto the ground. Vials of chemicals shattered as he shook the bag, filling the air with fumes. Matilda's mind jumped to the memory of emptying the pod after her arrival and, despite the situation, laughed at the absurdity of her mind's workings. The three men looked at her as though she were deranged.

The Bishop continued to empty the bag and with one final shake, Matilda's bible fell into the dirt. He tossed the bag aside and gingerly knelt down to pick it up.

"A peasant carrying a bible?" he asked, reading the cover. He flipped through the pages, frustration etched across his face as he tried to make sense of the text and images. "This is no bible. Plants and star signs. What pagan blasphemy is this?" he roared, waving the Book in the air.

Matilda worried that the Bishop would damage her precious Book and, in her panic, let her already fragile façade drop. Godfrey registered the new fear in Matilda's eyes and correctly judged the Book's value to her. With a devilish grin of pure spite, he grabbed Matilda's bible in both hands and tore it in two with an almighty wrench. He punctuated his vandalism by throwing one half of the Book forcefully into a nearby puddle.

Matilda felt her stomach twist. Something within her snapped and defeat swelled up within her.

The Bishop gestured threateningly at Matilda with the other half of the Book. "Your belligerence with the Baron was one thing but this blasphemy is unforgivable." He paused, tapping the tattered tome to his head. "But I've no time to deal with this properly…"

He turned to his thugs.

"Do away with her. I don't care what you do or how you do it, just make sure she's gone. I'll see that you are suitably rewarded for your services."

With that, Godfrey marched off into the street without a backward glance, the ruined Book still in his hand.

When it was clear he was gone, the two men exchanged a puzzled look.

"He wants us to do *what?*" the larger man asked.

"You heard him," the smaller man snapped, still clutching his arm. "Do away with the bitch."

He pulled a knife from his belt and the magnitude of the situation struck Matilda with an icy wave of pure terror. Her struggles to break free became more frantic.

"That's not what we agreed to," the larger man protested, barely registering Matilda's struggles. "That's murder! A mortal sin!"

"No it's not you idiot. We were *ordered* to do it, by a man of God. The bloody bishop no less. It's sanctioned by the Church so we might as well have some fun while we're at it."

The smaller man leaned in closer to Matilda, her already knotted stomach churning even further at the smell of his rancid breath. A trickle of blood snaked from the bite marks on his arm. He held the knife to Matilda's neck, pushing hard enough to prick the skin.

"You try any more funny business and I promise to make this as unpleasant for you as possible."

He pulled away from Matilda and she defiantly renewed her violent struggle but was still unable to escape the giant's grip. She had trained for situations like this but had never felt so powerless. So hopeless.

The smaller man grabbed Matilda's tunic and ripped his knife down the front, cutting through Ma's loaned peasant clothes. He tore them apart, expecting Matilda's naked body, but was met by chainmail instead.

"Woah," the weedy man exclaimed. "That's the fanciest mail I've ever seen! The Bishop's gunna pay us a fortune when we're done here."

He lovingly stroked the mail with the back of his hand, chilling Matilda to the core as it inched lower along her stomach. The Bastard paused as he reached for his belt and looked her dead in the eyes, his wicked grin revealing several missing teeth.

"Stop!"

A yell came from the road and all three heads jerked towards the sound.

"You stop what you're doing right now or, so help me God!"

Matilda's eye had already started to swell over from the attack but she felt an immense flood of relief as the blurry form of Stowey's kindly priest marched towards them, his wispy white hair flailing in the wind. The Bastard stepped away from Matilda and hope roared like a wildfire within her chest.

The Priest stood a full head shorter than the Bishop's two brutes but he showed no signs of intimidation.

"What in Christ's name are you two doing?"

His brilliant blue eyes blazed with a righteous fury that rivalled Godfrey's as he surveyed the situation. The thugs stayed completely still and silent.

"I might've expected this from foreigners but people from our own town? I've known you both since you were children. What would your wives say? Your mother? Your friends? God?"

He lowered the temperature of his voice but continued to stare the pair down. The smaller thug glared back defiantly but Matilda felt the larger man's grip ease.

"Let her go," the Priest commanded. The larger man released Matilda instantly, earning a reproachful look from his partner. Matilda's legs were jelly and she collapsed to the ground.

The Priest pointed threateningly at both of them. "You two leave this place right now. Return to your families and consider what you might've lost if the constable had found you rather than me. I'll expect to see you both at Mass on Sunday, you're both due for some serious penance."

The Bastard still looked ready to stand his ground but his hulking companion grabbed his elbow and dragged him away. They were both running before they rounded the corner onto the street.

Matilda remained crumpled on the ground, weeping uncontrollably. The Priest knelt down beside her and placed a gentle hand on her shoulder. She flinched at his touch.

"Hush, my sister. I am so sorry. I saw the Bishop and those two dolts rush down from the castle shortly after you left. I came searching for you as soon as their purpose finally dawned on me."

Matilda's whole body shook with her sobs. The Priest crouched down and tried to help her cover up.

"Don't touch me!" Matilda cried, shoving the old man away. He stumbled and fell to the ground himself. Matilda surged to her feet and tried to cover herself before hobbling away from the infernal ruin. The Priest looked up at her with a combination of shock and devastation.

Matilda threw up by the shack but ran as soon as she reached the road. Each step hurt and she didn't know where she was running to but she needed to be away from that place. Away from people. She was terrified that the Bishop would send his men after her again. She needed to find safety.

Knowing she couldn't appear in front of the Baron half-naked and with a swollen face, she turned away from the town and fled to the safety of the forested hills.

She ran through the woods until her legs shook and could move no further. Matilda dropped to the ground, willing the earth to swallow her whole. The reality of her ordeal set in and she was forced to relive the pain. The fetid breath. The hopelessness.

Everything had gone wrong. Harry was dead. Matilda's satchel was gone. The bible destroyed. She couldn't even defend herself.

Matilda was numb and time seeped by but as twilight fell she discovered a new fear. Faced the prospect of night alone in the forest, her mind failed her as she struggled for a solution to her predicament.

After an eternity, it finally recalled Pa and his promise of hospitality. Matilda forced herself up from the rotting leaves and headed in the rough direction of William's village. It was difficult to travel in the failing light but she eventually discovered some familiar landmarks and stumbled back towards Holford. Creepy forest sounds haunted her steps and were only drowned out when the heavens finally opened to release a torrent of rain.

Darkness had fully set in by the time she passed Holford's ruined mill. Matilda was freezing in her tattered clothes but the village's scattered lights promised warmth and comfort. She spotted the family's hut and hobbled towards it.

Just as Matilda reached the front gate, Rachel emerged from the building carrying a basket of dirty dishes. William's eldest sister was startled when she spotted Matilda but smirked upon realising who it was.

"Look what the cat dragged in," Rachel sneered, noticing Matilda's state of undress and swollen face. "You didn't get far. It looks like you got what you deserve."

"Rachel, please…" Matilda pleaded, only to be cut off.

"No!" Rachel barked. "We don't want your filth here, corrupting our home. You don't know a woman's place in the world. I've no idea how things are where you're from but parading around like you do just isn't right! So get out of here. Go!"

Rachel's scorn hit Matilda has hard as the Bastard's punch and tears welled in her eyes once more. She stood in dumbfounded silence but when Rachel started hurling bowls at her, Matilda ran.

Not knowing where else to go once again, she ran back into the mountains and hobbled toward the only other place she knew.

CHAPTER NINE
4 December 1123

William happily helped his family work in the fields, mindlessly slashing wheat with a scythe while his mind was occupied pondering deeper questions. It had been months since William first discovered Matilda at her cave yet he remained obsessed with the mysterious woman. Her visit had awoken something within him. Not the desire to understand things, that had already been there. Instead, she had shown that answers to his questions actually existed. It was only a matter of finding them.

Long days helping in the fields no longer felt tedious as William distracted himself by asking questions about the world around him and trying to intuit sensible answers. Matilda had explained how a bird could soar without flapping its wings, the answer simple and yet so complex. William found similar riddles everywhere he looked. A duck floating in a pond or ash flying up the chimney. The sheer number of puzzles might've been overwhelming and driven others to simply give up. William found them enthralling.

Each question prompted at least a handful more, just as it had when he'd met Matilda. William's family rapidly tired of his constant wondering and deflected his constant barrage of questions with replies of "so what" and "who cares". They sent him to cut the fields alone, claiming it was one of his increased responsibilities since turning sixteen but really just seeking a few moments of respite.

As always, Elizabeth was most sympathetic and often humoured William. Although she too had limits, some of William's questions – usually those related to plants – struck a chord and she also suffered bouts of staring into distant nothingness. Pa was similarly tolerant of William's incessant questioning. It seemed that merely spending time with the Redhead was enough to awaken the mind.

William was yet to revisit Matilda's cave, despite his inflamed curiosity and his promise that he would do so. He worried that returning to the cave would prove underwhelming. Or worse, remind him of yet another adventure he couldn't join.

Instead, William spent his rare free time to build experiments. He worked all day in the fields, using the time to concoct new ideas and consider the results from previous experiments. When the day was over, he raced home to start new projects, using Matilda's knife to cut or carve and burning things over a small fire behind the cottage. Ma's untrained eye only saw mess and his noisy work often prompted bellowed warnings from his weary family. But despite constant exhaustion, William knew he was learning.

Looking up from his scythe, William saw that the family had stopped work and gathered under the giant oak, their heads already bowed in prayer ahead of their midday meal. Losing his train of thought, he threw the scythe over his shoulder and traipsed over to join them.

The family had already started eating when he arrived. He sat down and Rachel tossed his food at him as he washed his hands. The bread roll bounced off his shoulder and onto the grass. Too tired to retaliate, William just picked up the bread and half-heartedly brushed it on his tunic.

"Stop that," Ma scolded Rachel, seeing the fatigue in her son's eyes. "You look exhausted Will. Why don't you take the afternoon off? Go find Ralph and explore the woods."

William's mind was elsewhere and he barely registered what Ma had said. "Um, yeah? Ok. That'd be nice."

"Good. But no more experiments. You need a break." Ma gave him a concerned smile before helping the rest of the family pack up and return to the fields.

William watched them leave and finished his food before heading to find Ralph. He was shocked to see that Ralph's family were weeks ahead with their harvest and already ploughing for their winter crop. Ralph yelled at William from the other side of the field. His voice barely carried across the distance but Ralph's wild arm movements screamed "go away".

With strict orders to relax but no one to accompany him, William decided to stroll through the woods alone. He visited some favourite childhood landmarks but found that they no longer sparked the same level of excitement. William knew he was procrastinating, avoiding the one place in the forest he truly wanted to visit. He changed course and headed towards Matilda's cave.

William enjoyed the pleasant trek through the woods. It was mid-afternoon when he arrived at the gully and casually strolled towards the cave entrance. He felt uneasy before he could pinpoint exactly why and stopped to look around. Something wasn't right.

The camp was different. Untidy. Matilda's stack of dry firewood by the door was gone, replaced by chaotic jumble of damp sticks. The neat circle of rocks around the firepit were scattered and carcases of small rodents had been haphazardly discarded and left to rot. The door to the cave hung ajar from a single strap.

William felt sick to his stomach. He cursed himself for failing Matilda and allowing someone to invade the place she had tasked him to protect. William had little doubt that her precious possessions would be damaged. Or stolen.

He was just about to run into the cave to check when another thought stopped him in his tracks.

Who was using the cave? Were they still in there?

William had been cautious about outlaws only weeks earlier yet was suddenly prepared to barge into the cave without a second thought. He'd been fortunate that Matilda was the original inhabitant but it was unlikely that the new residents would be so friendly.

Nevertheless, William's guilt compelled him into the cave. Plucking up all of his courage, he drew his knife and peered inside through a gap in the door.

William's eyes adjusted to the dark. There were no signs of life but inside was chaos. The intruders had looted the entire chamber and Matilda's furniture was strewn in pieces across the floor.

William headed inside but the smell of rotten food and human waste made his eyes water. William gathered what he could and piled anything salvageable at the foot of Matilda's cot. He eventually discovered Matilda's magical torch amongst her possessions which made the tidying process much quicker. William was on edge the entire time, listening for the smallest sound that might hint at the vandal's return.

He had just leaned Matilda's shovel against the cave wall when he heard shuffling sounds coming from deeper within the cave. He froze and listened for the noise. Everything was silent. Then he heard the shuffle again.

"Hello?" William called out delicately, casting the torch around the cavern and illuminating a cloaked figure crouched in the far corner. The figure shuffled again in the torchlight. Its blanket dropped and a matted curl of red hair fell out.

Matilda!

William flooded with excitement, his mind instantly racing with the questions he had most wanted to ask her. But as the reality of her ragged appearance sunk in, those thoughts were quickly replaced with concern.

"Matilda? Why are you here? Aren't you supposed to be in London with the King?"

Matilda brushed her hair back into the blanket. She ignored William's question, refusing to look him in the eye.

William considered the sight before him. The hunched figure was a shell of the brilliant woman he had met only weeks before.

"Are you alright?" he asked, his voice full of empathy. "Of course not, what am I thinking. Oh Matilda, what happened?"

She finally stared up at him with hollow eyes. Tears rolled down her cheek but still she remained silent.

"You should have come back. To my family," William continued. "We could've helped."

His final comment prompted a response, though not one William had hoped for.

Matilda glared at him with unbridled hatred before surging to her feet and storming from the cave. Still without a word.

William heard the door wrenched open and was left standing alone in the dark cave. He took a moment to compose himself and wondered what could've happened to Matilda. He was hurt by her sudden animosity. He'd only been trying to help.

Unsure what to do, he returned to the front of the cave and finished cleaning Matilda's mess. He organised the pile at the end of her bed and then swept out most of the accumulated filth. William left the cave door open as he departed, judging that the risk posed by the filthy air was worse than the chance of a wild animal getting in. With that, he made the long and lonely journey back to Holford. Confused as ever.

+++

William repeatedly replayed his encounter with Matilda over the following weeks. Analysing the interaction became more important than his thought experiments. William longed to tell his family about the Stranger's return but, feeling the news would only stir trouble, kept it to himself.

William returned to the cave several times over the following week, resuming his childlike habit of shirking family duties whenever possible. The weather had taken an early turn for the worst and the family urgently fought to save their crop. But William somehow felt the Stranger could help. He knew it.

William began eating only half of his meals and saved the rest for Matilda, determined to lift her from her malaise. His stomach always rumbled as he returned from the cave but he was sustained by the righteousness of the deed.

Matilda tried to avoid William at first. She quickly learned his schedule and was rarely at the cave when he arrived, though he sometimes spied her darting into the undergrowth like a startled deer. Undeterred, he left his small packages of food by the cave entrance and hoped that Matilda would return before it was snatched by some other forest inhabitant.

William felt dejected after each visit but stubbornly insisted on returning until he knew why Matilda wasn't in London with the King. He was driven by Ma's favourite saying, that even the hardiest cliff will be eroded by a gentle but relentless tide.

William gradually observed positive signs. The camp became tidier, firewood stacked more neatly and animal carcasses piled together rather than scattered around the fire. The door had been hung back on both hinges.

Matilda stopped running and they eventually reached an unspoken agreement that William could talk while Matilda ate. He shared his observations and the results of his experiments. Although Matilda remained silent, her interest in each given topic told William if he was onto something.

Things were looking up, despite the worsening weather and its devastating impact on the family's harvest.

Then Pa got sick.

It all happened too quickly. One day Pa was coughing in the fields and the next he couldn't get out of bed. His harvest responsibilities were all thrust upon his only son and William found it impossible to visit Matilda. Mama soon came down with the same ailment and it ripped through the village, killing one of the elderly men. Between the weather and the illness, Holford was miserable. But William had hope.

An endless drizzle had settled over the lands and the forest's once colourful leaves filled the air with the smell of rot. Rain lashed William as he trekked back to Matilda's cave.

"You're late," Matilda grumbled from her cot when William entered the cave. They were the first words she'd uttered since William rediscovered her.

William sat in his usual spot against the cave wall, water dripping from his wet clothes and pooling around him on Matilda's recently swept floor. Exhausted, he tossed her the package of food and leaned his head against the wall before closing his eyes.

They sat in silence, though William could feel Matilda's eyes on him.

"The harvest is going poorly. Pa and Mama are sick." He spoke casually, as though merely giving an update on threshing wheat. "I was wondering…" He paused, opening his eyes to look at the Stranger. "Do you know a disease that causes a rash across the chest? That wastes away even the strongest of men?"

Matilda stared back blankly, raising a chunk of cheese up to her mouth.

William ploughed on.

"I thought you might know how to fix it? Holford's midwife doesn't, she's never seen anything like it. We're already so far behind with the harvest and really need Pa back to help. I don't know how we'll feed the family through winter without him."

"Why would I help your family William?" Matilda asked mournfully. "Particularly your dear Mama, the rotten old hag. After the way she and her parrot treated me?"

William was confused. "They were unkind but their words weren't so bad."

"Rachel didn't tell you?" Matilda replied. "I was attacked by your beloved Bishop, may he burn in hell. And when I returned to your family seeking refuge? Your damned sister cast me away, hurling plates and laughing as I fled into the woods."

William sat in shock, his eyes wide with disbelief. The cave fell silent but the echo of Matilda's revelation continued to reverberate off the walls.

"We heard word that someone had performed a miracle for the Baron," William said to himself in little more than a whisper. "I thought it must've been you."

"It was. But I can't keep giving. I've given everything. My family and friends. My security. My mission. I don't know how I'm supposed to run around this land curing all ills and saving everyone. Lord knows that they haven't done the same for me."

Silence descended once more and William watched the ghost of Matilda with sadness.

With a sudden realisation, William stood and strode back towards the door.

"Where are you going?" Matilda called out, a hint of desperation in her voice.

William turned back to her as he reached for the latch.

"I am truly sorry for all you have suffered. I've already warned that Rachel's character is lacking but I apologise that you had to experience her wickedness firsthand. I pray that your wounds heal and your energy returns."

He gave a big sigh and blinked back tears of his own.

"Your refusal to help hurts. You came to us for a reason. You believed in it strongly enough to give up so much. Don't forsake us all. Don't judge the many by the actions of the few."

He paused again.

"This," he said, gesturing to Matilda's cave, "isn't living. What's done is done. There is no changing the past, unless you can make that egg of yours work again. Pick yourself up and plough on. It's what I'm trying to do. But I've got to take care of my own family now."

William wrenched the door open and strode from the cave. There was nothing more for him there.

CHAPTER TEN
19 December 1123

Tremendous gusts of wind buffeted Godfrey's carriage as it trundled along heavily guttered rural lanes, throwing the Bishop around uncomfortably. His attempts to accelerate the remainder of his parish tour had been riddled with fallen trees and swampy roads. Still travelling well after dark, the infernal tour showed no sign of ending.

Godfrey longed to be back in a proper town like Bath or Wells. He missed the comforts of his palace and the intrigues of court. He loathed the commoners' petty concerns and longed to be free from his cramped carriage forever.

The only thing that annoyed Godfrey more than the never-ending tour was the memory of the red-haired heretic. It had been weeks since their encounter yet he still rankled at the thought that a peasant woman would dare to challenge a bishop.

Such insolence!

Godfrey never discovered exactly how his two brutes had disposed of the Heretic but their roughness behind the shack reassured him that justice would be served.

The altercation was another reminder that Godfrey now lived in a savage land full of uncouth people. Things were more civilised back home on the European mainland. Godfrey hailed from the border regions of the Holy Roman Empire, the last bastion of the epic civilisation created by the Romans before the time of Christ. True, the Romans had murdered the Lord. But the durability of their empire, and aqueducts, was to be admired.

The Normans hadn't progressed much from the pagan tribes vanquished by the Romans yet even they had enhanced civility among the English after The Conqueror won his battle at Hastings. As far as Godfrey was concerned, the English were little better than the Nordic barbarians that raped and pillaged along the coasts of the North Sea. After his run in with the Redhead, Godfrey had promised to treat the English as the savages they were and meted out harsh punishments wherever possible to reinforce the costs of being uncivilised.

The Heretic's Book was an unexpected boon from the encounter. In his rage, Godfrey had left the ruined house still clutching the rear half and only realised when his temper cooled halfway back to the castle. The Bishop had considered discarding the heretical tome but worried that it might be picked up by a commoner. He laughed at himself for his foolishness.

As if an English commoner would know how to read.

It was during the journey to the next town that Godfrey first inspected the Book more thoroughly. Despite its blasphemy, the Book was a treasure. He first noticed the shocking realism of the Book's many illustrations, so stunningly lifelike that they appeared to be windows into another world. Godfrey held the Book at odd angles to try seeing more but the window's aperture was fixed. He was next intrigued by the Book's text, so perfectly uniform that the letters themselves were a work of art.

Godfrey was even further intrigued when he finally looked beyond the physical book and inspected its content. He discovered that the text was written in English rather than Latin. He could intuit some general topics or the occasional familiar name but this only further fuelled his interest. No words were needed to appreciate the pictures and Godfrey developed a morbid fascination with the Book's obscenely detailed anatomy sketches.

The Bishop was baffled that such an intriguing book could be written in English. The commoners' tongue. He knew of no English authors, let alone ones versed in such a broad range of topics. For weeks, Godfrey wondered how he would ever find a civilised translator to help decipher the text.

The Book quickly became Godfrey's favourite escape from the tedium of his parish tour. The more he daydreamed about it during services, the more he was convinced that it was a priceless treasure worthy of being stored in the Papal library. It might've been Godfrey's key to climbing further up the church hierarchy. If it was complete. He regretted tearing the Book in two, though he blamed the Heretic's stubborn silence for goading him into the needless act of vandalism.

And so his journey through the parishes continued. The same routine mass for the same greedy nobles with nothing to offer. Godfrey swore he would scream if he was offered one more fourth-born son to join his retinue as a trainee priest. And the commoners' requests were always the same. Heal my mother. Pray for a bountiful harvest. Deliver justice against the landlords. Godfrey did everything in his power to minimise contact with them.

Knowing exactly what he had to look forward to, Godfrey was in a foul mood when the carriage finally came to a stop. Wind nearly tore the door from its hinges as Peter leapt inside to give his regular pre-arrival brief.

"We've arrived at Babcary, Your Excellency. Another tiny village, though this one is set by a river." He called out louder, trying to be heard above the wind. "The local lord is Sir Simon and his wife is…"

Godfrey missed the next few words as the wind ripped the carriage door open again. Peter continued to talk as he heaved the door closed and fastened the latch.

"…and their youngest son is called John."

Godfrey impatiently waved his assistant along. "Peter, I don't care. Men are 'my son' and women are 'my daughter'. It's really not that difficult being a bishop. How long until we reach my estate?"

"Only a matter of days now. We'll rush through the service tomorrow and be off to the next village after lunch. Then just three more villages after that."

Peter opened the door and Godfrey followed him from the carriage, forgetting all decorum and running for the cover of the castle's tiny keep with his hand clasped tightly to his cap. The castle was fittingly small for such an insignificant village, its walls made of timber and the castle mound barely more than a molehill. The keep wasn't even made of stone and instead resembled an old English longhouse. Godfrey foresaw another dreary night.

An attendant closed the keep's heavy oak door behind them and the Bishop looked around the tiny castle's main hall. Although small, it was surprisingly homely and great care had been taken in creating the tapestries that decorated each wall. The wind continued to howl outside but a large fire roared in the hearth, its warm glow casting flickering shadows around the room.

The castle's lord stood to attention beside his wife, three sons and two daughters. Unlike the self-important lords of the larger landholdings, the minor nobility tended to know their rightful place and Godfrey approved of this acknowledgement of his superiority. Perhaps the evening would not be as dreary as he'd thought.

"Bishop Godfrey! Welcome. Our village is blessed to be graced with your presence. Please."

The lord ushered Godfrey toward a long dining table, giving him the seat at the head of the table closest to the fireplace. The Bishop's aching bones appreciated the gesture which partially compensated for the embarrassingly thin spread of food on offer. It was late but the family appeared to have waited to join the Bishop for his meal.

"Your Excellency, it is a pleasure to meet you," the lord interrupted as Godfrey chewed on a scrawny chicken leg. "I am Sir Simon, lord of these lands. This is my wife Ida and these are our children."

The family insisted on small talk and introduced themselves one-by-one. The eldest son was a knight and the second son training to become one.

"I've almost completed my first tapestry," the youngest daughter chimed. "Mother is helping finish the final stitches."

"And I'm John," finished the youngest son, average in every way. "Do you know of Plato?"

Godfrey bristled at being directly questioned and Sir Simon berated his over-inquisitive son. The lord correctly sensed that Godfrey's patience was wearing thin and asked the family to eat the rest of their meal in silence.

Simon offered to personally show Godfrey to his quarters as the table was cleared.

"I must confess, it's John's room. Our youngest son. It's small but it has the sturdiest bed. We prayed that you would understand."

Their prayers hadn't worked. Godfrey was offended, but he was too tired to rise to the slight. He set his jaw and entered.

The room was little more than a closet. It lacked the main hall's warm hearth and wind whistled through gaps in the wooden walls. Fresh flowers released a pleasant scent but it was like putting a dress on a donkey. The room was far beneath Godfrey's station.

The Bishop grunted goodnight to his hosts and was about to collapse into the small bed when he noticed a small desk in the corner of the room, covered with loose paper. Godfrey had seen some of the richer nobles learn their letters but never the third son of a poor minor lord.

Probably an over-zealous local priest, Godfrey thought, *looking to secure another victim to work for the church.*

The penmanship was scrappy. Among scattered Latin prayers and hymns were several pages of drawings and text that Godfrey couldn't read. They used the familiar Latin alphabet but the words made no sense.

Too tired to bother deciphering any more, Godfrey gave up and collapsed on the bed. Sleep took him instantly.

+++

Godfrey woke the next morning to the sound of Peter rapping at his door. He had once again overslept and was late for Mass. The weather remained miserable.

The village's tiny wooden chapel was already crammed shoulder to shoulder when Godfrey finally arrived. The building's sole chair had been reserved for the Bishop and he slouched in it, barely able to keep his eyes open. Godfrey's mind wandered as Peter led the congregation through a grating refrain of his favourite hymn. He found himself thinking about the writing from the boy's room and he tried to recall the names he had read.

Hrothgar. Grendel. They sounded English.

Epiphany struck Godfrey like a bell as the hymn finished and he bolted upright in his seat.

The boy could write English! He was transcribing scenes from Beowulf, the English epic.

Godfrey decided to overlook the boy's celebration of a clearly inferior language and was instead filled with an overwhelming sense of opportunity. He'd found someone that could write, and presumably read, English! Just the person he needed to decipher the heretical tome.

The Bishop contained his excitement and got through the rest of the service with enhanced vigour, taking care to mask his attempts to spot the average boy amidst the congregation. Godfrey tolerated the incessant requests from the villagers, blessing them absentmindedly as he started planning which parts of the Heretic's Book the boy should work on first.

The congregation thinned and eventually only the priests and the family remained. Godfrey seized the opportunity.

"I thank you for your hospitality," he said sweetly as he approached Sir Simon.

"I've never seen the chapel so full! My family and I should've arrived earlier, we almost struggled to squeeze in."

"Indeed, a most enthusiastic congregation. Now perhaps the issue of space is something I could help you with?"

Godfrey saw the local priest's eyes widen, no doubt hoping for a new church.

"Oh really?" Sir Simon asked, intrigued but wary. "How so?"

"Well, I realised while staying in your son's room..."

"We truly do apologise for that my lord," the wife interrupted. "Simon, we should have just slept on the floor."

"Not at all my dear," Godfrey replied impatiently. "I have realised that your son has a unique talent. One that could be very useful in the service of the Church."

"He does?" the eldest brother questioned. The whole family looked surprised.

"He does," Godfrey echoed. "Boy, how long have you been writing?"

"A couple of years," the boy replied timidly.

"Oh, writing?" Sir Simon said. "Father Reginald here has taught all of the family how to read and write Latin. John is particularly talented."

"But how long have you been writing in English?" Godfrey asked John.

"English?" Father Reginald asked with surprise. Everyone gawked at the boy.

"Not long," John conceded. "A few months perhaps. I was bored and wanted to try something new with the letters."

"He's not in trouble, is he?" the boy's mother interrupted again.

"No he's not, though he was lucky it was me who found out. Others may have been less...lenient."

The family milled around in an uncomfortable silence, not sure what to say.

"I propose," Godfrey continued, "that the boy returns with me to the cathedral in Bath. He can join the seminary and train to become a priest. He would be well taken care of and, if he continues to show promise, I will grant him access to my private library."

Sir Simon paused in thought as he considered the offer.

"No!" came an emphatic response, though it wasn't Sir Simon.

Everyone looked back at the boy.

"I don't want to go," he cried defiantly. "My home is here. My life is here."

His mother put her arm around his shoulder but the boy's defiance was already deflating under the Bishop's withering glare.

"Don't test the limits of my generosity Simon. Many have asked for such a privilege on my tour, to have their sons join the clergy to serve their Bishop. Others would have the boy flogged, perhaps even his eyes taken out, for daring to waste precious paper and ink to spread the commoner's tongue. I can ensure that his talents are put to a righteous use."

Simon was quiet, looking from the boy to Godfrey and back again.

"Ok," he surrendered.

The room melted into a storm of emotions. Godfrey felt triumphant. The boy cried out in despair. His brothers looked amused. The local priest looked robbed.

"Very good!" Godfrey clapped. "Well. Peter. John. Hurry now. We must arrive at our next destination earlier than last night."

"Yes Your Excellency." Peter ran off to prepare the carriage for their departure.

Feeling generous, Godfrey turned to his new recruit.

"Boy, take a moment to collect your belongings and bid farewell to your family."

The boy glared at Godfrey, his eyes oozing contempt for the Bishop. Godfrey mirrored the gaze but added a glimmer of triumph. John broke eye contact and accepted his fate with defeat, following his family back to the castle to collect his belongings.

CHAPTER ELEVEN
22 December 1123

It was cold. And wet. Matilda was sick and felt miserable.

She'd been jabbed with every vaccine known to man before journeying back in time. The Institute doctors warned that she would encounter innumerable viruses and bacteria, many that hadn't been seen for centuries. Each would assault her immune system, though the doctors assured Matilda that none were likely to cause any lasting damage to a woman in her prime.

They also warned that she would inevitably carry diseases from the future, despite their best efforts to quarantine her from the outside world. Any interaction with the new world risked the exchange of an unknown number of bugs.

But being forewarned had done little to help Matilda.

All the vaccinations in the world couldn't have protected against her encounter with the Bishop and his thugs behind the rundown shack. The attack was seared into her memory and she regularly woke in a sweat as the scene replayed on loop, her mind enhancing each nightmarish detail. The vice-like grip on her arms. The putrid breath. The mocking looks in their eyes.

Matilda was angry at herself for allowing it to happen. Even knowing that Harry would help keep her safe, she had spent years before her departure learning self-defence and sparring against classmates. Years training her body to fight. But there was little anyone could do to protect against a club to the back of the head or a man at least double her weight.

She'd let her guard down in her moment of triumph. And she hated herself for it.

Her depression had been building for years, the Bishop's attack was just the last straw. Leaving her family for the Institute. Studying so hard. The final sprint to prepare for the looming Drop. Leaving behind all that she knew for a plan that had failed. Harry's death. It was little wonder she had fallen.

William had been her saviour. Not some strapping man with a chiselled jaw, she'd never have stood for that. But she had been too deep in her depression to save herself, so instead she was rescued by a farm boy.

It had been difficult seeing William when he first returned to her cave. He was a reminder of Rachel's cruelty. And a man. Matilda hadn't yet forgiven herself for her moment of weakness with the Bishop and she'd been cruel in her grief.

Matilda regretted how she had treated the Boy. He'd asked for her help, to cure a disease that she had in all likelihood inflicted upon his village. Yet she continued to wallow. She had let down her only friend in an alien world and hadn't seen William for days since.

What was done was done.

There was something so final in his parting words. He wasn't angry. Disappointed was an understatement.

Matilda reflected on everything that had happened since she arrived back in time. All so different from the Institute's meticulous plans. Her mission was in tatters. The window for arriving in London to meet the King was long gone. Matilda knew that King Henry would be in Normandy to put down a rebellion and wouldn't return to London for almost a year. Even more time for her best laid plans to go awry.

Matilda thought back to the day of her arrival, when she had toasted the fact that she was the smartest person on the planet. She knew now, that all the knowledge and training in the world meant nothing without also knowing *how* to use it.

But she wouldn't be defeated. Dragging herself from her cot, Matilda gathered up her belongings and wrapped them in her blanket. She looked back at the empty cave as she closed the door. Few traces of her occupation remained.

There was no changing the past, William had said.

But that was exactly what she was there to do.

CHAPTER TWELVE
22 December 1123

The sun had barely risen when Margery stealthily prepared for another day of hard toil in the fields. She shuffled around the gloomy cottage, searching for her missing shoe while desperately trying not to wake Pa or Mama. Their strange illness seemed to have worsened overnight and the sounds of their laboured breathing filled the room.

William already waited outside but Ma and Elizabeth joined in Margery's wordless preparations. Rachel was also awake and had resumed her vigil at their grandmother's bed. She had long since forsaken work in the fields, instead playing the role of carer for their sick family members.

"How's she doing?" Margery whispered.

"Fine," Rachel hissed, though Margery heard genuine concern in her voice. "She was completely delirious last night, thought I was either Aunt Susan or Papa. I don't know what more to do. Astrid was no help, stupid midwife. This is all that wicked foreigner's fault. She brought her filthy foreign disease."

Margery hummed in vague agreement, not wanting to fuel further angst towards the Redhead. Barely a day went by that Rachel didn't mention William's strange visitor, though they'd luckily seen no sign of her since Pa escorted her away to Stowey. Margery guessed that her elder sister resented the Foreigner's unrepentant freedom. She shared the sentiment to an extent, though didn't dare raise the topic. Margery hated conflict and knew that Rachel's anger at the woman could easily shift to her.

Ma silently beckoned from the door so Margery gave Rachel's shoulder a squeeze of encouragement and rushed out to start the day. Ma handed Margery and Elizabeth tools for the day's work and hurried them along to join William.

Margery's brother sat out the front of the cottage, waiting impatiently for his sisters to emerge. He was antsy and already in a foul mood. The first weeks of William's adult life had been a trial by fire. He was the man of the house in Pa's absence and shouldered the majority of the family's work. Margery felt sorry for him but it was admittedly nice to see him finally pull his weight. He'd gotten away with the bare minimum for too long but the protections afforded by his extended childhood were gone. Now he too got to see the world for what it truly was. Warts and all.

"Where's Rachel?" William asked tetchily.

"She's staying behind again to look after Mama and Pa," Ma responded wearily. "They're both getting worse. And Rachel said she needs to 'perfect her tending skills' before her wedding."

There was an uncharacteristic hint of sarcasm in Ma's voice. The stress of their late harvest and sick family weighed on her too.

"But we need all the help we can get," William whined. "The cold weather's setting in and the crop's already starting to rot."

"Don't worry about it Willy, we need to get going. Besides, we'll get more done if you two aren't at each other's throats."

With a shrug, William conceded that Ma had a point and the four of them departed to the field. As they walked, Margery noted the thinning numbers of villagers that still worked their fields. Some had also succumbed to the mystery illness while others had already finished their harvest and awaited their turn with Holford's single plough before sowing the winter crop.

Most of the villagers had noticed her family's struggle, though none had offered to help. A few had given friendly smiles as the family trudged home after another long day, a mix of empathy, encouragement and approval at seeing William finally pulling his weight. But nothing more. Everyone was too busy caring for their own sick family members. One's own clan always came first.

Margery was concerned by William's mention of rot. It was a curse for the slow or lazy that accelerated with each drizzly day. It would determine how comfortably the family would live through winter. If at all. The family had discussed the food situation during the cold evenings and it looked dire no matter what they did. It was just a question of how dire. The promise of a hard winter, full of hunger and haggling for food, only further dampened their motivation to work in the fields.

The family made for glum travelling companions and even Elizabeth was silent. They were already flat upon arriving at their field. Before they'd even started working. They dumped their belongings beneath the grand old oak and, without a word, collected their tools and dispersed to begin their prescribed tasks. Each moved as if wading through honey.

William marched into the field with Pa's scythe and hacked at the crop with unusual ferocity, driven by some unspoken rage. Ma and Elizabeth took the role of baling the cuttings so Margery was left alone to thresh the family's semi-dry wheat with William's flail. She preferred it that way, being alone. She threw herself into the work, trying to extract every grain she could.

Burning arms today is better than an aching stomach in the winter.

The morning passed with its usual monotony. Other villagers started to arrive around midday to deliver food to the few remaining workers. Margery saw Joan Miller pass by with a basket for her latest love interest. Joan and Rachel were the queens of Holford's youth, friends one moment and bitter rivals the next. The only thing guaranteed to unite them was the promise of tormenting their younger siblings.

Joan's younger brother Henry was Margery's age and her only friend in the world. They were both outcasts after their elder sisters' endless taunts and the pair had established an alliance that blossomed into a friendship. Margery occasionally dreamed of it becoming something more. That would mean having Joan as a sister-in-law but she'd survived childhood with Rachel and could always build a nice little cottage on the far side of Holford. Margery wished Henry would bring her a basket.

Instead, her family paused beneath the almost naked oak for a dreary meal of the previous evening's stale bread. The conversation was as sparse as their food but Elizabeth did spot a rainbow, pointing it out to her solemn companions with child-like glee. It was the highlight of their day.

The family returned to their solitary tasks and worked until it was dark. The family collected their tools and Margery poured the day's takings into a sack. It wasn't even full.

They were all exhausted as they trudged back towards the house and the weather mimicked their mood, suddenly buffeting them with sheets of sleet. Ma and Elizabeth shared some weary banter while Margery and William lagged behind, preferring to walk in silence.

When they arrived at the cottage, Margery was irked that Ma and Elizabeth had paused at the front gate rather than going straight into their warm home. Eager to dry herself and the grain by the fire, Margery walked up to see what was the matter. And almost dropped their grain in shock.

The red-haired foreigner sat on a log beside the front vegetable patch. Water ran down her face and she was sopping wet but she squinted up at the family with a big smile.

"Hello there," she called jovially. "Back from a productive day in the fields I hope? Terrible weather."

"What are you doing here?" William hissed through gritted teeth, further shocking Margery with the hate in his voice.

"I tried to wait inside but Rachel threw me out. Something about causing your grandmother undue distress, though she used much more colourful language. So I pulled up a log to wait until you returned home."

The Foreigner's jolly mood didn't match the bleakness her surroundings.

"I don't care why you're on the ground," William spat. "Why are you here? Back in Holford? Shouldn't you be skulking in your cave?"

Margery gave William a curious look at the mention of a cave. *Wasn't she supposed to be in London?*

The Foreigner's head drooped like a chastised child. When she looked back up, her smile was gone and she spoke seriously.

"William, I've thought long and hard about what you said to me back at the cave. About how you've helped me over these past weeks when I couldn't help myself. And about how I repaid your kindness…"

The Redhead paused, suddenly aware that the family were all staring down at her.

"Anyway," she dismissed. "I owe you an apology. I owe you my gratitude. You were there when no one else was. You kept me company. And kept me alive. So I'm here to make up for being a complete ass."

Ma scowled at Matilda's foul language.

"I think I can help Pa, and Mama," Matilda continued. "If you'll let me?"

Margery's ears pricked up at the promise of assistance and her hope multiplied when she remembered that the Foreigner was an herbalist. Ma's scowl remained firmly set though her eyes also shone with anticipation.

But William stared at the Foreigner with distrust, weighing the sincerity of her words. He looked torn and even wearier than when they'd left the field.

"Fine," William eventually replied.

"Oh thank God," Margery exclaimed, butting through the gate and inside to escape the rain. She dropped the flail by the door with a thud and crept into the cottage, hanging up her wet coat and placing the grain by the warm hearth.

Pa gave a nasty cough and Rachel glared at her for the sudden disruption. Margery considered telling her sister about the Foreigner but decided against it. She would find out soon enough.

CHAPTER THIRTEEN

22 December 1123

Matilda's limbs ached from sitting in the cold for so long but Elizabeth helped heave her up from her log. Matilda hugged the friendly girl, grateful for the small kindness.

Margery had already barged into the hut and Ma promptly followed to check on her husband and mother. William passed next. He placed the family's scythe under the building's small awning with great reverence before wiping the rain off its long blade and gesturing for Matilda to enter the hut.

The poor boy looked exhausted. His face was grim and he avoided making eye contact. Matilda was relieved that he had relented and permitted her to join the family indoors. Sitting in the cold had given plenty of time to consider her strategy for mending things with William. There'd be a long, wet walk back to her cave if she failed. But William granting access to the hut was a positive step.

It was dark inside, the only window firmly locked to keep out the weather. It smelt terrible, the homely cooking aromas of her previous visit replaced with a revolting combination of stale sweat, bile and faeces. The family were either oblivious or had learned to cope. A smouldering log warmed the building's single room. It was nice to be out of the rain but the heat was stifling. Rachel must have been trying to burn the sickness out. Or summon the devil.

Stout Margery stood by the fire, drying her hair and talking to her eldest sister in hushed tones. Spindly Rachel knelt like a nun at the foot of Mama's bed. Her head was bowed in prayer, though she conversed with Margery through a series of dignified grunts.

Ma took Matilda's makeshift coat – her drenched blanket – and hung it by the fire. William closed the door with a bang, causing Rachel to jump.

"Be quiet, fool," Rachel hissed as she turned from Mama's lumpy form. "You'll wake them u…"

Rachel froze mid-scold when she saw Matilda. Her eyes burned with white-hot fury and she longed to scream but didn't dare wake Mama. Rachel regained a touch of composure before speaking.

"What the devil is she doing in here?" Her voice was perfectly level but it failed to mask the manic look in her eyes. "I wasted precious time keeping her outside and you just let her in like some mangy cat?"

She directed her question at Ma and Elizabeth, ignoring Matilda and William altogether.

Like the rest of the family, Ma was exhausted and in no mood to argue.

"Rachel, please. We know you don't like the girl but she's here to help. Isn't she Willy?"

William nodded.

"I don't care!" Rachel cried. "I've been helping here all day while you've been out messing around in the fields. It was me that tended to them, keeping them fed and watered and warm. Now you want some stranger, some wicked stranger, to come and try doing it better?"

"You know better than anyone just how much Mama is struggling," Ma continued. "And we won't finish everything in the fields without Pa. We need our family happy and healthy. So who are we to look a gift horse in the mouth? Here you are praying for assistance and we have an herbalist, who's supposed to be in London," Ma glanced at Matilda with a raised eyebrow, "miraculously arrive at our front door. We should at least hear what she has to say."

Rachel crossed her arms and pouted but didn't say another word.

"Well love," Ma said to Matilda, breaking the uncomfortable silence. "There's no point waiting around. Fix my family!"

Ma gestured to a shape lying by her feet just behind the door. Matilda realised it was Pa rugged up on a low cot.

Seeing Pa was even more confronting than the hut's smell. He was gaunt and his previously strong frame looked frail after weeks of wasting away in bed. He was covered in a sheen of sweat which felt wrong amidst the endless patter of rain outside. Matilda didn't know how the figure before her was the same man who'd singlehandedly carried three sacks of grain.

"Is Mama the same?" Matilda asked no one in particular, trying to keep the concern out of her voice.

William nodded and Matilda walked to the other side of the room to inspect the grandmother. Rachel blocked Matilda's path and belligerently stood her ground. Matilda tried to look unthreatening but it was only after a stern look from Ma that Rachel reluctantly stepped out of the way.

Mama somehow looked even worse than Pa. Her feeble chest shuddered with every breath and a trickle of spittle seeped from the corner of her mouth. She too was covered in sweat, despite Rachel's efforts to wipe her brow. Alongside a pungent bucket of vomit by the bed, Matilda noticed a bowl of water perfumed with flower petals and a small square of silk, a surprising luxury that would've been incredibly difficult for the family to come by. Rachel had taken her tending duties very seriously.

Matilda bent down to get a closer look at her more desperate patient but Mama's reaction was instant. Unable to make any intelligible sounds, Mama made an awful gurgling noise and attempted to roll her weak body away from Matilda.

Rachel's response was equally visceral. She threw herself at Matilda with an ear-splitting shriek, tackling her to the ground and dragging her away from Mama. She pulled at Matilda's hair and scratched with her nails, causing Matilda to cry out in a mix of shock and pain.

William and Margery leapt in to pull the young women apart.

"Quiet! Both of you!" Ma cried. "Come now! You're here to help, not make things worse."

The room fell silent again, except for Mama's agitated rasping breaths.

"Sorry Emma," Matilda apologised. "I need to see what is wrong. I can't help if I don't know what's causing this."

Ma gave a defeated sigh and threw her hands up in the air. "I don't even know anymore! Do whatever you can. Please. But stay away from Rachel and Mama, they clearly want nothing to do with you. Even if it means fixing this whole mess."

Ma sat down heavily at the table and started to weep. Elizabeth shuffled over and placed a comforting arm around her shoulder.

Matilda walked cautiously back to Pa for a more thorough investigation, rubbing a particularly nasty scratch above her elbow. She looked at the poor man with his wasted face and brow beaded with sweat.

"Rachel?" Matilda asked cautiously. "Why is it so hot in here if they're both sweating so much?"

Rachel replied with attitude. "They both feel like they're on fire yet complain constantly about being too cold. Whenever they can speak that is."

Almost on cue, Pa let out a hacking cough, his whole body shaking with the effort. Matilda placed her hand on Pa's forehead. Rachel was right, he was burning. She felt Pa's pulse and lymph nodes, recalling the years of medical training the Institute had drilled into all of its pupils. She placed her head on his chest and listened to his raspy breath.

"When did they get sick exactly? What happened?"

"Over a week before I asked you for help," William replied testily. "Pa was slowing down in the fields but thought it was just a cold. He was weary before the morning meal and completely exhausted by midday. A couple of days before I came to you he was completely bedridden. Said it felt like he'd been struck with a sledgehammer."

"Mama started later but got bad quicker," Elizabeth added.

"Has anyone else been sick?" Matilda asked.

"None of us," Elizabeth continued. "There's talk that others in the village have been confined to their beds and Old Man Cooper died but we've been so busy with the harvest that we don't really know what's happening."

Matilda nodded and ran the symptoms against her mental checklist, discarding possible diagnoses and determining the most likely suspects. Without thinking, she pulled down Pa's blanket and began to remove his shirt to inspect his torso.

The room erupted in protest.

"What are you doing!?" Margery yelled.

"You shouldn't do that," William advised.

"I told you she was a whore!" cried Rachel.

Poor Ma was lost for words and just sat in place, crying and shaking her head.

"Sorry everyone, sorry!" Matilda called, raising her hands in apology as she quickly realised her mistake. "I meant nothing inappropriate. I need to see what's causing this, if there are any signs on his chest or arms."

The family didn't reply. Their faces relaxed slightly, though their expressions remained scandalised. Matilda took their silence as tacit approval to continue her investigation and lifted Pa's shirt, bunching it around his head like a nun's habit.

Matilda saw in the dim light that Pa's chest was covered in red spots. Some of them had started to spread down his upper arms.

"Shit," Matilda exclaimed. "Typhoid perhaps? Or Typhus. It's hard to tell."

Matilda didn't know of any recorded outbreaks in the region and wished she could consult her bible. It would explain the darkness, the pair were probably both sensitive to the light.

"What's that?" Ma asked, her voice equal parts concern and hope. Matilda smiled, simply knowing something's name could reduce fear.

"It's a disease, caused by dirty water or fleas. It can be quite curable, with the right…concoctions."

Matilda cursed inwardly. She'd brought a small dose of antibiotics with her from the future that would've been perfect but they'd been in the satchel that the Bishop had stolen. She had an antibiotic culture somewhere back in her cave but it would take weeks to produce a new batch of the drug. They'd have to settle for merely managing their symptoms and preventing anyone else from getting sick.

She pulled Pa's shirt back over his head and joined Ma up at the table.

"I can find some herbs that will ease their headaches and coughs. Perhaps Elizabeth could help. They'll both need to drink plenty of water and replace the nutrients that they're, ah, passing. And we need to make sure they're eating well. A meat broth if you can manage it."

Ma blankly nodded her assent. The poor woman was shell-shocked. She picked up a knife and started shakily chopping root vegetables for the evening meal. Matilda reached over and took it from her.

"Here, Ma. I'll take care of that for you."

Matilda began chopping as she continued to share her prognosis.

"I'd like to see where you get water for drinking and cleaning. You'll have to start boiling it before using it for anything, not just drinking. You should probably tell your neighbours to do the same.

We'll also need to clean the hut and remove all possible nests for fleas and mites. The cats won't like it but they'll need a good scrub. We can make some soap. It could still take weeks for Pa and Mama to fully recover but if we can do all that, they should be healthy again in no time."

The mood remained uncomfortable but Matilda's confidence injected some energy back into the room. Margery and Elizabeth helped Matilda prepare a stew for the family, chatting with Ma to make her feel included. William remained by the hearth, whittling a stick with Harry's knife and watching the strange scene taking place in his home. Rachel returned to wiping Mama's brow.

When the meal was prepared and boiling by the fire, Matilda got up and collected her dry blanket.

"I'll be back in the morning to see what more we can do for them."

Matilda walked over to the door and pulled it open. It was fully dark outside and the rain had only gotten worse since she'd arrived. She didn't like the thought of the long walk back to her cave in such weather but also didn't relish being trapped in the mournful house, surrounded by illness and people who would rather she wasn't there. She'd already well and truly worn out her welcome.

"Oh no you won't!" Ma called. "You'll stay right where you are and eat some food. You can sleep here for the night and everyone will help you tomorrow. It's the sabbath so we can't work in the fields anyway."

Matilda started to rebut but was immediately cut off.

"Ma, we don't have enough food for another mouth!" William protested.

"I won't hear it," Ma said. "We wouldn't have a clue what to do if it weren't for this lady. The family's fate would be in the Lord's hands. Some worldlier intervention won't hurt."

Matilda saw that there would be no arguing with the woman and settled in for the night. William continued to stubbornly refuse to acknowledge her presence and the others avoided conversation, each wrapped up in their own thoughts. Ma thrust a bowl and spoon at Matilda who ate sparingly before settling into her lonely corner to sleep.

Matilda listened to the sounds of the hut as she waited for sleep to claim her. Mama's raspy breathing, William's snoring, Rachel's muttered prayers. Ma's relaxed breathing suggested that she at least was sleeping soundly.

+++

Matilda woke early the next morning and quickly set about her tasks.

William and Elizabeth showed her the stream behind their hut where the family collected their water for washing, cooking and drinking. Cupping her hands, Matilda inspected the cloudy liquid. Sediment stuck to her skin and Matilda only had to look upstream to see signs that it was used by others in the village for disposing of household waste. Matilda was mortified.

Next, she asked where to find some specific herbs for Pa and Mama. Elizabeth gleefully led the way, taking Matilda by the hand and guiding both her and William deep into the forest behind the family's hut. Elizabeth pointed out natural landmarks along the way. Odd plants with branches that jutted out at weird angles. Ancient trees that she swore were as old as the world itself. A patch of stinging nettles that would make an arm swell for a week. Matilda was impressed by the girl's knowledge.

They returned to the hut with armfuls of herbs and Matilda taught them how to brew a tisane to ease Mama and Pa's symptoms.

Rachel begrudgingly accepted Mama's cup but refused to let anyone else tend to her grandmother. The old woman spluttered as soon as the warm liquid touched her lips and Rachel pulled it away from her instantly.

"It's too hot!" she protested. "I'll give it to her later."

Pa downed his brew with gusto. He forced himself to lean up and swallowed the entire cup in a couple of gulps, challenging the disease to keep him down longer.

It's a start, Matilda thought. *And now we wait.*

CHAPTER FOURTEEN

25 December 1123

"He's gone, Father. Again."

Godfrey groaned but insisted on finishing his letter back to the mainland. He dotted the page with a flourish and lay down his quill before scowling at his assistant.

"How the hell did he get away this time, someone was supposed to be watching him! When was he last seen? Where?"

"In the library, Your Excellency," Godfrey's assistant replied cautiously. "The monks saw him before their mid-morning prayer but he'd left when they returned. They thought he might've gone for breakfast but he wasn't in the kitchen when they eventually sent someone to check."

"Daft monks. Too wrapped up in their prayers to worry about the real world. What of the Book? Don't tell me he took that too?"

"No Father, it was left lying on his writing table. Unaccompanied. Along with all of your notes."

"For the love of all that's holy, I don't have time for this!" Godfrey swore. "I want him found! I'll come see him after the Christmas mass."

"Yes Bishop," Peter replied. "I'll dispatch riders now and get some others to search the town. He can't have gone too far."

"No! Less people, the absolute minimum! We don't want rumours that we're holding the boy against his will."

"Yes Father. I'll only use our most trustworthy men. The boy shouldn't be too hard to find, it'll be difficult to hide the injury from his last escape."

"I don't know how I would manage without you Peter. And please, we've been working together for over a month now and your constant 'Father' just makes me feel old."

Peter left the room and Godfrey leaned back in his chair, applying pressure to his temples. He was weary. They had finally finished the parish tour and returned to his palace in Bath. The Bishop was excited to settle back into his regular routine and regain his creature comforts. His library and servants. Access to letters from the region's elite.

Most of all, he was excited to bid farewell to his infernal carriage. His buttocks still ached from the bumpy dilapidated roads and Godfrey maintained his new habit of carrying a cushion with him wherever he went. A small concession for his advancing age.

Unfortunately Godfrey had been thrust into planning the Christmas Mass, his first major service within the shell of the Bath cathedral.

The cathedral was the brainchild of Godfrey's predecessor who had spent his final years obsessed with its construction. Yet he had only managed to complete a partial shell surrounding the altar by the time he died, leaving Godfrey with an unfinished church, an expectant congregation and ever-growing debt.

Godfrey loathed the cathedral. He had only visited it once, when he was first appointed bishop. It had initially attracted him to the post and his excitement had grown as he journeyed to England and observed the new style of European churches under construction. What bishop didn't dream of creating such a physical manifestation of the Church's status and power.

But upon seeing the construction site, Godfrey knew that he would never see the cathedral finished during his lifetime. He lacked the blind commitment of his predecessor and resented the old man for committing Godfrey to such a large project, one that would only distract him from worldlier endeavours at the King's court. Or his work with the Novice to translate the Heretic's Book.

John was a wilful boy. Stubborn and fiery. Nothing like the timid child Godfrey had met on that first stormy night at his parent's pathetic castle. He had proven to be a handful since joining the Bishop and his attempts to escape started on their very first night.

Godfrey had excused John's early attempts at freedom, blaming them on the rashness of youth. However, weeks passed but the attempts to flee did not. Even a broken arm from one of Godfrey's overzealous guards wasn't enough to quash his spirit. John had looked at Godfrey with pure hatred when the Bishop set the boy's arm for him.

No appreciation at all.

Godfrey eventually shared the Heretic's Book in the hopes that curiosity might tame the wild boy. The Bishop further segregated

John from the palace's population to conceal any knowledge of the Book and its otherworldly contents. Isolation hadn't dampened the boy's desire for freedom but when he eventually tired of failed escapes and focused his mind on the Book, he was brilliant.

John deciphered more in days than Godfrey had managed in weeks. The broken arm had slowed his efforts but John confirmed that the Book was indeed written in a form of English, though many words were different to any dialect either had heard before.

Like Godfrey, John's efforts also petered out, though this was more due to content than the language used. The Book talked about stars and anatomy, religion and philosophy. Topics that no boy of seventeen could dream to comprehend. But in an attempt to build rapport, Godfrey had decided to expand the boy's intelligence and granted access to his personal library as promised. Godfrey shared his precious time with John to impart personal insights, though this too was met with a complete lack of appreciation.

And even then, the boy's attempts to escape showed no sign of stopping.

Still unsure how to break the boy's spirit, the Bishop sighed to himself and began preparations for the Christmas Mass. His attendants entered and dressed him in ceremonial attire before he departed for the cathedral. The incomplete building jutted from the ground like the exposed skeleton of some ancient leviathan. The congregation were gathered along an invisible aisle down the guts of the imaginary beast and Godfrey walked among them before stopping at the altar beneath the centre of the beast's ribcage.

The Bishop found himself surprisingly bored by the service, even amidst the embryonic cathedral and celebrations of Christ's birth, one of the grandest ceremonies on the Church calendar. As the congregation busied themselves with another hymn, he wondered when he had lost his passion for preaching.

Being stuck amongst the uninspired peasants of the Isles didn't help, he reasoned, and guiding the simpletons was of little interest compared to court politics. He had been personally tasked by the College of Cardinals to settle a longstanding dispute between the priests and the monks of the region when he received his appointment. And contribute information for the rebellion in Normandy. Mass was much less important.

It wasn't until after the service, as Godfrey was halfway through the local's petitioning, that Peter finally entered the construction site at a brisk pace. Godfrey excused himself from a tiresome conversation about wheat yields and moved to intercept.

"We found him," the Assistant whispered. "He was at the stables on the southern edge of town trying to convince the owner to lend him a horse."

"Industrious, I'll grant him that. I hope they didn't rough him up too much this time."

"No Fath…Your Excellency. They were under strict instructions to bring him back without fuss and even had the wits to slip the stablemaster some coin to keep his mouth shut."

"Good, we're learning. Bring John to the library and have him resume work on the Book. I'll meet him there when I'm finished with this lot."

Peter nodded, his silence hinting at an unspoken jealousy. The Assistant knew almost nothing of the Book, only that John assisted in some capacity and that the ruined tome occupied most of Godfrey's spare thoughts.

The Bishop eventually returned to his chambers and had his attendants remove the impractical ecclesiastical robes. He was amused by their reverence during the mundane exercise, reminding him of a pair of well-trained squires removing their knight's chainmail. His squires took his clothing from the room and returned with a simple afternoon meal of cheese, salted meat and freshly baked bread. It was much better than the basic fare he'd endured during his parish tour and Godfrey was further surprised to be served a full-bodied goblet of wine rather than the ale or mead he had grown accustomed to. *It was good to be off the road.*

Godfrey savoured the meal before leaving for the cathedral's small library to check on John. A single guard slouched by the door but bolted upright when he saw the Bishop approach.

"The boy's in there?" Godfrey asked.

"Yessir. Haven't heard a peep."

"Very good. Try not to be tardy," Godfrey reminded.

The Bishop slipped into the room and carefully closed the door behind him. The library was empty but for John, a small shelf of books and a monk working at a far desk. The boy was supposed to be isolated but Godfrey decided to ignore the monk.

"You made it further this time," Godfrey said, keeping his voice casual but injecting little warmth. "Almost good enough. I would appreciate if you did not try running again. My patience is wearing thin."

The Novice continued to write his notes in silence, his jaw set. Godfrey placed a small wrapped package on the table which finally prompted John to put down his quill.

"What's this?" he asked, his voice sullen.

A bribe to keep you in place, you wretched scoundrel, Godfrey thought before answering.

"A small gift to celebrate the birth of our Saviour. Something to help with your research."

John struggled to tear open the package with his one good hand but eventually exposed a small leather-bound book.

"A rare translation of Euclid's Elements," Godfrey informed. "I discovered it on my journey to England. What are you working on?"

The Novice ignored his question and flipped excitedly through the book. Godfrey interrogated his notes instead.

The pair had developed a basic understanding of the topics covered in their half of the Book. Some of the anatomical images were vulgar in the details they depicted and Godfrey wondered how the author had managed to learn so much about the human body.

The majority of the text continued to elude the pair but they had each begun deeper investigations of specific topics of interest. In addition to anatomy, Godfrey had taken particular interest in the tome's military-related aspects while John focused on a section about folk tales.

Godfrey's recent obsession was an image of five soldiers, each wearing increasingly sophisticated armour. The first two images showed familiar leather jerkins and chainmail, while the third image showed a collection of heavy-looking metallic plates. The fourth image regressed, showing a soldier wearing less of the plate armour over frilly clothing, while the fifth image was a complete mystery, appearing to be little more than rigid cloth. Godfrey guessed that the plate armour was the technological pinnacle and had commissioned a local blacksmith to develop a suit for him.

Flipping through John's notes, Godfrey observed that scribblings about mythology had been increasingly replaced with the bizarre mathematical symbols from the Book.

"It looks like you've had a change in interest. No more folk tales?"

John gestured to the monk in the corner.

"He had a look and gave some suggestions about what they mean. It's started to make some sense."

Godfrey was intrigued but also furious. The Novice knew that the Book was not to be shared.

"Monk, get over here," Godfrey commanded.

Without a word, the monk steadily finished his writing, blotted his paper and cleaned his quill before calmly walking over to John's desk. A middle-aged man with hair starting to grey at the temples, the Monk exuded control as he strode over to the Bishop and his young translator. Godfrey watched intently for any sign of insubordination but received only a pleasant smile.

"Yes Your Excellency?" the Monk asked sweetly.

"You were able to help John. You know these symbols?"

The Monk leaned down and looked at the page again.

"Not those symbols exactly. But I saw a similar formalism during my travels to the Holy Land. The Arabs use something similar to express numbers. Like roman numerals but much more efficient."

The Bishop scoffed – *as if that were possible* – but then grew suspicious.

"Who are you?" he asked warily.

"Adelard, my Bishop," he replied with another smile.

Realisation struck like a thunderclap. This was Adelard, the eccentric monk who was said to have travelled the entire world. Who was so favoured by Godfrey's predecessor. Opinion was split around Bath, half believing him to be brain-addled while others were convinced he was a genius.

"Oh!" Adelard exclaimed, seeing the new book in John's hands. "It's one of mine!"

"I beg your pardon," Godfrey asked incredulously.

"The boy's copy of Euclid, it's one of mine. I worked on the translation after my journey to Iberia. Wrote three of them, in this very room would you believe. I thought someone might've copied it but you've managed to find an original."

"Yes, well. I'm quite fond of books." Godfrey felt angry at both gifting such a treasure and paying a small fortune for a book that originated from a monk within his own diocese.

"You must be indeed. This ruined book you've found is a most remarkable treasure. Or part of one at least," Adelard added, stroking the torn spine. "I've travelled far in search of knowledge to explain God's miracles but I've never seen anything like this, in form or content. From the little that young John has shown me, this is advanced beyond measure."

"Is that so? And what can you tell us of its provenance, from the little you have seen?" Godfrey asked cagily.

"As I've said Father, it is well beyond anything I've come across. I don't know of any race sufficiently advanced to create such a work. As for the content, it appears to become increasingly advanced as the Book progresses. I'd truly love to see the first half, which might be slightly more accessible. Do you know anything of its whereabouts?"

Godfrey sat with an uneasy feeling in the pit of his stomach. He'd thought the same thing since he first flipped through the ruined Book as his carriage trundled away from the Heretic. He needed that other half of the Book. To think he had thrown it in the mud.

"John, I grant my permission to show the Book to Brother Adelard here. Work with him on your translations. Monk, I trust you understand that not a word about this Book is to be shared with a single soul outside this room."

The Monk nodded his agreement and Godfrey marched from the room, leaving them to a discussion about the strange numbers.

The Bishop sped past the slouching guard and down the corridor to find Peter. He was desperate to dispatch his fastest messenger to the sleepy little ambush town.

He needed the other half of that Book!

CHAPTER FIFTEEN

30 December 1123

William wanted to be angry, so badly. But he couldn't.

Matilda was back! The original Matilda, not the depressed mess from the cave. The lively woman who'd ambushed him by the campfire. The intelligent woman with an answer to every question. And she was just in time. At his family's darkest hour, there was suddenly hope.

The family's situation had miraculously turned around since Matilda's unexpected arrival on that miserable rainy day.

A part of William had been thrilled from the moment he first saw her sitting in the rain. He'd not forgotten her initial refusal to help the family but Matilda's helpfulness and renewed sunny attitude eroded his lingering resentment away day by day. William spied occasional remnants of her depression but just knowing that she was trying so hard made it infectious. William didn't know what had caused Matilda's sudden shift in mood but it didn't matter. She was back.

Matilda had completely abandoned her journey to London and now spent all of her time helping the family instead. Villagers refused to accept a stranger's medicine so she taught Elizabeth and Astrid – Holford's elderly midwife – how to make concoctions to ease symptoms and threw herself into helping with the harvest while they distributed doses.

She claimed to have never farmed before and asked endless questions about the most basic tasks, yet it wasn't long before she became a fully effective member of the harvest team. Matilda was uncoordinated and awkward when she began each new task but, channelling her determined enthusiasm, managed to match the family's performance in a remarkably short period of time.

With another set of hands to help and some novel new ideas, the family raced through the last of the harvest and lost much less of the crop than William had anticipated.

Despite being new to the work, Matilda asked pointed questions about the family's wheat yield, how much seed they had planted and the rate of crop rot before offering potential solutions. The family didn't take kindly to a novice trying to improve generations-old methods but Matilda's tactful demonstrations eventually convinced the family that her improvements made sense. William's family were bewildered at how she could know so much and regularly quizzed Matilda about her past.

"I'm just a quick learner I guess," she'd replied to their prying, suppressing a knowing smile as she looked over at William.

He'd kept her time-travelling secret, not that anyone would've believed him if he'd blabbed. William still questioned it himself before remembering all of the futuristic trinkets back at the cave that he'd seen with his own eyes.

When the harvest was complete and their bags of grain delivered to the Miller to be ground into flour, the family leapt straight into plans to plough the fields and sow their winter crop. They had long since forfeited their position in the queue to use Holford's sole plough-team – a pair of oxen that pulled the communal plough. They faced a long wait while the other villagers ploughed their fields and sowed their own winter crops. The plough-team had faced its own illness-related setbacks so the wait was even longer than normal.

While Matilda and William transported the last bags of grain to the Miller, the women of the family began futile attempts to turn the fields by hand. They shared a single wooden hoe between them so progress was excruciatingly slow but there appeared to be no other option. Nonetheless, they were all happy to finally work on anything other than their harvest chores and even minor progress was better than a completely untouched field.

Back at home, Pa's fever had broken within days of Matilda's arrival and he started to regain his strength. He eventually overcame Ma's protests and re-joined the family in the field. Their compromise was that he remained under the oak tree, providing guidance from afar and helping with menial tasks. Pa took great issue with being out-of-action – like some pregnant woman, he said – but the fresh air and human interaction further accelerated his recovery.

In complete contrast, Mama's condition had only worsened. She still suffered from the same nasty cough and had become fully delirious. She spoke to her dead husband, Holford's former miller, who Pa quietly told William had been even grumpier than Mama. She reminisced about the good old days, when people were God-fearing and had morals. A time before the young had ruined everything.

In Mama's few lucid moments, she praised Rachel as the sole beacon of hope for the future generation. Rachel still stayed behind each day to tend to her grandmother, wiping Mama's brow with her precious silk handkerchief and scolding anyone who made even the slightest noise.

Add some wrinkles and white hair, William thought, *and Mama would have a duplicate.*

Rachel and Matilda were never in the same place at the same time. William had believed that he and Rachel had a strained relationship but it was nothing compared to the thinly veiled hatred between the two women. Rachel tended to Mama during the day while Matilda joined the family in the fields but the moment they returned home, Rachel would finish her task and run away to spend the evening with the Brewers, her betrothed's family. She often failed to return before the family fell asleep, something that would've caused major scandal before Matilda's arrival. But Rachel's absence reduced conflict and the family didn't need to supply food for an extra mouth so no one really complained.

Matilda repeated her ritual of leaving for her cave every evening but the family wouldn't hear it. With the exception of Rachel – and Mama, who was too delirious – the family loved having Matilda around. She became a part of the family and had even joined them at Holford's Christmas Mass. While her beautiful singing had attracted some intrigued glances, Father Daniel treated her as just another of his flock.

No evening with Matilda was boring. She taught the family her bizarre songs and she told the most marvellous stories, the latest about a little man who had to destroy an evil king's enchanted ring.

"And then an apple flew out of nowhere and hit his head!" Matilda regaled.

Elizabeth and Margery fell into a giggling fit, so common around Matilda, which prompted a hacking cough from Mama and a disapproving groan from Ma. Matilda got up and helped Ma with the final preparations for their supper as everyone gathered around the table.

"Family," Matilda declared once everyone had started eating. "I've been considering the problems with the plough-team. I think I have a solution."

The family's interest was torn between the food on the table and what Matilda had to say.

"There are still four families ahead of you in the queue…" she continued.

Pa nodded, his mouth full of bread.

"…which will take at least four weeks, by which time our field will be a sloppy mess and practically unworkable."

"Mhmm," came their collective agreement.

"And you said we're not allowed to build an extra plough."

"Only if the Baron is happy to pay the King more taxes," William laughed.

"And there's no spare beasts to pull one even if we could," Margery added.

"So we're stuck waiting," Matilda continued. "Unless we can get the other families to work quicker."

"They're not going to do that," Pa said as he wiped his bowl clean with the last of his bread. "They're as worried about food as we are. They won't risk a tardy job just to help their neighbours, even if it's the proper Christian thing to do."

"That's so disappointing," Ma chimed. "Even after Matilda helped everyone with their sick."

"Well," Matilda said, "I have an idea for a heavier plough, something I've seen during my travels. One that would cut through the soil easier and allow the other families to finish sooner."

"Ha," Pa exclaimed, slapping the table. "Another one of your ideas! Look girl, you've been right helpful but we do things our particular way for a reason. And like you just said, we can't just build an extra plough without risking trouble with the Baron."

"Hear me out," Matilda reassured. "The Baron owes me a favour from my journey to Stowey…"

William's ears pricked up. Matilda never said anything about Stowey.

"…and we could bend the rules, just a little, and only destroy the old plough if my new one works. If not, we destroy the new plough and no-one would ever need to know of the little experiment."

Pa's furrowed brow revealed his disapproval of the planned deceit but Matilda either was oblivious or ignored it.

"Is there a blacksmith in the village?" she asked.

"There is," Pa relinquished, "but he's a shrewd man. Fair, but his work doesn't come cheap. And he demands proof of payment upfront. He charges me an absolute fortune for arrowheads."

Matilda paused to think and the family could see that she intended to see through her idea no matter what.

"I'll visit him tomorrow," she said adamantly.

+++

The family returned to the fields the next morning to resume their attempts to plough by hand. Wishing them luck, William took Matilda into the village square to introduce her to the blacksmith.

The pair walked in companionable silence, the frostiness of their relationship almost fully thawed. William caught glimpses of Matilda from the corner of his eye as they walked and savoured the feeling of having his friend back.

"But really," he asked cautiously, "were you born able to talk? How are you so intelligent?"

"I'm really not," Matilda replied with a laugh. "I guess, I do know more than most. Particularly here. But learning is just about keeping an open mind. Build upon a few basic principles and you can develop an understanding of just about anything. It's all just one little step at a time."

William longed to know what the basic principles were but they rounded the corner and arrived at Holford's blacksmith, an open lean-to with a giant stone furnace out the back.

Matthew Smith was already working out the front, beating a stove hook over his anvil. He was a stern man, younger than Pa and built like a mountain. William remained wary of the giant as their limited interactions had always been confrontational. Matthew hadn't appreciated William and Ralph's past attempts to play knights and bandits near his forge, particularly when the bandits pilfered his supplies.

The wariness was reciprocated and Matthew greeted them with a sceptical look as they approached.

"William Archer. What brings you to my forge?"

"Morning Matthew. I wanted to introduce you to Matilda, a guest from abroad. She's been helping my family finish up the harvest and would like to commission some of your work."

Matthew unashamedly looked Matilda up and down. His interest in the conversation grew noticeably.

"I don't know what a pretty thing like you would want with my modest work but please, see if there's anything you like."

He emphasised his final point by flexing his arms as he gestured to the assortment of metallic items scattered around the workshop. William cringed at the Smith's awkward attempts to flirt but Matilda kept a straight face. She picked up some pieces and examined them with an expert eye before turning back to the Smith.

"It's nice, considered work. Not bad."

Matthew dipped his head to accept the compliment.

"But I *definitely* don't see anything I like. I want a custom piece."

The Smith feigned disappointment and grinned sheepishly at William.

"Your guest really knows what she wants, no beating around the bush. But come now dear, what do you think I make here? Look around, I don't do jewellery. What could you possibly want customised?"

Matilda gave a sarcastic smile before proceeding to outline the plans for her plough in meticulous detail, down to the number of nails and the calculated weight of iron that would be required. The surprise on Matthew's face grew with each word, shifting from amusement to shock and then to absolute bewilderment.

"Right, you know your stuff! But how do you intend to pay for this…contraption?"

Matilda shot him a coy grin.

"Have you ever made chainmail?" she asked.

"Woah, hold up lady," Matthew said, motioning for her to slow down. "Look, your contraption is one thing but if you can't pay for the plough then I'd bet my forge that you can't pay for chainmail."

"I'd take that bet. Just answer the question. You know how difficult mail is to make?"

"I've never tried it myself, that's a job for the castle smiths. My master did show me a shirt he'd inherited when I was an apprentice. Fiddly work."

"Good," Matilda said, shocking both William and the Smith as she began to unfasten her top.

Matthew looked like Christmas had come all over again. William yelped to object but his warning transformed to a sound of pure awestruck amazement when he saw what was underneath.

"Mithril," William whispered in awe, recalling Matilda's story from the previous evening.

"Not quite," Matilda laughed, exposing more of her chainmail shirt. "It's a titanium alloy. Very high strength-to-weight ratio."

Matthew stood frozen in place, his mouth hanging open in amazement.

"Here," Matilda said, holding out the hem. "You can touch it."

The Smith closed his mouth and delicately grasped the chainmail in both hands. William found it comical for a man so large to show such care.

"I've never seen anything like it! Those links are the smallest I've ever seen. It's so light! And a four in one weave? With no rivets!?"

The pitch of the man's voice increased with each sentence. He dropped the mail and looked up at her seriously.

"What sorcery was used to create this?"

Matilda refastened her top.

"No sorcery, just additive manufacturing. And it's actually a six-to-one weave. I won't be able to show you how to make it for quite some time. Unfortunately."

The Smith wiped his brow and leaned back against his anvil.

"Lady, that mail is fit for a king. It's worth a fortune."

"You're right. And it could be yours."

Matthew almost fell over the anvil.

"You make this plough for me," Matilda continued, "and I'll help you sell copies to other plough-teams in the region. Provided I get a cut of the profits, of course. That should more than pay for my prototype. And if it doesn't work, within the year, I'll give you this chainmail."

Matilda's terms were the final straw and Matthew lost the ability to speak. His mouth opened and closed wordlessly like a fish.

"Do we have a deal?" Matilda asked, her hand outstretched.

Matthew nodded dumbly and shook her hand.

"Good. William, you're our witness. Now, this is our little secret ok? I've heard you're an honest man but there'll be no trying to swindle me out of the business or the chainmail. I promise it isn't the only protection I have at hand."

The trio agreed on some final details before Matilda and William left poor Matthew to recover his senses and marched off to join the family in the field.

"That was fun," Matilda said with genuine glee. "But he's a bit of a pig."

The exchange reopened the flood gates of William's curiosity and he hit Matilda with a completely fresh barrage of questions as they walked. What is titanium? Did everyone in the future wear metallic clothes? How did they keep warm?

William and Matilda arrived at the field to find Pa wrapped in a blanket under the oak, fashioning a second wooden hoe. The women were still turning the same tiny patch of land but stole the opportunity for a break.

"Did you have any luck?" Pa asked as they all approached.

"Sure did," William replied excitedly. "Matthew's going to make the plough for us and in return Matilda will let him copy the design for plough-teams in nearby villages."

"That's…unorthodox," Pa replied with a hint of disapproval.

"It'll work out for him in the long run," Matilda promised. "You'll see."

She sat down and recounted their exchange with the Smith. Matilda explained exactly how her device would cut deeper into the soil and gradually convinced each of them that the idea couldn't possibly fail. It took time but eventually even Pa was sold.

"It's often worth spending time to develop a smarter solution rather than pushing ahead with one that doesn't work very well," Matilda finished.

With the harvest complete and Matilda's plough all but guaranteed, the family's mood was jubilant. Not wanting to waste a day of work or Pa's new hoe, they took turns using the tools to turn the soil. Matilda made it into a race and the family were in hysterics as they cheered each other on in the spontaneous relay.

For the first time that season, the family decided to pack up early and were in a joyful mood as they returned to Holford. Seeing the plough-team working slowly in their neighbour's field no longer induced a feeling of dread and they were further heartened when

Matthew gave Matilda an enthusiastic wave as they passed through the village. There was a buzz of energy and excitement.

But it all evaporated in an instant when they entered the front gate and spotted Rachel weeping at the doorstep. The family stopped in their tracks and Ma rushed to console her.

"She died Ma. Mama's dead."

Ma wailed. Rachel wept into her palms. William felt conflicting emotions, sadness at the loss of his grandmother but also as if a cloud had lifted from their little cottage.

"What happened?" Matilda asked delicately. "When did she…pass?"

Rachel's head snapped up.

"What's it to you, snake!? You don't care about us!"

Rachel vaulted from the ground and threw herself at the Redhead. Matilda tried to raise a hoe in defence but Rachel slapped her in the face before anyone knew what was happening.

"This is your fault! All your fault! Revenge for not helping you that night."

She clawed at Matilda and pulled at her hair. It took all of Pa's effort to subdue his eldest daughter and he was exhausted by the time he separated the two.

"Be calm!" he commanded.

"No!" Rachel cried belligerently. "I won't stay another moment in the presence of this witch, with her loose morals and useless concoctions! I refuse to spend another night under the same roof as her!"

Wrestling herself free from Pa's grip, Rachel fled through the gate and ran off towards the Brewers' house.

The family were left standing in stunned silence. Ma stood alone by the cottage, mourning the loss of her mother. Pa dropped his hoe and gathered his wife into a tight embrace.

Matilda absentmindedly dabbed the scratches on her face. Then, as quickly as Rachel, she turned and fled through the gate. William didn't try to stop her and knew she was headed back to her cave.

William, Margery and Elizabeth stood frozen in place, wondering what had just happened.

Mama was dead.

CHAPTER SIXTEEN
4 January 1124

It had been five days since the family returned from the fields and discovered that Mama had died. Matilda hadn't returned to the cottage since. She wanted to give the family time to mourn together and knew that Rachel would stay away if Matilda was there. So she'd returned once more to her isolation at the cave. But this time she had purpose. She was working on a plan.

After weeks in the fields, Matilda had finally come to terms with abandoning her mission. Or at least postponing it. She enjoyed the simple life of helping the family with the harvest and it had revealed an alternate pathway to achieving her mission's objective.

Her encounter with the Bishop had demonstrated the fragility of her initial approach. One wrong move and the entire journey, and all of her sacrifice, would be for nothing.

Instead, Matilda reasoned that she could share her knowledge with the villagers, to get them started on the path to progress. Her Institute supervisors had always preferred a top-down approach that leveraged kings and cardinals to maximise the impact of a Chronomad's lessons. But King Henry had left London and would be abroad for at least a year so time wasn't an issue.

Matilda now saw that teaching lowly villagers would create redundancy for her mission. She would sow the seed of knowledge and hoped Holford would prove to be fertile soil.

Being back at her cave, Matilda had visited Harry's grave to share the idea and took his silence as tacit approval. It seemed like common sense but there would be obstacles. Rachel had rejected her, Mama was dead and Matilda was once again stuck back at the cave.

Trust Mama and Rachel to find yet another way to torment her.

"Shake it off! Shake it off!" Matilda bellowed as she floated on her back in the stream, watching drops of rain fall through the canopy. She was freezing but still had nasty welts where Rachel had clawed at her face and the cool water eased her aches. Being set upon despite her efforts to help the family had hurt almost as much as the physical injuries.

Matilda swam back to the bank and pulled her clothes straight on before running back to the cave. She rekindled her fire and started preparing the rabbit she'd caught that morning. Her stomach grumbled. Meat had become a rare luxury while living with the family. Matilda was roasting the creature over the fire when she heard scrambling from above and saw William making his way into the gully.

"Helloooo!" he called.

"Just in time," Matilda replied, glad to finally have some company. "It's scrawny but I'm guessing you haven't had meat for days?"

William nodded hungrily and sat on his regular log as Matilda cut her rabbit in half. The rain had eased to a light spit and the combination of a warm fire, hot food and company made it feel almost cosy.

"How's it been back at the cottage?" Matilda asked.

"Depressing," William answered, staring into the flames. "Ma cries all the time and Rachel is tearing the place apart searching for Mama's silk handkerchief, insisting that she can't be buried without it. None of us have left the cottage, other than bringing Mama's body to Father Daniel. It's lucky we finished in the fields when we did."

"And how are you doing?" Matilda asked lightly.

"I'm alright. We knew it was coming, after Pa got better while Mama only got worse. She wasn't the most pleasant person but, you know, she was family."

With a sympathetic smile, Matilda handed him the rest of her rabbit.

"Thanks," William said. "Looks like Rachel really hacked at your face. Sorry about that."

"It's not your fault. She's a real piece of work, that's for sure. It took everything in me not to fight back, but she had just lost Mama… So she's been gracing the family with her presence?"

"Unfortunately," William responded, the characteristic twinkle in his eye returned. "She's causing as much chaos as normal but I think Ma appreciates that we're all together. Rachel hasn't spent so much time with us since her engagement. Which means Alan has been spending more time with us too, insufferable twit."

Matilda let the boy vent.

"Ma and Rachel want to give Mama a proper farewell so they've delayed the funeral until tomorrow. People are still busy taking care of their own sick loved ones but Father Daniel said that it couldn't wait any longer…" William tried to put it delicately. "…for practical reasons."

Matilda tactfully changed the subject. "So the ploughing hasn't progressed?"

"Oh, that's why I'm here!" William said, sitting up excitedly. "Matthew was looking for you this morning! He has your plough knocked together and wants you to check it out."

Matilda was shocked. "Already!?"

"Yeah! He was really excited and said he's barely slept since our visit. Though I couldn't tell if that was about the plough, the chance to claim your fancy chainmail or the prospect of seeing you again," William teased.

"I'm not interested!" Matilda replied, more forcefully than she'd intended as a memory of rancid breath flashed in her mind. She saw William flinch and softened her tone. "Lord knows I'm not looking for anything romantic anytime soon. But it's great news about the plough, I didn't think he'd be done that quickly."

Matilda stared up at the sky to gauge how much daylight she had left.

"It's too late to go now but I'll come back to Holford tomorrow."

William squirmed. "Matthew will probably come to the funeral. The whole village will, Holford's a pretty close-knit community."

"Don't worry, Will. I won't come to the funeral. I'm trying to keep the peace and there's no chance of that if Rachel sees me. Plus, I don't think Mama would like the idea of me being there. We didn't exactly get along."

Relief flooded across William's face. "We want you back home though, once everything returns to normal. The funeral will be in the morning so they can bury Mama before the smell gets any worse. You could even catch Matthew before it starts and make any final tweaks while we're at the chapel."

"Sounds good," Matilda said.

William finished the last of the rabbit and threw the carcass into the fire.

"Excellent. I'd best be off, Rachel's probably torn the cottage to pieces by now. Sorry I took so long to slip away. It'll be great to have you back home, Holford's mighty dull with you back here."

With that, William raced out of the gully and back towards the village.

Matilda smiled as she stoked the fire. He'd asked her to come back. Home.

+++

Matilda woke early, sneaking in a visit to Harry and a morning run before walking into Holford. It was a nice day for the funeral. The drizzle had stopped and there was even the occasional patch of a blue sky.

Matilda whistled happily to herself as she walked back to the village, which felt odd given she was travelling towards a funeral. It had become increasingly easier to leave the cave, which felt less like home with each departure.

William waited for her at the ruined mill on the village outskirts, already dressed up for church. He wore his finest tunic, which was only slightly less faded and had fewer patches sewn into it. He'd even combed his unruly nest of hair.

"Looking good William," Matilda called, chortling at his boyish bashfulness at having his appearance complimented.

He ignored her. "You made good time. We can still see Matthew before the funeral starts."

Matilda didn't break stride as William matched her pace and they cut toward the blacksmith's forge.

"The Miller's boy dropped by again last night to see how Margery was doing," William started casually, laughing when Matilda raised her eyebrows at the juicy gossip. "She claims they're just friends but I think all Rachel's marriage talk must've rubbed off."

"It won't be long until there's only you and Elizabeth to keep your parents company," Matilda joked. "Maybe there'll be room for an old spinster like me to move in."

"You're not so old," William said with an awkward cough. "Anyway, Henry said his father has already ground our grain into flour. All of it! Something about commiserations for our loss, though I've never known the Miller to help anyone and Mama wasn't the most popular person in Holford. Regardless, imagine if Matthew's plough works *and* we can have all the flour accounted for. All in one day! That'd take the sting from an otherwise lousy day."

Matilda agreed but his plans seemed ambitious.

Matthew was laying out the final pieces of the plough when the pair arrived at the forge. William ran in to help assemble the heavy machine. Matilda provided directions from her perch on the anvil while the two men strained to lift the heavy components into place. They all stood back to appreciate the contraption when William suddenly discovered a grease stain on his leggings.

"Oh shit! Shit, shit, shit," he cried rubbing his leg vigorously.

"Careful boy, there's a lady present," Matthew teased as William turned red as a beetroot. "Whatcha think? Am I on track to inherit that fine chainmail of yours?"

Matilda stood up from the anvil and walked a slow lap of the plough.

"Not bad gentlemen, not bad at all." She stopped at the handles and gave it a vigorous shake. It barely moved. "Sturdy craftsmanship. Nice and heavy. You haven't skimped on the materials."

"So I've done good?"

"You've done well, Mister Smith. It looks good but the true test will come in the field. I expect you'll be joining us for the maiden run?"

"Wouldn't miss it!" Matthew replied excitedly.

Matilda paused in thought. "The challenge will be getting this heavy thing out there. And convincing the plough-team to even try it."

"I'll talk to the ploughmen after the funeral," William injected enthusiastically. "Perhaps they'll take pity on a grieving grandson?"

"I'll talk to them too," Matthew offered. "They use their cattle to help move some of my larger jobs and still owe me for some repairs. I'm desperate to see if this thing will work."

"We'll find out soon enough," Matilda said absentmindedly as she admired the machine. "You'd better get running to the chapel, we wouldn't want you being late."

The men set off, excitedly talking about the plough. Matilda smiled as William peppered Matthew with a flurry of questions about the type of metal he'd used and where it was mined. The Boy's thirst for knowledge really was insatiable.

Feeling odd standing alone in the empty forge, Matilda returned to the family's cottage and loitered around the front. Holford's lanes were dead quiet and it was eerie seeing the place so inactive. Realising she'd never been out the back, Matilda meandered around the building, eager to learn more about the minutiae of medieval life. She held her nose as she passed the outhouse, the smell making her want to retch even through blocked nostrils. Matilda couldn't teach the family about plumbing quickly enough.

The backyard was empty except for another small vegetable patch and a couple of apple trees. She was impressed by the size of the family's plot but underwhelmed by its mundanity. The humble backyard hadn't changed much in a thousand years.

Matilda was just about to return to the front of the property when she noticed a wave of colour in the compost corner beside the house. She walked over and was surprised to see Mama's handkerchief discarded among the compost. Matilda was amused that Rachel had inadvertently thrown out Mama's precious possession but the thought was quickly replaced by confusion as she recognised the composting contents surrounding the fabric.

The leaves of familiar plants were in various states of decay. Much more than should've remained from Elizabeth's preparation of Pa and Mama's medicines. Matilda pocketed the silk and shamelessly scrounged through the compost, unearthing even more of the rotting herbs. Too many. She had personally watched Pa take his doses and quickly deduced that there was only one possible explanation.

Rachel had thrown out Mama's medicine.

Matilda was furious. Beyond furious.

How could the stupid girl let a petty disagreement with Matilda kill the woman she worshiped? Her closest family member struck down by a baseless grudge. Matilda knew that this would only worsen their divide. There was no hope of Rachel accepting any responsibility herself, she would blame Matilda and use it to fuel an escalated enmity.

Matilda fumed. She threw down the composting slop and marched away from both the cottage and Rachel's foolishness. She was halfway down the road when she realised that she still had nowhere to go. She screamed out in frustration before pacing back and forth until her temper cooled and a plan started to form. Matilda decided to channel her anger into a more productive task and set off to find the Miller and start collecting the family's bags of processed flour.

Matilda had no trouble finding the mill, having helped William deliver the final bags of unprocessed grain when they completed the harvest. However, with the entire village at Mama's funeral, she was concerned that there wouldn't be anyone to release the family's flour. Matilda breathed a sigh of relief when she saw the surly Miller standing by the warehouse door, talking to his daughter and counting sacks with his fingers. He grunted when he saw Matilda.

"What're you doing here? Shouldn't you be at the old nag's funeral?"

"She's not from here Da," his daughter said with a look of disdain. "She's been helping the Archer family with their harvest. Helped William drop off their grain before the old lady died."

The daughter spoke as though Matilda wasn't even there and oozed entitlement from every pore of her over-inflated body.

"That's right," Matilda interjected with forced bubbliness, holding out a hand and hoping to overcome the Millers' animosity. "I'm Matilda, a pleasure to finally meet you Arnold."

The Miller grunted again, took a glance at her peasant clothing and left her hand hanging.

"I'm here to collect the Archer family's flour," Matilda continued. "Your son said you've already processed it."

"Over there by the wall. Just take it and be gone. I've got too much to do and can't have you getting in my way."

Matilda saw a collection of familiar sacks piled against the wall. Far more than she could hope to carry before the funeral finished. But feeling the handkerchief burning in her pocket, Matilda stiffened her resolve and picked up the first two sacks.

Matilda spent the rest of the morning repeating the same journey, carrying two large sacks on her shoulders and dumping them at the family's door before running back to collect the next round. She was fuelled by her anger with Rachel and her burning arms reminded her of training sessions back at the Institute gym which made her feel alive.

Holford was empty besides the Miller, his petulant daughter and a portly old man who made pottery outside his rundown shack. Matilda's journeys took her repeatedly past the Potter as she carried the heavy sacks back to the family's home and he watched her with increasing interest. He gave her an encouraging smile after the third trip and by the time Matilda returned from her sixth trip he was waiting for her with a bucket of water.

"Impressive to see such stamina in a young lady," he told her as he offered Matilda a ladle. "No need for concern, I heard your advice to the villagers and was sure to boil it first."

Matilda graciously accepted the water and took a seat at the old man's doorstep.

"Thank you kind sir. It's hot work, even harder than in the field. As much as we complained, at least the rain cooled us down."

The man gave a booming laugh. "Sir? I don't think anyone has ever bestowed that honour upon a lowly potter like myself. Please, call me Timothy."

"Nice to meet you Timothy, I'm Matilda. That looks like some fine craftsmanship," she said, gesturing to the row of pots drying behind him.

"Holford's specialty and my own unique curse. I learned it from my Pa and he from his before him. I'll still be making these same damn pots when the Lord returns to collect my withered skeleton on Judgement Day."

"Well at least you can show Him some quality work. Is it double glazed?" she asked, inspecting a finished sample.

"Ooh hoo hoo. A girl that knows her ceramics? What a find!" He looked at her with appraising eyes. "You and the Archers have done well to get so much flour, given the lateness of the season and Arnold's tendency to cheat his customers."

"The family put in a lot of hard work," Matilda replied modestly.

"I hear it was more than that, young Matilda. That a certain foreign herbalist worked a miracle. What land produces such hardworking women who know about boiling water, improved farming and ceramics?"

He let the question hang.

"The United Kingdom," Matilda responded. "I went to a prestigious boarding school. A place of learning where students live and are taught many things. Craft, agriculture, arithmetic, medicine."

Timothy raised his eyebrows enquiringly. "I've heard of many places in my time, even been to some distant ones myself. But I've never heard of a United Kingdom."

"It is very similar to here," Matilda replied, supressing a smile, "but also very different. And it's much further away than I would like. I doubt I'll ever return."

"I'm sure that if one as brilliant as yourself sets your mind to it, you'll get there."

"We'll see Mister Potter," she said, far from convinced. "So why aren't you at the funeral with the rest of the village?"

"You know why?" he asked in a whisper before yelling his answer. "I never liked the old bat!"

Matilda was shocked at his brutal honesty but couldn't help smiling as another wave of his deep laughter rolled over her. The shock on her face brought a tear to his eye.

"One of the perks of being old is you stop caring what others think. At my age, I've finally realised that life is too short to let others dictate how you feel or what you do."

"Amen to that. Though there's still time to keep making the same old pots?"

"Unfortunately so, a man must eat. But I content myself with a few moments away from the squabbles and petty politics of small village life. It gives me time to dream of what could have been. Making glass with my kiln perhaps."

"I've seen it done before, would you believe? If I ever finish with these damned sacks of flour I'd happily show you."

"At your magical boarding school, no doubt? Well, I'm interested but forgive an old man if I don't hold out much hope. Glass has always proven elusive to me. So you intend to stay in Holford then?"

"For now. The Archers have shown me extreme kindness, though I don't think they realise just how much. I'll be on my way eventually but for now, I have a debt to repay."

Matilda bid farewell to Timothy and returned to the mill to collect more flour. He resumed his pot making but called out friendly words of encouragement whenever Matilda passed. The bucket of water sat on his doorstep awaiting her return.

Matilda smiled inwardly each time she passed the Potter. She'd made a friend.

After several more trips Matilda guessed that she had collected about a quarter of the sacks and the pile finally appeared to be dwindling. But when she returned for her next load, Matilda was surprised to see the pile noticeably reduced. The Miller and his bald labourer walked away from the warehouse, sacks of flour in their arms.

William and Timothy's comments about the Miller's shady dealings flashed in Matilda's mind.

"Hey!" she called out. "Where's all the flour gone?"

Arnold turned and considered Matilda.

"I've taken the processing fee," he said simply, deeming the matter resolved and turning back to his discussion with the labourer.

"I thought you'd already taken it. What is the fee?"

"Every twelfth sack produced," he replied warily.

"And how sacks many were produced from the family's wheat?"

"Eighty-eight," the Miller replied instantly.

"Well I counted eighty sacks when I arrived, so you've already taken your fee. Now there's little more than forty!"

"You've been moving them all day, I don't know how many you have taken."

"I made nine trips with two bags each. There should be at least sixty sacks here."

Arnold did some calculations with his hands. Realising that Matilda knew more arithmetic than the average villager, the Miller changed tack.

"There's a double fee for priority processing. I had to push their grain ahead of several other families."

"That's ridiculous, the family never even asked to be bumped up the queue. Besides, even then you've taken much more than double."

"My son asked on their behalf," Arnold replied peevishly. "And it's too late, it's already done. Shouldn't you be mourning a family death or something?"

Matilda stood in silent rage, her hands clasped so tightly that it felt like her knuckles would burst.

The Miller sneered. "People usually know better than to question my practices, woman. This is the only mill for miles. It is what it is. Now, have those remaining sacks collected by sundown or there'll be an additional late fee. I can't have them crowding up my workspace."

He walked away with the family's flour still in his arms. Matilda found herself standing alone, baffled that the Miller could so brazenly steal their hard-earned harvest. He had a monopoly and he knew it. Matilda feared what else he'd taken from the other villagers.

With nothing else to do, Matilda collected another load of flour. She struggled to carry three bags but stubbornly resolved to do so just to spite the slimy Miller.

Matilda's arms screamed with pain when she reached the family's front gate. She dropped the sacks in triumph but the cottage reminded her of Rachel's role in Mama's death. She slumped to the ground, overcome by the injustice of it all.

"Living wasn't all that hard," Matilda's mother had always told her. "It was the people that made it most difficult."

So why were there so many shitty people in the world, Matilda wondered. *Why were people so selfish?*

An image of a portly old man with wispy white hair and kind brown eyes flashed into her mind. The echoing memory of his booming laughter was enough to prompt a smile.

The good people make it all worth it.

CHAPTER SEVENTEEN

5 January 1124

William felt a strange fatigue when the funeral finished. Emotional rather than physical. He would've gladly endured another entire harvest to avoid Ma's sobs and Rachel's excessive wailing. To skip the endless handshakes and insincere condolences. To top it all off, he still had grease on his pants.

Only the promise of testing Matilda's plough and collecting the family's hard-won flour had gotten him through the ordeal. William and Matthew played their part at the funeral, convincing the plough-team to try Matilda's creation when they returned to the fields. The team were sceptical but some significant outstanding debts to Matthew meant they couldn't say no.

Ralph had whooped with excitement when William told him about the development, drawing glares from nearby mourners. Ralph's family were already completely finished in the fields so he didn't even need to sneak away.

It felt like an age since William had seen Ralph and he realised that they hadn't spent time together since the day William first discovered Matilda. His childhood felt a lifetime ago but in reality was only a matter of months earlier. Time was strange like that.

Everyone organised to meet at Matthew's forge immediately after a post-funeral meal, giving the Smith enough time to prepare Matilda's device for transport. William impatiently waited for his parents to finish their solemn discussion with Father Daniel at Holford's small cemetery behind the chapel. They paid the priest and collected their children. It felt odd to return home with one of their number gone for good.

The family were surprised when they arrived and found Matilda sitting in the front yard, once again. She leaned against a large stack of flour sacks, her shoulders slouched. It wasn't the whole harvest but a remarkable effort for a lone woman to achieve in such a short time.

"Is that it? I thought you were supposed to be working while we were gone," William joked but he turned serious when Matilda didn't rise to his dig. "What's wrong?"

"Nothing," she replied flatly. "It's fine."

The rest of the family entered the yard and marvelled at Matilda's work but Rachel pushed past and headed inside without a word. Matilda gave her condolences to Ma and William found it refreshing to finally hear genuine sorrow for his family's loss.

William wanted to know what had Matilda so bothered but wasn't able to catch her eye as they all headed inside. Matilda told Ma to sit down and relax, pulling out a bag of freshly collected herbs to brew a tisane. Next, she withdrew a pair of rabbits and started preparing a particularly intricate meal.

"Something special to honour Mama's memory," she said with a weak smile.

Margery and Elizabeth helped Matilda around the hearth, chopping ingredients just so or watching the pot to ensure it didn't boil over. Rachel was in a foul mood and took every opportunity to snipe at Matilda, despite their visitor's obvious effort to commemorate Mama.

"How have you already ruined more of Ma's clothes? It would've been appalling to see you dressed in that filth at the funeral, all covered in flour. If you'd bothered to show up at all."

"Leave her alone Rachel," William defended. "She's spent the whole morning helping our family. Again. She didn't have to do that."

"Like you can talk, all covered in grease." Rachel shifted her gaze back to Matilda. "On second thoughts, I guess being covered in flour is still better than the filth she wore when she first arrived."

Everyone ignored Rachel but that only encouraged her attacks.

"Where are your fancy foreign clothes now? Did something happen at the castle?"

William saw the strain on Matilda's face as she fought to remain calm and refused to bite.

"Come on Rachel," Pa chimed. "Ease up."

Rachel looked directly at Pa before continuing.

"You call this food?" Rachel asked, poking at the foaming broth with her finger. "It smells terrible." She feigned a sudden epiphany. "I hope it's not another of your concoctions. We saw how good that was for poor Mama."

"Shut up!" Matilda cried.

The whole family snapped to look at their guest, shocked at her sudden outburst.

Matilda crumbled. "I can't take it! You wicked little she-devil. You sanctimonious bitch!"

"Woah, Matilda," William urged. "Ease up."

"No, I just can't take it! I've done everything I can to help this family and I taught Elizabeth how to help Pa and Mama recover. And yet Rachel still attacks my efforts? No!"

Matilda rounded on Rachel, her knife still in hand. William's eldest sister cowered slightly.

"That man," Matilda said, pointing the knife at Pa, "is alive because of what I did. Without me, your family would still be working the fields with little hope of saving even half of the crop. On top of that you probably would've buried two family members today."

Matilda paused for breath.

"You killed her Rachel. Mama is dead and it's all your fault."

William was shocked. Margery gasped and Ma's jaw dropped. She looked at Matilda with deathly serious eyes.

"What did you say?"

Ma's tone was as cold as stone. With four simple words she sucked all the wind from Matilda's sails.

"Those are some mighty large accusations, Foreigner," Ma spat. "You'd best be careful. What did you say?"

Lost for words, Matilda reached into her pocket and withdrew a strip of fabric. Only when Rachel tried to snatch it did William realise that it was Mama's handkerchief. Matilda swung it out of her reach.

"Emma, I…I found this out the back while you were all at the funeral. It was discarded in the compost heap, along with the remains of weeks' worth of ingredients. Rachel never gave Mama the medicine. She threw it all out."

Ma's deathly gaze swung to Rachel. Her eldest daughter truly cowered now.

"Is this true?"

Rachel kept silent and her eyes darted around the room as she tried to formulate a response.

"Rachel, you silly girl. Is this true?"

"It was poison!" Rachel protested. "We both saw it! Mama choked the instant it first touched her lips. She didn't want it and I wasn't about to force it upon her."

"That's not poison, you dolt!" Matilda muttered. "Mama was lying down and had a chest infection. Any liquid would've made her splutter!"

Rachel looked around the room for allies but seeing only stunned reactions and judgemental faces, she doubled down and went on the attack.

"I won't hear another of your ridiculous allegations, witch! You've been nothing but trouble since the minute you arrived here, with your loose morals and strange potions."

She launched herself up, fists clenched tightly against her side.

"You've turned my family against me! I know when I'm not welcome and won't spend another second under this roof with filth like you. Not when there's another family ready to accept me with open arms. A better family. I hope I never see any of you again!"

Rachel vaulted over her bed and ran from the room, slamming the door behind her.

The family was left in stunned silence, both at Rachel's sudden departure and the magnitude of Matilda's revelations. It was all too much for Ma who completely broke down with heavy, uncontrollable sobs. Pa and Elizabeth rushed over to hug her, one on each side.

William was surprised to see Matilda casually resume cooking. She chopped the remaining ingredients and passed the knife to Margery before wrangling the door open and walking outside.

William raced out after her.

Matilda paced back and forward in the front yard, both arms folded over her head and tears streaming down her face. Seeing William, she wiped her eyes and forced a smile.

"I'm fine," she said before William had a chance to speak. "It's been a big day for me too."

William nodded but just stood in awkward silence.

"It was the Miller too, you know," Matilda croaked eventually.

"What?"

"The reason I was so out of sorts when you all returned from the funeral," Matilda clarified. "When I discovered Rachel's…stupidity,

I started collecting the flour to channel my anger into something productive. I was making progress when I caught him stealing extra sacks. He's cheating the family."

William knew Arnold was a questionable character but was shocked that the Miller would so blatantly steal from his family.

"What scumbag robs a grieving family? Surely that isn't normal for this time?"

"It's not," William reassured her.

"It gets worse," Matilda continued. "He wasn't happy when I exposed his scheme and said he'd take even more as a fine if we haven't collected it all by sundown. I honestly don't know how we can avoid it."

"Shit." William felt kicked in the stomach. So many days of back-breaking work, only to have it stolen away from them.

The pair milled around uncomfortably out the front of the house. Matilda looked distraught but William's mind raced.

"Ok, I've got it," he said.

Matilda looked up at him quizzically.

"Matthew and Ralph are waiting for us to test your plough. If we help the plough-team get started, the four of us can run to collect the remaining sacks. How many did you say there were?"

"Forty-one, so ten trips."

"Less if we can find more volunteers! We can manage both that and the ploughing before sundown. Let's go!"

William shot Matilda his most encouraging smile and ran off towards Matthew's forge, beckoning her to follow. A small crowd was already gathered when they arrived.

"About time! Where've you lot been?" Matthew called as they approached. "Everyone's convinced it won't work. That I've wasted good iron."

William apologised. "Sorry Matthew, it's been a bit of ordeal. Ma's a wreck, Rachel stormed out during lunch and Matilda's had a run in with Arnold. We might need some more of your help."

"What's the sod done now? And who's this?" asked Luke, the leader of the plough-team. He looked at Matilda with uncertainty.

"Oh, yeah," William said. "Ploughmen, this is Matilda. She's been helping my family in the fields. This new plough was all her idea."

Matilda waved awkwardly.

"What's a woman know 'bout ploughin'?" another ploughman grumbled.

"You know Arnold," William continued, ignoring the rudeness. "He's up to his old tricks. He claimed a quarter of our wheat as payment for grinding it before the funeral and now says he'll take more if we don't collect it all by tonight."

"That's absurd!" Matthew protested.

"Like hell he will!" the Plough-Master chimed in. "I've had enough of that bastard thinking he can lounge around his fancy mill doing less work than us but take a bigger cut of the profit. Girl, help us get this thing working and my lads'll help you when we finish up."

Matilda smiled and they all leapt into action with newfound energy. They soon had the plough in the fields, assembled and hitched to Luke's cattle. Flanked by the plough-team, Matilda rode the plough into the field and showed them how to use it. The cattle strained to get the heavier load moving but the sharp metal blade cut deeper into the ground than any plough William had ever seen while a curved attachment turned the rich, dark soil.

Ralph and Matthew joined William to watch from the field boundary.

"So who's the Redhead?" Ralph asked, struggling to take his eyes off the woman working in the field. "Is she one of Rachel's friends?"

William forgot that Ralph hadn't actually met Matilda, just another example of how little time the friends had spent together recently.

"No, definitely not. A stranger, would you believe? Not even from the region."

Ralph was amazed. "Of course you managed to find the one interesting person passing near Holford. How'd you manage that!?"

"It was the day we tested the sling. She came past Holford some months back and needed to go to Stowey Castle so Pa offered to take her. She returned here afterwards and has been helping us with the harvest since. She's a wonder."

"Too right," Matthew chimed in dreamily. "It's rare to find a woman who knows her metal. She'd be one to walk the mountains with."

"I don't know how you do it William," Ralph said shaking his head. "But look at them go! A design so simple but I've never seen a plough glide through the fields so quick. The dirt is like butter! At this rate they'll be done here by tomorrow morning."

"That's the plan." William replied cheerfully. "And if they can do the Cooper's fields tomorrow then my family might get done by the end of the week."

The team ploughed on into the afternoon, stopping only to sing their praises of Matilda's invention. It washed over Matilda like a wave across a rock and William knew that she was already thinking about their next task. She managed to undo most of the plough-team's goodwill when she made them destroy the old plough. They all protested and Matthew even suggested hiding it at his forge but Matilda insisted that it wasn't worth risking the Baron's wrath. Not when they already had a superior design.

The plough-team finished their work well ahead of schedule and true to their word, joined William and Matilda to collect the remainder of the family's flour. The Miller was far from happy to see Matilda's reinforcements and even less so when one of the ploughmen stayed behind to keep watch while the rest of Luke's crew transported the sacks to William's home.

The sun had just set when the team collected the final three sacks of flour and said a jolly farewell to the surly Miller. William and Matilda thanked the plough-team and said goodbye to Ralph and Matthew at the forge before returning home. The pair walked in silence and William stared up at the stars as they walked, exhausted but amazed at how much had happened in the space of a single day.

Seeing him staring, Matilda broke the silence. "They're giant balls of fire, you know? Just like our Sun but burning thousands and thousands of miles away."

William looked up in amazement.

"They're the whole reason I'm here," she continued, looking upwards too. Darkness filled her eyes. "The Sun spat out its fire and licked the world. It was chaos."

"Truly?" William asked with disbelief. It sounded inconceivable but it was coming from Matilda. "But they just stay up there. Why don't they just burn out or fall from the sky?"

"Always asking the right questions," Matilda laughed. "You're a marvel. An absolute marvel."

Another silence fell as William looked up at the burning balls of flame through new eyes.

"Matilda? Will you leave us again, if you get sad or things get too hard? Rachel shouldn't be around anymore to cause trouble. Thank God."

She thought for some time before responding.

"I won't. Not until we've finished the ploughing and Holford has kicked the last of this miserable illness. I promise." She paused again. "William. I'm sorry for taking so long to come to your aid. You were right to ask for assistance, I was just too far gone to see it."

"It's alright. You came in the end. And it's really Rachel's fault that Mama's gone isn't it?"

"Don't be too hard on Rachel," Matilda said gently. "Fear can be a powerful motivator. For both her and Mama. I just wish she'd had more faith that someone could know better than her."

William was shocked to hear Matilda defend his vile sister. Someone who had been so wicked, who'd assaulted Matilda and caused the death of a family member.

"I feel sorry for Rachel," Matilda said. "It will be very lonely for her tonight."

William hadn't thought of that.

They arrived at the cottage and dropped the final bags of flour.

"What a long day," William said. "I'm exhausted!"

"Me too. But tomorrow's a new day. One filled with faster ploughs, pre-stacked flour and, hopefully, a later start. I'm sorry that Mama didn't make it."

Matilda gave him a quick hug and the pair headed inside. The family had packed up for the night and both Margery and Elizabeth were already asleep. Without a word, William and Matilda crawled into their beds.

William felt a weight of loss as he fell asleep listening to the heart wrenching sounds of Ma's weeping, as though he'd lost both his grandmother and a sister in a single day.

But Matilda lay on the other side of the room. She was like a new sister. One that understood him even better than the old one.

CHAPTER EIGHTEEN
15 January 1124

Godfrey had grown weary of his assistant's morning briefs. The man brought nothing but bad news.

"John has disappeared again," Peter shared. "This is the third time since you separated him from the Monk. I think you may need to concede their…friendship. I already have guards looking for him in all the normal places."

Peter nervously scanned his notes, searching for a safe topic.

"The blacksmith wished to inform you that his latest attempt at plate armour was unsuccessful. He said your changes made the plates too thin and they split during shaping."

Godfrey thumped the table with his fist.

Peter paled. "He wanted to remind you that he is still awaiting payment for the previous experiments."

Godfrey smouldered and Peter continued cautiously.

"Regarding money, the Jews have been asking how you wish to settle the debts for the cathedral."

"Settle the debts!? That was Bishop John's doing. He signed me up for their un-Christian money trap before he went and died. As if his cathedral debacle weren't bad enough. I hope he's writhing in hellfire!"

Peter blanched at the Bishop's casual mention of eternal damnation. "Well, they would like to know if you'll be continuing the arrangement or settling the debt. Without alternative means to pay them, I believe we have no option but to continue with the arrangement."

"I guess we don't," Godfrey huffed sarcastically. "We'll have to visit them and discuss."

"If you plan to leave the palace today, might I recommend a visit to the cathedral? There are more concerns with the design and a visit could boost the workers' morale. Masons have continued to leave as the pay issues drag on."

"Dammit man, have you no good news!?"

"Well," the Assistant said, rifling through his notes once more. "Your messenger returned from Stowey. There was no sign of the Book but he managed to locate the Foreigner's bag."

"That's something at least. Very well, it seems I am overdue for another tour of the town. Send word when my carriage is ready."

Peter was visibly relieved that they were finished. He handed Godfrey a sealed envelope before scuttering from the room.

"This arrived for you today."

Godfrey waited until he was gone and opened the letter at his desk. The wax seal was unadorned but he knew it was news from the rebellion in Normandy.

The Bishop read the letter twice before scrunching it into a tight ball and hurling it into the fireplace. More bad news. King Henry had arrived in Normandy and joined forces with his infernal bastard son, the Earl of Bristol. The rebels were in disarray but winter provided a chance to regroup. The cardinals wouldn't be pleased.

Godfrey poured himself a goblet of wine and drained it instantly. He was juggling too much and there were problems on all fronts. The tactical intricacies of running his bishopric were an annoying distraction from the cardinals' more strategic tasks. There was little he could do from afar to support the rebellion and, closer to home, the ongoing battle between priests and monks showed no signs of letting up. He poured another drink.

It was difficult to know what to focus on. Yet despite everything, Godfrey's biggest concern was John. The Bishop was convinced that the answer to all of his problems lay within the Heretic's Book and John remained the unfortunately uncooperative key. The Novice knew too much about the Book and its contents to be dismissed, yet also understood more than Godfrey and couldn't be…disposed of.

After months of deciphering the Book's contents, the well had run dry. John had translated all that he could and every avenue of investigation had reached a dead end. Their work ground to a halt and it became clear that they desperately needed whatever was in the first half of the Book to make sense of their half. Godfrey cursed himself yet again for tossing away the wrong half and blamed the Heretic for sparking his rage.

Peter was right. Dismissing Adelard had also slowed their work. The Monk had proven to be an insufferable know-it-all, frequently correcting the Bishop and claiming greater knowledge of the world.

The Monk did possess a unique intuition for deciphering the meaning of John's translations but Godfrey had thought it prudent to cut ties before he too learned too much.

John's renewed efforts to escape were an unfortunate consequence of the dismissal. The Monk and the Novice had developed a strong friendship during their secluded hours working in the library. The puzzle of the Book provided a shared interest and Adelard had kindled the comradery Godfrey had hoped to generate with John himself. But without translation work or friendship, John's efforts to escape became more frequent than ever.

Godfrey had personally requested that John's responsibilities be increased at the seminary and that the strictest masters keep a particularly close eye on him. It obviously wasn't enough and Godfrey needed to revisit the seminary to discuss further reducing John's freedoms. Yet another task.

Annoyed, Godfrey lay down his goblet and left his quarters to find the Assistant. He eventually found Peter in deep discussion with the palace staff but he wound up as Godfrey approached. The help dispersed with purpose. Despite often being the bearer of bad news, Godfrey admired Peter's fastidiousness and ability to make things run smoothly. He too was indispensable.

"Your Excellency!" Peter called. "I have the messenger here to see you. Shall we retire to the library?"

Godfrey nodded and followed Peter and the scruffy messenger to the palace's most secluded room. With John gone, the room was empty.

"So?" Godfrey asked. "Did you have any luck?"

The messenger looked nervous and eyed the door eagerly.

"Yes and no, Father. I spoke to the Priest again. A most friendly fellow."

"I don't care what he was like! Did he have my damned Book?"

The messenger flinched. "No Bishop. He said that books were rare in the town's castle, let alone in the streets. But he did have this."

The messenger revealed a familiar leather satchel, dusting it off before passing it to Godfrey.

"The Priest said he found it discarded in an alleyway during one of his walks through the town."

"That's convenient," Godfrey mused. "Did you press him on this?"

"No Father."

"Unfortunate." Godfrey gave a menacing look. "Did you ask the townsfolk if they had seen the red-headed foreigner?"

"No Father."

"Disappointing again!" Godfrey cried, brandishing the satchel. "This is definitely hers."

He opened the bag and rifled through, more delicately than the first time he'd held it. Nothing struck him as particularly useful but he thought the contents might provide a momentary distraction for John when he returned. Godfrey wiped his finger across a white crust and sniffed. It smelt caustic and burned Godfrey's nose.

"Well, better than returning empty-handed," he said, giving the messenger another intense stare. "Listen here. I want you to return to Stowey immediately and do your job. Properly this time. Don't return until you have asked every living soul whether they've seen the girl or heard word of my missing book. The Priest was right, something so precious would not be left abandoned in the street. Someone must have taken it."

The messenger bowed deeply and rushed to leave the room. Godfrey shouted a final command.

"Press the Priest for more information. It's too convenient that he found the satchel and nothing else. Search his chapel if you must"

The messenger disappeared and Godfrey looked over to Peter. "Is my carriage ready yet?"

The Assistant led his Bishop to the carriage waiting by the palace entrance.

Their first stop was to the blacksmith on to the outskirts of the town. He was not the finest craftsman but Peter assured Godfrey that he could be trusted to be discrete.

Godfrey longed to create the armour depicted in the Book, seeing it as the most direct way to assist the cardinals' rebellion in Normandy. Despite initial confidence that he would find a solution for the heavy plates, the Book lacked detail and none of the Bishop's efforts to recreate war instruments had worked.

Just as Godfrey had dedicated his limited time to deciphering the Book, so too had he devoted his limited financial resources to the project. He siphoned coin earmarked for cathedral construction to fund the blacksmith's endless attempts. Peter disapproved but was smart enough to hold his tongue.

"Still no luck, Bishop," the rough smith told Godfrey when he emerged from the carriage. "I don't know who's giving you these measurements but they're all wrong."

Peter gave the blacksmith a silent warning but he continued anyway.

"I don't mind tinkering with these experiments, so long as the coin keeps coming. I've got a family to look after you know."

"What would you suggest changing?" Godfrey asked, ignoring the man's insolence.

"Stop trying to do it all. Forget the helmet and fancy joints. Keep it simple. Perfect the breastplate and we'll go from there."

"So be it," Godfrey said, already returning to the carriage as Peter counted out coins.

Next, they stopped at the Jews' house to visit Godfrey's lenders. There was no established community of Jews in Bath but a single family from the wealthy community in Bristol had built a home in the shadow of the cathedral they had financed.

The Bishop would've preferred that they had remained with their kin in Bristol but he reminded himself that his various projects wouldn't be possible without the income generated from taxing the thrifty newcomers. And Christ had been a Jew. He begrudgingly respected the way that their culture instilled an understanding of numbers and letters in their young, even though it undermined the monopoly otherwise held by the clergy. It was little wonder that they could rise above the uneducated masses.

But they were different. Nobody ever liked different.

Godfrey was greeted at the door of a simple townhouse by a young assistant and shown into a room where an elderly man sat behind a large desk. Peter's face matched the shock Godfrey felt at seeing a room so lavish within such a simple building. There were even three books chained to a shelf, the expensive beginnings of a personal library.

"Welcome Your Excellency," the elderly man said. "Is this not the first time you have humbled my home with your presence?"

Godfrey nodded.

"I am Isaac. I trust you've come to discuss the terms for continuing the loan that was agreed by your predecessor. Ah, Bishop John. A truly inspiring man. Unorthodox but so dedicated to the health of his flock, from the lowliest peasant up to His Majesty himself."

"His death was a great loss," Godfrey replied stiffly.

"Quite," the Jew replied, eying the new bishop with suspicion. "So, you wish to continue our arrangement?"

"That's presumptuous," Godfrey said.

"Merely observant. I see no chests of gold and the cathedral remained incomplete when I last checked. What other reason could there be for your call?"

"Some astute observations. You are correct. We're here to express our willingness to continue the arrangement..." Godfrey thought on the fly. "...but I must also inform you of a new tax."

The old Jew looked displeased with Godfrey's sudden revelation but held his tongue like an expert diplomat.

"That is news to me Your Excellency. Please accept my apologies for our tardiness, I will see that you have full payment before you leave."

The elder waved over his shoulder, and his young assistant left the room.

"Will you also require the additional funds for the cathedral?" Isaac asked with a knowing grin.

Godfrey was once again baffled by the wealth contained within the simple building. He and Peter departed with a chest containing enough gold to fund three months of cathedral works, plus the tax Godfrey had invented only moments before.

His carriage had just departed towards their next stop when it was caught by one of the palace runners. Matching their pace, the runner shared a winded exchange with Peter through the carriage shutter. Peter barked some brief instructions and the runner changed course back towards Godfrey's palace.

"They found John," Peter said irritably.

"Well that's positive," Godfrey replied.

"It would be, if he'd just stop trying to escape. Back when I was at the seminary they had ways of breaking even the most insubordinate neophyte's will."

"You're right, a change of tack is required. We'll deal with him after the cathedral workers."

"Indeed. I've ordered he be confined to his room until we return."

"Very good," Godfrey approved.

The carriage pulled up at the cathedral. The master craftsmen insisted on repeating the same tired tour of the building's shell. The design complaints related to trivial details, though they seemed offended when Godfrey dismissed them as such. This was quickly forgotten when Peter presented the Jews' gold and Godfrey ordered them to pay the workers what they were owed, plus a month in advance. The Bishop personally delivered this news to the workers in a rousing speech and the worksite buzzed with renewed energy when he returned to his palace.

"Peter, I've been thinking about my Book," Godfrey said as the carriage trundled home.

The Assistant looked unsurprised. "How so?"

"It seems we are surrounded by incompetence wherever we turn. I wonder if the Heretic was perhaps not dealt with as permanently as instructed."

"Would you like me to put a call out for any information about a red-haired foreigner? And a missing book? I'll ask the parishes but we might have more luck if you offer a sizeable reward."

"Yes, that would be good. If I can't have the full Book then perhaps we can find a way to extract the information directly. If she is still alive."

The carriage finally pulled up at the palace. Godfrey was exhausted and craved more wine. But one last task remained.

Peter peeled away when they arrived and Godfrey went straight to John's room. A guard stepped aside to grant the Bishop passage. Noting the man's heavy chainmail mittens, Godfrey summoned him into the room too.

After a brief silence, the cold stone corridor echoed with John's helpless whelps but no one was around to hear them. Godfrey emerged with a grin. He saw little risk of ongoing disobedience.

CHAPTER NINETEEN
18 January 1124

Rachel's wedding was a lavish affair. Matilda had grown so accustomed to quiet rural life in the month since her arrival at Holford that it was a surprising assault on the senses. The reception was held in an unused field, with a giant bonfire at the centre surrounded by makeshift furniture and tents serving endless food to the guests. Musicians played pipes and lutes and drums. Barrels of ale, mead and cider flowed freely. Sober guests generated a buzz of conversation which was intermittently punctuated by drunken revellers who boorishly yelled out to one another or sang bawdy drinking songs.

Matilda had daydreamt of such a cultural experience during her classes at the Institute. It was just like the party scenes from her favourite novels and films, only the guest of honour wasn't turning eleventy one. Earthy smells from the field and warmth from the bonfire proved that the experience was very much real.

Despite the worsening weather, the wedding had been brought forward by months at the bride's insistence. Rachel hadn't set foot in the family cottage since the revelations about Mama's death and she had practically replaced the Archer family with her new in-laws. Poor Ma had been a wreck for weeks, having lost both her mother and daughter in the same day. But Rachel was blind to her mother's grief and only interacted to demand ever more as the wedding drew closer.

Despite the bride's well-known petulance, the whole region had turned out for the event. There were attendees from villages as far as Stowey. Many shared Matilda's views of Rachel's cruelty and Matilda even overheard one woman whisper that the bride and groom deserved one another.

Instead, it was the promise of an extravagant event that drew the crowds. Rachel's new father-in-law was Holford's brewer and had developed a reputation for producing some of the finest ales in the region. He'd spared no expense for his eldest son's wedding and rumours had circulated in the preceding weeks that there would be an entire season's production of ale, several whole cows roasted on spits, musicians travelling all the way from Devon and a bear fight.

People's excitement grew as each rumour turned out to be true – except the bear fight – and Holford was buzzing before the revelry had even begun.

The ceremony itself appeared a mere afterthought. Matilda unremarkably hadn't received an invitation to Holford's chapel and instead pottered around the cottage which had begun to feel like home. The family had adopted her as their own and insisted that there would be enough people at the reception for her to avoid Rachel's wrath.

Matilda snuck into the field when darkness had fallen and the party was well underway. She found a position on a hill at the edge of the celebration where she could watch the crowd. She'd always preferred people watching to being at the centre of things.

Despite the medieval twist on the gathering, Matilda was amazed by the similarities to large celebrations back in her own time. Embarrassing drunken family members and scolding wives were eternal. Revellers overindulged, volunteers cooked over hot coals and children wove amongst the proceedings on their own adventures. Just like home.

Watching the interactions between Holford's various social cliques reminded Matilda that politics was everywhere, even tiny Twelfth Century villages. Field workers and craftsmen, housewives and younglings. The fabric of medieval society. The villagers easily slipped into their places and Matilda enjoyed spotting the few people that belonged to multiple groups, stitching the whole community together.

Matilda had met enough of the villagers that her people watching became a medieval-themed game of Where's Wally. Rachel did the rounds with her new husband to thank their guests, though a peevish expression betrayed her displeasure at the lack of attention given by her groom on their wedding night. Ma and Pa were in deep discussion with Martin Brewer and his wife – Rachel's new parents-in-law – at the long bridal table. Margery sat at the fringe of a group of young adults talking with the Miller's son. Old Timothy held court with a collection of elderly gentlemen and Matthew Smith flirted with some out-of-town maiden.

Matilda eventually spotted William and Elizabeth walking towards her, each laden with armfuls of food and a big clay jug. They joined Matilda at the party's outskirts and lay out their takings.

"We tried to bring you one of everything," Elizabeth declared proudly. "So you'll know just how well Holford throws a party!"

The siblings insisted that Matilda try each of their favourite treats and they shared the jug of mead between them. Matilda felt as though she might explode, a sensation she hadn't felt since arriving back in time. Their stomachs also full, Elizabeth and William joined in her people watching and provided a running commentary.

"See the guy carrying two jugs?" William asked. "That's Herbert. Pa said he's so daft they had to tie his boots for him when fighting for the King. But he can fell a tree with a single swing of his axe. Works for the carpenter now."

"And that lady in the blue skirt is Widow Beatrix," Elizabeth pointed out. "Her husband worked a field near ours before he went missing off Kilve beach. William thinks Vikings took him."

"No I don't," William denied unconvincingly before quickly changing the topic. "That younger lady next to Beatrix is Mabel. Ma's not a fan, says that she..."

Matilda had just gulped a mouthful of mead when William finished his vulgar sentence and she snorted, making the amber liquid run through her nostrils. Elizabeth fell into hysterics, having sampled a fair amount of mead herself.

"I think I'd better get her back to Ma and Pa," William said, his face red. "She's well had it."

Grasping Elizabeth by the elbow, William led his sister back toward the bonfire. Matilda was left alone to digest her food in peace.

But as the pair melted into the crowd a voice sounded behind her.

"I thought I might find you here," said a familiar voice.

A chill ran down Matilda's spine as she turned warily towards the robed stranger. The bonfire's flickering light illuminated his face...and she was thrilled to recognise the friendly priest from Nether Stowey.

"Oh! So good to see you." Matilda shakily leapt up and gave him an awkward sideways hug before remembering that he was a priest and retracting herself. "I never caught your name!"

"Thomas, my dear," the Priest said with a laugh. "I see you've been sampling the Brewer's creations. He sure knows how to put on a party."

Matilda offered the jug but he politely declined with a raised hand.

"It's good to see you," Matilda repeated. "Do you come to Holford often?"

"I don't think I've been here for over twenty years. I'm a little too comfortable in my chapel. An old man set in his ways. When I heard of a great gathering in the hills, I absolutely had to try my luck finding the Baron's mysterious healer."

He stared off at the bonfire and the dancing villagers. A comfortable silence fell between them. Matilda sipped from the jug.

"The Baron missed you that day," Thomas said. "It's not often that a miraculous healer denies him the chance to bestow a reward."

"I needed to be away from that place," Matilda explained with a hiccough. "From those vile people. I've never felt so afraid in my life."

The conversation put a rock in Matilda's stomach.

"I can't even begin to imagine. I'd bet it's hard to believe but they're not bad people. One is the most loving father and the other dotes over his aging mother. It was that vile Bishop's doing. Power can make even the gentlest of people do horrendous deeds."

The flames of the bonfire reflected in his eyes.

"Not that it forgives their actions," Thomas continued. "Not at all. I just thought you ought to know of their remorse. Neither has missed a single Mass since."

The priest was right, they weren't forgiven, but the enduring rock in her stomach did lighten slightly.

"I'm sorry for shoving you, behind that shack," Matilda said with an apologetic smile. "Some way to thank my saviour."

"Not to worry child, no harm done. I'm just glad to find you here in one piece." Thomas paused. "You should know that Bishop Godfrey has been looking for you. Three times now I've had visits from his messengers asking about that afternoon. Now he's put out a call to the parishes seeking any word of a red-headed foreigner."

"Oh," Matilda said dumbly. "That's not good."

"Not ideal, no. I told them I have no idea where they might find the woman they described. I'm staying with Father Daniel in Holford's chapel tonight and will have a quiet word with him before

I leave. It seems you've helped the village more than enough for him to see the value in holding his tongue."

"Thanks Thomas. You're kinder than I deserve."

"Kindness begets kindness. Anyway, this old man needs his bed. Do come back to Stowey someday. I've no doubt that Baron Walter still wishes to give you your reward. And I could always use an extra hand sweeping my chapel."

He began to set off but suddenly stopped in his tracks.

"Fool! To venture so far only to forget the reason why! Old age, I tell you."

He reached into the cloth bag slung over his shoulder and pulled out a bulky object.

"Might this belong to you?" he asked with a cheeky smile.

"My bible!?" Matilda cried as she beamed up at him. "How?" she managed to choke out.

"I wasn't about to leave your belongings lying in the mud. I flicked through the Book myself but couldn't make the slightest bit of sense out of it. I unfortunately had to surrender your bag and its contents to the Bishop's men but I somehow convinced them that I hadn't seen your Book." There was a naughty twinkle in his brilliant blue eyes. "Take care of it. It sounds like Godfrey will move Heaven and Earth to get his hands on it. And be careful referring to it as your bible, some might find that to be poor taste."

Matilda couldn't help herself. She leapt up from the ground again and pulled the old man into a tight embrace.

"Thank you Thomas!" she gushed. "You have no idea how much this means."

Even in the dim light, Matilda saw a blush on the man's cheeks.

"No worry at all," he blustered. "I know the value of a good book."

The Priest headed off back into the crowd, leaving Matilda to pore over her beloved bible in the firelight. The spine was torn, pages were falling out and a crust of mud obscured the embossed cover. But it was the most precious object she'd ever seen. A reminder of the world that was.

She sat in a stupor for what felt like hours, soaking in the familiar pages and remembering exactly where she'd been when she wrote her various notes. The rock in her stomach had completely dissolved, replaced with a warmth that emanated throughout her entire body. She felt reborn.

Matilda was so absorbed that she barely registered William, Margery and Elizabeth's return.

"I couldn't get Elizabeth to stay with Ma," William complained. "She kept chasing after me. She's calmed down a bit now, just hide the jug."

"Shut up Willy!" Margery interrupted, pointing at Matilda's bible. "What's that?"

"You got your Book back!?" William asked excitedly.

"You've a book!?" Elizabeth cooed.

"You know how to read!?" Margery cried.

The trio descended upon Matilda and watched completely enthralled as she flipped through the pages. She told them that a kindly priest had returned it to her but omitted the details of how she'd lost it in the first place.

"Can you teach me to read?" Margery begged. "I've always wanted to learn!"

"Definitely," Matilda replied with enthusiasm.

They were still poring over the pages when a pair of elderly villagers passed by as they retired for the evening. Intrigued by the suspiciously quiet gathering of young people, they strolled over to see what was happening.

"Ho ho! Look at that Stephen, a book!" Timothy Potter exclaimed.

"Well I'll be. You don't see many of them in little old Holford. Not enough people that know reading."

"Always beyond me," Timothy replied. "But no surprise that this one can. Stephen, this is the girl I was telling you about. The one that carried all that flour. Who *claims* to know how to make glass," Timothy added teasingly.

Matilda flipped roughly through her bible until she found the page with photos of glass blowing. She thrust it up at the elders.

"Would you look at that!?" Stephen said. "She might just be telling the truth Timothy. Amazing."

"So did you salvage the family's flour?" Timothy asked, still inspecting the image of glass.

"Most of it," Matilda replied. "The Miller charged another obscene fee but we left someone standing guard while we moved the last of it. I don't know how Holford lets him get away with it."

The two old men looked at each other and burst into laughter.

"*Let* him get away with it? Ha! Dearie, there's no other choice!"

"It's just the way it's always been," Stephen added. "We work until we're blue in the face. The Miller swoops in and takes a hefty portion, just because he can. Then the Baron takes a bite, and sometimes the King too. We're left with barely enough to get by. It's the circle of life."

"But it doesn't need to be that way!" Matilda complained.

"I'm afraid it does," Timothy told her with grave sincerity. "There's no other way, never has been and never will. Every miller since the dawn of time has known that they have the power. Arnold runs the only mill within miles so nobody is willing to risk losing access."

"What about the old mill, the ruined one on the way to Stowey?"

"That hasn't worked since my Pa was a kid. Folks say it's cursed. Look, no one likes a miller. These kid's grandparents knew that well enough, no offence. But there's nothing anyone can do about it."

On that cheery note, the old men wished the young ones a good evening and resumed their journey back to Holford. The siblings all returned to the Book, flipping through its pages and marvelling at the lifelike pictures.

But Matilda sat in silence, staring into the flames of the dying bonfire. The Miller's stranglehold over the village was so unfair…

CHAPTER TWENTY

25 January 1124

Winter had well and truly set in. It rained constantly. Margery's family were confined to the cottage, though Rachel's departure lightened the mood and made it slightly less crowded. Margery quite enjoyed the confinement but poor William bounced off the walls like a caged animal.

With little to do outside, Margery and her remaining siblings pestered the Foreigner to teach them how to read and write. Margery was the most diligent student and raced ahead of the others, though William stubbornly struggled to keep up and excelled at Matilda's lessons, particularly numbers. Elizabeth didn't mind either way and was just happy to spend quality time with the family.

They practiced writing by drawing with their fingers in the cottage's dirt floor. In less than a week they'd memorised the letters of the alphabet and could spell out each family member's name when quizzed. They loved the lessons and while Margery focused on learning ever more complicated words, William had already started multiplication.

The Foreigner's Book was in high demand and the family were placed on a strict rotation policy. Margery used her time to stare at new words and sound each one out loud, driving everyone insane with her endless mumbling. William spent his time looking at the Book's pictures which only fuelled his annoyingly endless stream of questions. Elizabeth spent her time focused on the Book itself, flipping through the pages and wondering what the tree that produced it might've looked like.

"We can try making paper when the rain clears up," Matilda promised her. "Then you can bind it into a book of your own. That'll make our writing lessons easier, particularly if Ma and I can make some inks."

To further break up the winter monotony, Matilda also taught a series of new crafts and activities to help around the house. Each morning started with Matilda's bizarre routine of strange full-body stretches followed by mock fights. She showed Pa designs for sturdier tools using metal from Matthew and taught Margery how buttonholes could enable tighter-fitting clothes.

One rare sunny afternoon, Matilda took William to her secretive cave in the forest and returned with a bag of exotic plant seeds which she used to teach Elizabeth how to cultivate seedlings in the warmth of the cottage. Greenery soon sprouted from every available space.

Margery especially appreciated that the Foreigner devoted particular attention to Ma, who struggled most with winter malaise and adjusting to life without Mama and her eldest daughter. Matilda first tried teaching Ma new recipes. The family benefitted from mouth-watering delicacies but Ma remained a wreck. Margery hinted that textiles were Ma's great passion and it was only when Matilda discussed making an improved loom and long-lasting dyes that Ma finally forgot that she hadn't heard from Rachel since the wedding.

Although they'd lost Rachel, Matilda had quickly become a part of their clan. She joked with them over family meals, helped out with chores and showed appropriate levels of scandal when listening to the scarce village gossip. She was thoroughly more enjoyable to be around than Rachel had ever been. Margery thought it was the best winter ever.

Although normally full of energy and willingness to help, Margery noticed that the Foreigner's mind was often elsewhere. She regularly needed questions to be repeated or stared off into nothingness. The cause of her silent musings was revealed as the family sat down for their meal on yet another dreary morning.

"I've been thinking about the Miller," Matilda raised in an overly casual tone as she ladled a bowl of porridge. "I think I've got a plan."

Margery stiffened in her chair. The Foreigner knew of Margery's friendship with Henry yet persisted with her crusade against the Millers. Margery wished Matilda would just let it go.

Pa lay down his spoon and interrupted her with a sigh, "Not this again?"

"I know," Matilda continued. "You can't risk Arnold blocking your access to flour. But isn't it ridiculous that a single man can hold the entire village hostage when there's another mill lying in ruins? That he can live a life of luxury, barely lifting a finger, while everyone else lives on meagre rations? Holford deserves better."

Margery had heard it all before. She scoffed the last of her watery porridge before fleeing the cottage without a word.

The Miller's house was nestled by the stream that ran through the village. It was nicest building in Holford, meticulously crafted by

Stowey stonemasons generations earlier and its roof tiled by Timothy Potter. Only the brewery was bigger.

Margery raced there to find Henry and knocked on the door, feeling self-conscious standing before such a grand building. As always.

She prayed that Henry would open the door rather than any of his miserable family. Margery and Henry often bemoaned their two wicked sisters but at least the rest of Margery's family were pleasant. Henry wasn't so lucky.

Margery's prayers were answered.

"Oh, hi," Henry said simply. "Wasn't expecting you today. It's raining."

"I know," Margery said impatiently, pulling him outside and towards Arnold's warehouse. "Quick, I've got to tell you something."

Henry followed and sat upon the sacks of grain as Margery closed the door behind them.

"Matilda's up in arms about your Da again," she blurted.

Henry looked up at her dumbly. "Oh, I thought you might want to try kissing again."

"Not now Henry. Trouble's afoot."

Henry looked disappointed. "Well, what's she up to?"

Margery paused, feeling sheepish. "I didn't stay long enough to listen. But she's been worked up for days. Your Da's antics during Mama's funeral really bothered her. She's going to do something."

"She can't do anything," Henry replied with certainty. "No-one's brave enough to mess with Da."

"I don't know Hen. This woman doesn't play by the normal rules."

"But what can we do? Da's already in a foul mood today. He won't listen if we say something's just going to happen."

Henry was right. Margery paused again.

"Ok, let's go hear what she's thinking. Surely your Da will appreciate some warning."

Henry looked hesitantly at the rain but followed Margery outside. The pair were halfway home when Margery caught a glimpse of red hair also darting through the rain, followed closely by her little brother.

"Quick, over here!" Margery whispered, dragging Henry behind a hedge as William knocked on their neighbour's door. "Sneak up and see what they're up to."

Henry looked unconvinced but Margery pushed on anyway. She shuffled from cover to cover, hiding behind hedges, barrels and fences. Henry made too much noise but they eventually got close enough to listen.

"…but surely you want things to change? You just said how much he's taken from you. Shouldn't we try stopping him?"

"It's a noble undertaking but he's a cruel man, plain and simple. I wish you luck but I want no part in it."

Margery heard a door slam shut.

"That's two now," William told Matilda. "They'll all agree with you but no-one's brave enough to challenge him."

"Come on Will," Matilda pleaded. "We've got to try."

The pair ran back into the rain and onto the next house. Margery followed behind, taking care to remain unseen.

William knocked at the next door. "Hello Beatrix, sorry to bother you. This is Matilda, she's helped out with the harvest and wanted to ask you some questions."

Beatrix eyed the Foreigner warily. "Yes?"

"I'm concerned about Arnold Miller and want to bring an end to his unsavoury practices."

Widow Beatrix happily told Matilda about her experiences with the Miller, down to the exact amounts of flour he'd taken over the previous three harvests. But she clammed up the instant Matilda asked for help.

"Nope, won't do that. A corrupt miller is still better than grinding wheat by hand."

Matilda thanked the Widow and resolutely continued to the next houses. She got a long list of evidence but only Matthew Smith and Pa agreed to join her and William to confront Arnold.

Margery listened as the group discussed their plan of attack and Pa urged once more that Matilda let the matter lie. She considered him briefly before shaking her head and marching off towards the mill. The men cursed and ran after her.

Margery and Henry followed, running into the yard as Arnold exited the mill. William acknowledged their arrival with a surprised look.

"Morning Arnold," Matilda started glibly.

"What do you want?"

Margery felt Henry cringe beside her at seeing his Da already riling up. He was well acquainted with the man's temper.

"Just a friendly chat," Matilda replied sunnily. "I've compiled a detailed account of the villagers' takings from the fields. And the fees you charged each of them." She held up her Book with a flourish. "As expected, things didn't quite add up when I ran the numbers. You're taking much more than you should."

"I take what I'm entitled to," Arnold replied petulantly.

"I don't believe that. Numbers don't lie."

"Well, what are you going do?" the Miller challenged. "You're not even from here, why do you care?"

"I loathe bullies," Matilda replied with a shrug. "Tell me, does the Baron know? I'm sure he still makes a tidy profit but is he aware of the scale of your greed? Does he know how much more he could be getting from the villagers?"

"I pay more than I ought to."

"Hmm, we'll see. Baron Walter owes me a favour and I'll be sure to raise this issue with him. Unless I can have your word that things will change around here, of course."

Matilda let the words hang and Arnold paused in thought. With a silent look, Margery asked Henry if Matilda had done enough. He shook his head just as the Miller's expression hardened.

"The fees are what they are. They're not up for negotiation. Not that it'll matter to your lot," he said, gesturing to Pa and William. "I won't be dealing with you again and if others don't like it then they can try going elsewhere too."

"Oi!" Matthew shouted, "That's not fair!"

"Be reasonable Arnold," Pa implored coolly.

The Miller sneered as he turned back to the mill.

"Holford is united," Matilda bluffed. "Lose one and you'll lose them all."

"Ha! I'll take my chances," the Miller called over his shoulder as he returned to work.

"That's unfortunate," Matilda responded calmly. "I'd hoped he'd want to avoid this but I guess there's no option. Come William, time to see the Baron."

The pair strode off in the direction of Stowey.

"Are we really going to see the Baron?" William asked excitedly.

"Yep."

"And he really owes you a favour?"

"Yep."

The rest of the group were rooted in shock and Matilda had disappeared around a nearby building before any of them moved.

"Shit, I don't think she's joking," Matthew said, tugging at Pa's arm. "We should stop them before this gets out of hand."

The men ran off.

"Should we follow?" Margery asked Henry.

"I dunno. Da looked pretty mad."

A sense of adventure seized Margery. "But Hen, do you think she's really going to see the Baron? In his castle?"

Henry hesitated. "You go. I'll make sure Da's alright."

Margery didn't argue and ran off in pursuit, leaving her friend standing alone. She caught up with the group as they entered the forest. Margery heard William's endless questions from a mile away.

"Margery?" Pa noted with interest. "What are you doing here? Where's Henry?"

"Back with Arnold. I couldn't miss this!"

Margery joined the group, listening in awe as Matilda batted away every concern or objection. They were halfway to Stowey when they heard running.

"Come to talk some more?" Matilda asked with genuine interest as Arnold and Henry came into view.

"I don't know what you're hoping to achieve here, woman," Arnold huffed as he caught his breath. "Cease this foolishness and be on your way. The damned family can keep using my mill."

Matilda thought for a second.

"No. Not good enough."

She turned and resumed walking.

To everyone's surprise, Arnold vaulted forward and grabbed Matilda from behind, childishly trying to restrain her.

Matilda's response was equally unexpected. The moment the man touched her, she dropped to one knee and used the momentum of his large frame to pull him effortlessly over her shoulder and fling him to the ground. She pinned him down with her forearm tightly across his throat.

The group's shouts of concern quickly transformed to amazement.

"Touch me again and you'll wish you were dead," Matilda hissed.

The Miller stopped struggling.

"Good. Now, you've proven to be the slimy weasel I'd expected. It's time someone put you back in your place. Scurry home, little ferret."

With a shove, Matilda pushed herself to her feet and casually resumed walking. William trotted after her while the others stared in shocked silence. Matilda wasn't ten yards away when Arnold called out.

"No!" he cried, pushing himself from the ground. He followed after them again, not even bothering to brush himself off. "I won't let some *woman* drag my name through the mud."

"You've done that yourself," Matilda said. "But suit yourself. It'll be fun to hear what Walter has to say to you."

The mood was tense as the group continued towards Stowey. Margery fell in line with Henry and greeted him with a bewildered smile. Arnold walked alone at the rear of the group, muttering to himself.

They arrived at the town and headed straight for the castle. Their tense party drew strange looks as they traipsed up the castle hill but no one interrupted them.

Margery had never been inside the castle and was filled with anxious excitement. She couldn't believe that Matilda had the nerve to just stroll up to the guard and was let through without breaking stride.

Margery soaked in the sights as they raced through the castle. Five of the most magnificent horses she'd ever seen stood unused in the stable and the stone buildings were finer than any in Holford. Even the Miller's house looked shabby in comparison.

The Foreigner strode confidently up the keep staircase without a care in the world.

"Hello again Grumpy," she said with surprising familiarity to the surly guard. "I'm here to see the Baron. Is Sir Phillip in?"

Margery was amazed by her casual tone and even more so when the Constable actually appeared. Sir Phillip was legendary around the region for his valour while serving the King and for being the Baron's righthand man. Margery had only ever seen him from a distance.

He greeted the Foreigner with a big smile and a friendly embrace.

"So good to see you again! We thought you'd left for good. The bag of clothes you left made for an odd parting gift."

"I ran into some unexpected troubles," Matilda replied cagily.

"I pray it was nothing too great."

"I've mostly recovered," Matilda reassured. "I've been helping with the harvest in nearby Holford and seek an audience with Walter on a related matter. Is he in?"

"Locked away in his study but I'm sure he'll excuse an interruption for his prodigal physician."

The Constable welcomed the group, ushering them inside and out of the cold. They gathered around the hearth of the biggest fireplace Margery had ever seen. It warmed her in an instant and she gawked around at the cavernous interior of the keep as they waited.

"Lady Matilda,' Sir Phillip eventually called. "He's ready to see you now."

He guided the group into a grand hall where the Baron waited expectantly on a simple wooden throne. It would've held at least four of the family's cottage.

"Matilda!" the Baron called joyfully. "A pleasure to see you again."

The Foreigner marched forward and gave a graceful curtsy worthy of a seasoned noblewoman. It looked odd in her well-worn farm clothes.

"Good to see you too my lord. How is your finger?"

"As good as new," he said, rubbing a finger on his left hand. "Though I've taken to wearing the ring on a chain."

"Very prudent," Matilda approved.

"And who do we have here?" the Baron asked.

Matilda motioned the group forward.

"Villagers from Holford, my lord. I've been assisting with their harvest since helping you." Matilda's voice cooled. "And this is Arnold, Holford's miller."

The Baron's expression hardened as he realised Matilda hadn't come for a straightforward social visit.

"I don't have many mills on my lands," he interrupted. "I don't recall ever having missed payment from this mill."

"No my lord," Arnold replied, "you have not."

Matilda glared at him. "I'm sure he's paid precisely what you have asked. But I've found that he is heavily cheating the villagers and have little doubt that he's also cheating you."

The Baron looked displeased and stared warily at the Miller. "This is a concerning allegation. One that will require further investigation. Do you have evidence?"

"Yes, testimony from countless villagers. I would welcome an investigation, but I've also come with a potential solution."

The Baron was intrigued but wary. "Go on?"

"Competition ensures that villagers can get the most flour from their grain. And more flour for them means more taxes. I beg your permission to renovate the ruined old mill at the outskirts of Holford."

"You can't do that!" Arnold cried.

"*I* can't?" the Baron asked, irked by the Miller's boldness.

"There...isn't enough work for two mills," Arnold pointed out. "And the taxes! To the King. Surely you will need to pay double the taxes if you allow this woman to operate another mill."

"He has a point," Baron Walter told Matilda.

"He does, my lord. But I'm confident your investigation will show that he's stealing from the village which should easily cover any increase in taxes. And as for demand, Holford's crop will improve next year. Matthew Smith here has already improved the farming equipment and I'll teach the villagers how to better manage their fields to improve yield. I'd happily teach your other villages too."

Margery marvelled as silence fell over the room while the Baron considered what the family's guest had said.

"One other thing," Matilda added cheekily. "You did promise me a favour for saving your finger."

Baron Walter looked displeased at being reminded of a debt. Even Margery knew that Matilda was pushing her luck but the Foreigner doubled down.

"I ask for ownership of the ruined mill as my reward. I can have it operating within the year and your income from Holford will more than double by the next harvest. I promise."

The Baron paused again. Sir Phillip whispered something to him.

"Fine," the Baron said. "You may repair and operate the mill, but it remains my property."

"My lord, you can't," Arnold pleaded, earning him a glare from the Baron.

"I can do what I bloody well like. Sir Phillip will visit Holford to investigate the truth behind Matilda's claims. Be warned Miller, I don't take kindly to being cheated. Now all of you, be gone!"

"Thank you, my lord," Matilda said with another grand curtsy. "I'll have it working in no time."

Margery watched in awe as the Foreigner left, as though what had happened were the most normal thing in the world.

How could she ever be like that?

CHAPTER TWENTY-ONE

30 January 1124

Sweat beaded on Matilda's forehead as she worked on the ruined mill. She wiped it off with the back of her filthy hands. The clouds had mercifully cleared to grant a rare three days of respite from the endless winter rain. The ground surrounding the mill was churned from William and Matilda's early renovation efforts but it became less boggy with each sunny day.

She tore one last vine from the exterior wall before stepping back to appreciate all they had accomplished in the week following the Baron's decision. After a wet march to collect tools from her cave, they had barely stopped working and even camped in the ruin to maximise their use of the pleasant weather. It was starting to look like a tidy crumbling ruin, rather than just filthy and overgrown. *Her* crumbling ruin.

Matilda was ecstatic that her gamble had actually worked. There had always been some human elements outside of her control but the case against Arnold seemed tight. Harry had always been the best at negotiating but Matilda had rolled the dice and come out with a spectacular win. Plus her bag of clothes from Sir Phillip. Pa was furious at Matilda after Arnold had cut off the family's flour, if only for an hour, but Matilda still felt an inner glow at challenging the Miller's unjust stranglehold over the village.

It was only when Matilda first stood before the ruined mill and inspected it with an owner's eye that she realised the true scale of her task. She was glad that King Henry was still in Normandy and her mission on hold. It would take months to repair the building, let alone getting the mill back to working condition. And that was provided she somehow convinced Holford's tradesfolk to help her without upfront payment. She would need all the charm she could muster.

Matilda had been pleased to discover a surprisingly solid structure after clearing the dense undergrowth surrounding the mill, though the exterior plaster had started to crumble after years of neglect and sections of the tiled roof had caved in. The building consisted of a long single-storey stone warehouse that ran parallel to Holford's small stream. The millhouse stood on the southern end, a semi-submerged three-storey building that housed the grinding mechanism and a small loft.

The mill's waterwheel was a mess of rotten timber but Matilda was relieved to find that the grindstone and internal mechanisms were mostly intact, despite the majority of the millhouse roof having collapsed. A little less charity she would need to ask of the townsfolk.

William emerged from the warehouse with a large bale of brambles over his shoulder, Matilda's hatchet tucked into his belt. He tossed them onto the ever-growing pile of refuse before the building. They planned to have a bonfire. While it wouldn't rival the one at Rachel's wedding, Matilda hoped an accompanying party might entice a few prospective tradesmen to inspect the project.

"These blackberries are never ending," William complained. "And so spikey. Ma's going to kill me if she finds another hole, she's still mending my other tunic."

"It'd be nicer if there were berries," Matilda sympathised. "But it looks like Elizabeth's got lunch!"

William's youngest sister skipped towards the mill, humming to herself with a basket draped over her arm. She'd been the most supportive family member, making food deliveries rain, hail or shine.

"Wow," Elizabeth marvelled as she lay down her basket. "You two have actually managed to make this place look presentable."

"Thanks Beth," William said, already pilfering from the basket. "It's been a big week. It'd be easier with some extra help…"

"No way," Elizabeth replied, swatting William away. "I'm not risking Pa's wrath. He's already tetchy that I'm delivering your food. Says we have to get everything prepared for next season, that we don't have a second to waste. It feels like winter's barely started."

"That's my fault," Matilda said. "He's worried about the Miller, that you won't have anywhere to take grain next season and will have another hungry winter. It'll take time for me to earn back his trust."

"Nah," William countered. "Just get this mill fixed and the whole village will love you."

"I still can't believe the Baron gave it to you in the first place," Elizabeth marvelled as she unpacked the food. "Everyone knows it's haunted."

"Haunted?" Matilda asked with a raised eyebrow.

"People say its cursed," William explained. "The old miller was murdered here, years back. Pushed his apprentice too hard, they say."

"Mama's husband was trained by that apprentice," Elizabeth added. "Even Mama was scared of him."

"Well there's been no ghosts yet so never mind all that, little sister," William beckoned excitedly. "Come see what we've done."

William's excitement was hard to ignore so they led Elizabeth inside to show off their progress. She was impressed before they'd even entered.

"You can actually open the door!"

"We. Sure. Can," William replied, using his shoulder to fight the rusty hinges. "Not that we could do much when we finally got it open. It took a day of chopping down bushes and clearing debris before we could even get inside."

After days of work, the dim warehouse was now a dry cavernous space. Cobwebs still hung from the exposed rafters and beams of sunlight shone through gaps between the roof tiles. Half of the room was still filled with brambles but William had worked through them with remarkable efficiency.

"You could fit all of Holford in here!" Elizabeth marvelled, her voice echoing off the distant walls.

"And then some," William said proudly. "It's much bigger than Arnold's warehouse and even he can only fill half at any time. We'll need to patch up the walls. Inside and out."

William gestured to a particularly bad stretch of wall, where fallen plaster lay in large chunks on the dirt floor.

"We need to do something about these windows," Matilda added, motioning to the four large shutters on either side of the long warehouse walls. Fighting another rusty hinge, she forced one open to let sunlight and fresh air stream in. "I'll see if Timothy wants to start making glass. After some roof tiles that is."

A rat scurried along the wall as the trio continued the tour.

Elizabeth squealed.

"Any chance you could lend us one of your cats?" Matilda asked Elizabeth, only half joking.

They reached the far end of the hall and William wrenched open the double doors to the millhouse. A small step took them up to a floor made of heavy wooden planks. The gaps between them were still caked with flour that had long since spoiled.

The room was particularly bright compared to the dim warehouse as light poured in through the partially collapsed roof. Shattered roof tiles lay scattered across the floor. Sifting through them to recycle any that remained intact was another task on Matilda's comprehensive to do list.

The giant millstone sat in the centre of the room and a shaft pierced the floor, leading to the primitive gear system that drove it. It was the pinnacle of medieval engineering. William had already quizzed Matilda for hours to understand how it worked and how she planned to improve its efficiency.

Elizabeth was much more intrigued with what was above.

"A loft! How fun!"

Like a little child, she raced up the ladder and onto the small platform. Matilda chuckled at herself for missing the novelty of a second storey for someone who lived in a hovel.

"It's so dusty," Elizabeth called from above. "And high. And spacious!"

"Missing half the roof will do that," William called up. "It was miserable there when we first arrived and rain was pelting down."

"That's where my bed will go," Matilda told them casually.

"What?!" the siblings cried in unison. Elizabeth's head comically popped over the edge of the loft.

"You can't expect me to stay in the cottage forever?" Matilda asked.

They continued their blank stare.

"On a cot in that cramped little corner of the house? With your whole family?"

William's mouth hung slightly open.

"When there is all of this space just waiting here?"

The siblings remained silent. Matilda decided to wait them out.

"Well that changes everything," Elizabeth said matter-of-factly as she jumped down the final rungs of the ladder. "This will need to be much homelier if you ever intend to live in it. I'll help you plan."

The trio exited the main millhouse door and sat down for lunch.

"What will you do with all the spare space?" Elizabeth asked as she unfurled a rug.

"I was thinking of starting a school," Matilda replied.

William and Elizabeth stared at her blankly once more.

"A shared space where people could come to learn how to write," Matilda explained. "Or make paper. Or study animals. Anything really."

The siblings loved the idea, provided they could be among the first pupils. They discussed other ideas for the empty space. A hospital. A laboratory. An inn. A workshop. In the end they decided the mill was probably big enough for a little bit of everything. The siblings didn't mind, so long as they were involved every step of the way.

"A hospital will need a proper herb garden, for the medicine," Elizabeth realised excitedly. Apple still in hand, she ran to the mill and began to pace out the space needed to grow sufficient produce for whatever Matilda's building eventually became.

"Naturally," Matilda agreed, jumping up to join the excited girl in her pacing.

They planned the layout for a generous garden, complete with herbs, berries and an orchard. William shouted half-hearted encouragement from the picnic blanket before tiring and lying back to watch the clouds.

"And you'll need pretty flowers too, not just practical ones," Elizabeth insisted. "It's got to look nice after all."

William groaned loudly but Matilda agreed enthusiastically.

As her finishing touch, Elizabeth marched to the 'orchard' and dropped to her knees. She scooped away several handfuls of mud and placed the core of her half-eaten apple inside the hole.

"There," she said proudly, wiping her muddy hand on her dress. "If the sun and rain continue like we've had this past week, it'll be a nice shady tree for your pupils to study under in no time."

With their planning done, Matilda helped Elizabeth pack up the remnants of their lunch and thanked her for trekking to the mill yet again. As always, Elizabeth was just happy to assist.

Matilda decided to join Elizabeth back to Holford, leaving William to continue his clearing work. The two women happily chatted the whole way back. Elizabeth told of her favourite walks through the forest and Matilda recalled the amazing nature she'd seen on her travels.

Matilda bid farewell to Elizabeth when they reached the cottage and went to tell the Blacksmith her ideas for the mill. Matthew was beating away at pieces for a second plough when Matilda arrived.

"Our first order," he proudly informed. "Lots of people asked about it at the wedding. The plough-team couldn't help bragging."

Matthew had already agreed to help with the mill but regretted his premature offer when Matilda outlined her plans.

"We'd have to sell many more ploughs to make all of that happen," he told her. "Though you could always part with your chainmail."

"Not a hope in hell," Matilda countered. "I'll talk to Timothy about the roof. William suggested Holford's carpenter might also help? What do you think?"

"I'll ask. Walt's a fine builder but a touch fickle. One day he's helping a neighbour for free, the next he refuses paid work from his own mother. He might take issue with working for a woman but I'll see if he might help for me. Surely he can't turn down a project this grand."

Matilda thanked Matthew and continued on to Timothy's house. The elderly potter was away so Matilda simply left a broken roof tile by his kiln, trusting he would know who it was from. Deciding to delay another awkward apology to Pa for another few days, Matilda turned back towards her mill.

An endless stream of calculations ran through Matilda's head as she meandered back. She had grand plans for the mill. Mechanical bellows. An automated sawmill. Electricity. Technologies all at least a century away from discovery but she had a chance to introduce them prematurely. The prospect of a tangible project was much more stimulating than theory learned at the Institute.

But the small waterwheel could only power one. *Which to choose.*

She sauntered through the bare trees but her mind snapped to attention when the mill came into view and she saw four strangers gathered around the building. She was too far away to see exactly what was happening but her gut told her it wasn't good. She picked up her pace to a jog.

As she drew closer, she saw William boldly standing between the men and the mill. She was still too far to hear what he was saying but could hear the defiance in his voice. The men antagonised him, mocking his courageous stand. In an escalation of their sport, Arnold's bald assistant stepped in and punched William in the face before expertly bouncing back to dodge William's sluggish counter swing. Matilda broke into a sprint.

"Hey!" Matilda called as she drew closer to the confrontation. "What the hell's going on?"

The men turned to face her.

"Look here boys," the Miller sneered. "The bitch is back."

Matilda slowed and was relieved that the men's attention had shifted away from William. She felt the familiar rush of adrenaline that preceded a fight. This time, having not been ambushed or clubbed over the head, she could handle them. Any lingering fear was quickly overcome by rage.

"What're you doing at our mill?" she asked through gritted teeth.

"The bitch has teeth," Arnold jeered. "Listen to her growl!"

"You're more confident with friends around," Matilda noted. "Surely you don't want a repeat of our journey to Stowey?"

The Miller's men threw him questioning glances.

"What are you going to do? Take us all?" Arnold challenged with bravado.

"I'm not going to take any of you, as much as I'd like to. The Smith and Carpenter are on their way to measure up our new waterwheel," Matilda lied. "I don't think they'll take kindly to your bullying. Or we could just start now, it's probably fairer to you."

The mood remained tense. Matilda continued to stare down the Miller, her eyes blazing with fury and defiance.

Arnold buckled first.

"Watch yourself girl. Sir Phillip just visited my mill and took a huge fine because of your meddling. You've got powerful friends and achieved more than I'd ever thought possible. But you can't keep going. You won't. Know your place."

Arnold shoved past Matilda and signalled for his gang to follow. They each glared at Matilda with varying levels of menace before following their leader like a pack of browbeaten dogs.

Matilda ignored them and rushed over to William. He had a bloody nose and would get a nasty black eye but he was fine. Matilda grabbed a bucket of water and handed William a rag to clean his bloody face.

"Who were they?" Matilda asked as she handed a rag to William.

"You know the chubby blonde one, Margery's friend Henry. The scrawny twitchy one is his apprentice Joshua and you've already met his labourer at the warehouse. The bald one. He does all of Arnold's dirty work, both at the mill and around the town."

Matilda's blood boiled as she watched the men disappear into the woods, pumping themselves up at having threatened a woman and beaten up a boy.

Her gut told her it was far from over.

CHAPTER TWENTY-TWO

2 February 1124

William stirred upon the lumpy earthen floor outside the warehouse. He was absolutely exhausted after weeks of slaving away at the mill and his brain urged him to stay asleep. For at least a little longer. But something prickled at his subconscious, dragging his mind from its slumber.

Aren't you supposed to be on watch? it asked. *What's that crackling sound? Is that smoke?*

A smoky smell cut through the inertia of William's sleep. His eyes burst open and he sat bolt upright. He pushed himself up from the ground and wrenched open the warehouse door. The sight within made his blood run cold.

The millhouse wall at the opposite end of the warehouse glowed with orange light. It streamed through cracks in the doors and out onto the empty warehouse floor, casting a long shadow from the lump of Matilda's slumbering form.

"Matilda!" William cried desperately. "Matilda, wake up!"

It was like someone had slowed down time. Matilda must've been in a deep sleep as she also stirred, refusing to wake. She only began to move in the same instant William noticed smoke billowing in from the mill.

"Matilda! Fire!" William called as he ran towards her.

Matilda jerked awake and snapped into action. Time resumed its normal pace as Matilda pushed herself to her feet and stumbled towards the fire without a second thought. William raced to catch up with her.

"What the hell William?" she shrieked as she ran. "What happened?"

William's silence spoke volumes. He'd failed his guard duty and fallen asleep. Matilda shot him an anguished look and sprinted on towards the fire.

Flames had already started to lick through the doors when Matilda reached them. Not waiting for William, she tore the doors open and was engulfed by a ball of flame that burst into the cooler air of the warehouse.

Matilda remained upright when the flames cleared and William smelt burnt hair. Her dark silhouette stared into the hellish inferno on the other side.

William drew up alongside her and marvelled with morbid fascination at the sheer energy of the blaze. Plaster fell from the walls and heavy beams crackled. William could see through the charred floor and into the burning machinery below.

"What do we do?" he asked, noticing that Matilda's hair was smouldering.

Matilda didn't respond and stared up at the flames in the loft instead.

"Get help," she eventually croaked. Her voice was devoid of emotion but her face was etched with fury and her eyes screamed devastation.

Then she ran in. Matilda was darting across the burning floorboards before William could stop her. Dodging piles of fiery debris, she pushed outside through the mill's main door and quickly returned with a bucket and wet rag. William watched the woman with admiration, dwarfed by the burning building but prepared to fight nonetheless. David versus Goliath.

"Go!" she commanded, seeing William rooted in place. "I'll save what I can but we need help to stand any chance of salvaging this. Go!"

William didn't need to be told again and sprinted back through the warehouse. Flames had started to lick the rafters.

He passed through the warehouse door and was running down the laneway towards Holford when he heard a tremendous crack, followed by something heavy crashing through wooden floorboards and a hideous scream. Worried for his mentor, William whipped back towards the mill but when the smoke cleared Matilda's silhouette dashed out of the building to collect more water.

"Go!" her voice echoed across the yard as she ran back inside.

William sprinted towards the village, racing until his chest and legs burned. And then some. He was furious with himself.

How could he have fallen asleep?

William and Matilda had both slept at the mill since Arnold's thugs' attack, taking turns to watch for any sign of sabotage from the Miller. They'd even informed the Baron of their concerns but received no reply. Just William's luck that the attack had fallen on his watch.

The sun was just beginning to rise and a light drizzle had started when William finally arrived in Holford. He welcomed the cool mist on his singed arms. He circumvented a few of the closer houses and headed straight for the family cottage.

Still at full sprint, William pushed through the front gate and burst into his parents' home.

"Wake up everyone! Wake up!"

Margery groaned and urged him to go away. Pa leaned out of bed, staring up at William with concerned bleary eyes.

"Wassup now?"

"Matilda's mill's on fire! Everyone, please!" William begged. "Arnold set the mill on fire. There's a chance to save it but we need help."

There was a rush of activity as the family assembled outside.

"Rags, buckets, shovel!" William urged. "Anything you can get. Head there now and I'll get more help. Please, as fast as you can. Matilda's all on her own!"

The family hurried off, Pa in the lead with Elizabeth close on his heels. Relieved to have reinforcements on the way, William ran off to find more help.

The Carpenter's house was nearby so William went there next. He decided against barging in but drummed wildly on the door until Walt emerged, wiping his eyes and cursing like a sailor.

"What in blazes do you want?" he asked bluntly.

"The old mill's on fire! Total inferno. We're trying to fight it but we need help."

Walt's expression changed instantly. Fire was a carpenter's mortal enemy.

"Rightio then." He ducked inside and quickly returned with a coat. "You get the Smith, he'll wanna protect our investment. We didn't spend these last weeks helping out for nothin'. I'll gather me boys and meet you there."

William was already leaving before he finished.

The commotion prompted villagers from their homes and William yelled for assistance as he ran past. He had no idea if they would care but he'd take whatever help he could get.

Matthew was already awake and standing outside when William arrived at the forge.

"What's this about a fire?" he asked and was already moving when William answered. "Grab some tools and let's go."

Matthew piled buckets and shovels on William before collecting his own stack of equipment. They raced to the mill together, hindered by their awkward loads.

The fire still raged when they arrived, though the flames appeared slightly smaller. The site was a hive of activity and William was pleased to see that several villagers had joined the fight. The millhouse had been conceded to the inferno but several people beat flames up on the warehouse roof and a chain of others passed buckets of water up from the stream. More still darted in and out, salvaging items from inside or clearing debris.

Matthew and William approached the crowd and distributed their equipment before joining the fight themselves. It was manic and time passed by in a blur. Other than a roiling sea of orange that gradually calmed to black and grey, William's only memories were of Matilda.

The woman fought like a lion, beating at flames with a wet rag and tossing buckets of water with precision. She bellowed orders, with little regard for the weariness of her volunteers. Her face was covered in soot and chunks of her hair had burned away. Her clothes were covered in holes and skin peeled from her hands.

And yet, she was everywhere. Fighting the fire from the front line, improving the bucket bearers' efficiency, guiding the placement of salvaged items. She ran everywhere, slowing only after the flames were completely extinguished. Even then, she prowled around the building to survey the damage while everyone else milled around in the warehouse.

With the fire extinguished, Elizabeth and Margery ran back into Holford to collect food for the weary volunteers. They returned bearing a basket of bread and were soon followed by the Brewers who distributed casks of ale amongst the crowd. Rachel stayed at home.

Matilda finally sat down as the last of the bread was being handed out. She'd lost her eyebrows and walked with a limp. Her toes poked through one of her fine leather boots. Most concerning was the peeling skin of her blistered hands and a nasty burn across her upper left arm.

Despite Matilda's harsh directions, the volunteers were concerned for her wellbeing. She dismissed all offers of assistance and sat shaking uncontrollably with her hands in a bucket of fresh water. She ignored everyone's gaze and smouldered with anger and grief.

"How bad is the damage?" Matthew eventually asked gently, coaxing some life from Matilda.

"The millhouse is gone. The grinding stone fell when the floor collapsed. The remaining roof fell too. There's nothing but the stone shell, though the walls should be salvageable." She droned on. "The majority of the warehouse was saved. Whoever thought to remove the roof tiles and fight the fire from above is a genius."

Matthew passed her a cup of water and she paused to drink, though her shaking hands made it difficult.

"The mechanism is a chunk of charcoal but the grinding stone's still intact, despite the fall. I hope Walt hasn't started the new waterwheel yet…" He shook his head. "…because this might be an opportunity to build something even bigger and better than before. More power. More machines. More options."

William admired her optimism but didn't share it.

"Just get yaself better," Walt told her with unusual tenderness. "We'll make whatever design ya throw at us."

The crowd sat in silence, trying to absorb everything she said.

"But how did it happen?" the Brewer asked bluntly.

All eyes turned to William and Matilda. Matilda slouched and avoided William's eye so he started.

"I woke up to the smell of smoke. Next thing I know the whole building was on fire."

There were disconcerted murmurs among the crowd.

"Did you leave a candle lit?" Widow Beatrix asked. "People say you've both been working like dogs, day and night, to get this up and running."

"It was all of the dust," Matilda replied mournfully. "We never stood a chance. The place must've gone up in an instant." She conceded a look at William. "It was that bloody Miller. He threatened us after beating up Will. Said we'd never fix it. Then he burned it down to make sure."

"No!" came the collective cry from the crowd. Some were outraged, others refused to believe Arnold could stoop so low.

"We know he's an evil whoreson but surely not," called another neighbour. "He could've killed you and the boy!"

Matilda grunted, pulling herself upright and shuffling to the salvage pile. She scrounged around before returning to throw an object into the centre of the crowd.

"It's well within his twisted capabilities. There's your proof."

Everyone peered at the unidentified object.

"Oh," Timothy exclaimed thoughtfully. "Yes, that's his alright."

Matilda blinked at Timothy with a vacant expression, taken aback that someone had accepted her theory so easily. "What?"

"That's one of my oil lamps. That glaze was a custom request, tricky to get the colour right. You're right, it was for Arnold."

Matilda blinked twice as she registered Timothy's affirmation of her theory.

Then, for the second time that morning, she ran.

She didn't wait for anyone or say where she was going. She just left.

But William knew exactly where she was headed and ran after her, calling back to the others that she was after the Miller. Luckily her limp made it easier to catch up.

"Matilda! Stop!" William called, but the Redhead limped on with determination. "Surely this is a matter for Baron Walter?"

"You don't understand William. This man is a parasite, a cancer on the village. Now either come and help me or get out of my way and leave me alone."

William continued his pursuit. Several of the villagers raced to catch up and also sought to dissuade Matilda from a confrontation with the Miller.

"He's too powerful."

"What can you possibly achieve?"

"Give it up"

"You've still got your health, mostly."

But there was no convincing Matilda who continued her resolute limp back into Holford. A crowd swelled behind her.

The sun had fully risen by the time Matilda reached Arnold's house. She slammed against the front door while calling out for the Miller. His daughter eventually opened the door slightly.

"Get. Him. Now," Matilda hissed.

Joan timidly closed the door and disappeared in search of her father. Matilda paced around the door as she waited, like a big cat waiting to be fed. The crowd continued to swell. Even villagers who hadn't helped fight the fire started to arrive and asked their neighbours what had happened. Word of the fire was spreading.

The door eventually opened. Matilda stopped her pacing and waited with the crowd. William walked over to stand beside her.

Arnold emerged, his head held high. His family filed out after him, dressed for Mass and standing in silent support. William saw Margery catch Henry's eye and give a subtle wave. The blonde boy looked terrified.

"What's the meaning of all this commotion?" Arnold demanded. He saw Matilda standing at the head of the crowd and smirked when he noticed her burnt clothing. "I thought I heard the dog barking. Why have you interrupted our breakfast and brought a mob to harass my family? I thought a strong independent woman like yourself didn't need reinforcements."

Matilda scowled at him.

"You know exactly why I'm here, pig. You lit my mill on fire!"

The Miller stood unswayed. "I did nothing of the sort. I've been here with my family all morning. The sabbath is a day of rest."

"Then what's this?" Matilda asked, throwing the ruined oil lamp at his feet.

"That's your evidence? You're deranged, woman. Circumstantial at best."

It started to drizzle again and yet the crowd didn't move, not wanting to miss the most monumental exchange in Holford's living memory. Not a soul spoke up and Matilda raged at their apathy.

"Come on people, wake up! You know he did this!" she cried at their vapid faces. "Why aren't you angry? This man has a stranglehold over your lives. He takes what he wants and you just let him. His family stands before you in their finery while we eat soggy bread and live in fear. He's nothing without us. For the love of God, wake up!"

Arnold's labourer arrived as Matilda pleaded with the crowd and roughly elbowed his way towards her. William smelled smoke on the bald man's clothes as he pushed past.

Without warning, the brute lunged at Matilda in an effort to silence her. Even with her limp, Matilda deftly dodged his first two blows but his third caught her off balance and struck her sharply in the jaw. She fell to the ground but the bald man dropped and continued his assault.

It was the Labourer's brazen attack on a wounded woman that finally jolted the crowd into action. William and two other men hurled themselves at the bald thug and tore him off Matilda while the crowd hurled insults at the brute. The Labourer broke free and lashed out at the villagers which only earned him greater scorn. Three more men dived into the melee before he was subdued.

Pa called for order but the mob was incensed.

With the help of a few nearby villagers, Matilda picked herself up from the ground and calmly brushed herself off before turning back to the Miller.

"You can't even do your own dirty work," she scolded before turning to the crowd. "Do you see?"

The crowd's anger grew and their shouts shifted towards the Miller and his family. Concern finally dawned across Arnold's face and he urged his wife and children back into their extravagant stone house, calling for silence as they fled.

"Quiet! Quiet.' He paused and waited for the crowd to listen. "So you've sided with the flame-haired bitch? Yes, we burned the mill…"

There was an angry ripple through the crowd.

"…But what are you going to do? You need me. And more importantly, so does the Baron. There isn't another miller within a hundred miles of here. This chicken shit doesn't count," he said, spotting his apprentice in the crowd. "If I go, so does your flour. And the Baron's taxes. But it won't happen. Wealth talks so you can't touch me."

The crowd grew silent as his message sunk in. And then the scrawny apprentice threw a stone, hitting Arnold square in the chest.

The blow shattered the Miller's arrogant façade and he stared at his apprentice in shock. Then a second stone hit him. And another. The crowd's barrage of abuse resumed, now joined by stones and any other object the mob could find. The villagers took up Matilda's message and demanded that he leave Holford.

"Be gone," they cried. "Never show your face here again!"

Arnold fled within the house and barred the door, abandoning his labourer to the angry mob. They surged forward and surrounded the house, beating at the door and window shutters. William looked around in awe, he'd never seen his neighbours so incensed.

The crowd turned their anger back to the Labourer but two of Pa's fellow jurors took the bald man away. Pa eventually managed to restore order by promising to talk to Arnold. William watched with pride as his father calmly knocked on the door and led the remaining members of the village court inside to mediate.

The mob's anger simmered but it wasn't long before the door opened, reawakening the crowd and their insults. Pa emerged from the house and called for silence.

"Holford has spoken and the law of the land is clear. Arnold Miller freely admits that he caused the wanton destruction of our lord's property and upon that confession the Holford court finds him guilty. He's to be banished indefinitely and his mill will be passed to the care of his apprentice until a replacement is found."

There was a cheer from the crowd. The Apprentice looked dumbstruck.

"Now please, allow the Miller family clear passage as they leave. Any additional assault will be handled accordingly."

A fragile peace settled over the villagers before the Miller and his family gingerly emerged from their house, laden with all the worldly possessions they could carry. Arnold's wife wore five layers of clothes, making her look even more rotund than usual.

The crowd was on its best behaviour and they followed the Miller family to the village limits with only the occasional outburst of abuse. They formed a line as they reached Holford's outer boundary. Arnold turned for one final word.

"You are the dumbest flock of sheep I've ever had the misfortune to meet. You'll regret this day, mark my words."

He defiantly cast his gaze over the crowd before finally settling on his apprentice.

"Boy, you've been the bane of my existence but come now. We'll start a new mill, away from this rabble."

The Apprentice looked terrified but puffed his chest and answered with a simple emphatic, "No."

The crowd cheered and issued one last volley of abuse. They hurled insults and stones as the Miller and his family fled into the forest.

The abuse died down and the Millers had almost completely disappeared through the trees when a final cry erupted from the crowd.

"Wait!" Margery shouted. "Wait for me! I'm coming too."

Before anyone could react, William's older sister ran off into the forest after the Miller family and her best friend.

Just like that, another sister was gone.

CHAPTER TWENTY-THREE

2 February 1124

Matilda was stunned to see Margery run off into the forest, ignoring Pa's calls and chasing after the Miller family. The frenzied crowd redirected their abuse at the fleeing girl, hollering insults and good riddance. The sudden loss of another daughter was too much for poor Ma who collapsed into Pa's arms. William and Elizabeth ran to her side.

The Miller family disappeared from sight and the crowd's yelling subsided. Pa lifted his distraught wife to her feet and they joined the remaining crowd heading back to Holford. The charged atmosphere was extinguished as drizzle turned to rain and the crowd dissipated. Ma's wracking sobs drove the villagers even further away.

Everyone was silent as they walked down the muddy road back to Holford, processing the morning's tumultuous events. Deciding that the family would be absorbed by their own loss, Matilda darted into the forest to get some space of her own. She caught William's eye and shot a look urging him not to follow.

She cut towards the smoking remnants of her mill and it was only when Ma's weeping was replaced by forest sounds that Matilda realised just how weary she was. Her jaw ached from the Labourer's brutal attack and her burns throbbed. Already feeling woozy, she threw up after looking closely at her blistered fingers. They'd already started to smell.

Matilda was terrified of infection and headed straight to the mill-pond, grabbing a bucket and a coarse rock to clean herself as best she could. She stripped off her clothes but took particular care with her tunic which had crusted onto her shoulder from pus.

She cleaned herself meticulously, using twigs as makeshift tweezers to remove every strand of fabric or ash from within her burns. Each new discovery made her retch.

Convinced that she'd cleaned most of the filth, Matilda went for an awkward swim to wash out her wounds. The cool water soothed her burns but she began to shiver uncontrollably and suddenly became lightheaded.

Clutching onto consciousness, she dragged herself to the safety of the shore. She caught her breath and collected her burnt clothes before staggering naked back to the mill, head foggy and legs like jelly.

Several times she found herself dropped on one knee. She arrived to the safety of the warehouse and was drying herself with her blanket when she was hit by a particularly strong wave of nausea. The dirt floor rushed up to meet her and everything went black.

+++

It was dusk when Matilda woke. She hated her body's weakness and for letting the Miller's sabotage rob her of a day's work. She ignored her rumbling stomach and went straight to wash herself again before donning fresh clothes and fashioning bandages for her burnt hands.

Matilda stubbornly resumed her work and toiled well after the sun had set. The fire was extinguished but her anger remained ablaze, at everyone and everything. She tore charred lengths of timber apart to salvage whatever building materials she could. Some of them were still warm.

The clouds cleared and moonlight streamed through the completely collapsed roof, allowing Matilda to continue her work late into the night. It was only after a third fall, when Matilda landed heavily and burst a giant blister, that she finally conceded the futility of her efforts and begrudgingly sought some rest. She was asleep almost as soon as her head hit the dry dirt floor.

+++

Matilda spent the next morning poring over the wreckage of the mill and cataloguing the full extent of the damage. She determined that the fire had been deliberately concentrated around the mill mechanism which meant there was little left but the stone shell of the millhouse. Luckily the majority of the warehouse was unscathed.

By midday, Matilda had created a decent stack of salvaged timber in the warehouse. She was wrestling with a particularly large beam when William arrived carrying Elizabeth's food basket. Matilda was ravenous but refused to pause her work and continued to wrangle with the timber.

William placed his basket on the warehouse floor and vaulted down into the mill's basement to assist. The pair had almost succeeded when the task required Matilda to break her stubborn silence.

"No, push to your left!"

With one final shove, they hauled the beam into the warehouse and sat down, exhausted.

"You look terrible," William told Matilda bluntly. "Have you stopped at all?"

"I cleaned myself up when I got here," she replied simply. "There's work to do."

"Not yet, you need a break. I'd bet you haven't eaten since the fire."

Matilda's stomach growled viciously. "Fine."

William started preparing her a meal of bread and cheese. He'd even smuggled the family's precious supply of honey.

"I didn't know whether you'd prefer to eat it or use it on the burns," he told Matilda as he passed over her meal.

Matilda mellowed with each hearty bite. It was heavenly.

"Thanks Will," she said, feeling more herself. "You were gone awhile, what've you been up to?"

"Taking care of Ma," William replied. "Trying to at least. She's a wreck. That's two daughters gone now. Plus Mama. Poor Elizabeth hasn't been allowed out of her sight which is sucking the life from both of them. I've never seen Pa so angry. He put Arnold's brute in the stocks to await Sir Phillip. Overnight! Arnold would be either brave or stupid to set foot back in Holford."

"What about the villagers? Did they continue their rowdiness?"

"Not without you to fuel their frenzy. They all went their separate ways as soon as we returned. The reality only settled in today, now that the excitement's worn off. Everyone's on edge, asking how we'll grind flour or how the Baron might seek vengeance. Some even talked about finding Arnold and getting him to come back."

Matilda felt her hackles rise. "Over my dead body!"

"It won't happen," William reassured. "Pa won't let it. Nor I. Or Joshua, the Apprentice. But he'll need your help. Poor guy's in way over his head. He was so proud to finally stand up to his boss and even moved into Arnold's house. But people are already banging on his door demanding their flour. Some are even asking for their grain back. But he just sits there, trying to understand Arnold's ledger. I don't think he can even read. Perhaps he could be one of the first students here at your school."

William shot her a cautious smile.

"I'm sorry for falling asleep. I really tried to stay awake, I swear."

Matilda knew she'd asked too much of the Boy. "It's not your fault. I pushed you too hard. Myself too. Arnold was bound to get his way eventually."

"True," William said thoughtfully. "I guess it's only upwards from here then. We certainly can't sink much lower. What will you do with the place now?"

Matilda had given it a lot of thought and told William that as terrible as the fire was, it presented an opportunity. The pair walked around the site as Matilda shared her plans to build a completely new mill, one with a much bigger waterwheel and a more efficient mechanism that could drive all sorts of machinery. A mechanical bellows for the Smith *and* a water-powered saw for the Carpenter. Perhaps even an electrical generator. It would be revolutionary. Provided they could fund it of course.

Matilda was just explaining how falling water would more efficiently drive her improved design when she heard thundering hooves racing towards the mill. Baron Walter rode into the yard at full gallop, flanked by Sir Phillip and another knight. He sat atop the tallest horse Matilda had ever seen. It was solid muscle and lathered in sweat from a hard ride. The Baron reined in his steed, smoothly dismounted and marched towards them.

"What in damnation is this?" he yelled, waving at the charred shell. "I give you a building that lay untouched for decades and within weeks it's burned to the ground?"

"It hasn't…" Matilda was cut off as Walter continued his rant.

"And my miller? MY miller! I hear he's been kicked off MY lands, by MY own peasants no less! How can my quietest hamlet turn so suddenly to chaos? I ordered you to keep the peace!"

"We tried. My lord," Matilda added stiffly. "William and I kept to ourselves, just clearing the mill. It took weeks but we were almost done. The village craftsmen were already making replacement parts."

"But did you tell the Miller what you were doing? Did you tell him *why* you were clearing it?"

"He witnessed your decision!" Matilda replied angrily. "Of course he knew what we were doing…"

"So you flaunted that you were usurping his position in the village?" the Baron asked matter-of-factly. "No wonder he attacked you, I would've too!"

Matilda resented the Baron's insinuation that they'd deserved the attack but, channelling all the lessons from the Institute's diplomacy curriculum, she strained every fibre of her body to hold her tongue. She stared at Walter in tense silence, waiting for his temper to burn out.

"I will say my lord," Sir Phillip interjected, "It may be missing a roof but the building *is* much clearer than last time I rode through."

The Baron let out a reluctant sigh.

"Right you are Phillip," Walter said pensively. "Well, it's done I guess. Now what are you going to do about it?"

Matilda seized the opportunity and gestured with an injured hand. "It's been a painful ordeal, but there are positives that can come of it."

The Baron stared at her with disbelief.

"The blaze cleared out the remaining areas much faster than William or I ever could. The destruction of the mill's mechanism is certainly a loss but we can install a more powerful design when we rebuild a new mechanism."

"Why would we need to build a new mechanism," Walter asked impatiently. "There's already another mill, without a miller!"

Matilda took a deep breath, letting the frustration of the man's obstruction flow over her.

"I hope to work with Holford's smith to create a mill-powered forge capable of producing stronger metal and with the carpenter to create a mill-powered saw. Among other things. I guarantee that no other region in the entire Kingdom has access to that technology."

Matilda led the Baron and his men around the site, showing them the extent of the damage but taking care to paint it in a positive light. She explained how her plans for a more efficient mechanism would work and how it could allow the mill to do more than just grind flour.

"This is all fine and well," Walter chimed, "but with neither mill operating the villagers can't process their own flour. You promised me double output but now expect me to go without any income? It's unacceptable!"

"I could train the Miller's apprentice…" Matilda started but Sir Phillip interrupted.

"I must say, this contraption is well beyond me but she does seem singularly knowledgeable. Your mind is a valuable commodity Miss Matilda. Walter, if she succeeds with this, maybe she could revive other projects. The old copper mine perhaps?"

"Oh no, one project at a time," Matilda insisted but Walter's eyes had already lit up.

"Now that's an idea," the Baron mused. "It could certainly compensate for the reduced milling revenue."

"And longer term…" Sir Phillip hinted.

"Yes!" Walter cried without a second thought.

Matilda protested. "There's no way I can complete both projects at once. Any time spent on the mine would be less time to restart the mills. I can teach the Miller's Apprentice but not both."

"I won't hear it," Walter said. "You will inspect the mine and make it profitable again. The damned Miner is still wallowing around somewhere nearby isn't he?"

"He is, my lord," Sir Phillip said, giving Matilda an unusually sympathetic smile.

"Then Matilda will find him and have him show her around the mine. And you'll also help the Apprentice. Yes. Cease your work on this ruined endeavour this instant and don't return until the Apprentice has dealt with the flour."

The Baron's last statement was issued as a command, his tone concrete and eyes set.

Matilda paused. There was no way around it.

"Okay, my lord. I'll inspect this mine and see what can be done. But I make no promises of success. And I'll help the Apprentice get his affairs in order while also continuing planning with the village craftsmen." Matilda's tone was concrete and her eyes set. "At least permit *them* to progress so we can begin repairs when the apprentice boy is trained."

Walter nodded and turned toward his horse.

The exchange left an unpleasant taste in Matilda's mouth so she decided to push her luck.

"My lord, the mill has rightfully remained your property. As will the mine. But may I request compensation for my output?"

Sir Phillip shot Matilda a cautioning look but she continued.

"I've proven myself to be both capable and honourable. I request full authority to make alterations at both sites as I see fit, with the specific goal of maximising your long-term output."

"That seems fair," Baron Walter said warily.

"And I would request half of the profits," Matilda continued with a completely straight face. "To finance the work."

The Baron baulked. "Half!? You're daft woman!"

"Only of the profits," Matilda reassured. "Surely my efforts are worth something to you. You're asking me to turn dead and unprofitable sites into golden geese. If I leave…" She looked at him pointedly "…or something happened to me, the sites would remain untouched. Wasted. Useless."

"She *has* proven to be an asset Walter," Sir Phillip confirmed. "Perhaps half of a half might be fair?"

"Careful Phillip," the Baron warned, only half-jokingly. "It appears you and the Redhead are in league with one another." He sighed. "You're a wilful woman Matilda but fine, half again. An eighth of the profits to distribute as you see fit. I'll hear no more on the matter."

"Yes my lord," Matilda said with a grateful curtsy. The mere promise of income would encourage cooperation with the villagers.

Satisfied that his interests were no longer threatened, Walter mounted his horse and started back to Holford at a more leisurely pace. Matilda gave a knowing nod of gratitude to Sir Phillip as he too mounted up and departed to detain Arnold's labourer.

"By all that is holy, how did you manage that?" William exclaimed as the knights disappeared from sight.

"I don't know," Matilda said with a big grin. "I guess it rarely hurts to ask? Come on then, we'd better earn our keep and see what this apprentice has gotten himself into."

William helped Matilda hobble back to Holford and they quickly made the rounds. Timothy was glad to see Matilda in one piece and excited to make more tiles for a new roof, a welcome change from the endless pots that were his namesake. His one condition was that Matilda finally show him how to make glass. Knowing of its future utility for her projects, she agreed instantly and wondered if David's celebratory champagne bottle was still in her cave.

Matthew was harder to convince. He'd been happy providing minor support but his frown deepened as Matilda explained what they would need for the new waterwheel and mechanism. His interest grew when Matilda promised to teach him how to forge larger components and he became genuinely excited when she explained how the larger waterwheel would drive large saw blades for Walt and automated bellows for Matthew's mechanical forge.

"You can do that!?" he cried.

"Sure can. We could even try making steel," Matilda baited.

"Why do I sense there's more..?" Matthew asked warily.

Matilda sighed. "Well, the Baron gave me another task. He was quite insistent that I find the Miner and revive his old copper mine. Do you know where to find him?"

The joy in Matthew's face disappeared. "That old mole. He owed me a lot of money. Good luck getting a coherent sentence out of him, he's the Brewer's older brother and rarely without a drink. I'll try to find him for you. He's either sulking in some cesspit near the Brewer's or at his hovel near the mine."

Matilda thanked Matthew and left to find Walt. She needed a much bigger favour from him and wracked her brains for the best approach.

"Na, can't help ya," he said. "Ya'd need my entire stock of dry timber."

Matilda ended up having to literally beg for Walt's assistance. He was intrigued by the idea of a saw mill but it was the Baron's promise of future funds that eventually convinced him to provide enough wood for at least the roof. Even then he demanded a hefty cut of profits.

Matilda was satisfied with her progress but her head throbbed and her burns ached as they made their final stop to help the Apprentice. She shivered as they passed the Miller's empty house, her mind replaying the previous day's confrontation.

The mill was in complete shambles when they arrived. Bags of grain were strewn across the floor and fallen stacks of flour had torn open. The Apprentice was covered in the white powder, making his hair look prematurely grey. Combined with his gaunt eyes and scrawny physique, he looked like an elderly man.

William and Matilda spent the rest of the day helping Joshua get the place in order. William restacked the grain and swept up the flour while Matilda worked with the Apprentice to decipher Arnold's needlessly complex accounting system. Having spent the winter teaching the family, she was shocked at Joshua's lack of rudimentary numeracy and helped develop a schedule to put his customers' minds at ease. Matilda suggested significantly reducing the Miller's overinflated fees to further alleviate any concerns.

Next they worked with the mill itself, helping Matilda intuit how the machine was supposed to work. They managed to grind their first bag of flour after hours of experimentation and had the site working – though still far from smoothly – by sunset.

"Well it's official," Matilda announced. "I think we can call you Joshua Miller now."

Joshua gushed with gratitude and his eyes had regained some life by the time William and Matilda set off for the cottage. They were both weary but felt they'd accomplished a lot.

They were almost home when an arm grabbed Matilda and dragged her behind a hedge. William cried out with a mixture of shock and warning. Matilda acted out of instinct and, despite her burns, swept her assailants feet before landing a flurry of punches.

"Ow! Stop it!" Matthew cried, trying to push Matilda away.

"Oh, sorry," Matilda replied sheepishly. "I don't like surprises."

"Noted," Matthew wheezed as he clutched his stomach. "I found the Miner for you. Want to see who you'll have the pleasure of working with?"

The pair followed the Smith to a pigsty behind a nearby building. Matthew gestured to a lumpy pile of rags.

"There's your miner," he said, barely hiding his amusement at Matilda's disgust. "Looks like you've got serious work to do."

CHAPTER TWENTY-FOUR
6 February 1124

John stared longingly out of the library's small window. The sky was grey and dreary yet people passed through the palace gate below and into the town of Bath. Coming and going as they pleased. John envied their freedom.

The scratch of Adelard's writing drew John's focus back indoors and onto the stack of parchment before him. Progress on Godfrey's Book had slowed to a crawl and John had resorted to consolidating his notes to search for additional clues he might've missed. Yet still the text made little sense.

"This is impossible!" John cried out, tossing his quill onto the writing desk. It ricocheted onto the floor, the sound reverberating around the Bishop's small library.

"Impossible you say?" Adelard asked, looking over at John with a hearty chuckle. "The impatience of youth. It's undoubtedly slower than you'd hoped, but translating a text is difficult work. Let alone from an obscure dialect that no soul speaks. Add in the complex subject matter, then remove the first half of the text and the task seems nigh on impossible. It's a wonder you haven't torn out your remaining hair. You've done well to get this far. It'll just take time."

Adelard's compliment cooled John's frustration. "But how long Adelard? I don't have time!"

"Ha! You've got plenty of time, boy! I'm afraid the Bishop has you firmly in his clutches. From where I stand, you're barely off your mother's teat and will see many more moons yet. I suspect the Book will take years to fully comprehend, even if it was in Latin."

John sighed in resignation. "I'll still be locked in this room when Godfrey's cathedral is finished, though with luck we'll have a new bishop by then. Father Cuthbert will probably still be teaching us initiates. I don't think death could stop him."

"Religious life isn't such a bad existence," Adelard reassured. "There's food in the kitchens and a solid roof over your head. Put in a few tough years now and you could escape to a rural parish, out from under the Bishop's thumb."

John pondered the idea. "It doesn't sound totally abhorrent... I was always destined to become a priest, being father's youngest. But what I really want is to travel the world, like you."

"Ah yes," Adelard said wistfully. "Life on the road is uniquely free. Each day brings a different sight and new people. I can see the appeal to a caged sparrow like you. It's not easy though. There are many long hungry days and danger always keeps you on your toes. I don't know how you'd fare...the priest life has turned you soft," Adelard poked with a twinkle in his eye.

"I could join a Crusade," John countered. "Surely they could use a budding priest to sanctify their journey, in exchange for my passage and a bit of protection."

"I don't know which is funnier," Adelard roared. "The thought of *you* whipping the masses into a zealous frenzy or scrawny little John armed with spear and struggling under the weight of a shirt of mail. Either way, the Holy Land would fall in days!"

They both burst into laughter. Adelard always knew how to lighten the mood.

John collected his quill before begrudgingly turning back to the impossible task of cataloguing the unfamiliar words and strange topics locked in Godfrey's tattered Book. Adelard strolled over and rustled through John's notes.

"What I would give for that other half..." Adelard said wistfully.

"What I would give to meet the author!" John rebutted. "How did he learn so much, about so many topics? I wonder who he is?"

"A singularly strange man," Adelard agreed. "Why write such a masterwork in English? Surely it would reach a wider audience in Latin, or perhaps Arabic. Even the script is strange. I've never seen such perfectly formed characters, repeated identically page after page. Your writing isn't quite as good but the practice is paying off. Your notes are pristine!"

"It's never enough for Godfrey," John replied grumpily. "This cursed splint doesn't help either. How much longer must it stay on?"

"You want to be certain it has fully healed this time, those guards didn't hesitate to re-break it," Adelard noted with concern. "I'd guess another week or two."

"It could've been worse," John said. "Who'd have thought that all those years of fighting my older brothers would help some day. I even managed to give a little back in return," John added with a grin.

"Yes but was it worth it?" Adelard asked, sage as ever. "The Bishop's guards are brutes at the best of times but now their eyes blaze with bloody murder each time they catch sight of you. I've heard them. They hold no love for you. Watch yourse…"

As if on cue, the library door burst open and one of the Bishop's guards strode into the room. He was quickly followed by Godfrey himself, dressed in frumpy formal robes for a busy day of errands. His pompous assistant followed on his heels.

"What's this chatter?" Godfrey barked impatiently. "There's work to do. You've progress to report?"

"We were just discussing John's work to date, Your Excellency," Adelard answered diplomatically. "And pondering the tome's origin. The author must be a truly unique and knowledgeable man."

Godfrey paused, a rare look of mirth in his eyes. "Like no man you've ever met, I'd imagine. Novice, show me your work."

The Bishop swept over to the desk by the window and peered over John's shoulder. His clammy breath flowed past John's neck, making his stomach churn.

"Dammit boy!" Godfrey cried, clapping the back of John's head without warning and making him bite his tongue. A metallic taste filled his mouth. "Those are the same pages you showed me yesterday. I need something new!"

Despite his aching tongue, John made to respond but Adelard came to his aid. "We're reviewing the previous work, Bishop. To confirm there's nothing we've missed."

"Very well,' Godfrey said, unconvinced. "Cease the chatter and get back to work, these endless delays are testing my patience." He looked at John. "You'd better have something new when I return this evening. There are others who can speak English."

John seethed but Adelard gave a silent look of warning as he ushered the Bishop from the room. "Leave it with us Your Excellency. I was just telling Brother John how laborious translation work can be. But there's good progress, I'm sure of it."

The Bishop grumbled as he was led from the room but didn't give a backwards glance.

Adelard closed the door and John cried out in frustration. "He's impossible!"

Adelard hushed him urgently, a concerned eye glued to the door. "Quiet boy!"

They waited until the Bishop's footsteps had disappeared. Only then did Adelard relax.

"I can't do this Adelard," John said, tugging at his sore tongue. "The seminary. This stupid Book. I just want to be home, with my family."

Adelard stepped over and gave John a consoling hug. "I understand, friend. Change is hard. Yet it is the only constant in life. Life itself is change. Best to focus on things we can control. Shall we go for a walk?"

"No, thanks. I just need some time alone. This is all so infuriating."

Adelard understood and gave a consoling look. "It will get better, with time. But have some space, take care and I'll see you for supper."

John cupped his head in his hands as Adelard gathered his things. He heard the door close and waited again for the footsteps to fade away.

Then he leapt into action.

Godfrey's casual abuse was the final straw. He needed to leave. For good.

John had learned from his previous escape attempts. There would be no witnesses this time. No sack of belongings. He'd memorised the guards' movements and knew where they loitered. He had a plan. This time he would break free.

John collected his cloak and pocketed what possessions he could, taking trinkets to trade on the road but leaving enough to mask his illicit departure. The righteous voice in his head made him feel guilty for stealing but the wicked voice urged him to take the Bishop's prized Book too. John considered the greater theft but eventually judged it an unnecessary risk that would only heighten Godfrey's desperation to hunt him down.

With bulging pockets and nothing but the clothes on his back, he set out for Bath's outer districts.

John's heart pounded as he peered into the corridor, confirming that it was empty before scurrying along the wall like a stealthy mouse. He avoided Godfrey's grand staircase and instead took the steep servant's stairs, throwing himself behind an old barrel near the pantry as a pair of monks headed towards the kitchen. The smell of a hearty lunchtime stew made his stomach rumble but John tore himself away, knowing that most of his fellow clergymen would also be drawn by the food and not wanting to waste his opportunity.

There was a precious window of time before someone came looking for him. Godfrey would assume that John was diligently at work and Adelard would be gracious enough to give him space.

John scampered into the palace courtyard and skirted around its circumference towards the gate, keeping to the shadows to avoid attention and finding a crate from which he could keep watch. He spied Adelard talking in animated discussion with a pair of elderly priests across the courtyard and prayed that his friend wouldn't be punished for John's departure. That he would understand John's need to escape.

The courtyard was busy despite the promise of a midday meal and a constant stream of clergymen and servants flowed through the main gate. John watched and waited, growing increasingly desperate as time passed. Godfrey's guards cast a watchful eye over each passing person and John had little doubt that they had been forewarned to look for the Bishop's troublemaker.

He was still waiting for an outbound group that he could join when a burly farmer entered the gate carrying a large sack. John paid him little attention, cursing his bulk for obstructing the view. But the man headed straight towards John's shadowy corner and showed no sign of stopping. Not knowing where else to go, John scrambled onto the low rampart of the palace walls and hurled himself against the ground to keep out of sight. The farmer unceremoniously dropped his sack mere feet from where John had hidden and casually exited through the gate.

John's heart was still racing at the near miss when he realised he'd made a terrible mistake. Guards lazily patrolled the ramparts on either side of him, though they were luckily less attentive than their brethren at the gate. John crawled up against the crenelated wall and tried to make himself as small as possible.

He prayed for an escape, or just time to think, but a patrolling guard turned and headed back towards John. He was trapped from either side and trapped from below. There was nowhere higher he could go. In desperation, he looked over the wall and judged the distance. *It wasn't so high.*

The guard drew nearer and John realised he didn't have a choice. His throat was dry as he crouched onto the ledge and awkwardly lowered himself down using his good arm. He closed his eyes and, with a deep gulp, let go.

The fall was over in less than a heartbeat. John landed heavily with a muffled thud but picked himself up and brushed himself off as the guard above passed by without a care. John marvelled at his fortune to survive two near misses and prayed that his luck would hold out.

Finally free from Godfrey's inner sanctum, John refocused his efforts on escaping the second layer of his hellish prison. Bath's city walls had four gates. John's family lived southwest of the town and it was at the southern gate that Godfrey's men had caught him procuring a horse during his previous escape. John reasoned that the Bishop and his guards would assume that he would head for his family once more. So that was exactly what he did.

John darted down back-alleys away from the Bishop's palace before joining a main street and casually strolling towards the southern gate. He made no secret of his presence, stopping at stores to inspect their wares and greeting familiar faces. He told anyone who would listen of how he'd been asked to collect plants in the southern forests to freshen up the Bishop's library.

The false trail was weak but John wagered that an angry Bishop wouldn't pause for rational thought.

John was about to loop around to the western gate when he spotted the master of the southern stable. The man looked to be on hard times and yellowing bruises suggested that he'd also been punished for his uninvited role in John's earlier escape attempt. Their eyes met and John snapped still, rooted in place. Then the damnable man started to yell.

"Fugitive! That's the Bishop's boy, somebody stop him!" He called for his stable boy and hobbled towards John.

John saw people turn toward him but didn't wait to explain. He ran.

Fleeing only brought more attention and John heard others join the stablemaster's pursuit. Hands grabbed at his arms and robes but John tore himself away and ran faster. He wove through the crowd and made for the maze of quieter backstreets, running northwest as though his life depended on it.

Tall buildings muffled the shouts of John's pursuers and he slowed to a brisk walk. Oncoming strangers gave him questioning looks as he rushed by but he tried to even his breath and remain inconspicuous, as much as possible for a tonsured priest with a broken arm. Deciding that the western gate was an obvious place for Godfrey to set up an ambush, John changed course and headed north. Returning to his family could wait, first he just needed to escape.

John darted across another main street which prompted fresh cries from his pursuers, spurring John back into a run. He dodged past bewildered onlookers, apologising when he knocked a basket of bread from an old lady's hands. He wanted to help gather her belongings but the shouts of his pursuers drew closer and John could only manage an apologetic smile.

John sprinted down unfamiliar streets, wishing he'd had a chance to explore the city before attempting another escape. He rounded a corner and barged straight into the chest of the city's Jewish elder. The man's attendant shouted his disapproval but the Elder met John's gaze with a quizzical look.

Utterly exhausted, John gave a wordless plea.

A cry from one of his pursuers echoed down the alleyway. They were getting closer. The Elder gave John a knowing smile and stepped aside to grant him passage, prompting more disapproval from the underling. John didn't think twice and ran through. When he looked over his shoulder the Jews had resumed their casual stroll and shortly after John heard bickering and shouts as they impeded his pursuer's path.

John's chest was tight and his robes drenched with sweat when he finally arrived at the northern gate. He was relieved to see that it was calm and news of his escape had not reached the northern walls. John dropped back to a casual walk and stepped into the street. Hiding his sling in his sleeve, he brazenly strolled directly to the gate and stepped through as if it were nothing. He didn't dare to even breath until he was a stone's throw from the wall but Bath's guards remained idle and paid him no attention.

Wanting to obfuscate his path further, John clambered down into a ditch and skirted back around the town wall towards the western gate. He joined the steady flow of travellers on the road towards Bristol and breathed easier as buildings faded to empty fields.

He fought not to break into a run, though in truth he was physically spent from his dash through Bath. Instead, he maintained his brisk walk and searched for a decent place to hide but there was only an endless patchwork of fields and a sparse scattering of trees.

John walked for miles and passed several small villages. He began to enjoy his freedom. The sky seemed brighter and the air fresher. He planned where he might go when he arrived in Bristol and who might be willing to purchase some of his stolen trinkets. He imagined the look on his mother's face when he returned.

John passed through a small forest before reaching another plain of fields. He marvelled at the industry of his fellow man, being able to bend the Lord's land to the task of feeding the masses. Just another thing to be thankful for.

It was then that he heard horses, thundering at full gallop rather than the leisurely clip-clop of regular travellers. John looked over his shoulder and his stomach sank. A trio of horsemen wearing the Bishop's colours bounded down the road, their eyes firmly fixed on him. John desperately looked around for cover but even the sparse trees were gone.

Knowing there would be no escape, he turned and defiantly awaited the inevitable.

Godfrey wouldn't be happy.

CHAPTER TWENTY-FIVE
11 February 1124

William didn't know how it had happened but he'd been tasked with babysitting the Miner while he sobered up. Matilda and Matthew often disappeared to work on their other projects, leaving William alone with the human garbage. William resented their casual abandonment, as though he wasn't knowledgeable, talented or old enough to assist with their more technical work. He resented them being able to spend time alone. Together. But most of all, he resented the Miner.

In his sixteen years living in Holford, William had heard scattered gossip about the Brewer's ne'er-do-well older brother but only ever caught glimpses of the man. Ma had quite rightly protected her children from the Miner's sinful existence and the old copper mine had always been out of bounds for children. While this normally would've served as a challenge for William, even he knew not to risk his parents' wrath by breaking that particular rule.

To call the Miner a pig of a man was an insult to swine. The man was sin personified, guilty of gluttony, greed, sloth, anger and jealousy. William had little doubt that, given the chance, the Miner would've also been guilty of lust but his long hair was matted, his odour repulsive and his language would make a maid blush.

The only sin he couldn't be accused of was pride. Despite William's efforts, the man remained almost always drunk and he had stashes of food and drink scattered around Holford. His filthy clothes strained against the mass of his stomach and were covered in drippings from meals months prior.

From a young age Ma and Pa had preached the importance of looking presentable and keeping clean at all times, not just when going to church.

"People respect a clean person," Pa would say. "It shows the world that you're in control."

Living with Matilda had further reinforced the importance of hygiene, for both reasons. She taught William that Ma and Pa's daily cleaning rituals actually served to kill jurms, tiny invisible devils that made people sick.

"The fleas that live on fleas," she described them.

The Miner knew none of that and lacked any hint of self-respect. He was quite comfortable rolling around in filth and cared only about the source of his next meal. His younger brother, Holford's successful Brewer, had always provided.

That would change today, William thought. *Today you'll earn your supper.*

"Get up, slug," William grunted at him, nudging the seemingly unconscious man with his boot.

"Gerroff me," the Miner groaned.

"Up!" William ordered as he tossed a bucket of water over the man. "You're showing us the mine today and we want to get out of that death-trap alive."

The sopping Miner bellowed in anger and tried to surge at William. He hauled himself upright but only managed a couple of staggered steps before he collapsed back into the mud.

"Fine, you win. At least give a man some water, to drink this time."

It was the first time he'd requested anything but alcohol so William happily obliged. The Miner guzzled half the bucket, water streaming down his face.

"Tha's better," the Miner said before letting out an almighty belch just as Matilda and Matthew arrived.

"Classy," Matilda said with a look of disgust. "Is he really ready?"

"I'm fine," the Miner slurred. "Bit wet but tha's the boy's fault."

"Ready as he'll ever be," Matthew judged, turning to William and looking impressed. "I haven't heard him string so many words together for years. Well done."

"He still looks under the weather," Matilda noted with concern. "I hope he's lucid enough to know what he's doing."

"He'll be fine," Matthew said as he wrenched the wretched man to his feet and wrapped an arm around his shoulder. "Here Will, help me keep him steady."

William walked over and supported the Miner's other side. The man smelt even worse up close up.

The group set off towards the mine at a slow pace, wading through a dense fog and battling against a fierce wind. Matilda detoured to the burnt shell of her mill and ran inside to collect tools for their inspection. William was disheartened to discover that Matthew and Walt had already moved their own equipment into the yard. His monopoly of Matilda's time was over.

They resumed their slow journey, regularly stopping for the Miner to urinate, throw up or curse. Matthew tired of the vulgar antics and walked ahead with Matilda, leaving William to endure the Miner's putrid body odour alone.

"So what happened to your mine?" William asked the Miner, hoping conversation might distract from the smell and Matthew's obnoxious flirting. "No one ever talks of it but it must've been bad to do…this."

"Wha's there to say? There's nothin' there. Either empty or underwater. Dunno why you lot are interested all of a sudden."

"The Baron didn't really give us a choice," William said tetchily. "He's convinced that Matilda can resurrect it."

"The Redhead? More copper in her hair than left in those rocks."

"Surely there's something still down there?"

"Nah. We worked it for ages. My Da's grandad dug down there, an' even he weren't the first. Never a huge production, mind you. Not enough to warrant bickering between the lords. But good enough. My brother's brewin' only started cos we had enough scrap ore for him to make his brewin' cauldron. Never thought it'd become the family business."

"So what happened?"

"The damn thing flooded," the Miner said bitterly. "We dug deeper'n deeper. My workers refused to go down after the cave-ins started. Only a handful remained when I took over from Da an' they left when I couldn't pay 'em. I got stuck with a wet hole in the ground."

William sensed growing agitation and dropped the subject.

The group broke out of the tree line and entered a gusty stretch of fields. The Miner directed them up a slight hill towards a lonely outcrop of trees with a dilapidated hovel that had suffered years of neglect. Disused equipment in varying states of decay was scattered around the structure, the remnants of a once thriving work site.

The mine was a stone's throw from the hovel's front door, a deep gash straight into the flat ground. The sloping gradient straight into the earth reminded William of Matilda's cave but while her gully appeared to have been gently scooped away with a spoon, the mine looked like it had been hacked with a knife.

The group gathered around the mine and peered down into the entrance. Matilda looked uncharacteristically uneasy. She too eyed the support timbers that framed the mine's entrance, their rot matching the decay of the surrounding site.

"Nope," Matthew said bluntly. "I'm not going down there. I work with metal by the light of day, by the light of my forge if I'm really pressed for time. But taking ore that's still trapped in rocks straight out of that hellhole? No thanks, I'm not ready to be buried just yet."

The Miner shrugged and returned to his hovel.

"Suit yaself," he called over his shoulder. "Long way to come just to chicken out now."

"Better a chicken ranging freely above ground than a lion buried in stone," Matthew defended. "Those timbers look like the gates to Hell!"

"How 'bout the rest of ya?" the agitated Miner asked, brandishing a handful of makeshift torches at them. "Ya drag me away and hide all me drink. Ya'd better not bail on me now."

William's inner voice screamed with terror but he resolutely stepped forward and claimed a torch, determined to prove that he was braver than Matthew.

The Miner went to pass a torch to Matilda but she shook her hand.

"No thanks, I've got my own," she said as she withdrew her magical light box from her pocket. She wound its delicate handle a few times before motioning for the Miner to lead the way.

The Miner looked perplexed but shrugged. He stepped under the rotten logs and into the cramped passage of the mine, using the walls to keep upright. Matilda gave William an encouraging smile as she followed. William's stomach was a knotted mess but he followed too.

The world was muted the moment he stepped into the artificial cave, the howl of the outside wind replaced by the muffled echo of the trio's footsteps. Matilda switched on her torch, it's sharp beam of cool light further enhancing the otherworldly feel.

The mine was so tight that not even bats dared to explore it. The jagged rock walls narrowed as they walked, to the point that William's shoulders scraped against them no matter which way he leaned. The narrow passage was carved through solid rock with a slight bulge on the sides. The shape of a coffin. Every visible surface was the same stony grey and covered in chisel marks, creating a disorienting monotony that was only broken by the occasional smear of coppery green.

New branches of the mine infrequently came into view as they walked on. Some took awkward turns, weaving to and fro or veering off at odd angles.

"Followin' promising veins of copper or dodgin' the harder rock," the Miner explained, his voice echoing off the walls. His answers to Matilda's many questions grew more authoritative as they delved deeper, completely different to the incoherent slob from the surface.

Other tunnels were dead straight and went as far as the eye could see, ending in a distant coffin of darkness. William's mind ran wild imagining what demons hid in the shadows, just out of sight. He longed for the safety of daylight.

Even then, the most terrifying tunnels were those with collapsed ceilings. Hidden worlds of darkness lay behind the fallen rocks, formed in an instant of crushing destruction. William's desire to run back to the surface increased with each one that they passed but he forced himself onward, refusing to abandon Matilda or be outdone by the filthy Miner.

Not that he had a choice. The journey had taken so many twists and turns that William had no idea how to return to the surface. The thought of wandering aimlessly in the dark was even more terrifying than being crushed.

The passage grew progressively narrower, first requiring them to crouch and eventually turn their bodies and shuffle awkwardly. The dry dirt floor became muddy and more waterlogged with each step. Still they shuffled on, until the Miner abruptly stopped.

"This is as far as we can go without swimmin'. We dug deeper but the tunnels are flooded"

"I've seen enough," Matilda said.

The Miner gave her a shove. "Come on then. Move along boy, back where we came."

The group turned around and walked back into the smothering darkness. The Miner pushed past as soon as the corridor widened and the knot in William's stomach started to unfurl.

The return journey felt much quicker and it wasn't long before the glow of sunlight overcame their makeshift torches. William heard Matilda turn off her torch.

The first breath of fresh air was the sweetest of William's life. The sound of wind passing through the trees was wonderous and even the cool fog on his exposed skin made him feel alive.

"You made it!" Matthew called as he pushed himself up from a mossy rock, his face flushed with relief. "You spent long enough down there. I was worried."

"Not worried enough to come looking for us," William sniped.

"What d'ya think?" the Miner asked Matilda, ignoring the bickering. His exaggerated gruffness seemed to mask a faint glimmer of hope.

Matilda thought for a bit. "It's hard to say, but there's potential. I saw signs of missed copper and we should be able to lower the water level…"

"We bloody tried that!" the Miner snapped. "An' it took workers away from actual minin'."

"I can try building a pump. And hoses," Matilda replied. "But first I'd be interested to see the refuse pile. With a bit of experimenting we might be able to extract even more copper from the stone."

The Miner straightened up even further. "Don't know why ya'd wanna do that but sure, I'll show ya round back."

Matilda and the Miner disappeared, leaving William and Matthew standing in frosty silence.

"I'm worried about those supports," Matilda added as they returned. "You've been lucky to avoid accidents so far but they'll need reinforcing before you resume any major mining activity."

"Easier said than done," the Miner parried. "Wood and tools aren't free ya know. Hard when ya not pullin' anything from the ground."

"I know," Matilda reassured. "That's why Matthew's here. He can provide the tools…" She held up a hand to halt Matthew's protest. "…and I'll talk to the Baron about payment. What would you need to get the site back up and running?"

The Miner paused. "A couple of gents to start. Three I guess. A set of tools for each of us, maybe some wood for makin' ya supports."

"Is this possible?" Matilda asked Matthew. "On top of everything we discussed back at the mill?"

"Perhaps, if we can find some additional hands to help at the mill. At this rate I might need to take on an apprentice."

Matthew looked at William appraisingly.

"No way," Matilda objected. "I need him, you find someone else. That said, it wouldn't hurt for him to learn a bit more about what you do…"

William felt like a goat being auctioned at market. It was nice not being ignored but he wasn't sure that he liked that type of attention.

Matilda turned back to the Miner. "Get this place cleaned up and put a call out for your team. It'll take some time to get everything in order but it'd be good to start as soon as winter breaks."

The Miner beamed with disbelieving gratitude and practically bowed at Matilda.

"And you must know," Matilda added, "knowledge is my currency. My advice isn't free. I'll expect the first loads of copper for my own projects and will take a percentage of what is produced after that."

William saw the Miner deflate.

"Don't worry," Matilda promised. "Even with my fee, it'll be well worth your while. Just ask Matthew."

"She's right," Matthew said. "It's already been a blessing and she's only been in Holford a couple of months. Plus, surely anything beats the endless drinking? Eh Edric?"

The Miner paused, unsure if he should be insulted. "Ya, there's truth to tha'," he conceded.

With everything agreed, William joined Matilda and Matthew on the trip back to the village. Edric stayed behind and had already started tidying the yard as they left. He'd found a broken broom and swept furiously, as though desperate to remove the years of personal neglect.

The trio walked back to Holford side by side. Matthew was impressed at William's willingness to venture into the mine and both he and Matilda were interested to hear what he'd learned from Edric on their outbound journey.

William felt appreciated. *Finally.*

CHAPTER TWENTY-SIX

23 March 1124

"Noooooo!" Joan Miller shrieked. "I won't go!"

Margery looked up from her miserable bowl of gruel and struggled to keep a straight face as Arnold's spoilt daughter performed her daily ritual. Watching Joan's struggle with the 'hardships' of normal life made the tasteless gruel almost palatable.

"We can't afford another night here," Joan's mother insisted. "The landlord threatened to summon the constable."

"You think this backwater has a constable?" Joan cried "No! I want a roof over my head. And proper food."

"You think I don't?" Arnold thundered back at her. "We lost all that when bloody Holford took my bloody mill. The world isn't fair." He calmed himself and made his voice sickly sweet. "But I'll find work, I promise. Then things will get better. Ok precious?"

Arnold's pandering made Margery want to throw up but Joan settled down. Margery was baffled that Joan was stupid enough to buy Arnold's same line every morning. But she did and so the ritual continued. The Miller family finished eating, packed their meagre belongings and started another day of walking.

The day slipped away, both fast and slow at the same time. There was no break for food – they had none – leaving Margery to ponder the time since her hasty departure.

It had been almost two months since Margery impulsively elected to follow the Miller family as they fled from Holford's frenzied villagers. In the emotionally-charged aftermath of the mill fire, fear of losing Henry had loomed larger than anything. Her only true friend. She hadn't paused to consider the consequences. But she dearly wished that she had.

Since then, the Millers had trudged from village to village, through the depths of winter, without a plan. Arnold had relied upon the hospitality of friends and his network of neighbouring millers but always managed to wear out their welcome.

His stubborn pride prompted several premature departures in their first weeks. Arnold took offence at being told that Holford's revolt was his own doing or that there was little chance his mill would be returned. When he finally acknowledged his family's desperation and looked for work, Arnold took offence whenever told there was nothing for him and that he should try the next village. He was deaf to his peers' voices of reason and instead decided that the world had turned against him.

Like his daughter, Arnold was also prone to tantrums and exploded each time word of his underhanded business practices preceded the family's travels. His biggest outburst was at Stowey Castle the day after his eviction when Baron Walter showed little sympathy for Arnold's situation. The Miller's arrogance was such that he ranted at the Baron, demanding a new position and prophesising that Holford would be doomed without him.

Arnold's harsh words only irked the Baron, who asked why he would need a miller stupid enough to be *caught* sabotaging his competition. The confrontation ended with Baron Walter telling Arnold to leave Stowey by nightfall or face his dungeon. That was the first of many nights the Millers had spent without a roof over their heads. And so began their arduous life as nomads.

The winter had been relentless. The Miller family were buffeted by storms as they crossed fallow fields and the bare forests provided little shelter. Margery's teeth had chattered constantly and she worried that she might never be dry again.

The Millers had been forced to leave Holford in such a hurry that they were poorly equipped for life on the road. Arnold's wife Edith had prioritised collecting her finest clothing and jewellery which did little good when stomachs rumbled in the evenings. The fool resisted parting with her finery to raise funds for food or shelter, preferring that her family stayed hungry rather than harm her delicate pride.

The resulting conditions were far from ideal but were less of an adjustment for Margery than they'd been for the Miller family. Margery was shocked to discover that they didn't know the basics of survival, things that Ma and Pa had instilled in their children from a young age. The Millers struggled to start a fire outdoors and Edith often spoiled their meagre supplies in failed attempts to cook.

Margery was forced to adopt a leading role in the family. She took time to teach them how to prepare food or find an appropriate place to set up camp. No longer able to just hide in the shadows, Margery became the family spokesperson and helped negotiate prices at markets or politely asked fellow travellers for directions and gossip. Unfortunately for Margery, the Millers' entitlement was so strong that these tasks were soon just expected and her lessons were quickly forgotten. As was any appreciation for Margery's efforts.

The biggest letdown of the entire fiasco was Henry. The whole reason she'd even left in the first place. Margery and Henry had been close for years, enduring bullying by Holford's older children fuelled by the taunts of their older sisters. The pair stuck together out of necessity and eventually discovered that they enjoyed each other's company.

But their time together had been limited and Margery always returned to her family's cottage at the end of the day. There was no respite now that their time together was uninterrupted, meaning that once niggly annoyances ballooned into full blown irritations. Like the rest of the Miller family, the pair were often peevish with each other and their previously easy-going companionship was frequently strained.

Henry barely spoke to her anymore. None of them did. The Millers all blamed Margery and her family for their plight. For bringing Matilda to Holford. They treated her with ever growing coldness and tolerated Margery's presence only as a source of food and shelter.

Margery couldn't fend off all of their animosity and it started to colour her own feelings. Her family *had* been the one to invite Matilda into Holford and Margery's own taunts had so often driven William away.

Perhaps she was guilty.

The Millers' animosity made for an incredibly lonely existence and there was ample time for introspection during the long days of walking.

Margery trudged on but eventually realised that, despite the dying sunlight, the Miller family still had no plans to set up camp. She was about to make the decision for them when she spotted a small wooden chapel nestled in the woods.

The Millers raced towards the building, each member eager for a night out of the rain with a roof over their heads. Margery followed slightly behind, amused at their almost primal need for comfort.

As they drew closer, Margery saw that the chapel lay on the outskirts of a tiny hamlet. There appeared to be no more than four rundown huts gathered at the bottom of the valley, each made of mud and even more dilapidated than Holford's worst house.

The Millers gathered around the door of the chapel and waited for Margery to assume her role as their voice. Motioning for them to wait in place, she lay down her meagre belongings and poked her head through the chapel door.

"Hello?" Margery called out. "Father?"

There was no response, just the eerie quiet of the dark and lifeless room. A musty odour paired with the unnatural stillness to make Margery feel uneasy but she didn't relish the thought of another night in the wilderness. Or a repeat of Joan's tantrums.

"Father? Are you there?"

A shuffling sound came from a room behind the altar, putting Margery further on edge. An incredibly elderly man stepped into the room, his face gaunt and skeletal arms straining with the weight of a large candle. Margery called out again but he paid her no attention and continued his shuffle around the altar.

Margery walked to the altar and tapped the priest on the shoulder. The poor man nearly leapt out of his skin.

"Sorry Father, sorry!" she said, raising her hands unthreateningly.

"Oh my Lord," he said, holding a skeletal hand up to his chest. "You nearly scared the life out of me."

Margery didn't doubt it. "Sorry to startle you Father. I'm here with a family. We wondered if we might shelter here tonight."

"I'm a little hard of hearing, dear," he told her with a vacant smile. "What did you say?"

"Can we. Please. Stay here. Tonight." Margery said loudly.

The priest stared blankly before spying the Millers huddled by the door. Realisation flooded across his face.

"Of course my dear, of course. My door is always open. Please, invite them in."

Margery ran over to summon the family but Joan barged through before she'd said a word, deliberately knocking Margery as she passed. The others filed in and the priest's eyes lit up. He seemed unaccustomed to having so many guests.

The poor man's hopes of a willing congregation were dashed when the family sat far from the altar and immediately began unpacking their evening meal. Seeing that they were occupied, the priest resumed preparations for his evening prayers. His shoulders were slumped and his movements even more sluggish than before.

Margery obediently prepared the evening meal while the Millers waited impatiently. They devoured their portions without conversation and dispersed when it was finished, eager to put another day of their nightmarish new existence behind them.

One-by-one they fell asleep, leaving Margery alone once more to contemplate her thoughts. She approached the altar and prayed for guidance through her hardship, taking solace in another familiar ritual. When she finished, she sat upon a simple wooden bench and looked around the small chapel. It was strange. There was no question that it was poor. There were no hangings on the walls and only crudely carved adornments on the altar. But the room was spotless and its few contents were meticulously placed. Each bench was perfectly aligned with the altar.

As Margery cast her eye around the room she spotted something on the pulpit that she hadn't expected. A Bible. Bound in gnarled old leather, it looked particularly out of place in such a poor chapel. It was the largest book she'd ever seen, even bigger than Matilda's. An absolute treasure, tucked away at the edge of the world.

The book called to her. Only upon seeing it did she realise how desperate she was to read again and how much she'd missed Matilda's lessons. She succumbed to the book's silent siren song and crept toward the pulpit.

She carefully opened the book and peered at the letters, struggling to make out the words in the flickering light of the priest's candle. Most were different to those Matilda had taught during her lessons but Margery sounded them out nonetheless and quickly recognised the clergy's Latin. She was thrilled every time she spoke a familiar word. It made the book come alive, the scribbled symbols suddenly more relevant to her everyday life.

Margery was completely entranced and lost track of how long she'd stood whispering to herself. She was halfway through her third page when a frail voice broke the silence.

"Most impressive, young lady."

Margery gave a muffled squawk and slammed the book shut, the sound reverberating off the bare chapel walls.

"I thought you were hard of hearing," she said defensively.

"I am, my dove. But it's easier when I know I ought to be listening. And I could see your lips move which helps."

The priest let silence linger, foolishly hoping for Margery to break it.

"Forgive me, I'd not taken you for a lady," he finally continued. "I would've offered you my humble quarters, had I known." There was sincere regret in the man's eyes. "You keep very lowly company," he noted, motioning to the slumbering Miller family. "It is so rare to see women of the nobility who can sing the sounds of the letters."

Margery almost laughed. "I'm no noble Father. Only two moons ago I was ankle deep in mud, fighting to harvest a rotting crop."

The priest looked taken aback. "No? But it is rare for the nobility to read, let alone a peasant woman. Where did you learn such a thing?"

"A question for a question," Margery teased playfully, enjoying the genuine shock on the skeletal man's face. "Why does such a simple church have such a wonderful book?"

The priest smiled, a distant look in his eyes. "A remnant from a past life. From before I moved to this sleepy hamlet. That was a life of nobles, though admittedly not one that I miss."

"Frustratingly cryptic Father but very well. Our village had a visitor who stayed with my family. She had a Book of her own. Well, half a book. Seeing my family's struggle with the harvest, she stayed to help. She taught me and my siblings to read as payment for food and lodgings."

The priest was intrigued but didn't know where to begin so he quizzed Margery on everything. Her family, the strange visitor, the fire, the Miller family, life on the road. It felt so nice to have someone finally listen and Margery spilled everything that was on her mind. They only stopped when Arnold woke to relieve himself outside.

"Well my dear, I think it is time that we both got some rest. My head pounds when I'm overtired and I'm sorry to say there is no mill nearby so you have another long day of walking ahead of you. But do not fear the future. You have a strong head on your shoulders and I've little doubt that you'll find a way out of your current predicament. Goodnight dear."

The priest pushed himself gingerly to his feet and blew out the large candle before hobbling into his small room behind the altar. Arnold returned from outside and quickly fell back to sleep.

Margery was left sitting in darkness before the altar, staring at the silhouette of the bible on the simple pulpit. Finally voicing her concerns about leaving Holford and causing the Millers' plight had lifted a weight from her soul. But as she stared up at the Bible, she still felt guilty.

As though she had said too much.

CHAPTER TWENTY-SEVEN
23 March 1124

Winter had finally ended. The gloomy grey skies became regularly interspersed with patches of blue and Holford's mood noticeably lifted as the temperature increased. Spring came into full bloom. As the flowers and trees began to blossom, so too did the project seeds that Matilda had sown across the village to fill the long winter nights.

Matilda was busy from dawn to dusk and the relaxing days while waiting for her ankle to heal became a distant memory. Matilda lived permanently at her mill, waking at the crack of dawn only to be pulled across Holford from person to person until the sun disappeared from the sky. Even then her work continued. In the absence of stock to fill her warehouse, Matilda created a tracing floor which she used to scrawl new designs for the following day's activities by the light of her torch. Matilda remained exhausted each morning but the tangible progress towards her revised mission spurred her to work even harder.

Teaching Matthew to make bulk basics like screws or an improved drill for Walt had wowed Holford's craftspeople but it was Matilda's more complex designs that left the entire village speechless. People came from all over to try her rudimentary bicycle and Matilda had used Holford's Spring celebration to unveil her bizarre musical instrument.

Holford had gathered to celebrate the end of a particularly miserable winter. Ever the businessmen, Martin Brewer ordered Rachel's husband to roll out barrels of beer and cider to sell to the assembled crowd. Rachel begrudgingly helped with the sales but her surly expression betrayed her preference to be drinking with the revellers.

With the whole village in attendance and the Brewer's products flowing, it wasn't long before the springtime air was alive with traditional folksongs and rowdy drinking ballads. Matilda mingled with the villagers who eventually insisted that their out-of-town visitor share her own local tunes. William had pre-warned Matilda that this might happen so she had fashioned a makeshift instrument over the preceding evenings, aiming to produce something like her old guitar but which sounded more akin to a ukulele.

Matilda entranced the crowd with classic songs from her past and the crowd quickly grasped the strange lyrics and sang along. Matilda smiled at the memory of Elizabeth falling from her stool while drunkenly belting out Hallelujah and the joyful tears streaming down the Carpenter's face while singing Over the Rainbow. Matilda's Institute teachers had never truly appreciated the value of these little gifts from the future.

The Brewer's concoctions were surprisingly strong and everyone eventually retreated to their beds. Almost everyone.

As she returned to her mill, Matilda had discovered Edric stumbling towards the mine, catatonic from his brother's brews and barely able to stand.

Matilda was devastated. Only days earlier, as she had installed his new pump, he'd shared that he felt like a new man. How the mine had brought renewed purpose to his life and that he would never drink a drop again. Matilda had been thrilled by his revelation, having spent the previous week cannibalising her old parachutes to make hoses for the hand-cranked pump that Matthew had prioritised over their other projects.

The man's weakness angered Matilda but she helped her fallen colleague back to his hut, lifting him each time he fell and waiting as he stopped to throw up.

"Why Edric?" she asked, unable to hold her tongue. "You were doing so well."

"The flamin' pump's busted again," he lamented. "A great split down the pipe. Everythin's fillin' up with water."

Matilda struggled to calm the Miner, reassuring him that they could patch the hoses and promising to develop a more robust design.

"So sorry, Ma'tilda," he hiccoughed as they reached the hut. "A miner lapse. Ha! It won' happen again."

"I hope not, Edric," Matilda replied soberly. "Think of the Boy. He's starting to look up to you. What if he'd found you..?"

Edric stopped in his tracks. "Ya right. He's a good lad."

Matilda helped the man inside and watched him collapse into his cot. When she was convinced that he was asleep, she combed every inch of his hut for illicit stashes as the Miner's snores reverberated off the walls. She poured her findings behind the smelting furnace before finally heading back to her own bed.

+++

Matilda awoke even groggier than normal and had little doubt that most of Holford would feel the same, buying some precious time to finish her sketches. She scrawled away furiously, channelling her annoyance from the evening's unwanted discovery. Edric had been doing so well, a walking embodiment of the improvements she sought to achieve for the village. She cursed the vile Brewer for enabling his brother's addiction.

Matilda eventually looked up from her sketch, finally happy. Time had become a precious resource and Matilda needed a way to schedule her many appointments around Holford. She would've loved to build a working clock but ironically lacked the time. So sundials would have to do. Her sketch would allow Matthew to mass produce the stylised iron shapes which she could scatter around the village. They lacked precision but people could at least guess the rough time. She took a mental image of the design and set off to find William.

The sun burst over the treetops as Matilda left the warehouse and she paused to soak in the view of her progress. The charred trees nearest to the mill had sprouted new leaves up the entire length of their trunks, giving them an alien appearance. Much like the charred forest, there were signs of growth on the building itself. The Carpenter and his team had already installed new rafters across the millhouse and Timothy had almost finished making ceramic roof tiles.

There was other new growth in the area around the mill. Holford's various craftsmen had built a small village of shacks to store their tools closer to their work. Each reflected its maker. Timothy's had a neat tiled roof. Walt's was simple but sturdy. Matthew's was open to the world.

The once boggy yard was dry and Elizabeth had used Harry's box of seeds to convert most of it into a well-stocked garden. William's sister tirelessly toiled to transplant her seedlings and cuttings. Any excuse to escape Ma's increasingly smothering attention.

Many of Elizabeth's plants had never been seen in Holford and her excitement grew as they did. A diverse crop of leeks, rhubarb and cauliflower was already taking shape and her bamboo was visibly growing each day. She sketched each variety in her hand-bound notebook. Her apple core miraculously managed to survive the fire and the happy memory of her excited squeal upon discovering its tiny green tendril still echoed around the clearing.

With a smile, Matilda tore her gaze away from her mill and headed into Holford to meet William. The village was just beginning to stir when Matilda arrived. There were few signs of life at the cottage.

"Hello?" she called when she reached the door.

Ma emerged with a basket of dirty dishes under arm, her face grim.

"They're just tidying up inside. You're taking him away *again*?"

"Just for a bit," Matilda replied with her sunniest voice. "He's been such a help around the village. We all missed you last night."

"Didn't feel up to it," Ma shrugged before nudging past Matilda to empty the food scraps behind the house.

Matilda stepped through the open door and into the cottage. The change of energy was jarring.

"Morning!" William called, earning a grunt of disapproval from Elizabeth.

"Please, shut the door," she begged Matilda, though she too managed a weak but welcoming smile.

"Still recovering from your big night?" Matilda asked with a cheeky grin before quietly closing the door and sitting at the table. "Ma still seems out of sorts."

"She misses Margery," Pa agreed mournfully. "And it doesn't help that Rachel barely speaks to us anymore."

"She's just being dramatic, that was all months ago" William said matter-of-factly. "They'll both be back. Unfortunately."

"We didn't see you last night either," Matilda told Pa.

"Didn't want to leave Em by herself. And I was weary from the jury's trip to Stowey yesterday. Finalising the exile of Arnold's labourer," Pa added. "Which reminds me, Sir Phillip said the Baron wants to see your mill again. You've made some powerful friends."

"I don't know if I'd call Walter a friend but thanks for the warning. Come on Will, enough lazing about. Time to start the day."

They were just leaving when Rachel barged through the front gate. Tears streamed down her face but, with a special fury reserved for Matilda, Rachel wiped them away and pushed past her. Despite their animosity, Matilda was concerned. The tears looked genuine.

"Ma's out the back," William told Rachel's back. "Hey Ma! Rachel's here!"

Matilda heard Ma drop her basket and run around the cottage to give Rachel a big hug. She was finally smiling.

William and Matilda left them to their embrace and started their routine circuit of the village. Holford had looked to Matilda for leadership and guidance ever since the Miller's expulsion and many had welcomed her ideas and improvements, be that designing a new mechanism for the Smith or teaching a child how to tie a knot.

With William's help, most of Holford's youngsters had been rallied to assist with different projects. Even the girls. A handful of the older children refused to help out of principle but most welcomed a distraction from the winter monotony. Matilda feared encouraging child-labour but figured that temporary apprenticeships had to suffice until her school was established. The young workers had enthusiastically set about their tasks, guided by craftsmen to learn trades and assist with increased workloads.

Many of the youngsters had gone to help Walt with his carpentry, having been exposed to woodwork basics through their families' day-to-day existence or during their own adventures in the forest. The Carpenter tasked the children with splitting logs or shaping timbers and had breezed through Matilda's tasks with the extra help.

Walt had always boycotted the Brewer's concoctions so his rough voice already rang across his worksite when Matilda and William arrived. It was uncharacteristically gentle as he taught his newest apprentices how to work the timbers safely.

"Careful lad, I just sharpened that chisel so it'll take your finger if you let it."

He brandished a hand at the boy to show off his missing digit before giving a welcoming wave.

"Didn't think I'd see you two up and about any time decent."

"Your lot are up early too," Matilda noted. "There's too much work to stay in bed feeling sorry for myself. How're things coming along?"

"Always straight to business," Walt said with a shake of his head. "Your new waterwheel is taking shape. It took a while to get our heads around your complicated design but I'm beginning to see how it'll come together. The lads are just finishing the shafts for the mechanisms, so are you sure you don't want me to make the gears? They've been made of wood at every mill I've ever seen."

"I'm sure Walt. Wood burns. I've got Matt Smith working on metal designs which should be much more durable. Save your time for things of beauty. I need furnishings for inside. Tables, chairs, shutters."

Walt disapproved of Matilda's continued insistence to break from convention but perked up at her suggestion of beautiful wooden furnishings.

"Speaking of things of beauty, last night's music was breathtaking. Never heard anything like it. Yet performed with such a crude instrument."

Matilda explained her ukulele and described other instruments she had seen from the future. Walt was enthralled by the possibility of even more beautiful music and promised to carve a fiddle based on Matilda's descriptions.

"Only after the new tables," Matilda insisted as she and William set off to their next visit. He begrudgingly agreed.

They'd barely rounded the corner when William burst into laughter.

"*Speaking of beauty*," William mocked. "I think he fancies you!"

Matilda agreed. "I don't think his wife would like that. Besides, I got the feeling last night that there's others I should be more concerned about."

Matilda had attracted quite a lot of attention from Holford's male population. She wasn't sure if it was her height, her accent or just her general foreignness but it only became clearer as the Brewer's drinks continued to flow and the men became less subtle. Matilda didn't know when they expected her to find the time for romance and the scars of her encounter with the Bishop meant the thought still made her stomach churn. Fortunately it wasn't something she needed to worry about with their next visit.

Timothy Potter sat outside his home. He skilfully wrestled a large ball of clay and specks were stuck in his bushy white beard. A gaggle of young helpers darted around the yard behind him, laying fresh rooftiles out to dry or unstacking freshly fired ones from the kiln. There were hundreds of them.

"Almost done, little missy," he told her jollily. He gave the clay a wet slap. "Three more lumps like this and your roof will be done. The crew pretty much navigate themselves now. They'll start on floor tiles for your warehouse next. Can we finally start your next lesson?"

Whoever said you can't teach an old dog new tricks had never met Timothy. Matilda thought that teaching the basics of glass making would keep him busy but the elderly man threw himself into the task with unrestrained enthusiasm. After surprisingly few failed attempts, he was well on the way to mastering the skill. He'd already blown small glass bottles for Matilda's other projects and she'd vowed to next teach how to make flat panes for windows.

Matilda promised Timothy another lesson, provided he first make a prototype of Matilda's gravity-flushable toilet. Recalling the stench of Holford's outhouses, she couldn't over-emphasise how valuable it would be. Timothy needed some convincing and then insisted on showcasing his entire inventory of tiles before Matilda and William could finally move on to their next visit.

Things were quieter at the blacksmith. Matthew had only taken on one apprentice, William's friend Ralph.

"Quality over quantity," Matthew had said when Matilda had offered more. "There's too much to teach, plus smithing is dangerous. One will do, for now."

As always, Matthew had pushed the boundaries and argued again that William should be his apprentice but Matilda wouldn't hear it. William was much too important to her broader plans but she suggested Ralph instead, arguing that he had the bulk to throw into the heavy smithing work. Matilda was amazed how quickly Ralph's puppy fat had converted into muscle.

"We're ready to cast these gears you're so excited about," Matthew reported. "Edric already dropped by and said he'll deliver his first load of ore within the week. He's recruiting *more* newcomers for the mine, sounds like they're practically eating through the rock. But when can we get started on Walt's saw blades?"

Matilda sighed. She'd promised to teach him how to make stronger steels for giant blades that would allow the Carpenter to rapidly saw beams. Matthew understood the benefits of the stronger material but unlike Timothy wasn't quite up to the task.

"Patience Matthew, one thing at a time. Perfect these gears first and then we'll get started on the blade."

Matthew wasn't happy with the delay but he lapped up Matilda's praise for his other projects. He'd mastered extruding molten metal to make wires and screws, even modifying Matilda's design to make it more efficient. He was back to his usual overly charming self by the time they left.

Matilda and William continued their visits for the rest of the day, checking that Joshua was still managing at the mill, waving at Pa and Luke ploughing the fallow fields, and visiting Edric. Looking bashful, the Miner said nothing of the previous evening and they managed to repair Matilda's makeshift hose, which was sucking water from the mine again when Matilda and William finally left.

It had started getting dark and they were both weary by the time they reached the cottage for a long overdue meal.

"Surely there's a better way to do this?" William asked.

"I was thinking the same thing," Matilda said. "All this running around is time we could spend actually working and everyone's *almost* doing everything themselves. They just need coordination. Perhaps we could establish a council?"

"Huh?"

"You know, a gathering of the key townsfolk to discuss our progre.."

"I know what a council is. I mean what's that? Listen."

They stopped walking and Matilda strained her ears. Then she heard it. Yelling. Tears. They'd just passed the Brewer's house near the centre of the village and the commotion was coming from the building next door. Rachel's house.

The pair stood rooted in place, unsure what to do. The yelling continued, occasionally punctuated as thrown pottery crashed against the wall. There was one last thunderous yell before the door was thrown open and the Brewer's son stormed outside. Even in the darkness, they saw that Alan's face was warped with fury.

Silence fell over Holford once more, broken only by the loud sobs of William's sister alone in her new house. Matilda instinctively wanted to console Rachel but knew that her presence was likely to only make things worse. She gave William a look, asking what they should do.

"It's late," he said. "Let's get home."

The pair trudged home in silence, unsure what to make of what they'd just witnessed. They pushed solemnly through the front gate, only for Ma to open the door and greet them with a broad grin before dashing back inside to prepare their food.

Matilda was glad to see Ma in better spirits.

"Have you heard the exciting news?" she called over her shoulder. "Rachel is pregnant!"

CHAPTER TWENTY-EIGHT
27 March 1124

Godfrey fidgeted as his carriage trundled back to the palace after another long morning of menial tasks. His head thundered but he was relieved that the day's obligations were behind him. It had been months since his consecration and life had settled into a comfortable but dull routine. The monks and clergy had reached a tentative truce, he had negotiated agreeable terms with the Jewish lenders, and cathedral construction required minimal intervention. The Bishop's only failure had been his efforts to extract value from the ruined Book.

This still irked Godfrey. He had been sure that the Book contained precious secrets but after months of effort it had proven to be little more than a drain of both time and money. Despite great personal investment, he finally conceded that nothing more could be done. The Book sat gathering dust amongst more valuable tomes on his bookshelf, its tattered spine the only reminder that it was even there.

Godfrey had finally succeeded in breaking John's spirit after the last escape attempt and moved him back into the seminary to fully focus on his training. The Bishop occasionally felt pangs of guilt at tearing the Novice away from his family. But then he remembered all the trouble the boy had caused and that John's usefulness had proven underwhelming. Seminary training was more than he deserved.

Godfrey was relieved when the carriage finally reined in at his palace. He marched into the grand building and made for the solitude of his study, not even breaking stride as he informed the servants that he would take his lunch there and should be otherwise undisturbed.

He was dismayed to find a sealed envelope waiting on his sitting table. He sat down heavily and opened it. Another message from the Cardinals bearing bad news about the rebellion. The Bastard Earl had won several victories after the winter hiatus and Godfrey's technical assistance remained unappreciated. The Bishop leant back in his chair and applied pressure to his temples. His headache raged from the busy morning and required several goblets of wine to take the edge off.

Godfrey was on his fourth cup when the servants finally arrived to deliver his midday meal. He silently smouldered as they clumsily set his table, banging dishes and clattering cutlery. The Bishop was pleased when they finally left him in peace. Godfrey's mouth watered at the smell of the rich feast and he was carving a particularly plump mutton shank when there was a knock on the door.

Peter warily stuck his head into the study.

"I said no interruptions!" Godfrey scolded before his assistant could utter a word.

Peter looked reproachful but continued to enter nonetheless.

"Apologies Father, it's just that…"

"I swear, if it's that damned boy again, so help me God…"

"It's not about John, Father. It's something you'll definitely want to hear for yourself."

Godfrey looked at him quizzically. Peter was intelligent enough to know that the mere disruption was enough to risk the Bishop's wrath. And yet he stood his ground.

The Bishop stuffed a chunk of mutton into his mouth and lay down his fork. After some drawn out chews, he took a swig of wine for good measure.

"This had better be good," Godfrey warned. "Spit it out!"

Peter flinched but continued timidly. "You'd best come and see Your Excellency."

Godfrey's blood boiled. "I finally have time to enjoy some *basic* sustenance and you tear me away? Dammit man, what is so important that it cannot wait?"

Godfrey watched the Assistant weigh his options.

"We have a visitor, Father. An elderly priest from a distant, inconsequential hamlet. He's deaf, incredibly frail and shaking like a leaf. But he walked all the way from his tiny chapel as fast as he was able. He has a message for you. Only you. Concerning a red-haired woman. With a book."

Godfrey's interest was instantly piqued but he refused to let himself get over excited. He had already received two enterprising visitors since putting out the call for information about the Book. Both had suffered his wrath.

"Very well," he said with a measured tone. "I will speak with this priest. Have the servants bring my meal down to the garden courtyard. Tell them to bring more food, the priest has travelled far. And more wine."

Feeling wobbly from his drink, Godfrey made his way downstairs and waited impatiently as his servants re-laid the generous platter of food. He sampled each item to take the edge off his appetite before calling for the priest to be let in.

The man was ancient. Peter didn't jest about his frailty. A solid gust of wind would send him flying.

"Welcome brother," Godfrey greeted in his most regal voice. "You have travelled far. Please, join me for a bite to eat."

The Elderly Priest required a nudge from Peter but he shuffled into the room and gingerly took the seat Godfrey had gestured to.

"Some wine?" Godfrey asked, offering the decanter.

"No, thank you," the priest said, a little too loud. "Much too rich for me, it would upset my stomach. Just water will be fine."

The man sounded like an old tree. Gnarled and ancient. Painfully slow.

"My assistant tells me you've news from afar."

"Yes Your Excellency. Though would you prefer that we discussed it in private?"

The old man gestured at Peter with a gentle nod of his head.

"Not to worry, brother. Peter has my trust."

Godfrey's assurances put the Elderly Priest at ease and Peter joined them at the dining table.

"Very well. Where to begin? My parish doesn't get many visitors. It's a backwater. Like a flea bite on the arse end of a mangy hound."

"Very...colourful," Godfrey said irritably. "It's a poor village, I understand. Go on."

"A family arrived four nights ago. It was already getting dark and I was setting the altar for the evening prayer. They startled me half to death, barging into my little church without knocking. But Saint Peter says we should offer hospitality without grumbling and they looked desperate. So I let them stay."

"Naturally," Godfrey said impatiently.

"They were an uncouth bunch," the Elderly Priest continued, "using the chapel purely for its roof. The adults exuded an air of entitlement, though they displayed little reason to deserve any status. Their clothes were filthy and tattered, as though they'd been on the road for months. None of them showed the slightest respect and they promptly fell asleep after gorging on their meagre supplies. Except for the girl."

Godfrey leaned forward excitedly. "The red-headed foreigner!?"

"Oh no. Nothing that exotic."

Godfrey slumped back into his chair and gnawed on a chicken leg. Peter started fidgeting with a spare fork.

"Just a regular peasant girl. More grounded than her companions, comfortable in her well-travelled clothes. It was clear that she wasn't part of the family."

The priest paused and shakily sipped his water.

"I only noticed her because she so differed from her brutish companions. She alone bowed her head in prayer before sleep. My hope in humanity lifted, temporarily. Because then she walked up to my bible at the lectern and started reading out loud."

"What?" Godfrey spluttered, tossing down his chicken. His interest reawakened.

"You have a bible?" Peter asked inquisitively.

"My thoughts precisely," the Elderly Priest answered Godfrey, ignoring Peter. "Where does a peasant learn to read? And a young woman, at that. I confess that I was initially bewildered and watched closely to be sure that my age wasn't playing tricks. But there she was, sounding out words from somewhere in Psalms. Rather clunkily, but they were definitely the right words. She celebrated with a dainty little dance each time she recognised a new one.

"I'll tell you, I wasn't pleased that this young peasant woman had her filthy paws on my most precious possession. A gift from my years in London. It was just unnatural, a woman reading. I immediately sought to distract her, when I finally realised what was happening."

"Was she ashamed at being caught?" Peter asked.

"She was, like a teen caught singing when they think they're alone. I ignored the reading altogether and steered the conversation back to proper Christian behaviour, asking instead what she had been praying about. That was when it got really interesting."

Peter stopped fidgeting. Godfrey was on the edge of his chair.

"She admitted that she didn't belong with the family. That she'd made a horrible mistake. She had joined the family in exile, feeling partly to blame for their predicament. I pried for her to explain but she simply replied that she mocked her little brother too much."

"What older sister doesn't?" Peter asked, his voice oddly raw.

"I said the same thing. She confessed that she and her sister taunted the boy, driving him to spend time in the woods, away from them. It meant more work for the girls but it was rare to get time alone to discuss inane things like attractive boys without their brother's constant eye rolls. All had been fine, until the boy came home one evening with a stranger, around the feast of All Hallows."

"Who was the stranger?" Godfrey begged. "What did she say?"

"She was a foreigner," the Elderly Priest started, a twinkle in his eye. "With curly red hair."

"Yes!" the Bishop cried, bolting upright and knocking his chair back. Peter and the Elderly Priest stared at him, aghast at such behaviour unbecoming of senior clergy. Godfrey sheepishly sat down, clearing his throat and gesturing for the visitor to continue.

"I'd hoped you'd be interested. Well, the Foreigner's arrival sent a shock through the girl's small and respectable family. There would've been scandal if word escaped that her brother had come home with an unmarried woman. Let alone one that dressed inappropriately and spoke so strangely. The peasant girl was relieved when her father escorted the stranger away the next day. He took her to a town called Stowey under the pretences of delivering taxes but in reality he was under strict instructions from his wife to ensure that no ill would befall the family.

"The peasant girl was relieved to see the Foreigner gone. The Redhead was different. Too different. But she was gone, never to be seen again."

"But?" Godfrey asked with desperation. "Please tell me there's more."

The Elderly Priest gave a fox-like smile. "The peasant girl couldn't shake the feeling that that they hadn't seen the last of the foreigner. Her elder sister was coy but said with absolute certainty that the woman had gotten what she deserved. The girl sensed there was more to the story but the Foreigner remained nowhere to be seen and life returned to endless harvesting and gossiping about boys."

"Quit playing with me priest," Godfrey warned. "That's it?"

"It was, until the peasant girl's father and grandmother took ill. It was dire. The grandmother was on her deathbed and the family stood no hope of surviving the winter without the father. Then the Foreigner reappeared.

"She was different to before. Reserved. Mournful and morose. But she did what she could to help the family. She provided remedies and joined them in the fields while the father recovered. Each day she emerged further from her shell and the family actually grew to like her, despite her eccentricities.

"The Foreigner cared nothing for convention and upturned the village's entire life. She introduced new techniques to hasten the harvest and healed sick villagers with strange medicine. She possessed half of a book and taught women and children how to read." The priest didn't mask his disapproval. "It was all too much for the girl's grandmother, a proper Christian woman, who returned to be with the Lord. It was the Foreigner who eventually raised the village in rebellion against their miller, the boorish visitor who slept in my chapel.

"The peasant girl blamed herself. If she'd only been nicer to her brother, the Foreigner might never have come. Her grandmother might still be alive and the mill still run by its rightful owner. For all of its downsides, life in their village would've at least been normal."

Godfrey had heard enough and swooped in with his most burning question.

"Did the peasant girl say where she was from?"

"She did, my Bishop."

Godfrey leaned forward hungrily.

"Do you know the Quantock mountains my lord? An outstanding example of the Lord's natural creation to be sure, though I haven't been there for decades."

"I've heard of them," Godfrey said impatiently. "Go on."

"Well, in the eastern foothills there is a town called Nether Stowey. A small town but it has a modest castle with a stone keep and holds a full market once a month. The town where the peasant father took the Foreigner."

"Get to the point priest! Stowey is where I last encountered her. She's not there."

"No, she wouldn't be. Only a fool retouches a pot after being burned."

Godfrey didn't care for the priest's attitude. But they were so close.

"A short walk northwest of Stowey, nestled in the Quantocks themselves, lies a tiny village. With a mill. A new miller. And a red-headed foreigner. A village called Holford."

The room was silent as Godfrey digested the final piece of information. Holford. The name whipped around his head like a ship in a storm. Finally, a new lead. And she had the other half of the Book! The smouldering ashes of his passion project reignited into a raging inferno.

Godfrey returned to his senses.

"You've done well, priest. More than well. This is truly the Lord's work and He will no doubt bestow His greatest blessings upon you. But please, name yourself a more earthly reward. A horse for your journey home? A transfer to my new cathedral to live out your days in peace and prayer? What would you like? Name it."

The priest gave a gentle smile.

"None of that will be necessary my Bishop. I ask only that you keep our little end of the world in your prayers and do what you can to quash this Foreigner's unseemly ways. And perhaps a new goat, ours died during the winter."

"It will be done," Godfrey promised with absolute sincerity, thinking the man a fool for not requesting more.

Peter escorted the Elderly Priest out of the room, leaving Godfrey to his thoughts. His mind raced. The possibilities of the complete tome were tantalising but to capture the woman and extract information directly was even better. He wondered where John was.

Peter returned to the room.

"That went well," he said with a grin.

"Better than well," Godfrey agreed. "I want to know what that woman is doing. Where she eats, shits and sleeps. Get one of your men there. To Holford. Now!"

CHAPTER TWENTY-NINE
7 May 1124

It was dark. And cold. William was terrified.

The flame of William's rush-light guttered as he ran along the dark corridors of the mine, lost and afraid. He longed to wake up but it was no nightmare. His torch struck the wall as he rounded a corner and finally went out, smothering him in complete darkness.

The malicious laughter of William's tormenters echoed off the tunnel walls. William dropped to the floor and sheltered in place, willing the wicked noise to stop. It eventually faded as his pursuers tired of their sport but was replaced with an even more terrifying sound.

Absolute silence.

William crouched in the darkness, unable to see even his hands. He was just a mind in a world of dark. He fought for a way out of his predicament but he couldn't see any solution.

His terror rose with each heartbeat but after an age of ever diminishing hope, the tunnel appeared to lighten. It was faint at first but its intensity grew and William started to see the stone walls around him. He didn't care if it was his tormentors returning, anything was better than the dark prison.

He called out.

A torch rounded a bend in the tunnel and the friendly Miner came into view.

"Roger an' Warren up to no good again?" Edric asked solemnly.

William nodded, squinting up at him.

"Bloody mongrels. I never shoulda taken 'em on. Pity Roger's so good with a pick. Sorry 'bout that."

It wasn't William's first run in with the pair. He didn't know what he'd done to earn their enmity. The out-of-towners had recently arrived in Holford, answering Edric's calls for extra assistance in the mine. They'd taken an instant dislike to William and quickly set about making his life hell. Offering to help find Edric, only to abandon him in the tunnels, was just the latest escalation of their bullying.

"Don't mind 'em boy," Edric told William. "Yar worth twelve of 'em. Everyone's seen how ya been helpin' the village. I'll give 'em a good crack over the head. Bloody dolts."

They reached the surface and William breathed a sigh of relief. He'd never been so happy to see the sky.

"Ah lad, you'd best get changed," Edric said, noticing William's torn and muddy pants. "Take it easy and I'll see ya at the Council meetin' tonight."

William was further humiliated by Edric's dismissal but didn't object. He slunk back towards Holford, trying to avoid the judging eyes of the mine labourers. Most were new arrivals, their faces were unfamiliar. He was halfway home before he realised that he'd forgotten to ask about Edric's production forecasts, the whole reason he'd risked the dreaded mine in the first place.

William slipped into his family's cottage, hoping to find it empty.

"You're back early," Ma chimed with surprise. She sat by the hearth, preparing another batch of cloth for Matilda's new dyes. William was still unaccustomed to seeing Ma with a spring in her step but news of Rachel's baby had lulled her back to life.

"Are you alright?" Ma asked with motherly concern.

William mumbled a response but Ma saw straight through him with her well-trained maternal eye.

"Will..?" she asked pointedly.

William relented and told her about the whole incident and the labourers' ongoing torments. Ma was furious, her colourful language so unusual that it forced a reluctant laugh from William. Ma washed his pants and dried them by the fire. The pair chatted the afternoon away, trying to solve the world's problems while Ma continued working on her cloth. Just like old times, the mere act of talking reenergised William. Edric's brutes were almost forgotten when he finally departed for the Council meeting.

The Council was Matilda's idea and that evening was only their third meeting. A necessary evil after coordinating Holford's many activities became too much for her and William. They had stubbornly persevered for as long as possible but a growing series of accidents eventually forced them to concede the need for more assistance.

"Plus," Matilda had added with a smile, "we can pressure the participants to finally learn their numbers and letters."

The new group built upon the leadership of Pa's jury, though Matilda insisted on keeping the groups separate. It was held in the Brewer's hall, the only room in Holford large enough to fit the participants.

William sat at the long trestle table in the barrel-lined cellar, directly across from Martin Brewer and his son. Martin had made clear his dislike for William, saying that he was too young for a prestigious leadership position. But Matilda wouldn't hear it and pointed out the important role William played in accelerating Holford's progress. William defiantly returned Martin's glare. Yet another bully.

He breathed a sigh of relief when Pa entered the cellar, deep in conversation with Elizabeth's friend Astrid, the woman who had brought William into the world. Pa caught William's eye and slid onto the bench next to his son, inviting Astrid to sit next to them. It was her first Council meeting and the shy midwife declined, taking a seat at the farthest end of the table instead. William gave her a small wave.

Timothy and Walt arrived next, deep in discussion about the warehouse roof. Timothy sat next to Astrid and gave her hand a friendly squeeze while continuing his conversation. Luke Ploughman, Father Daniel and Joshua Miller gradually filtered in one by one and sat.

The Brewer glared as each person entered, daring them to challenge his authority and ensuring that they took the seats he deemed appropriate. He smothered conversation and everyone milled around uncomfortably. Except for Timothy and Walt, who were either oblivious or just didn't care.

Matilda finally arrived with Edric Miner and Matt Smith in tow. Timothy and Walt stopped their conversation as Matilda stood behind her seat. She looked around the table, dissatisfied.

"No, this won't do at all. Everybody up, we're going to mix this around."

Martin looked incredulous. "Dammit woman! You can't tell me where to sit in my own building!"

"I can actually, if you wish to remain a part of this group. And if you want me to continue helping you and your family. But if you insist on being obstructive, we can move our meetings to my warehouse. It'll mean a longer walk for everyone but might rid us of some dead weight."

The pair stared off in uneasy silence until Alan grabbed his father by the elbow and urged him to stand.

Matilda scattered the attendees around the table, breaking up the cliques that had already started to form.

"I'll say this once more, then let it be done forever," she said. "You're all key members of Holford, the few with the power to advance the interests of the many. I've asked you here to lead, to guide the village to prosperity.

"We're all working towards the same goal. A prosperous village will improve each of your individual lots. But more importantly, it will also improve the lives of your family, friends and neighbours. I won't have petty squabbles in this group. I can't have us fragmenting so leave the petty politics behind. We're all one team in this so if you're unwilling to cooperate, know that we will go on without you."

Martin made a face to his son across the table, though Alan ignored him and remained intently focused on Matilda. Annoyed by the lack of acknowledgement, the Brewer turned to his brother and whispered something behind his hand.

Matilda noticed too.

"Any problems?"

Edric shook his head and William chuckled as Martin cowered at Matilda's gaze, avoiding eye contact.

"Good," she said cheerfully. "Well, first I'd like to welcome Astrid. I've been teaching her more medicine over the past week so she can assist with the injuries that are becoming increasingly frequent amongst your workers. She's also been helping Elizabeth grow some new plants that should be of interest to all of you. Haven't you Astrid?"

The Midwife gave a nervous nod to Matilda, only to quickly look down again at her clenched hands.

"Well it's good to have you here," Matilda said with genuine warmth. "Don't be afraid to chime in, we need more women in this group. Ok, let's make this more productive than the last meeting. We'll start with an update from everyone so let us know what you need from William and I over the coming week. Then we'll discuss our approach for Baron Walter's upcoming inspection. Our revision of numbers and letters can wait until next week."

They went around the table, each member sharing what they'd been working on. Walt and Timothy were almost finished with the roof of the warehouse which would free Timothy to focus on glass for the windows. Walt had finished the waterwheel components and awaited Luke's plough-team to transport them to the mill.

Father Daniel had progressed work on Matilda's design for an automated writing machine. He'd shown great interest in Matilda's Book and was delighted when she taught him to make one of his own. Walt's young assistants had helped carve hundreds of tiny letters into wooden blocks which Father Daniel had painstakingly arranged to tell the Genesis creation story. He promised to have initial prints for the Council's reading lessons by the next meeting, provided others supplied ink and paper.

Martin didn't have anything to contribute but Alan had used an old cauldron to scale up dye production for the priest's writing projects and Ma's cloth. He'd also been working with masons – recently arrived from Stowey – on Matilda's plans to separate Holford's waste and drinking water.

His father scoffed at the idea. "Why anyone would waste time making an artificial river, only to bury it underground?"

When Alan explained how it would improve the quality of their brews the Brewer went quiet once more.

Matilda scrawled notes with charcoal on a precious blank page of her Book. "That paper and ink couldn't come quick enough," she told them with an exaggerated sigh.

Joshua, Luke and Pa were all progressing well. Joshua had processed Holford's backlog of grain and started work on Arnold's personal hoard which would be needed to feed all of the new arrivals. Luke and his team were almost finished ploughing the fallow fields, well ahead of schedule thanks to Matilda's improved plough. Pa was working in the fields to cut hay before sowing the next crop.

Matthew and Ralph had finished adapting the new mill mechanism to drive their automated bellows and had started sharpening the blades for Walt's sawmill. With Matilda's help, Matthew had finally succeeded in casting stronger steels and Ralph was experimenting with magical steels that wouldn't rust. Matthew hoped to use them to make an even better plough, which made Luke whoop out loud.

Edric shared the production estimates William had forgotten to ask for that morning. Matilda's improved pump was keeping the water out of the mine and the Miner's team had already exposed promising new ore-veins. Edric welcomed Astrid's assistance as the hasty excavations made his inexperienced miners prone to clumsiness.

Soft-spoken Astrid finished with an update on her work with Elizabeth.

"Matilda's tomato plants are starting to grow fruit so we're expecting our first harvest soon. Nowhere enough to address the food shortages but a step in the right direction. Matilda promises they will be unlike anything we've eaten before so perhaps we could share that with the Baron?"

Matilda laughed. "That's a great idea, let's make him a pizza! It'll blow his mind." The blank faces around the table made her laugh even harder. Then she grew serious. "Astrid and Joshua have touched on the food issues but we need to discuss the new arrivals. We're becoming victims of our own success and it won't be long until Baron Walter starts getting complaints from the other lords. Even more people have arrived from the region seeking work but we have nowhere to house them. Some Holford families have kindly shared their homes but we can't rely on their generosity forever."

William took his cue and spoke up. "We can establish new lodging for the newcomers which will mean even more help for our projects. And if we do it well now, we could design a larger village so it doesn't get crowded like Stowey. Should we ask the Baron for assistance?"

There was a general murmur of assent from the Council, though Timothy uncharacteristically grumbled that too many outsiders would change Holford's character.

"Come now Timothy," Matilda chided. "The only constant is change. Engage with the newcomers from the outset and you can teach them the Holford way of living. Just like you showed me when I first arrived. Plus, aren't half of your new assistants from other villages?"

Timothy dipped his head in defeat.

"Very well, we can discuss designs and timeframes over the coming days. We'll need extra land and materials so I'll raise this with Walter when he visits. Now, all of you go home!"

The Council members filed out of the cellar, their conversations charged with possibility. William and Pa waited for Matilda to gather her belongings and the three of them then made their way home.

"That was an improvement," Pa noted.

"Much better," Matilda agreed. "It'll require firm guidance to keep our more belligerent members focused but momentum should keep us on course once we're all moving together."

"We can try," William countered, "but I think the Brewer family will always want to branch off on their own. They don't really care about anyone else."

Pa met William's pessimistic realism with a contemplative nod.

They were all exhausted from another long day and it was a relief when they finally entered the cosy cottage. William reflected on the various changes as they settled into their usual places. Pa sat on a new stool from Walt, Ma dished up food in crockery provided by Timothy and Matthew had even crafted forks for everyone. The family's role in welcoming Matilda to Holford was appreciated. By most.

The biggest change of all was in Ma who was almost back to her same old self since hearing that she would become a grandmother. She was full of energy as she rushed around the cottage in the mornings and evenings, cooking and cleaning to make sure that everyone was ready for their busy days of work.

"We've got to have Holford in a good state before my grandchild arrives," she joked.

Ma was busy herself during the day and William didn't know how she managed everything. He often saw her dashing around the village to visit her friends and coordinating the efforts of the Holford women. She had started building an improved loom with Matilda's guidance and Walt had privately vented his frustrations to William at Ma's incessant insistence that he prioritise her work.

William didn't complain of Ma's work ethic whenever her latest food creation was inflicted upon him. With just regular ingredients, Matilda had taught Ma how to make delicious concoctions but Elizabeth's new produce only further enhanced their meals. That evening was no exception. William's mouth was alive with new sensations. It felt on fire!

"Do you need some water Will?" Ma asked, still enjoying the novelty of being able to offer clean drinking water.

"Not water," Matilda said. "That'll make it worse. Is there any milk?"

"How was the meeting?" Ma asked while ladling William some milk. "Better than last week?"

"Much better," Matilda said. "Everyone's making progress, it's so good to see."

"It's honestly amazing to see how much everything has changed. I don't know how I never noticed, but there's something in the air. Everyone has a spring in their step, even more than you'd expect in the leadup to Summer. You've really worked some magic Matilda."

"You're too kind Emma. I've just given gentle nudges here and there. Everyone else is doing the actual work and William is running around to keep them all on task."

William felt himself blush at his mentor's compliment.

"Another of your enchantments," Ma replied. "We love our William to death but Lord knows we never thought he was capable of working so hard."

"Hey!" William protested half-heartedly.

"Not at all," Matilda said with a smile. "I knew he had a good head on his shoulders when I first met him. I think he was just bored."

Matilda got up and rinsed her clay bowl, placing it on the new shelf Walt had built to placate Ma until her new loom arrived.

"That was delicious Emma, it's hard to believe you've just started cooking with chilli. Astrid said the tomatoes are getting close so I'll show you some more recipes soon."

Elizabeth was excited at that announcement.

"Ok dear family, it's getting late. The evenings keep getting lighter as summer draws closer yet somehow it's always dark when I finally return to the mill."

"You take care of yourself, Til," Pa said protectively. "You always say it's fine but keep your wits about you. Martin's made it clear that not everyone is happy with your changes."

"Thanks Pa, I'll be careful."

The young woman strode out into the twilight and the family settled into their regular evening routine. William was amazed how different the building felt with Rachel, Mama and Margery gone.

Everyone seemed less on edge and life in the cottage was smooth. Easy.

William remembered the morning's traumatic events and suddenly felt exhausted. He settled onto his small cot and quickly fell asleep to the sound of the happy family pottering around the house. The horrors of the mine were forgotten amongst the warmth, light and sounds of home.

Life was good.

CHAPTER THIRTY

1 June 1124

Rachel was frustrated.

"No Ma," she urged. "You don't understand, they're ruining everything! Martin says they've completely changed Holford."

"Come now dear," Ma said absentmindedly as she stirred a pot of red sludge above the hearth. From the Foreigner no doubt. Rachel's stomach betrayed her with a hungry rumble. "You're being silly, not all change is bad. Just look around, I've never seen our neighbours working so hard. And yet also so happy."

Rachel looked at Ma with disbelief and finally realised that she too was a lost cause. Just like the others, Ma had succumbed to the guile of the red-headed bitch. Rachel gave up. She accepted the aromatic bowl from Ma and nodded along as Ma nattered about her work with the village women. She scoffed her sludge and fled at the first opportunity.

"Don't forget," Ma called out after her, "The arguments will subside if you just *talk* to Alan! Take care of that grandchild of mine!"

Frustrated at Ma's obvious advice, Rachel left the cottage and walked the familiar roads back to her new house. There were signs of change wherever she looked. Neighbours' hovels had been renovated with tiled roofs or rehung doors. Strange tools were propped beside buildings and gardens brimmed with unusual plants. Matilda's 'bysicles' increasingly whizzed along the paths and every second face she passed was unfamiliar.

The whole village had gone mad. The Foreigner's arrival had upended Rachel's entire existence. Matilda was confident, independent and beautiful. She could travel wherever she liked, whenever she liked. Even her clothing hinted at a femininity that Rachel had always been forbidden to embrace, yet the Foreigner showed no fear or shame. Rachel hated her for it.

As if on cue, Matilda marched across the village square shadowed by followers who interrupted each other to ask questions before darting off to another corner of Holford. It was madness. There was a time when Rachel had been followed by a gaggle of admiring followers, younger girls wishing to be her or admiring boys wishing to be with her.

But that was no longer the case. One by one Rachel's friends had tired of her efforts to expose how things had been better before. They too had abandoned Rachel, pointing to their own second-order benefits from Matilda's efforts. Now even Ma had joined their side. Rachel felt her lonely world shrink even more.

She missed Margery. Her younger sister would've at least heard Rachel's point of view and always had some pearl of wisdom that could be hatched into a full-blown plan. But Margery was gone. Rachel admittedly could've been kinder to her sister when among Holford's adolescents. But surely Margery understood that Rachel only sought to improve their family's social standing. Countering the embarrassment that William attracted with his constant antics.

Rachel's feet carried her along while her mind was elsewhere and she eventually found herself standing before Mama's headstone at the chapel cemetery. Rachel visited the grave most days. Mama's passing was another loss brought upon by Matilda's arrival. Another voice that Rachel could no longer rely upon for counsel.

Mama had understood the importance of social standing. Had experienced the harsh sting of its loss. Mama was buried beside her wealthy husband beneath a grand headstone carved by Stowey's masons. But her final years as a widow had been a drought compared to her lavish life as a miller's wife. For years, Rachel had witnessed the pain of that fall.

Rachel startled as she felt her baby move around inside her. The intrusive reminder of new life was a complete contradiction to graveyard around her. She lovingly clutched her visibly extended stomach. The baby was her one glimmer of hope. Her chance to finally have the happy family she'd always dreamed of.

She hoped it was a son. Life was easier for a man.

Ma and Pa had always wanted a son. Even as a child Rachel had been all too aware of that. It was the reason they'd tried to have so many children. The four that made it past infancy and the many that didn't. Rachel had watched them try all of the Midwife's schemes for conceiving a boy. The potions and prayers. The position of stars and chants. It had bordered on heresy.

But they'd received Rachel and her sisters instead. Their eldest daughter was constant source of trouble, as Pa had reminded Rachel all too often. Her efforts to secure Alan's attention had required the Midwife's other fertility services on several occasions. Pa accused Rachel of bringing shame upon the family but he too failed to see that she actually sought the exact opposite.

It was inevitable that Rachel would end up with Alan. The Miller's son might've provided even greater wealth but he was socially awkward, an outcast. Plus, he was closer to Margery in age so why not double the family's chances of a good marriage? Pa had suggested several respectable boys from nearby villages but Rachel knew it had to be Alan. As Martin Brewer's eldest son, he was guaranteed to inherit a lucrative trade and, more importantly, he was well respected amongst his peers. He was undeniably a bully but Rachel didn't care whether it was respect or fear that underpinned his social clout.

Despite years of insisting that Alan and Rachel weren't mature enough to marry, Pa was finally prompted by Rachel's third visit to the Midwife to make a proposal to Martin. Pa promised a generous dowry to the Brewer – much more than he could afford – on the condition that they be married after Alan's eighteenth birthday. The sole positive of Matilda's arrival was that the date had been moved forward.

Rachel had been so happy in the lead up to the wedding. Her soon-to-be father-in-law spared no expense in organising the event and she was the talk of the entire region. All of the details she and Mama had discussed for years finally came into place, though it was a knife to the stomach that Mama wasn't there to see it herself.

In contrast, life after the wedding was far from what Rachel had dreamed. She had tried to be the perfect wife. She prepared meals just as Ma had shown her, tweaking the recipes to accommodate Alan's specific tastes and using the expensive ingredients available to the wealthy. Sugar, caraway, pepper. She worked harder than ever before in the first weeks of marriage to make a beautiful home, only for Alan to return from the brewery, inhale his meal and provide little more than grunts as conversation. He would retire to bed and have his way with her before rolling over without a word. Every day was the same.

Rachel always knew that Alan was a brute – selfish and aggressive – but foolishly hoped that the love of a new marriage would cool his temper and warm his heart. She learned that he was a sad man, cursed by his alcoholic father and the weight of responsibility. Even amongst his cruelty and neglect, Rachel discovered that she felt sorry for her husband.

Martin Brewer had managed to establish a successful trade despite being a younger son without claim to a large inheritance. Martin had built his brewery through tenacity and hard work, overcoming doubters and debtors alike. But the endeavour took a toll and he'd heavily sampled his own brews to cope. Much like his brother Edric, Martin was a mess behind closed doors. Responsibility for keeping the brewery running had fallen to Alan years prior.

It was a heavy burden for a young man and Alan also used his product to blunt his worries. He spent most evenings away from his marital home, drinking with friends while Rachel obediently awaited his return. Alone.

Rachel bore the loneliness for as long as possible but each day became harder. Her pleas for companionship fell on deaf ears, enraging Alan who saw them as yet another responsibility he was forced to bear. Each confrontation drove Rachel's husband further into his drink. The new couple's limited interactions were often spent fighting and there were many nights that Rachel fell asleep in their lavish house with tears streaming down her cheeks, praying that her husband would wrap her in a warm embrace.

For so long, marriage had been a beacon of hope. A chance for her to escape the oppressive life with her parents and William's constant irritating presence. And yet it had soured so quickly. *But it was alright*, Rachel told herself, *she had her baby*.

Realising that she'd been away from the house for too long, Rachel raced from the graveyard and back home. She rushed to have food ready for Alan's return that evening but knew deep down that he would be late. Again.

Rachel sat in silence by the warm hearth while she waited for her husband's return, cradling her stomach and dreaming of the life her baby would have. She no longer felt alone, as she had in the early weeks after the wedding. She had hope.

It was well after dark when Alan finally stumbled into the house. Rachel had fallen asleep against the wall and he was so drunk that he didn't even see her at first. Rachel stood up, her eyes still bleary.

"Welcome home dear. It's late," she observed wearily.

"Don't you start," Alan slurred. "I've already had an earful from my father."

"That's no good. Why don't you take a seat and tell me about it? I made beef stew. Just how you like it."

Alan grumbled but dropped into his seat. Rachel ladled stew into his bowl and lay it in front of him.

"What happened with your Pa?" she asked cautiously.

Alan ignored her, his unfocused eyes fixed upon his bowl as he ate.

"Was it another busy day?"

She waited. Again there was only silence.

"I visited Ma today. I told her how the Foreigner is ruining the village. That too much is changing. She didn't believe me and said Holford is actually improving."

Alan scoffed.

A response! At least it was something.

Alan finished his food and lay down his spoon before clumsily pushing himself up and shuffling towards their bed.

Rachel plucked up her courage and spoke plainly to her husband.

"Please talk to me."

Alan staggered around and stared at her.

"Please?" she begged, hating the desperation in her voice. "I don't want much, just to hear about my husband's day."

Tears welled in the corners of her eyes.

Alan swayed and gaped at her. His addled mind processed her words. And then his face scrunched up with rage.

"You don't…want much?" he hiccoughed. "You got me, didn't you? What more could you want?"

Rachel saw what was coming and tried to back down.

"No Al, that's not what I'm saying. Never mind, we can talk another night."

"No!" he yelled. "You got what you wanted. You got me! You made your stinking Pa talk to mine and they hatched their grand scheme to lock me away. For life!"

Alan stepped toward her, menace in his eyes.

Rachel cowed before him. She'd never seen him so worked up.

"And now they gang up on me in front of the Redhead? This is all your fault."

He struck her across the face.

Rachel cried out in shock and fell to the floor. She tried to pick herself up but Alan shoved her back down.

"It's all your fault!" he cried.

Rachel looked up and caught a glimpse of his eyes. An unfocused cocktail of devastation and fury.

Then he attacked.

Rachel's drunk husband rained blows down upon her. He struck with an open fist but each blow rang her head like a bell.

"No!" she begged. "Please? Stop! The baby!"

Her last words cut through her husband's rage and he stopped, shoving her to the ground one last time.

"Get out," he hissed. "Now. Go to your parents. Go to mine. I don't care. Just get out and leave me alone."

Rachel's ears rung and she barely heard him.

"Now!" Alan yelled.

Rachel didn't need to be told again. She lunged for the door and tore it open before running aimlessly into the night. One hand wiped tears from her eyes, the other cradled her baby.

She had no idea where she was going, she just ran. Away from Alan. Away from her parents. Away from all the people who'd let her down.

Rachel ran past the village boundary, until she couldn't run any more. She was suddenly woozy and the pain in her head made her drop to the ground. She threw up and crawled to a hedge at the side of the road, hoping to use it to stand back up. She propped herself up but anything else was too difficult. Tears streamed down her face.

Her swollen eyes were starting to close over when a light appeared on the road, coming towards her from the village. Fearing it was Alan, Rachel scrambled again to stand up but her body refused to obey. She was forced to lie in a heap by the hedge, filled with dread.

Rachel realised it was a woman as the figure drew closer. Some lucid part of her brain wondered what woman would risk walking the outer roads so late. Then she glimpsed the red hair.

The Foreigner was the last person Rachel wanted to see and she was mortified that Matilda would see her in such a state.

Rachel saw Matilda notice the shape by the side of the road and watched the shock register on the Foreigner's face as she realised it was a person. Matilda rushed towards Rachel, her otherworldly light searing Rachel's swollen eyes.

The Foreigner propped Rachel up, her voice urgent but speaking in calming tones. Rachel was numb and too sore to push away the assistance but noted with morbid amusement the shock on Matilda's face as she recognised William's sister. Yet still the Foreigner helped.

"Oh Rachel," Matilda soothed, "what has he done to you? I knew it was bad, but this?"

Rachel was surprised by the genuine concern in Matilda's voice. Despite her hatred of the Redhead, Rachel relished being cared for.

"We're not far from my mill," Matilda told her. "We'll fix you up there."

Matilda carefully coaxed Rachel up from the ground and led her back to the mill. It was slow going and Rachel stumbled several times but Matilda held her with a firm yet gentle grip.

Rachel hadn't been to the mill since the fire and was amazed by the small village that had grown around it. Even by the moonlight, she saw the tiled roof and freshly plastered walls. It was the grandest building in Holford.

Matilda brought Rachel to her bed in the completed corner of the warehouse and lay her down gently.

"Wait here," she said kindly.

Matilda disappeared and returned with a bucket and cloth. She delicately wiped Rachel's face, reminding Rachel of her own efforts to care for Mama. Tears flowed once more.

"Shh," Matilda hushed. "Stay still. Be calm. You're safe here."

Her soothing worked and Rachel felt herself starting to relax.

"It's alright Rachel. It's going to be alright. I'm here to help."

Rachel closed her swollen eyes and savoured Matilda's deliberate strokes.

"Tell me what happened Rachel. It'll help." Matilda paused with the cloth. "I'm not here to judge. I honestly don't understand the animosity between us but I wish it were gone."

Rachel stayed silent. Matilda resumed wiping and eventually got up for fresh water. She returned with a salve and when she'd finished applying it, Rachel spoke.

"It was Alan," she confirmed.

A dam broke and Rachel poured her heart out, telling Matilda everything. She didn't care anymore. She told Matilda about Alan. About her marriage. About the baby. She told Matilda about her loneliness and the changes in Holford. She told of her hatred.

Matilda just listened, stroking Rachel's hand the whole time. Rachel felt Matilda tense as she described Alan's attack.

"You poor thing," Matilda said. Her voice was full of compassion but her eyes were aflame. "No one should have to go through that. You deserve so much better." Matilda took a deep breath and centred herself. "You stay here tonight ok? Get some sleep. We'll work out a longer-term solution in the morning. You're safe here, I'll keep watch."

The Foreigner stepped out of the warehouse and stood by the door.

Rachel felt empty but she couldn't explain why. It was a good empty, as if a weight had lifted from her shoulders.

Finally feeling safe, Rachel permitted her eyes to shut.

Sleep came instantly.

+++

All was silent when Rachel woke the next morning. Only one of her eyes would open and her head pounded but she forced herself up and silently left the warehouse. Matilda lay asleep by the door, still wearing her clothes from the previous night. Rachel felt embarrassed at letting her former rival see her so weak. She fled.

Rachel limped back into Holford, hoping to avoid anyone familiar but the roads were mercifully clear. She considered going to Ma and Pa's cottage but dreaded the awkward conversation. Ma had said only the previous day that it was her duty to obey her husband.

Instead, Rachel turned towards her marital home beside the brewery. She stood at the door for what felt like an age before finally lifting the latch and entering.

Alan was nowhere to be seen. The house was a mess, their belongings strewn across the ground. Several items lay in pieces. Alan's dirty bowl still lay on the table.

242

Rachel didn't know what had happened but she spent the rest of the day putting the house back in order and tidying up the mess. Matilda tried to enter the house at one point but Rachel yelled at her hysterically until the Redhead retreated. Rachel calmed down and spent the rest of the day baking bread and refreshing the stew for her husband's eventual return.

She'd spent all day trying to figure out the right words to say but Rachel's apprehension evaporated when Alan opened the door and she saw his face. It too was covered in bruises. His eye was black and he carried his left arm by the wrist.

Alan stopped in his tracks and looked around the recently tidied house. At the stew by the hearth. He glared at Rachel and disappeared into the bedroom.

Without a word.

CHAPTER THIRTY-ONE
2 June 1124

Matilda had been at the end of her tether when she returned to her mill, suffering mental whiplash from another day of being jerked all over Holford. She fantasised about a weekend escape back to her cave. Swimming in the stream, visiting Harry, carving a chair and enjoying the forest solitude.

She needed the retreat. Unexplained acts of vandalism had become increasingly frequent as more strangers arrived in Holford. Her morale was chipped away as days of concentrated toil were ruined in an instant of mindless destruction. Matilda had asked Pa and his fellow jurors to investigate but the culprits remained at large.

Matilda was almost back at her mill when she noticed the unexplained mass beneath a hedge. She initially thought it was a wounded animal but ran when she realised it was a person. She reeled when she discovered it was Rachel.

Despite Rachel's history of antagonism, her story was heartbreaking and instantly filled Matilda with rage. Matilda's hands shook as she cleaned Rachel's battered face and she made for Holford the second Rachel fell asleep. Her fatigue was completely forgotten.

Rachel's house was dark and completely still when Matilda arrived. She vaulted up the stone steps and threw herself against the front door until it broke. Her efforts woke Alan who was standing dumbfounded by his bed when she entered. He smelt of stale beer, sweat and vomit.

The pair exchanged a momentary look before Alan sneered. The single expression, so reminiscent of his father, personified everything wrong with Holford. Rachel's bruised face. The mindless vandalism and endless work.

Matilda surged forward.

The coward tried to run, flinging objects and upending furniture in a vain attempt to slow Matilda but she took down her prey with the grace of a lioness.

Matilda showed Alan as much mercy as he'd shown his wife and their unborn child. She rained down punches and threw in her knee and boot. She didn't hold back. Alan landed several feeble blows of his own which only fuelled Matilda's rage.

"How dare you harm your wife?" she snarled between blows. "How dare you harm your unborn child? Scum!"

Alan eventually yielded and broke down in tears. Matilda landed a few extra blows for good measure before subduing him, bending his arm uncomfortably behind his back and forcing his head into the tiled floor. She smelled urine and saw a pool form on the floor tiles.

"You're disgusting," Matilda hissed, jerking Alan's arm further back to get his attention. "You lay a finger on them again and I will be back. I won't be so gentle next time, the world doesn't need garbage like you. Do you understand?"

Alan wept into the floor.

"Do you understand?"

"Yes!" he'd cried. "I won't touch her again."

"You promise?" Matilda asked, pulling his arm tighter. She felt a pop.

"I promise," the snivelling worm cried.

"I'll be watching you," Matilda said coolly. She threw him to the ground and stepped into the night without a backward glance.

+++

Matilda was dejected when Rachel was gone the following morning. She searched her mill and the surrounding buildings, hoping against hope that her guest had merely moved somewhere more comfortable or secure. But Rachel was gone.

A wave of weariness and remorse hit as Matilda recalled the previous night's events. She'd exacted revenge and taken her anger out on Alan but it wasn't becoming.

Eager to clear the fog from her head, she gave up her search and went to bathe in the mill pond. The cool water soothed her knuckles and the few places where Alan had landed decent blows. They hurt to touch but each flash of pain filled Matilda with vindication. Alan would be much worse off.

A cloud of red hair billowed around Matilda as she floated in the pond, calculating what to do next. She didn't need to worry about Alan. He'd be feeling sore and sorry for himself, though his father wouldn't be pleased. Rachel was Matilda's priority. She would've either retreated to her parents' cottage or returned home to her abusive husband. Knowing the social expectations of the time, Matilda feared the latter was more likely.

Matilda needed to act fast and while the odds of finding Rachel with her parents were slim, the cottage had to be her first stop. An overly judgemental reaction from Ma could do lasting damage but Matilda hoped that a discrete discussion with the family's matriarch might prevent any additional trauma.

Matilda made her way into Holford, careful to time her arrival just right. Late enough that the others would've departed for their regular daily routines but before Ma left to visit the local women. Matilda sneakily approached from the rear of the property to avoid any unnecessary conversations.

Ma was already outside emptying breakfast scraps into the muckheap. She gave a quizzical look as Matilda clambered through the vegetable patch, taking care not to trample Elizabeth's crop.

"What's wrong with using the front gate?" Ma asked. "Surely you're not that important yet?"

"Too many admirers out there," Matilda joked as she awkwardly unhooked herself from a blackberry bush. "Have the others left yet?"

"They have," Ma said curiously, staring into Matilda's soul. "Come inside and have something to eat."

Matilda followed Ma indoors and graciously accepted a fresh loaf before searching for a place to sit amongst the giant loom and knee-high stacks of paper awaiting transfer to Father Daniel's ever-hungry press. Even more sheets hung drying from the rafters. Ma stared at Matilda expectantly, waiting for her to spill whatever she'd come to say.

"You really don't miss a trick," Matilda said.

"It comes from raising a litter of rascals. What brings you here?"

Matilda picked at her bread as she decided how to put it delicately.

"Have you heard from Rachel?"

"She was here yesterday. Stayed for a good talk, just like old times. I gave her some pasta. She didn't say much but I thought it was tasty."

"Did she say anything about Alan?" Matilda asked delicately.

Ma's mood darkened. "Look, I know you two aren't friends but you shouldn't snoop into other people's business. It's not proper."

"I'm not snooping Emma, I promise. It's just…Rachel slept at my mill last night."

"That's…unexpected," Ma said with genuine surprise.

"It was for me too." Matilda took a deep breath. "I'm afraid there's been some problems."

Ma didn't look surprised. "I know, Rachel told me yesterday. It's quite normal for newlyweds to have issues in the early months. It's a big adjustment living with someone new. But it will be water under the bridge in no time."

"I'm afraid it's more serious than that. Alan's beating her."

"He never!" Ma exclaimed in disbelief.

"I'm afraid so. Rachel was collapsed by the side of the road when I travelled home. Well past the village boundary. Her face was bruised and bleeding."

Ma looked grim. "I knew he was a brute but I never thought him a wife beater. My poor girl, it's started so early. What of my grandchild?"

"The baby didn't seem hurt," Matilda reassured Ma. "But Rachel was gone before I woke up. I'd hoped to talk with her before she decided what to do next."

Ma's expression hardened. "You be careful there, young Matilda. Don't you go putting dangerous ideas in her head."

"But…" Matilda began.

"No, I won't hear it," Ma said firmly. "You've made some fine changes in this village, truly. But not this. Things might be different where you're from but Rachel made her pact with God. She will stand by that boy, that dreadful violent boy, until death separates them. Don't think I like it, I'm her mother! But a promise is a promise. We can merely pray that Alan sees the error of his ways, repents and redeems himself. The Lord will judge an appropriate punishment."

Matilda toyed with telling Ma about her late-night encounter with Alan but thought against it. Better that someone else tell her, while Matilda was far away. Matilda knew that Ma wouldn't be swayed.

"Ok Emma. I won't tell her to leave Alan. But please, Rachel needs kindness. The life she described to me last night sounded agonisingly lonely. She could really use some company. Free from judgement and expectation."

"You're a confident young woman Matilda," Ma conceded, shaking her head. "Overconfident, I'd say. But I appreciate what you've done for my daughter. For the family. The whole village for that matter. Just know that we do things for a reason. You can't change everything."

The finality of Ma's statement signalled that the conversation had ended.

"Now. If you'll excuse me, I'm showing some of the local ladies how to use Walt's loom. And Father Daniel needs this paper to print more exercises for tonight."

Ma got up and showed Matilda the door. Matilda left, her bread still in hand. She was still processing Ma's blunt acceptance of Alan's violence as she meandered onto the road. She was trying to work out what to do next when a cry came from behind her.

"Oi, Matilda!"

Matilda turned to see Joshua Miller. "Oh, hi."

"So glad I found you, you're harder to pin down than a rabbit in heat. I wanted to ask about…"

"Oh sorry," she interrupted. "I'm actually in the middle of something. Can we talk before the meeting tonight?"

Joshua looked taken aback, like he'd had a prize snatched straight from his hands.

"I guess," he said. "It's actually about that, and some mill stuff. Looks like there's going to be trouble."

Matilda stopped in her tracks. "What makes you say that?"

"My new assistant said Alan was attacked last night. That Martin's out for blood. Alan's locked in the brewery, terrified that he'll be attacked again. People are saying it was someone from the Council but Alan's refusing to name them and my boy didn't know either."

"Shit. Thanks for letting me know," Matilda said, already starting to run away. "I'll drop past yours on my way to the meeting!"

Matilda had worked up a slight sweat by the time she arrived at Rachel's house. At least Alan was unlikely to interrupt.

She knocked at the door and waited, wryly noting that she'd stood on the same spot only hours earlier. She heard shuffling from within.

"Rachel? I know you're in there."

The shuffling stopped but there was no response. Matilda grabbed the latch and started to open it.

"Rachel, I'm coming in."

"No!" came a hysteric cry from inside and the latch slammed back down. "Go away! How dare you show your face here after what you did to my husband. I know it was you. Leave us alone!"

Matilda was confused. "But Rachel. What about last night?"

"Leave me alone!" Rachel screamed.

Matilda was used to Rachel's outbursts but this was particularly manic. She wondered if Rachel had directed similar intensity at Alan or whether she railed at Matilda to vent unspoken frustrations. Either way, Matilda felt Rachel's words lacked their usual scorn and just stood with her head against the door, letting Rachel wail until she tired herself out. Matilda let the silence settle.

"Ok Rachel. I'll leave you be. Just know that there are people who want to help. Who want what's good for you. Remember last night, you can always visit my mill if you need anything."

Rachel remained silent, the latch shut. Accepting defeat, Matilda turned away to start what was left of her regular day.

She bounced between tasks with less energy than normal, stifling yawns as she provided advice and staying on her feet lest she fall asleep. She longed for her bed and vowed to take a multi-day retreat to the cave for a long overdue break.

As promised, she went to Joshua's mill before the evening Council meeting. She helped diagnose problems with the mill mechanism and offered some of the spare parts Walt had made. He hung off her every word.

Realising they were late for the Council meeting, the pair ran to Martin's brewery. Matilda was apprehensive about her reception but they found everyone sitting at their assigned positions in a particularly tense silence. Pa's jury colleagues were also in attendance. An air of intrigue hung over the table and people looked everywhere but their injured companion.

Alan looked miserable. Astrid was tying his arm in a rough sling and his face was swollen. Both of his eyes were black. Alan's father was furious.

"You mongrel!" Martin cried the moment Matilda entered the room. "How dare you attack my son! In his own house!"

The Council bristled.

"Martin!" Pa called out in rebuke. "That's a mighty big allegation. And of Holford's most outstanding citizen too."

"No Mark, it's true." Matilda replied without remorse. "I did it. And I'd happily do it again."

The room fell dead silent and several attendees looked at Matilda as though she actually were a mangy dog.

"Oh," Pa said, taken aback. "Matilda, that's serious assault. What would possess you to do something like that?"

Matilda looked at Alan. "Would you like to tell them or should I?"

Alan glared at her through his swollen eyes.

"Suit yourself," Matilda said with a shrug before turning to address her audience. "In addition to being a coward, young Alan here beats his wife. I found Rachel as I returned to my mill last night. She was lying in a heap by the side of the road. Her face was bloody and she cradled her unborn child as she wept."

There were scattered looks of disapproval along the table. Matilda was surprised by their muted response and had to remind herself of Twelfth Century norms. Pa's reaction was most visceral, sitting stone still with his jaw and fists clenched.

"I brought Rachel back to the mill," Matilda continued, "where she told me what had happened. Everything, from her wedding until last night. It turns out Alan has been a far from honourable husband. So I went to visit him while his wife and baby rested in the safety of the mill. He showed no remorse and ran the second he saw me. Still took his fair share of swipes too. Hitting one woman wasn't enough."

She lifted her shirt and chainmail to show bruised ribs before looking at each of the attendees.

"I came here to help improve your village, you've all seen this. But improvement isn't just about farming or construction. There's room for social improvement too. Who of you stands for Alan's thuggish actions? For the brutal treatment of a dutiful wife? Is that the sort of behaviour to be tolerated in Holford?"

She cast her gaze around the table. At Pa's jury friends. There was a general mumble of disapproval.

"What happens within the privacy of a man's house is of no concern to you," Martin told Matilda. "No-one appointed you constable. Does knowing some cheap tricks entitle you to rule Holford with impunity?"

There were mumbles of agreement at his second statement, including from Pa.

"I dunno," Luke Ploughman quipped to Matt. "Double my wheat and give me three new ploughs and I reckon she can break the odd arm."

"No, no. I am not above the law," Matilda agreed sheepishly. Humanity had a tendency to allow a privileged few to exert influence over the masses. She couldn't allow her Council to promote that. "But you don't deny that your son struck his wife? And their unborn child?"

"So you should be punished!" Martin cried victoriously. "And Alan no doubt had reason for his actions." He looked to his son for confirmation. Alan gave a slight nod.

Matilda couldn't believe what she was hearing.

"What of the Jury? Which of you would see such an assault punished? We can call upon Rachel to provide further evidence but I fear she needs rest now more than ever."

Pa's colleagues grumbled their agreement and everyone but Alan and Martin raised their hands, earning Edric a scowl from his brother.

"Please, just the Jury. Which of you would see Mister Alan disciplined for his cruelty?"

The Jury raised their hands again.

"And who of you," Matilda added, "feel that the punishment already served was sufficient?"

There was some surprise from around the table, most of all from Alan himself.

"I'd say you gave the boy the walloping he deserves," Walt said with a smirk.

There was a murmur of assent from the crowd and the matter seemed resolved.

"And who agrees," Pa added with a certain twinkle in his eyes, "that *no-one* should be taking justice into their own hands from now on?" Matilda was sure to look appropriately chastised.

"Very well then," Pa declared. "Assault will not be tolerated. Alan has served his punishment and the Jury will decide a suitable penance for Matilda. But for now, let's get on with it."

The rest of the meeting went smoothly, though Alan and his father remained sullen and both contributed little more than grunts.

Everyone shared updates of their projects. Matthew and Walt had tested the saw mill on some smaller branches and waited on Matilda before they tested a full trunk.

Though flushing still needed work, Timothy's first toilets had proven a great success and he'd also started shaping his finest samples of glass into lenses. He proudly withdrew a rough pair of spectacles that comically magnified his eyes. Matilda couldn't help but laugh, exactly what she needed after such a trying day.

They concluded the session with a round of reading and writing exercises using Father Daniel's worksheets. Matilda was impressed at the rate they had all picked up the skill. Even Martin kept up with the class, determined not to be outdone.

It was Pa who called the meeting to a close, noticing Matilda's increasingly frequent yawns.

"That will do for tonight. Time to retire."

Matilda shot him a silent look of thanks and helped Father Daniel collect his worksheets as the rest of the Council filed out. Only Martin stayed seated and he tightly grabbed Matilda's thigh as she walked past to collect his paper.

"This isn't over," he hissed under his breath.

Matilda was shocked at his venom and swatted his hand but he dug his fingers in deeper. Seeing that no-one else was watching, she wrenched her leg away and flicked Martin on the forehead. His eyes went wide with shock.

"Yes it is. Grow up old man and realise when you've lost. Your time has passed and there's a new way of doing things around here. Go with the flow and you might retain some influence. Oppose it and you'll be swept away like the old driftwood you are."

Matilda gave him a sickly-sweet smile and was on the other side of the table before her words had even sunk in. The Brewer hobbled hastily out of the room, his son in tow.

"You're not stirring trouble again already?" Pa asked as they left.

"Me?" Matilda replied sweetly. "Never!"

CHAPTER THIRTY-TWO
4 August 1124

The morning sun was still climbing but sweat already trickled down William's back as he walked towards the mine. He enjoyed the walk, a chance to escape the chaos of village life. Holford was a hive of productivity and William rarely found time to relax between project work, Council meetings and helping Matilda. He often thought back to the dull monotony that was his life almost a year earlier. Even on the busiest of days, he couldn't dream of going back but it was nice to have the odd chance to escape.

Despite scattered objections about his age, William was a recognised leader in Holford and responsible for coordinating several projects of his own. Villagers came to him whenever Matilda couldn't be found and he was increasingly vocal at Council meetings. He'd learnt so much just by following Matilda around for months and she bestowed increasing responsibility upon him as her faith in his abilities grew.

The metal-related projects at both the mine and the blacksmith was an area that made particular sense for William to manage. His friendship with Ralph had been the main driver but he'd also developed a strong relationship with Edric. The Miner had a soft spot for William and still joked that the Boy had literally helped him get back on his feet.

Edric's transformation was as magnificent as Holford's. With the newfound purpose from his revived mine, he'd gone from the town drunk to a thriving member of society. He tied his unruly hair into a tight ponytail and worked with the energy of three men, spending more time underground than above. Besides sleep, attending Council meetings was probably the only time he spent on the surface.

William entered a familiar outcrop of trees where a layer of grey dust covering the undergrowth indicated that he was approaching the mine. He marvelled at the flurry of activity at the site as he approached. Edric had continued to take on whatever additional help he could find, eager to restore the greatness of his family's once prosperous mine. Barring the occasional burst hose, Matilda's pump design had solved the issue of groundwater and Edric's workers had begun crafting their own rudimentary hoses, allowing them to delve ever deeper. William heard plans for new tunnels with each visit.

Edric's decrepit hut now served as both sleeping quarters for the Miner and a lockable storage room for his valuable ore. His labourers seemed content to sleep under the summer stars, though some had started to construct basic huts from whatever spare wood they could scavenge. They'd set up a long trestle table and benches where the whole mining crew gathered for their dusty communal meals.

Despite the heat, Edric's smelter blazed every day to free the valuable copper trapped within the ore. William was still amazed each time he witnessed its red-hot contents scraped out. Melting rocks to form nuggets of metal was a special type of sorcery that predated Matilda's arrival.

It was for those nuggets that William had journeyed to the mine. He'd followed Edric's progress for months, monitoring the mine's output with an eagle eye. If his calculations were correct, he would finally have enough to finally start his biggest project.

Matt Smith didn't understand Matilda's desire for delicate threads of copper. *A weak metal,* he'd said, *colourful but useless for anything practical.* He had still built a wire extruder according to Matilda's specifications but used it for steel, refusing to process Edric's early batches of copper without knowing why it was so important. Matilda said he'd just have to wait.

Edric's labourers paid little attention when William arrived and continued going about their tasks. With so many newcomers, William struggled to recognise any of the workers and his stomach dropped when the only familiar face was Warren, one of his frequent tormentors. Certain that Edric was nowhere to be seen, William reluctantly approached Warren and asked where the Miner was.

"Where d'ya think?" he said, surly as ever. "Down the mine. I ain't helping you with nothing so go find him yaself. Careful tho', Roger's down there too…"

William was unsurprised by Warren's taunting tone and left before the animosity escalated.

The mine entrance had been reinforced since William's first visit but his stomach churned as the darkness loomed before him. Taking a breath to steady himself, he withdrew the precious device Matilda had bestowed upon him and ventured underground.

William's biggest project all came back to Matilda's tiny magic light box. The one she'd first shown him at her cave – he was still the only soul who knew her true futuristic origins – and used when they first explored the mine. After months of constant badgering, Matilda had finally judged that William knew enough to understand the device and explained how it worked.

"It's a torch," she'd said simply, as if it were the most unremarkable thing in the world. "Electricity runs through a diode, or a bulb, and generates light."

William didn't understand half of the words but was amazed nonetheless. His family could rarely afford candles so the day ended when the sun set. Matilda's device promised endless light and William's mind exploded with the possibilities of what he could do with limitless daytime. The things he could learn.

Matilda showed him how to dismantle the torch and described each component. The bulb, the crank, the casing. Most important was the battery, which Matilda said could do so much more than make light. William thought she was joking but Matilda explained how she planned to use the mill to make a much more impressive device. Powering lights was just the beginning.

Matilda ended up gifting the torch to William, knowing how much time he spent at the mine and how much he hated being underground. William cherished the gift as he delved deeper in search of Edric.

He interrupted two groups of workers before finally stumbling across the Miner. Edric hummed one of Matilda's tunes as he squatted by a stone wall, the steady ring of his pick adding percussion to the base of his voice. He was far too comfortable in the cramped surroundings.

"Ho, William!" he called, pushing himself upright with a grunt. "Fancy seeing you down 'ere, all by yaself. None o' the boys offered to help?"

"I can manage on my own," William replied defiantly.

"That you can. Here for the nuggets?"

Edric brushed past William and headed back outside without waiting for a response. William scurried after him, terrified of being left behind. Darkness swallowed everything behind him.

"Matthew didn' happen to give ya any o' the tools we been waitin' for?" the Miner asked, his deep baritone echoing off the walls.

"No, he didn't mention anything."

"That's a shame. We're all back to rotatin' shifts til we can get more. Been workin' so hard that we went through the whole month's supply in only two weeks. Almost too many of us now. But Lord has it been worth it. You shoulda brought that mate of yours to help carry it all back. You'll be hurtin' when you sleep tonight."

Edric's hearty laughter echoed around the mine. William feared he was right but couldn't help smiling at the reformed man's energy.

William breathed a sigh of relief when they reached the surface, though the wall of humidity made him miss the cooler depths. Almost. Edric pulled out a long iron key that matched his hut's heavy lock – another of Matilda and Matthew's more recent creations – and unlocked the door before rifling around under his bed and withdrawing four bulging sacks. They looked small but William noticed that even Edric strained as he lifted them onto his bed two at a time.

"That should do for now," the Miner said. "I'm not sure you'd be able to carry much more to be honest." He eyed William's arms. "The Redhead has ya running around too much. You're too scrawny. Ya should come down and swing a pick with us for a while. It'll do ya some good."

"Uh, thanks for the offer," William stalled. He couldn't think of anything worse. "Maybe if I find some spare time. But I'd better get going, Matthew's waiting."

"Me too," Edric said, eager to return underground. "Always more to do but never enough time. See ya tonight," he called over his shoulder as he marched back into the earth.

William shook his head in disbelief at the Miner's enthusiasm. So different to the slob he'd met in a pigsty.

Edric wasn't exaggerating about William struggling to carry the bags back to Holford. His arms ached before the mine was out of view but he soldiered onwards, refusing to let the labourers see a soft villager fail at such a simple task.

His frequent stops reminded him of another interrupted journey between the mine and the village, though this one had less vomit. His arms were ablaze by the time he arrived at Matthew's forge.

"I just don't understand," the Smith said as William dumped the sacks by the forge. "Why copper? She can't make anything with it!

Perhaps cheap jewellery but our time would be better spent improving the steel or recreating her chainmail."

"Not the chainmail again?" Ralph asked impatiently as he joined them, handing William a pitcher of water and the magnetic lodestones Matilda had requested. "Haven't you preached that there's more to this noble craft than warfare?"

William downed the entire pitcher and massaged his sore arms while the blacksmiths continued to spar about the noble art of metalwork.

"How long until the wire's ready?" William interrupted.

"A few weeks perhaps, depends what Matilda wants to prioritise," Matthew said. "I've made my arguments but it seems that even my apprentice is against me. Insubordination I tell you!"

"You can ask at the Council meeting tonight, but I'm sure she'll say it's the priority. She really wants to get started on this next mill project. Trust me, it'll be worth it."

"Look at you," Ralph mocked. "All high and mighty knowing what the secret project is." He looked to Matthew with a smirk. "I'm sure one of those iron rods could get him talking. You heat it in the coals and I'll pin him down?"

Matthew picked up a rod with a flourish and William was feigning terror when there was a sudden commotion from the village square.

"Heeeelllppp!!!" a desperate voice cried. "Someone!? Anyone!?"

The three men ran out of the forge to see what was going on. Several other villagers emerged from nearby houses.

One of Edric's labourers stood alone in the village square. He was covered from head to toe in dust and looked around frantically.

"What's going on?" Matthew asked the man, cool-headed as always.

"Cave in! Down the mine. Most got out but there's people trapped down there!"

Matthew and William reacted instantly, running towards the mine. William stopped only a few strides in.

"Matthew," he called. "Tools! Edric said they're low on tools. Have you got more?"

Matthew stopped too and took Ralph back to the forge to grab them. William ran on, urging the labourer back towards the mine. The crowd continued to swell and he spotted Elizabeth and Astrid.

"Tell Matilda to come to the mine. Astrid, with us! Now!"

Elizabeth sprinted towards Matilda's mill and William urged everyone else to the mine.

"What happened?" William asked the labourer as they ran. "I was just there."

"One of the old shafts collapsed. Only just reopened. Ed's been pushing us hard to beat his quotas so we didn't have time to redo all the supports."

William cursed Edric's stubborn determination to redeem himself and thundered towards the mine.

When they finally arrived, the mine was a different type of chaos to what William had witnessed that morning. Cries of pain tore through the trees and people ran everywhere. Two men groaned on the long benches, covered in even more dust than usual. One was bleeding profusely from his head. Astrid rushed over to help.

William did what he could to coordinate the rescue efforts and, lacking any other leadership, the frenzied labourers quickly updated him on the situation. One of the older tunnels had collapsed. Edric had ordered it reopened a week ago. Reinforcing timbers had been used for huts. Two men had already been dug out, one was dead. Four more were missing, including Edric.

William was consulting with Astrid when Matthew and Ralph arrived with additional tools. William tasked them with coordinating things on the surface before rallying some familiar labourers and running down into the mine. Despite the clear risk of another cave in, William's mind noted with amusement that he felt no fear as he delved underground once more.

The air was dusty and the floor littered with debris. William pushed his way to the front of the rescue effort and used Matilda's torch to illuminate the space for the workers. He barked orders, organising a human chain to remove debris and telling others to find additional wood to reinforce the walls.

Progress felt excruciatingly slow and William lost track of how long they'd been digging. Larger rocks had to be levered out and the diggers tired quickly. William made them swap and started digging as well.

William finished a third rotation before returning to the surface. It was much calmer and he found Matilda walking around and tending to the wounded. He ran over to give her an update.

"Well done," Matilda said. "It sounds like you've got things under control. I think we…"

There was a sudden commotion from the mine entrance.

"We've found one!"

Midsentence, William ran back into tunnel.

It was one of the labourers. They'd exposed most of the man when William arrived but the man's crushed chest made it clear that he was dead. William stepped aside as the body was delicately extracted from the rubble and carried back up to the surface.

Digging resumed with renewed vigour and it wasn't long before they found a shoe and its accompanying foot. They initially thought it was another casualty but the toes wiggled as they brushed dirt away. The group accelerated their efforts and hastily extracted the man.

It was Roger, William's other tormenter. He was in a bad way, his breathing ragged and his torso purple. He was barely conscious but his eyes pleaded for help. William ordered that Roger be carried straight to Matilda and resumed digging.

The debris became finer and William's team eventually carved a hole through to the other side of the tunnel.

"Hey!" came a weak cry from the other side.

"Gregory!" a female labourer called out with relief. William had never met either of them.

"My legs are busted," Gregory announced. "Hurry! I've managed to dig Edric out but he's not good. Stay with me Ed…"

Wary of the insecure ceiling, William ordered that the roof be braced before they resumed digging. They dug as fast as possible, carving out a hole big enough for the female volunteer to slide through. She reported that neither man was in a state to clamber up the debris so work resumed to carve a hole large enough for a stretcher.

They cut though in no time, the woman digging from one side and the rest of the team from the other. William pushed through and scrambled down to Edric. The torch beam passed over the Miner's face, coated in dust and flittering eyelids barely open.

"You'll be alright," William urged.

Edric couldn't speak but gave a weak smile upon hearing the familiar voice.

Warren helped William fumble in the dark to assemble the makeshift stretcher. Edric grunted in pain as they loaded him onto it and was fully unconscious when they passed him through the hole.

William ignored the gaping abyss behind him and focused on Gregory who was bathed in sweat and moaned as he clutched his shattered legs. They bundled him onto another stretcher which Warren and the woman guided through the hole while William pushed. When he was through, everyone scrambled out and William followed, relieved to be back on the safe side of the collapsed roof.

"Out!" he cried. "Everybody out! Now!"

The few remaining volunteers ran out of the mine. William was the last to leave the godforsaken tunnel. Darkness lapped at his ankles.

The atmosphere was subdued when he reached the surface. Two bodies lay on Edric's long trestle table, coarse cloaks draped over their faces. Astrid wept uncontrollably.

"William!" Matilda cried from the door of Edric's hut. "Get over here!"

William rushed inside and was shocked to see the floor covered in blood and Roger lying on Edric's bed. The intrusion in Edric's abode felt wrong

"I've done everything I can but he's still looking pretty bad," Matilda said. "Keep an eye on him while I check Edric and the man with the broken legs. Just remember what we discussed in the winter, pressure and pulse."

Matilda ran out of the hut, leaving William alone with his tormenter. William wasn't entirely sure what to do but he diligently watched over the man, willing him to stay alive. William's hands shook uncontrollably but he refused to take his eyes off the injured miner.

Matilda eventually returned and relieved William of his terrifying watch.

"That'll do Will, I'll take it from here."

William gladly stepped aside and let Matilda perform a quick check of her patient before she knelt down and started to clean Roger's grimy face.

"How were Gregory's legs?" William asked.

"Shattered," Matilda said with concern. "There's a chance they'll heal but they'll never be straight again. I'm afraid he'll be crippled for the rest of his life. We may even need to amputate but he'll live. I'm not so sure about this one."

She gestured to Roger.

"He's tough," William conceded. "A real arse but I'm sure he'll make it. And Edric..?"

Matilda stopped mopping Roger's brow.

"I'm so sorry Will. Edric didn't make it…"

William's blood froze.

"He was gone before he reached the surface. The other labourer died too. I asked poor Astrid to take over when Roger reached the surface but she was well out of her depth. I fear I've caused her great trauma today."

Matilda paused and looked up at William, her eyes full of compassion and concern.

"He died doing what he loved," she said. "A man in his mine, not a drunk in the mud. You've done so well William. Helping him get back on his feet. Keeping him motivated. Organising this rescue all by yourself and leading from the front." She paused. "I really don't know what to say. I'm so proud."

William gave her a weak smile. Despite everything, the sincerity of Matilda's praise meant a lot.

"Go home and get some rest," she continued. "God knows you deserve it. I'll stay here with Roger. He looks stable but I doubt he'd survive the journey to Holford. There's no way in hell I'm letting another soul slip away. Not today."

William didn't need to be told again and fled the cabin. A crowd had assembled outside. They'd wrapped the bodies and loaded them onto stretchers. William huffed impatiently for them to move but it was only after a nod from Matthew that he realised they were waiting for his directions.

"Ah, alright then. Back to Holford."

William led the mournful procession back to the village, all the way to the parish church. He was glad someone had run ahead and warned Father Daniel, meaning he only needed to give a cursory explanation before the crowd dissipated and William could finally return home.

Ma, Pa and Elizabeth's faces were etched with concern but they didn't press him to talk. Still fully clothed and covered in dust, William dropped to his bed without a word. His arms ached but consciousness left him almost immediately.

He slept like a rock.

CHAPTER THIRTY-THREE
5 August 1124

After months of travelling, the Miller family finally abandoned their delusions of reclaiming their previous life. They settled in the large town of Taunton, where Arnold hoped the sheer number of people would mask his history. He took a labouring job at one of the town's three mills, which provided at least meagre food for his family.

They received permission to occupy an abandoned hovel on the outskirts of the town. The floor was littered with droppings from its previous animal inhabitants and large chunks were missing from the walls but it provided *most* of a roof over the family's head. The hovel was much cruder than Ma and Pa's cottage but it wasn't too large an adjustment for Margery. For the Millers, it was hell.

Joan struggled most with adjusting to her new lifestyle. She constantly complained about the smells and her routine tantrums continued even as their new life solidified. Not a day went by that she didn't remind everyone that she missed her mirror.

Her mother also partook in the whining. Edith regularly complained of boredom but did little to help herself. She refused to interact with the townsfolk – fearing it would reinforce her family's new position in the world – and instead hid away indoors. She only left for Sunday Mass and even then returned home as soon as possible.

Edith's confinement ate away at her. Mind and body. She seemed feebler with each journey and started to remind Margery of Mama.

The Millers now viewed Margery with open hostility, despite her continuing to shoulder all of the chores required to keep the house functioning. Edith enjoyed watching as Margery slaved away, criticising her technique or choice of ingredients but never helping. Margery had always done something wrong and Edith told anyone who would listen that she could've done better.

"You're chopping it too small!" Edith snapped as Margery prepared a scrawny rabbit for the evening's stew. "You'll ruin it. We won't be able to taste a thing and you know we won't get meat again until next week."

Margery sighed and adjusted her chopping. It was easier that way, giving in. She let the little woman have her little wins and kept her head down. After all, she was fighting a bigger fight.

It wasn't long after Margery's evening discussion with the deaf priest that she'd resolved that her days with the Millers were numbered. Speaking her concerns aloud had been liberating and the mere act of vocalising them solidified thoughts that had rattled around Margery's brain for weeks.

Replaying her interaction with the Elderly Priest always brought a smile to her face. A part of her felt uneasy about the encounter but her memory was fuzzy and she couldn't pinpoint the exact cause. Margery instead savoured the conviction the discussion had provided which always flooded her with a calm sense of purpose.

Her feelings of guilt had also evaporated since the conversation. She no longer blamed herself for the Millers being driven from Holford. Merely setting foot within their hovel revealed the true reason. It was a spiteful place, full of negativity and, ever so slowly, regret. Although Margery was often the target of the family's displeasure, they were also prone to turning upon each other. Even Henry treated her poorly and the former friends barely spoke. Margery realised that the Millers' terrible personalities were the real cause of their problems. Holford had been right to expel such toxicity from their community and now Margery planned to be rid of them too.

Having travelled with the Millers for so long, she knew the hazards of the road and just how dangerous it would be to go alone. But it needed to be done, like lancing a boil. Margery prepared by pinching the odd coin from the family whenever shopping at Taunton's market, telling Edith that prices had been higher than expected. Margery surprisingly felt no guilt at the theft. It wasn't hard to argue that she deserved payment for enduring the Millers' wretched behaviour.

Margery still didn't know how to escape the world she'd so foolishly created for herself but she left the hovel as often as possible and analysed every situation in search of the ideal escape. Washing the Millers' clothes. Shopping at the market. Attending Mass at the church. Each offered opportunities to escape, though none presented a sure enough option to justify the risk. And so she always ended back at the hovel. Washing and cleaning and cooking.

Margery finished chopping the chunks of rabbit and slid them into the boiling pot over the fire before starting on the vegetables.

"Not the onion, save that for tomorrow," Edith barked. "And carrot tops are garbage, not food."

Arnold walked in, covered in dust from his morning's work at the mill. He sat heavily on the bench that Margery had just wiped down.

"Why's supper not ready? I'm starving!"

Margery trembled with pent up anger at his entitlement. She reached around him to scrape the carrots into the stew but knocked the pot's flimsy handle, causing it to drop and spill the contents into the fire.

"Oi!" Arnold bellowed.

"You stupid cow!" Edith wailed. "Why'd you do that!?"

"Sorry!" Margery cried as she tried to salvage as much as possible. Only half remained in the pot. "I've saved most of it. See?"

"You dolt," Edith cried hysterically. "You've wasted our rabbit! Just after I said it was precious, you did that deliberately. No, we'll take the pot. You eat whatever you can salvage from the flames."

Margery stood dumbfounded as Edith's words washed across her. Jean giggled and Henry looked away. She snapped.

"You're not serious!?" Margery cried. "Why would I do that deliberately after slaving away for you!? You expect me to eat ash!?"

The Millers all looked at quiet-spoken Margery in shock.

"Now you listen here," Arnold told Margery, grabbing her tightly by the wrist. "Don't you ever speak to my wife like that again. You're lucky to have a roof over your head so be grateful you get any food whatsoever!"

Margery ripped her hand free using one of Matilda's self-defence tricks and shocked the former Miller by continuing her attack.

"You call this a roof? You can't even provide for your family, you impotent old man."

Arnold's face was frozen in fury but Margery pushed the big man hard in the stomach and fled from the hovel before the adults could compose themselves.

Not knowing where to go, Margery ran to the town square and hoped to get lost in the crowd. Taunton was much bigger than

Holford, even bigger than Stowey. It still amazed her to see so many people in one place. Every day was like Rachel's wedding.

Margery walked amongst the crowd until her heart stopped racing and she was sure that she hadn't been followed. Her stomach rumbled and she cursed her foolishness under her breath. She definitely wasn't getting any of the rabbit.

Deciding to give the hovel time to cool, Margery retreated to her favourite place in Taunton. The tavern reminded Margery of Holford's brewery, with its long tables and walls lined with barrels. In a town as big as Taunton, the tavern was always busy and there was a constant stream of people coming in for a meal and a drink or three.

Unlike Holford, Taunton's tavern could afford to hire permanent staff, paying decent coin in exchange for pouring drinks and waiting tables. Margery had proposed working there to bring in some extra money but Arnold and Edith had forbidden the idea, telling her it was an evil place that would corrupt her soul. That only encouraged Margery and she visited whenever she could.

Margery stepped into the tavern and was greeted by the familiar attack on her senses. The noisy patrons, the smell of stale ale, the heat of a fire that roared year-round.

It was quieter than normal and Margery ordered a mug of mead from a familiar serving girl before taking her favourite seat in a distant corner, out of the way but with a great view of the room and its constant flow of patrons. Margery sipped her drink and watched people pass by. She recognised regulars scattered around the room but a party of four unknown adolescents eventually claimed a nearby table.

They were around Margery's age, give or take a year, which was a surprise as the younger crowd rarely had money and usually only arrived as night set in. Unlike Edith, Margery had made a point to know the townsfolk, particularly those around her own age. Anyone that might aid her escape from the miserable Miller family. Yet these folk were unfamiliar. Intrigued, Margery tried to eavesdrop.

"…it's surely more than two days? Three at least," a brunette girl said.

"Yes but they'll already be on our tail," the older boy said.

"Baron Hugo already snatched Paul," a younger girl interjected.

"Exactly!" the older boy exclaimed. "He doesn't want his serfs running away to work another lord's land. But they don't know where we're heading. Taunton was a fair bet, it's one of the larger towns. But where we go from here, they'll have to guess. Down to Exeter? Up to Bridgwater perhaps? But surely they wouldn't guess Nether Stowey."

Margery almost dropped her mug when she heard the familiar town.

"Shh," urged the smaller boy. "Quietly..."

"What I'm trying to say," the older boy whispered, "is it'll be harder for them to track us if we stick to the forest. It'll take a bit longer but then we can muddle our way in slower time."

"And what about bandits?" the younger boy asked him matter-of-factly.

"I'd rather risk the possible chance of bandits than the guaranteed threat of Baron Hugo. "

"Is this even worth it Guy?" the older brunette asked. "Risking all this just for a *chance* of better work? Based on nothing but the word of a tinker?"

"You saw his knife, didn't you? Not a speck of rust. Granted, it's not much to go off. But surely you don't fancy the life of our parents, slaving away for a Baron who raises taxes each year on a whim. I don't. The tinker said there's work in a copper mine. We've only just arrived and have already learned it's near a village that evicted its miller and that there's a mysterious red-headed foreigner involved. It's the talk of the town!"

Guy's mention of Matilda was all Margery could take. Emboldened by her mead and the confrontation with Edith, she moved towards their table and interrupted their conversation.

"Excuse me," she said timidly. The group stared up at her. The younger boy looked terrified at being interrupted but the older two just looked annoyed.

"What do you want?" Guy grunted.

"I couldn't help but overhear. The town with the redhaired woman? It's Holford, not Nether Stowey."

The younger boy was practically fell off his chair but Guy looked at Margery sceptically.

"How would you know that?"

"I'm from there, originally. I'm living here with their old miller and his family but my little brother was the one who first invited the Foreigner to Holford. Her name's Matilda by the way."

Realisation that she was telling the truth dawned on the group's faces. The younger boy's mouth hung open.

"I could take you there if you want," Margery offered casually, feeling a little more confident. She gestured to the older girl. "She's right, it'd only take a day if you really pushed and I can show you a way through the forest."

Guy weighed her offer.

"Why the sudden desire to go back?" he asked. "Why are you even here in the first place?"

Margery felt her face flush with embarrassment.

"Leaving with the Millers was a hasty decision. A big mistake. Life hasn't been pleasant since I joined them but it sounds like things are much better in Holford. I miss my home. And my family."

Guy still looked unsure.

"I could introduce you to her," Margery added hastily. "To Matilda. My brother and her were close friends. She lived at our house. She could help you get work."

"Ok," Guy said after a pause, "but we leave today. I won't risk being captured by Hugo, not when we're so close. We can camp in the woods this evening and make our way to…Holford in the morning. That fine with you?" he asked with a serious stare.

Margery breathed a sigh of relief and didn't need to think twice. Within a heartbeat she promised herself never to set foot in the Miller's hovel ever again.

"Let's go!"

"You're not going to collect your things?" the younger boy asked.

"There's nothing for me back there but misery and scolding. Best we just leave now. I know a cave where we can set up camp before night falls."

The older girl insisted that the group at least finish their drinks before leaving so Margery used the time to get acquainted. Guy was the oldest male and as such, the group's default leader. The older girl was Gemma. She was slightly older than Guy and the younger boy Adam was her younger brother. The quiet girl was Guy's little sister Anabel.

Although the others quickly warmed to Margery, Gemma remained wary and watched the newcomer closely. The rest of the group happily shared what they'd heard about Holford – most of it fanciful – and Margery told them more about Matilda's arrival in return. They spewed a flood of questions and their collective excitement continued to grow well after their drinks were gone. Adam squeaked with excitement when Margery shared that Matilda had taught her how to read.

Margery was beginning to revel in being among friendly and energetic people, so different to the Millers, when the tavern door burst open. Her stomach dropped to the floor.

Arnold.

Without a word, she slid under the table and crawled behind her new companions' feet until she was wedged against the wall.

"What you doing down there?" Anabel asked excitedly.

"That's the Miller!" Margery whispered, gesturing wildly at the door.

Gemma kicked Anabel and resumed their conversation, pretending Margery wasn't there. Margery looked past Adam's feet and saw Arnold's boots marching around the room. The friendly serving girl's skirt moved to intercept him.

"Can I get you a drink sir?" she asked.

"No," Arnold responded gruffly.

"Would you like anything else?"

Arnold stopped scanning the room and looked down at her angrily. "I'm looking for my…daughter. I know she comes here, when she's trying to hide. Blonde, about your age. Have you seen her?"

"No sir, I haven't. I'll keep an eye out."

Arnold gave the serving girl a dismissive huff and took a final glance around the room before striding outside without another word.

"That was close," Margery said with a giggle as she clambered out from under the table. "Thanks for that," she said as the server cleared their mugs.

"No problem at all," she said with a wink. "It happens more often than you'd think and us girls have to stick together. You'd better get going, in case he comes back. But remember this if I ever come looking for a mining job!"

Margery promised she would. They quickly paid and darted out of the tavern.

Margery's new friends had left their own meagre possessions behind a large rock on the outskirts of the town. They collected their things before cutting across fields towards the Quantock mountains in the distance.

Margery felt freer than she had in years, running alongside newfound friends. Towards her family and home.

She didn't look back.

CHAPTER THIRTY-FOUR

5 September 1124

After months of preparation, Matilda's quest to generate electricity was almost complete. She returned from Matthew's forge laden with spools of copper wire and a small package wrapped in Ma's rapidly dwindling paper. While the package made Matilda crave fish and chips, it actually contained a most precious and delicate cargo.

She passed a gaggle of women carrying bolts of cloth dyed in vibrant purple and red, Ma's newest colours. Matilda juggled her awkward load to wave but received a split of smiles and scowls. The mood in Holford remained sombre in the weeks following the mine collapse and the village was divided. Some praised Matilda and William's rescue efforts while others blamed her for the incident occurring in the first place. A loud few, led by the Brewers, had even called for her expulsion.

The critical reaction particularly hurt because Matilda agreed. She could've paid more attention to the mine, if she hadn't been distracted juggling Holford's many other projects.

She'd had plenty of time to ponder potential alternate timelines during the week that she tended to William's tormenter in Edric's cabin.

Yet even then she failed, so intent on seeing Roger live that she had delayed returning to Holford. By the time she arrived, the man with shattered legs was in a bad way. There was no winning. Matilda was forced to amputate one of Gregory's gangrenous legs and the other was unlikely to ever fully heal.

A solar eclipse on the day of the operation had done little to enhance Matilda's standing with the village. Matilda cursed herself for losing the other half of her Book, which contained several decades worth of upcoming celestial events.

When half of the sun disappeared in the mid-morning, as though devoured by some dark demon, neighbours saw it as a sign from God that the amputation should not go ahead. It was only when Matilda emphasised to Gregory that he would otherwise certainly die a painful death that he reluctantly agreed to the procedure.

A big crowd had gathered for the amputation. Most came for the gory spectacle though Astrid led a small group who were determined to learn from the ordeal. Astrid hated herself for buckling under pressure at the mine and had doggedly done everything in her power to improve her craft, going so far as to personally lead a group in dissecting animals to better understand the body.

Matilda's patient had glared at her with unbridled hatred as she prepared his leg, maintaining eye contact throughout the procedure until he eventually passed out from the pain. The surgery went surprisingly well, given the unsanitary conditions, but Gregory's hatred still smouldered when he eventually woke. Not even Matilda's promise to make him a wheelchair softened his mood.

Margery's return was the only thing to cut through the lingering gloom. Holford still buzzed about the heart-wrenching reunion, when Margery casually strolled back into the village and Ma screeched through the streets with uninhibited delight as she sought her prodigal daughter.

Margery was appalled to have missed so much in the six months that she was away and told Matilda that Holford was almost unrecognisable. From a vantage point overlooking the Holford valley, Margery marvelled at the warren of stone-lined drains and the raised water-tanks which fed the flushing toilets installed at every other house. She lamented the loss of thatched roofs and noted the constant traffic entering from nearby villages. Most of all, she was scandalised that so many had overtaken her ability to read and threw herself into past editions of the village newspaper that Father Daniel had churned out with his printing press. Matilda soon had yet another follower vying for her time.

Margery's new friends were another bonus and a welcome addition to the village. Each was passionate and pragmatic, eager to assist and grateful for every opportunity. Margery took them under her wing and they moved into one of Walt's recently constructed workers' huts. Funded by voluntary contributions from Holford's collective economic exploits, each hut contained a pair of bunk beds which gave Matilda flashbacks to her dorm at the Institute. She apologised for the basic furnishings but the four youngsters gushed thanks as though she had bequeathed the Tower of London.

Matilda passed Walt's organised grid of huts as she left Holford, their fresh unweathered timber contrasting with the forested landscape. Walt's apprentices now coordinated themselves and, using an assembly line, each new building went up quicker than the last. Almost quick enough to keep up with Holford's new arrivals.

Matilda was surprised at the scarcity of interruptions as she returned to her mill. One silver-lining of the mining accident was that Holford had marched on without Matilda's guiding hand. Council meetings continued and projects progressed while she tended to Roger. There had been some mistakes and she would've done some things differently but it was reassuring that Holford had continued to grow without her. Thoughts of resuming her mission to London were no longer tinged with guilt.

Matilda's arms burned when the mill finally came into view and she rushed towards the millhouse. Labourers in the surrounding buildings were packing up for the day, oblivious to the magic Matilda and William planned to unleash that evening. The setting sun reflected off Timothy's newly installed glass windows and the mill's giant new waterwheel continued its tireless rotation. The new wheel was much more efficient than the tiny original design. It already drove both Walt's sawmill and Matthew's bellows but that evening Matilda would connect the most impressive project yet. A true glimpse of the future.

"You took your time!" William called as Matilda lay down her cargo. He was seated beside the millhouse hearth, coiling endless loops of copper wire. He lay down his spool of wire with a thud and walked over as Matilda unwrapped her precious bundle to reveal hundreds of jet-black loops.

"That's Elizabeth's bamboo?" William asked. "Looks more like your hair after the mill burnt down."

"Not far off," Matilda agreed, the fire still painfully fresh in her mind. "They're called filaments. Matthew roasted them in his furnace for days. Each should provide as much light as a candle, maybe more."

William tried to inspect one but the graphite disintegrated at his touch.

"They're very fragile," Matilda warned. "The tungsten in my satchel would've been better but the Bishop stole that. Let's finish putting this thing together and test it out."

The pair resumed their coil winding, working through sunset and then by the firelight. The last of the labourers left the yard and closed off the mill pond, stilling the waterwheel and its attached machinery.

The room was eerily quiet at night without the rattling of the waterwheel, the scrape of the grinding stone and the rasp of the sawmill.

The pair worked on in determined silence. William finished first.

"Done!" Matilda cried with a final flourish. "Let's see if it worked."

William helped her fix the rudimentary generator onto the mill's main shaft before running outside to reopen the water channel. Matilda checked that all the lodestones were in places and the wires attached correctly before hollering to William. The waterwheel began to spin but the only hint that the experiment might've worked was a slight smell of burning from the primitive technology.

William ran into the room but gave Matilda a quizzical look.

"Did it work?" he asked. "It seems…underwhelming."

Matilda had to agree and tried to think of something that would convey the true gravity of what she was about to show him. It eventually came to her.

"Take my torch and sit by the hearth," she said as she doused the fire with water, closed the shutters and collected the two copper electrodes. She returned slowly to let the atmosphere build.

"Switch it off," she said, her voice fey.

William did, smothering them in complete darkness.

"Ok. In the Bible, Jesus says you are the light of the world. This invention will make that true. Literally."

Matilda made sure she had a good grip on the wires.

"Other than me," she continued, "you are the only person who knows this secret. Savour this moment, it will be remembered in history for centuries to come."

Matilda's assistant was silent but the darkness was charged with anticipation.

"William, what was God's very first commandment?" Matilda asked in little more than a whisper.

William was puzzled. "Huh? Oh, Genesis? Let there be light?"

At that, Matilda brushed the two wires together, emitting a flash of light that made William whoop with excitement. She moved the wires slowly together and allowed the electricity to arc through the air.

"Unbelievable!" William exclaimed, crying out with each flash of light. "Lightning! You've made lightning! Just like Thor!" He paused. "But where's the thunder?"

Matilda laughed. "There's still work to do before I can claim to be a Norse god but it's a start. A neat trick. But let's try something more practical. Here, have a try while I grab the filaments. Just be careful."

She set off with the torch and William was still cackling with glee when she returned. Matilda sat back and watched, savouring his simple pleasure. She admired how quickly he progressed from aimless playing to experimentation, slowly moving the electrodes closer until he too discovered the point that arcing began.

"That'll do, let's try the real experiment."

William let the wires droop. Matilda cleared the floor of sawdust and debris from the floor before laying down a spare glazed tile. She wouldn't risk another fire.

"You've asked how all this could possibly justify so much work. And the deaths. Well, this lightning is electricity, just like the torch. Anyone might find it an intriguing piece of magic but as you've seen yourself, there's nothing special to it. Anyone can do it. Yes?"

William hung off her every word. He nodded.

"Lightning is fun but we can control the energy to make it more useful. The filaments can become a candle that will last for months but that is just the beginning. You could do all sorts of things. Horseless carts. Speaking to people in London as if they were right here. Creating cold in summer and heat in winter. There's endless possibilities, but first we need to control it. And so, the humble filament."

Taking the uncharged wire from William, Matilda carefully wound around one of the delicate black filaments. She gently placed it back on the tile.

"When I tell you to, touch your wire to this end," she said, showing William how to complete the circuit. Matilda switched off the torch, plunging them back into darkness.

Matilda's heart raced, reminding her of another poorly lit history-defining experiment that started her whole adventure. She held her breath. She'd done the experiment many times before, both at the Institute and at home with her father. The stakes had never been higher.

"Do it now William."

She heard the Boy fumble around but then he stopped. Darkness combined with the weight of expectation to smother her from all sides.

And then she saw it. An orange glow. Faint at first but it flared to full brightness in a heartbeat, momentarily illuminating William's concentrating face and the room around them.

William cried out in surprise and accidentally broke the circuit, plunging them back into darkness.

"No!" he commanded. "I've got it, hold on…"

The light returned, longer this time. Long enough for Matilda to catch William's eye and return his toothy grin. The filament burned out and the room went dark once more. The pair cried out in celebration.

Matilda hurriedly switched on her torch, its light cold and sterile compared to the warmth of the bamboo filament.

"That was bloody amazing!" William exclaimed, each word dripping with awe.

"There's plenty more where that came from," Matilda reassured him with a gesture toward the remaining package of filaments.

She placed another on the tile and William reapplied the electrodes. Matilda switched off the torch but William had already bathed them in a warm orange glow. The current was far from steady and the filament lasted just long enough for Matilda to notice a slight flickering before it once again burst into flames.

"They should last longer than that. Let's try something different."

The pair experimented with the electricity late into the night, eventually achieving sustained success by using one of Timothy's glass flasks to enclose the filament. Most of their filament stockpile remained intact.

William and Matilda sat around their makeshift light globe, basking in its orange glow. William was full of questions and already thinking of the next big development but Matilda brought him back to earth so they could plan their next step.

The reveal.

+++

Over the following week, Matilda and William worked like they were possessed. Matilda spread word of a gathering to celebrate Holford's many achievements. All were invited. She called in favours from across the village and William ran around collecting everything they needed to create a night to remember.

Matilda placed the mill under a shroud of secrecy, entrusting only a select few to help with the preparations. Margery and her friends became custodians of the generator, insulating wires to hang from the warehouse rafters while Matthew created more filaments and a weary Timothy slaved away to produce more glass jars. He apologised for the sloppy work but each handcrafted bulb was a work of art. Walt built large trestle tables that ran the length of the tiled warehouse, blustering with frustration when Matilda denied him entry to set them up.

Gossip and rumourmongering swept through the village. Why had Matilda insisted on hosting the event at dusk? How had she paid for it all? Why, after almost a year of slaving away, were they suddenly being rewarded for their efforts? Holford's more sceptical villagers saw Matilda's party as an attempt to win back good will after the mine debacle. Others just looked forward to a free meal.

The big day finally arrived and guests flooded to the mill. Martin Brewer begrudgingly cracked kegs while Ma coordinated a gaggle of Holford women as they finalised an enormous exotic feast, for the entire ever-expanding village and then some.

Food and drink were flowing by the time Baron Walter and Sir Phillip arrived at dusk. Awaiting sunset, Pa gave the guest of honour a tour of the site before guiding them inside the warehouse at Matilda's signal. Once they were seated beside villagers at one of Walt's tables, Matilda started the formalities from the front of the room.

"Welcome everyone. Thank you all for trekking out from the village this evening. It will be a dark walk home but I promise it will be worth it.

"Tonight is a chance to give thanks for all your hard work, particularly to everyone who helped restore this brilliant building. I haven't seen so many people here since the day it burned down. A dark day, one of many since I arrived in Holford. But it is great to have you here under better circumstances.

"We are joined by Baron Walter…" Matilda paused for the villagers' polite applause, "…who generously approved the mill's renovation. He's becoming a familiar face in the village and will no doubt celebrate Holford's increased productivity.

"On a more personal note, I want to thank the Archer family. You welcomed me into your home as a guest, then extended an invitation for me to become one of your own. We've been through so much together.

"Finally, dear William. You were the first person I met while journeying through these lands and it was you who brought me to Holford. Your thirst for understanding is unquenchable and you've helped shape Holford's fortunes more than anyone."

Matilda raised her goblet to him.

"And because of that, I invite you to reveal the results of your personal project. The real reason we're all here tonight."

At Matilda's signal, Margery and her friends extinguished the torches around the room. There were some disconcerted cries, including a yelp from Walt, but the audience held their breath in anticipation.

There were mutters in the darkened room as William made his way to the light switch by the millhouse door. Matilda's disembodied voice filled the uneasy silence.

"William has worked for months on a project to…further illuminate the village. He has bounced tirelessly between the forge, the carpenter and yes, the mine. Everyone's efforts have contributed to this work, in some way. So William, over to you."

The Boy paused and let the crowd mill uncomfortably in the dark.

"Father Daniel," William eventually called out. "What was the Lord's very first commandment?"

"Ah?" Holford's elderly priest stammered, not expecting to be called upon. "Let there be light?"

William flicked the mill's rudimentary switch, powering the hundred glowing glass spheres that dangled from the rafters above. The room filled with a mix of screams and cries of delight as the crowd was instantly bathed in a warm light. Baron Walter almost fell out of his chair in surprise.

Matilda stared up and judged the bulbs. They were far from optimal designs and would be lucky to last the evening. A couple had already burned out. But the crowd didn't notice. They were mesmerised by the gently pulsating lights and every neck was craned up toward the rafters.

Matilda gave William an encouraging thumbs up and was pleased to see him basking in the audience's awe. He gave her a cheeky smirk and flicked the switch once more, plunging the room back into darkness. There was a collective cry of disappointment.

"Not to worry!" William reassured. "It's easy to put back on! Who else wants to try?"

He flicked the switch again and the glow resumed. There was a sudden scramble to join William by the door, starting an endless flickering of lights that lasted the rest of the evening.

The Baron barged his way towards William and enthusiastically flicked the lights on and off, singlehandedly destroying at least ten of the weaker bulbs. Satisfied with the invention, he graciously passed the control on to the next villager in line and summoned Matilda.

"I'll be damned. I'd have sworn it was sorcery if I hadn't made it happen with my own hands. I don't know what I did to deserve you Matilda but praise the Lord you stumbled across this little village. First you save my finger, then salvage a ruined mill and now this? I want one, you hear. Back at my castle. You will make it happen?"

"I'm afraid not, my lord. This design requires the mill to work and we've exhausted our entire stock of copper, for now. But with longer summer working days, I can start on a wind-powered design and begin construction for you once we've mined more copper. We may need extra timber as well…"

Baron Walter looked at her incredulously. "Woman, you can have the whole forest for all I care! Everything you touch turns to gold! Get to work, we'll talk again soon."

The Baron and his entourage exited the building, leaving the villagers to revel in the flickering lights. Sir Phillip gave an encouraging wink. With the Baron gone, a weight lifted from Matilda's shoulders and she could finally enjoy the festivities. She gathered some food and sat to watch Holford gather around the switch. Even her most ardent critics were in line.

"A nifty trick," came Timothy's deep voice from behind Matilda, causing her to jump. "I never dreamed I'd see something like it in my lifetime. Truly blessed."

The old man sat down on the bench next to her.

"And to think I've contributed! I wish you'd told me though. The light amplifies all the imperfections in my work! I'm proud Matilda. Amazed and truly proud."

Timothy couldn't know how much his approval meant. The pair sat in companionable silence and savoured the joy in the villagers' faces as they flicked the lights on and off.

"Matilda," Timothy said seriously, breaking their silence. "As grand as it is, one can't help but wonder at the cost. Of all this." He pointed to the far corner of the room where Gregory sat in his wheelchair, deep in discussion with Astrid. "There's several lads that can't enjoy this wonder. Most were new to Holford but I'd known Edric since he was a boy. He would've cherished seeing his precious copper being put to such great use."

Matilda felt a lump rise in her throat.

"What I'm saying," Timothy continued, "is that I'd wager more of them might've lived if all that medical know-how wasn't locked away in your head. Only your head. Astrid did her best, bless her, but Lord knows she could've done more."

Matilda nodded thoughtfully. "You're right, Timothy. I've been so caught up in everything around Holford but it could save lives and needs to be prioritised. I could've taught her more. About the body. And the medicine and tools."

"Tools sounds like something for young Matty Smith and I think Astrid knows her fair share about the medicine by now. But the body... Perhaps that's something I could help with?"

Matilda looked up at the old man, confused.

"Look girl, let's talk straight. We both know my days are numbered. I've had a good life and have seen such wonders, particularly over this past year. You taught me how to make glass!" He gave a booming laugh. "But I think I could do one last bit of good, after I go. Your students might benefit from seeing what a real person looks like inside. Not some pig or goat or chicken."

An awkward silence settled over their conversation.

"That is…very generous," Matilda stumbled. "But what about the afterlife? The resurrection?"

"Ha! Surely you remember our first conversation, the day of the grandmother's funeral? You see the world differently, when you've been around as long as I have, and seen the things I've seen. Once you've asked the scary questions and let them rattle around for a decade or so. I like to think that a merciful God, capable of creating the heavens and Earth, would be capable of stitching me back together. If He's all-knowing, He'll see that it was done for a just cause."

Matilda paused as she considered her dear friend's words.

"Ok Timothy. I graciously accept your offer, but only because you're correct that it will benefit the whole village. You'll get the chance to give one last gift. *When* the time comes. But until then, and may that be many moons from now, have Astrid take a look over you. Just to make sure nothing's amiss."

The old man bowed gratefully and departed without a word, humming jollily to himself as he limped away.

The conversation left Matilda feeling uneasy and the rest of the evening passed by in a blur of congratulations and apologies for past doubts. Matilda continued to feel out of sorts when she woke up the next day. She dreaded the thought of her dear friend's departure. And having to fulfil the morbid promise he'd asked of her.

Matilda spent the following weeks bouncing more slowly around Holford, developing plans for the Baron's windmill and taking time to build upon Astrid's evening medicine classes.

Almost two weeks after their conversation, Timothy Potter died. Matilda was up early changing some bulbs that had blown during the previous evening's anatomy lesson when one of Timothy's apprentices ran into the mill and delivered the news. Matilda dropped everything and sprinted to the old man's house, vaulting over the bucket that still sat by the doorstep. A stained-glass window lay unfinished on his table. Matilda approached the bed and saw that the precious man had passed away in his sleep. His face looked content.

Mentally noting the need to personally carve another headstone, Matilda complied with Timothy's final wish and put out word of another special gathering at the mill the following evening.

A dissection.

CHAPTER THIRTY-FIVE
23 September 1124

John sat amongst his fellow novices in the choir of the Bishop's half-built cathedral. Although still early into his training, he'd already committed all of the songs to memory and the monotonous routine of clergy life made him want to scream. It didn't help that his superiors were all daft, regularly contradicting each other or talking in circles during their lessons.

The remainder of Bath's population stood on the opposite side of the altar in the cathedral's nave. The more fervent parishioners sang along with the clergy but most were engaged in other business. Mass provided a venue where social run-ins were guaranteed, perfect for cornering slimy debtors or jilted lovers.

John longed to be among the crowd and watched them with envy, though his view was increasingly impeded as construction on the cathedral progressed. While being a member of the clergy meant he never needed to worry where his next meal would come from, at least every day in their world was different. Not just an endless repetition of the same boring mass.

The hymn finished and John sat back on his pew. The parishioners remained standing, their dealings uninterrupted but slightly more hushed. Broken by endless beatings, John had learned to conform. Obedience continued to rile the rebellious part of him that remained deep within. It pined for freedom as he peered through the cathedral's incomplete walls and out into the streets of Bath. *No, those thoughts only led to more pain.*

Instead, John tried to focus on the morning sermon, which was delivered by ancient Brother Cuthbert rather than the Bishop. Even Godfrey's assistant was absent, despite scolding the novices only moments before the service began. Their absence piqued John's interest. Something different. Other priests had also noticed and highlighted the irregularity using their subtle system of coughs and shuffles in the pews.

The priests' restlessness reached its barely audible fever pitch when they spotted Godfrey's assistant striding down the side of the cathedral towards the choir. Peter ignored the sermon and rudely strode straight past the altar. Even the parish noticed something strange about that.

John was still pondering the possible reason for Peter's unorthodox interruption when the Assistant strode directly to John's pew and quickly sat beside him. Peter had the decency to allow the crowd to refocus on the sermon before talking to John in a hushed voice.

"His Excellency requires you in his chambers. Now."

John was surprised. Godfrey had unceremoniously dismissed him months ago, without a word of explanation. "But, the mass?" was all John managed.

"Godfrey's chambers," Peter repeated firmly. "Right now."

He stood abruptly and waited by the end of the pew. John dragged himself up, already missing the boring monotony of moments before. He felt the eyes of the entire congregation upon him as he followed Peter towards the cathedral's incomplete entrance. Even the businesspeople and socialites paused as John passed.

John's stomach churned as he wondered why he had been summoned so urgently. Would he be punished? He wracked his brain trying to think what he might've done. He shot questions at the Assistant as soon as they emerged from the skeletal cathedral.

"What does Godfrey want? Did I do something wrong? I've done everything asked of me, I swear. Is it about the Book?"

Peter ignored him and marched towards the Bishop's palace, though John's final question caused him to break stride.

So it was something to do with the Book. That was a start.

The pair rounded the final corner to the Bishop's palace and John was surprised to see a small herd of horses gathered out front. An army of attendants were saddling them while another exchanged a peasant's shabby pony for a fresh mount. The beast had been ridden hard.

Peter and John were climbing the steps when Godfrey emerged. He beamed upon seeing John.

"John my boy!" the Bishop cried out excitedly, bundling John into a tight embrace as though they were dear friends. "We've found her!"

John was dumbfounded by the Bishop's sudden camaraderie.

"The girl," Godfrey continued. "Matilda. The author of our Book! She lives!"

"I've sent riders ahead of us to organise a raiding party," Peter said. "They'll be waiting when we arrive."

The horses suddenly made a lot more sense.

Godfrey thanked Peter and led John to a horse near the ragged peasant.

"As you can see, we're going to catch her before she can disappear again. And more importantly, before she desecrates the corpse of a fellow Christian."

John was only further puzzled but Godfrey introduced the peasant.

"John, this is Warren. He hails from just outside Bath but has been reporting on Matilda's activities for some months now. He saw the earth swallow his fellow workers as they strove to meet Matilda's unquenchable thirst for metal. Like me, he witnessed the woman's barbaric attempts at *medicine*."

Godfrey's spy nodded eagerly, "Chopped 'em right up, she did. To be fair, a couple survived but ovvers weren't so lucky."

"Bah, disgusting!" Godfrey spat. "Warren tells me that she is now teaching her barbarism to others, by carving up her deceased neighbour no less. Sacrilege! I won't stand for it, she must be stopped! And you're coming with us."

John blanched but stood rooted in place.

"Me, Your Excellence? Why me?"

Godfrey looked at John impatiently.

"I considered Adelard but I don't trust the self-righteous monk. Warren here has also reported all manner of bizarre developments in the village, some nothing short of magic." Godfrey dropped his voice "The sort of thing only found in a very rare Book. You will identify any useful knowledge or equipment that might reinvigorate our own investigations. I'll be busy securing the woman so I want a complete update when we return. Go on then, up you get."

Godfrey shepherded John onto a horse before vaulting atop his own. John was still trying to find a comfortable position in the saddle when they set off at a quick pace. Godfrey and Peter rode ahead with the Spy while John rode behind, flanked by a pair of Godfrey's guards.

The Bishop continued to interrogate the Spy as they rode. They made an incredibly odd pair, the Spy wearing his ragged travel-stained cloak and talking coarsely while the Bishop rode a fine steed and wore the magnificent robes of his Office.

They travelled hard throughout the day and reached a secluded camp in the woods at sunset. Peter's contact waited for them with a dozen mercenaries gathered around a wagon, all armed with spears and clubs. Peter greeted them with a pouch of coins and the group quickly planned their raid. The Spy told them of Matilda's hideout, a ruined mill she'd rebuilt after a deliberate fire. He told them of the villagers, estimating how many would attend the dissection and which were likely to resist the Bishop's ambush.

With a plan agreed, the party set off into the twilight on foot. They left Peter and two of the mercenaries behind to guard the horses and the wagon. Godfrey ordered them to be ready for a quick escape.

The Spy looped them around the village, eager to avoid any prior warning of the impending raid. They completed the last of their journey by moonlight, traipsing through the forested hills that surrounded the woman's mill. The group stumbled through the undergrowth before coming to a stop at the clearing surrounding the mill.

It was much grander than Godfrey's spy had described. John had imagined a fire-damaged building with some patchy repairs but instead, the mill looked practically new. Even in the moonlight John saw new tiles mounted on the roof and fresh plaster applied to the building's exterior. The smell of sawdust filled the air and the echo of water rushing over the waterwheel filled the clearing.

But most shocking of all was the light. Night had long since fallen but sunlight streamed from the building's windows, bathing the entire clearing in an otherworldly glow. It had the same warmth as sunlight but its unsettling pulse suggested something supernatural. The men whispered amongst themselves, unsettled by the unnatural sight.

The Bishop took in the spectacle before signalling for the group to advance towards the building. As they drew closer, John marvelled at the wealth displayed by the building and its surroundings. Each glass window had external shutters and heavy curtains hung inside. The party passed through the perfectly manicured garden that surrounded the building, carelessly trampling over strange-smelling herbs. The group divided to stand on either side of the building's tall glazed windows.

The first mercenary to peer inside let out a sound of disgust, earning sharp rebukes from his companions. The reason became clear as they each reached their window.

John threw himself against the wall and peered into the room. His eyes were first drawn up to the ceiling where a multitude of glowing spheres radiated warm light down upon the unfazed crowd. John's jaw dropped in disbelief.

Villagers were crowded in the hall, seated on long wooden benches that made the gathering look like a church service. Many wrote in paper notebooks, each worth a small fortune back at the seminary. John was amazed that so many people could write but also saw some sketching surprisingly lifelike forms.

It was as his gaze shifted to the front of the room that John's blood ran cold. A woman stood before the crowd on a raised platform, her vibrant red hair tied back into a bushy ponytail. She stood at a long table, upon which lay the naked body of an elderly man. As if that wasn't perverse enough, the man had been sliced open from throat to stomach and the red-haired woman had her entire arm inside the poor man's chest.

John watched the scene for several heartbeats before throwing up violently at his feet. He leaned against the wall, hands shaking. Some of the mercenaries had similarly visceral reactions but the Bishop was unfazed as he stared into the room, barely blinking as he took in the woman's every movement.

Godfrey stood transfixed until one of the men gave a muffled cough that jerked the Bishop back to the present.

"Ok men," he called out in a whisper. "We're too late to prevent this abomination but let's end this heresy before her corruption can spread any further. Break in at my signal."

The mercenaries gathered and lit the torches they'd carried from the wagon. It was too bright inside for the villagers to notice. Godfrey ordered four men to the windows on either side of the building and led the rest to the entrance at the far end of the hall. John and the Spy cautiously followed.

Godfrey paused at the door to give the men time to loop around the building and then tested to see that it was open. He took a deep breath.

With a sudden burst of energy he threw the doors open and marched into the hall with his chest thrust out.

"Stop!" Godfrey cried. "Cease this heresy immediately!"

The crowds' heads whipped around and the woman stopped what she was doing, entrails still in her hand.

"This is the work of Satan," Godfrey boomed. "How dare you desecrate the body of your fellow man? By the power of the Church, I order you to stop!"

At the sound of the Bishop's voice, the mercenaries started to break the glass windows and tossed their burning torches into the heavy curtains before leaping in themselves.

The reaction from the crowd was instant. Seeing the armed men breaking into the mill, they leapt from their seats and fled, streaming past the corpse and out the one remaining door.

"You escaped me once, hag," the Bishop called as he casually strolled towards the front of the room. "But not this time."

"Bishop Godfrey!? No!" the Redhead cried out in horror as she recognised Godfrey and placed down the entrails.

"Yes!" he cried greedily. "Seize her!"

His men swept forward, driving the straggling villagers out of the room. The room filled with smoke as the curtains caught alight but a handful of villagers gathered around the woman and prepared to fight back with improvised weapons.

The mercenaries leapt into action, working together to beat back their poorly armed opposition. John marvelled at the villagers' tenacity. Despite being outnumbered and outmatched, they fought like demons to protect the Redhead. John saw a large man go down as a spear pierced his leg. Another fled clutching a gash in his arm while a boy, about John's age, went down as a spear shaft glanced off his head.

"Stop!" the woman screamed.

Such was the power of her voice that everyone in the room obeyed, some of them in mid-swing. Even Godfrey stopped in his tracks.

"I yield. No more death. End this madness."

The villagers reluctantly backed away and the mercenaries advanced on the woman. Godfrey marched toward her, his eyes blazing with victory.

"There will be no more of your filth," he gloated. "Take her away!"

One of the mercenaries struck the woman over the head with his spear and she collapsed to the floor. Another man crouched over her limp body and bound her before tossing her over his shoulder. The Bishop's party rushed from the burning building without a backward glance.

Outside, villagers milled around unsure what to do. Several aided injured fighters while others were already coordinating efforts to extinguish the fires. None dared to approach the raiding party who ignored them altogether and followed the Spy straight through the village, no longer bothering with stealth.

As the party disappeared into the darkness, John realised with a bolt of dread that he'd forgotten to collect any artefacts of interest in the excitement of the ambush. He cringed at the thought of Godfrey's reaction when he found out but feared that the unconscious woman's fate would be even worse.

CHAPTER THIRTY-SIX
23 September 1124

William woke to screams and smoke. Someone was shaking him.

"Get up boy, the mill's on fire! They took Matilda!"

The last statement cut through his grogginess and Walt helped him to his feet. His head pounded and his vision was blurred but he staggered out from the burning building. The Carpenter urged him to help put out the fire but William knew others would take care of that. Someone needed to help Matilda.

William pushed past the tide of people rushing inside to fight the fire and broke out into the courtyard. The cool evening air helped clear his head and the yard came into focus. Elizabeth crouched by the millhouse, tending to a nasty gash in Matthew's leg.

"Matthew!" William cried. "You alright?"

"The Bishop's men got him pretty bad," Elizabeth reported as Matthew bellowed obscenities.

"Where'd they go?" William asked urgently. "They had Matilda?"

"They ran towards Holford. Nobody stopped them, they were too well armed. One of the bigger men had Matilda slung over his shoulder."

"Shit." William paused for a moment and then sprinted away. "I'll try to keep up with them. Send help, I'll leave a trail."

"But Will," Elizabeth protested. "Your head's bleeding!"

"Never mind," he called over his shoulder. "Get word to the Baron!"

William raced back to Holford, an unexpected energy pumping through his veins. Small clusters of people were gathered in the village square discussing the ambush.

"William!" Father Daniel called out. "They've got Matilda."

"That's justice for you," Martin Brewer sneered.

"Which way?" William asked, ignoring Martin.

"East. About ten of them, maybe more. I'd say they're headed to Stowey or Bridgwater. Moving pretty quick. Boy, your head's bleeding."

"Thanks Father," William cried back. "I'll be fine. Tell someone to send help!"

He raced out of the village and into the fields which were illuminated by an almost full moon. The vast emptiness emphasised that he was alone, chasing a group of armed men. He was hit by a wave a doubt but stubbornly pushed on.

The shadow of the distant mine teased potential reinforcements, though the miners had little love for William and Matilda since the accident. Not sure what else to do, he used stones to craft a crude arrow in the middle of the road before continuing his run.

Unsure how far ahead the Bishop might be, William climbed a hill for a better vantage point and scoured the landscape. The moonlit fields aided his search and he eventually spotted a shadowy mass moving in the distance. He was relieved that they travelled at a reasonably gentle pace, slowed by a few stragglers and their precious cargo. William's chest burned from the run and his head pounded but spotting the group gave him another burst of energy and he resumed his pursuit.

Concerned that he might be seen, William kept the group just in sight while trailing them for miles through the fields. The Bishop skirted around the edges of Stowey town and headed towards a small thicket of trees.

The silhouette of Stowey castle stood tantalisingly close. William wracked his brain for a way to signal the Baron for help but the Bishop's men disappeared within the thicket, forcing William to resume his chase. He crafted another arrow in the middle of the path using some fallen sticks and prayed that the Baron might find it.

William entered the thicket, thankful for the cover of the trees. He recalled his childish games of ambush with Ralph as he darted from tree to tree, using the dense foliage as cover as he searched for the raiders.

Loud celebrations betrayed their position and William soon spotted the light of a campfire. He snuck towards it and peeked through the undergrowth. The raiders were gathered around a fire, gnawing on tough trail bread and recounting their exploits while the Bishop angrily interrogated a younger priest. William gasped when he spotted Warren's familiar face among them. *Traitor*!

William was surprised at how established the camp was. A tent had been erected for the Bishop and a handful of horses were unsaddled and tethered beside a large wagon, revealing the raiders intention to stay put. Weapons were propped against the wagon and inside lay a lumpy form with a mass of matted red hair. William's stomach flipped.

He held his breath as he watched Matilda, willing her to show any sign of life. It was an eternity before she finally began to stir. Unable to move with her hands and legs bound behind her, she threw up and was forced to rest her head near the pile of vomit. William felt indignant on her behalf but was relieved that she was alive.

William longed to free Matilda but the situation looked dire. He was vastly outnumbered and Matilda lay in full sight of the Bishop's men, preventing William from sneaking up to check on her.

The Bishop eventually noticed that Matilda was conscious and ordered a thug to drag her to the fire. She didn't resist but looked shaky on her feet.

"It's late," the Bishop said with a yawn, "but I really must know. The lights? Can you do it here? Now?"

Matilda met his gaze but didn't speak.

"Answer me woman."

Matilda remained silent. Defiant.

"Answer me!"

When Matilda showed no sign of moving, the Bishop gestured to his brute. And then the fire.

Matilda started to resist but the man grabbed her with ease and dragged her hand above the coals.

"Tell me," the Bishop commanded.

Matilda struggled to escape but her lips remained sealed.

The Bishop nodded and his brute lowered her hand. Matilda's cry echoed through the trees. William wanted to rush in and help but a rational part of his mind forced him to refrain.

"Stop!" the Bishop finally yelled. "Anything to say now?"

Matilda stared up at him defiantly, though she let out an involuntary whimper.

"Very well then," Godfrey replied with disappointment. "That will do. I'll have the time and tools to do this properly back in Bath. Until then…" he taunted as he retired to his tent.

His men returned Matilda to the wagon and posted a pair of sentries before curling up beside the fire. When everyone else was asleep, the Bishop's younger priest visited Matilda to offer food, bathe her hand and clear away her vomit. William hated the Young Priest for his association with the loathsome raiders but was at least thankful for that.

Unable to devise a workable plan, William prayed again that Elizabeth had found reinforcements. He knew it would be almost impossible for them to find his clumsy signs in the dark and cursed himself for not laying more. He settled in to keep watch and urged himself to stay awake as relentless waves of fatigue rolled over him.

+++

The sun had already risen when William woke and he struggled to recall where he was. His head throbbed and his legs ached. Memories of the previous evening jolted him awake and he pushed himself to his feet, cursing his weakness.

The camp was abandoned. The fire had been doused and wagon tracks led to the east. William didn't know the way to Bath but Bridgwater was the largest town in that direction. The wagon needed to keep to the roads so there was still a chance of finding them. William hastily crafted another arrow with charred wood and set off towards the rising sun.

William's stomach growled as he marched along a rutted road but he pushed on, stopping only to ask farmers if they'd seen the raiders pass by. Each greeted him with bewildered looks but one eventually confirmed that he wasn't far behind.

He picked up his pace and the wagon soon came into view, trundling along at a comfortable pace. William breathed a sigh of relief and eased the intensity of his pursuit, keeping out of sight and watching them from afar.

William's blood boiled as the Bishop intermittently rode back to admire his prize and gloat about her capture. Matilda remained stoic, letting the Bishop's petty words flow over her without getting riled up by the cantankerous old man.

The group skirted around Bridgwater and continued travelling until they happened upon a particularly picturesque clearing as the sun reached its zenith. The raiders kindled another fire beside a babbling brook and prepared a morning meal, showing no concerns of being pursued. William resented both their complacency and being forced to watch as they enjoyed their food. The Young Priest shared his meal with Matilda and William found himself begrudgingly starting to like the man.

Godfrey's men had just started packing up when the sound of galloping horses echoed through the trees. A handful of heavily armoured knights thundered into the clearing on mighty warhorses, Baron Walter leading from the front and a ferocious Sir Phillip at his side. The Bishop's men quailed at the sight of Sir Phillip and William had to consciously refrain from revealing his position with whoops of excitement. The Baron looked resplendent in his shimmering chainmail and brightly coloured tabard. His face was a portrait of rage.

"Godfrey! What is the meaning of this?" the Baron demanded.

The Bishop calmly strolled towards the Baron, hands clasped behind his back. He walked right up to the Baron's horse, showing no sign of being intimidated by the beast's might nor the Baron's collective strength.

"Baron Walter, I am most surprised to see you so far from your castle. Are your men always so heavily equipped for hunting?"

"Don't be coy with me Bishop. Unhand the woman and be on your way."

The raiders held onto Matilda, eager to keep her well within reach.

"Unhand her? I think not. She has been found guilty of heresy and sacrilege. These men can vouch for that, as can many from your own village. She comes with me to face the Lord's justice."

"No," the Baron snarled. "She's mine."

"Walter! I'm not property..." Matilda objected, only to be silenced by the Baron.

"You'll be quiet," Baron Walter snapped, "if you know what's good for you!"

The Bishop also glared at her before continuing his debate with the Baron.

"Regardless of *who* she belongs to, the woman has committed grave crimes and must be punished. Do you truly crave association with a blasphemer and heretic?"

"I don't know what crimes you think she's committed but I've watched her work for months. She's introduced much good to my village. To the entire region. So no, I won't hesitate to be associated with the woman and her works."

The Bishop began to object but the Baron continued.

"And nor will Earl Robert. He's followed my letters about Matilda's work with interest and will no doubt oppose your ill-informed actions. I wrote him last night, as soon as I learned of your attack."

William's ears pricked up. He knew the Baron and Sir Phillip had closely followed Holford's progress but never thought that word would reach as high as the Earl. Matilda looked surprised too.

"The King's bastard?" Godfrey noted with disbelief. "I don't care what your earthly ranks might be, this is a matter for the Church. My men and I will defend that right."

William saw the Bishop's men weigh the strength of Walter's recently-arrived cavalry and eye their spears by the wagon. Their faces paled as the Bishop spoke on their behalf but their hands hung by their knife belts and the Baron's knights shifted in their saddles.

The tense silence shattered as thundering hooves echoed around the clearing once more and another horse burst into view. The horse panted from the hard ride, though the rider carried himself with poise. His livery was even finer than the Baron's.

"Baron Walter. Bishop Godfrey. How…convenient to catch you both in the same place," the rider said diplomatically. "I come bearing word from Earl Robert."

The messenger withdrew a scroll from his bag but looked unsure which noble to give it to. The Bishop reached out for the message but Walter nudged his horse forward and plucked the scroll from the messenger's hand. Still astride his saddle, he unrolled it and read silently to himself.

"Ha!" he exclaimed victoriously. He unceremoniously tossed the scroll to the seething Bishop. Walter gave him a moment to read before announcing its contents to the crowd.

"We've been summoned to the Earl's court in Bristol. Earl Robert acknowledges the right of the Church to punish religious misdemeanours, but also insists that he be appropriately informed of high-profile crimes occurring on his own lands before any punishment is given. What say you Bishop? His Majesty would no doubt agree."

The Bishop shook with silent fury but his body betrayed defeat.

"You are correct," he said through gritted teeth. "You ride ahead and inform your lord to prepare for my audience. I shall see the woman safely to Bristol."

Baron Walter seemed to consider the Bishop's proposal but William couldn't allow that.

"Nooooo!" he interrupted, bursting out of the bushes and startling priests, nobles, horses and raiders alike.

"What is the meaning of this?" the Bishop cried.

"It's the witch woman's apprentice," Warren informed him.

Sir Phillip recognised William instantly and gave an impressed smile.

"William? Elizabeth delivered your message, that Matilda was in trouble. Remarkable for you to still be on the trail!"

William ignored him. "You can't let the Bishop take Matilda! He's been cruel and hasn't fed her. Or tended to her wounds. She'll be lucky to make it to the Earl at all, let alone in a condition for an audience."

"I hope this isn't true Godfrey?" Walter said, finally noticing Matilda's bloody hair and cradled hand. "Playing with your prey like a cat with a fieldmouse? You couldn't hold your barbaric foreign ways in check until judgement was delivered, could you?"

"You're getting what you want Baron, don't anger me further."

"Fine," Walter conceded. "You hold her but we travel directly to Bristol. Together. My men and I will accompany you, every step of the way," he added, looking directly at William as he spoke. He turned to the messenger. "Tell your lord that we're coming. I give my word that we'll make haste."

The messenger wheeled his horse around and galloped from the clearing. William knew that he wouldn't receive any further concessions from the Baron but was pleased with the guaranteed audience with the Earl.

"Well then," the Baron said awkwardly. "No reason to dawdle. Let's get to Bristol and get this farce over with."

Matilda gave William an encouraging smile as the raiders loaded her back into the wagon. They rebound her hands, in front of her this time. Not knowing where he was supposed to go, William glanced around the clearing and vaulted into the back of the wagon.

Sir Phillip barked orders to the knights, establishing an escort and sending a man to inform Stowey of the new travel plans. The Baron settled into the rear of the formation where he could personally keep watch over Matilda.

The wagon lurched forward and they started the long journey to Bristol.

Matilda gripped William with her good hand. "You little champion. You followed me, all this way? What did I do to deserve a friend like you?"

William didn't know what to say so he merely smiled, content with knowing she was safe. Feeling suddenly weary, he lay down among the spears and was asleep in a heartbeat.

CHAPTER THIRTY-SEVEN

24 September 1124

Matilda would've quite enjoyed the day-long journey to Bristol, had it not been for her throbbing hand, pounding head, and general existential dread. She soaked in the views of the medieval countryside, watching peasants work fields that looked pristine and unspoiled. The wagon trundled lazily along dirt roads, some heavily rutted and others little more than animal tracks.

Godfrey was in no rush to reach Bristol and greatly slowed his pace after Baron Walter arrived. The two groups watched each other warily, the Bishop's men knowing they were outmatched and Walter's men not trusting Godfrey with his hostage. Matilda felt odd being the centre of such focused attention but tried to make the most of the strange situation.

Away from Holford's frenetic pace, Matilda could finally reflect on the bigger picture. She judged it had been almost a year since she had bid farewell to her family. Since Harry had died. Matilda hoped they would approve of everything she'd achieved. The mill. The village. The people.

Despite her immediate predicament, Matilda was proud of how she had adapted, no longer married so rigidly to others' plans and able to think on the fly. She would've particularly loved to show her Institute mentors how well her alternate approach had worked.

Although completely different to the original plan, Matilda was confident that her revised approach had sufficiently progressed society. Holford was on the path to increasingly advanced technologies and William could lead their work. Even if she never left Bristol…

Matilda refused to let her mind sink into melancholy and instead allowed the Boy to distract her. His transformation was even greater than Holford's. The impatient youth that stole Harry's knife was long gone, replaced by a measured and intelligent young man. They used their most complex modern English vocabulary to discuss their predicament, enjoying the stupefied looks from Godfrey's minders.

"What stratagem will you employ upon our imminent arrival at the misbegotten's domicile?" William asked, struggling to keep a straight face.

Matilda chuckled but shook her head. "Alas, my cognitive faculties are presently engaged in formulating a satisfactory resolution, rendering me quite uncertain at this juncture."

She also appreciated the quiet company of the Young Priest who also sat within the cart, watching them intently but reluctant to engage. He'd shown kindness after her abduction, a single ray of hope as she lay hogtied in a pool of vomit. Matilda wondered how the compassionate priest could be in league with the Bishop but his companions' animosity towards him suggested that he too wasn't there by choice.

The density of man-made structures ebbed and flowed as the group passed through the countryside but consistently increased as they neared Bristol. The town was much larger than Holford. Its cramped streets were lined with multistorey buildings containing stores dedicated to all manner of unique goods. Matilda found it strange to see so many people in the one place but the putrid smells of stagnant refuse were strangely endearing. Just as she'd always imagined.

She longed to escape the convoy and explore but they were escorted straight to the castle. Townsfolk were stunned to see a bishop and a baron arrive unannounced and they stopped to watch as the strange company passed by. Matilda gawked right back at them with even greater intensity.

Matilda's stomach dropped as the castle came into view, reminding her of the seriousness of their journey. Located beside the River Avon, the party were led across a drawbridge and through the castle gate.

The afternoon sun was low in the sky when the wagon pulled up at the keep. An elderly steward emerged, followed by an army of attendants who quickly collected the party's horses and led them to the stables. Godfrey's men dragged Matilda from the wagon before it too was led away. The steward watched with veiled disapproval but maintained a diplomatic facade.

"Greetings Bishop Godfrey and Baron Walter. My lord has just returned from a hunt. He was expecting your arrival so won't be long. Please make yourselves comfortable inside."

The steward led the unusual party into a large antechamber and made polite small talk before leaving to attend to other matters. Another army of servants arrived bearing chilled water and bread.

The two groups milled around awkwardly, uncomfortable at such close proximity to their opposition. Matilda was stuck in the middle, wondering what fate awaited her behind the hall's heavy oak doors.

Godfrey scowled whenever she caught his eye and she received little more warmth from the Baron. When the bread and water was gone, Walter strolled up to her and spoke in a hushed voice for the first time since her rescue.

"Earl Robert is a serious man. Canny and just, but not known for leniency. Just keep your mouth shut and let me do the talking."

Matilda started to object but was silenced by the Baron's glare.

"Did you really write to the Earl about Holford?" she asked to fill the silence.

"Yes," Walter replied. "But only on the night of your capture. I wasn't about to let anyone steal my golden goose."

Their conversation was interrupted when the elderly steward emerged through the inner hall's main doors.

"The Earl will see you now," he told them simply, before turning and leading the party into the hall.

Godfrey dismissed his mercenaries and entered with a pair of priests in his wake. Walter waved away his knights, permitting only Sir Phillip to enter with him. William made to follow the pair into the hall but Walter irritably shooed him away.

"The Boy comes," Matilda said firmly.

Walter was struck by her boldness but reluctantly conceded when Matilda stood firm. William rushed after the men into the hall. The Bishop followed with Matilda in tow, escorted by a priest on each arm.

The Earl's hall was also just as Matilda had imagined. Tapestries depicting grand battles hung on stone walls, nobles awaited their own audience and spear-wielding guards were stationed around the room. A fire crackled within a large fireplace, filling the hall with a smoky haze.

Earl Robert sat on a throne upon a raised dais at the head of the hall, still dressed for hunting. A woman sat on a smaller seat to his right. *His wife*, Matilda guessed.

Everyone watched with genuine intrigue as the unusual group of petitioners entered the courtroom. The Earl appraised them with an intelligent gaze which gave Matilda hope.

"So *this* is the cause of your quarrel?" he mused as they approached.

"My lord," Walter started with a deep bow. "Thank you for granting this audience at such short notice."

"You made decent time, Baron," the Earl noted. "My riders updated me on your progress. And Bishop Godfrey, we meet again."

The Bishop didn't bow. "We do indeed. You were absent at the Feast of the Assumption."

"I was still returning from Normandy, as you were no doubt aware. But I shall attend your Christmas service as compensation. Please, tell me about this woman."

Intrigued by their stilted interaction, Matilda vaguely recalled reading of a feud between the Earl and his stepmother – England's new Queen and Godfrey's former charge.

Walter leapt in before the Bishop could speak. "My Earl, three nights ago, Bishop Godfrey slipped into my territory to abduct this woman. Like so many other barbaric foreigners before him, Godfrey set fire to her dwelling and spirited the woman away under the cover of darkness.

"This woman is precious to me. She has brought great prosperity, teaching my villagers new skills and my craftsmen new technologies. She has singlehandedly increased the output of my lands. Threefold."

"I see," the Earl said thoughtfully. "Bishop Godfrey, by what right do you think it acceptable to apprehend another lord's peasant?"

"You will find she is a foreigner, not one of his serfs," Godfrey replied in a bored tone. "This is a matter for the Church, transcending the petty laws of Man. The woman is an enemy of Christendom."

Scandalised gasps issued from the crowd. Matilda knew it was a serious accusation.

The Earl quietened them with a raised hand. "A bold claim, Godfrey. On what grounds?"

"Sacrilege and heresy. Baron Walter has failed to mention that my men and I arrested her as she butchered a fellow man. Cutting him up before a willing crowd of the Baron's villagers, no less."

The Earl's expression hardened and his wife blanched. "Is this true?" he asked Walter.

"I knew nothing of it," Walter stammered while looking at Matilda in horror.

"Such little awareness of his own lands," the Bishop chided. "*I* have been watching the woman for months. Our paths first crossed at Stowey castle where I was assisting the Baron after a…hunting accident. I had almost finished my treatment when she suddenly arrived, claiming first to be a healer and then to have cured the Baron with a cheap trick. It was then that I first became suspicious."

"Does she have a name?" the Earl's wife squeaked.

"I beg your pardon?" Godfrey asked tetchily.

"The woman standing before us in chains. What is her name?"

"Matilda, my lady," Matilda replied, earning a sharp look from the Baron.

"Carry on, Bishop," Earl Robert said with intrigue.

"I listened for news about the mystery healer, knowing she was bound to stir up more trouble. Then, several months ago, I learned of a sleepy village transformed by a red-headed woman, as if by magic. So I tasked someone to watch her. A friend she would never suspect."

A chill ran down Matilda's spine. *Warren was no friend. Who could it have been?*

"My source's messages grew stranger with every week. There were unusual plants that grew a yard each day. Mysterious metals that didn't rust. Women and children learning to read.

"The entire village was besotted with the woman and her power over them was absolute. Villagers who spoke up against her were beaten or banished. Lives were lost in her overworked mine, some at the hands of her misguided attempts at healing.

"But it was only in the past weeks that my concerns truly ripened. I received reports of artificial suns, orbs that hung in the night sky to make a room as bright as day. Such a feat could only be explained by sorcery. I admit that even I was fearful to confront such unnatural power. But then my source's messenger arrived at my doorstep.

"He arrived by horse, exhausted from travelling overnight with dire news. An elderly villager had died and was so tightly gripped by the woman's spell that he had volunteered his earthly body for her vile healing lessons. She planned to cut him to pieces before a willing crowd."

"Goodness, no!" the Earl's wife cried.

"I'm afraid so, my lady," Godfrey said with surprisingly genuine sorrow. "We were too late to stop her desecration; may God have mercy on the poor man's soul. But we interrupted her butchery and clapped her in irons before setting the building alight to cleanse her unholy presence.

"We were travelling to the sanctity of Bath Abbey when Baron Walter interrupted and ordered that we bring the woman to see you. I really must insist that I resume my holy duty and see this *abomination* safely dealt with on sacred grounds."

A shocked silence hung over the hall as Godfrey finished his account. Even Matilda shared their scandal at the Bishop's convincing recollection. He looked victorious as he soaked in the crowd's horror.

The Earl sat deep in thought, a troubled look on his face and his hands propped up before him.

"A most disturbing account, Bishop. Very disturbing indeed. Walter, did you know of this?"

Matilda watched the Baron's options tick through his head. His hesitation didn't fill her with confidence.

"Ah… No, my lord. I knew of her improvements in the village and our increased taxes. But of the dissection, I knew nothing."

"Curious," the Earl said. "A mysterious woman bringing unknown, and unnatural, gifts from a foreign land. How bizarre." He stared at her with a grave expression. "Who are you Matilda? Where do you come from?"

Matilda felt every eye in the hall turn to her, projecting the room's collective curiosity and disdain. The Earl's questions sounded rhetorical and yet she felt compelled to answer. She gave a wry smile to William before turning to address the Earl.

Her situation was dire. It was time.

"The future, my lord."

The room's silence was absolute, so quiet that Matilda could only hear the fire crackle. Then, like a rolling wave, the crowd started to grumble and then grew into shouts.

"Don't play games," the Earl warned. "Your life is at stake."

"It's the truth my lord," Matilda replied calmly, though her stomach felt like lead. "I am from the future. The year two thousand and thirty-seven of our Lord, to be precise. I was sent to help, to avoid a calamity that devastated my own time."

The Earl stared at her in disbelief. "*Woman*, you continue this farce?"

"The proof is in my work, my lord. The developments I have introduced are nothing unnatural. Anyone can do it. Young William here can replicate many of my achievements and Walter himself has made the orbs shine. Simpler than lighting a candle, with the right tools. There is no need for magic."

The Earl eyed William before settling his sceptical gaze on her once more. He was intrigued.

"Don't believe a word she says, Robert," Godfrey chimed. "She has already enchanted many. Any sane person can see that she calls upon the supernatural."

The crowd grumbled disapproval and warning at the Earl, giving Matilda little doubt that they sided with the Bishop.

"Your father will die!" she cried with desperation. "Eleven years from now, eating lampreys." All eyes snapped back to Matilda and the Earl stared intently. "His death will throw the Kingdom into chaos and war. Your cousin Stephen will betray your sister and claim her throne."

The room erupted once more.

"You *prophesize* His Majesty's death as your defence against supernatural activities?" Godfrey sneered in disbelief, savouring the chaos.

"Quiet!" the Earl ordered, pale as a ghost. Godfrey flinched at the rebuke. "How does a foreigner know of his love for lampreys?" he whispered.

"It is one of many things recorded of your time," Matilda said simply. "I know that you have just returned from a campaign against rebels in Normandy, though many here already know that. But I also know that you have Sir Amaury imprisoned in your dungeon at

Gloucester. Tell me, if the Bishop has watched me for months, how could such a secret reach an inconsequential village like Holford?"

The Earl baulked and even Godfrey looked shocked at this revelation. A hush fell over the room.

"I don't know what is more difficult to believe," the Earl croaked, "that you are from the future or in league with Satan. Perhaps both?"

"I can prove it, my lord." Matilda said delicately. "I've travelled far to share knowledge from another time. I intended to show your father, before Godfrey's first assault disrupted my plans. I've given up too much to be scuttled by a jealous bishop. Please, I humbly request a chance to prove myself. A week to show what we have made in the village and how it works. Let me prove my innocence, and I will teach your subjects all of my tricks."

The Earl mulled over Matilda's words. Walter looked particularly displeased by Matilda's final offer.

"This is indeed an issue well beyond my jurisdiction," the Earl started, prompting a flash of victory from Godfrey. "But you have little hope of a fair trial at the hands of the Bishop...."

"There is no question Robert, this woman is guilty!" Godfrey howled. "To even consider her story would be heresy."

Cries of assent rippled around the hall but the Earl raised a hand.

Matilda's hopes rose.

"You see? No chance for justice." The Earl glared at Godfrey before gesturing to Matilda. "This woman could be a valuable gift to the Kingdom, if you are indeed what you claim. The King's very life may depend on you." The Earl looked at Matilda pensively. "Very well. You may show us your secrets, though priests will supervise you at all times to ensure you try nothing untoward or ungodly. I am a busy man and cannot be traipsing to some country hamlet for a week. You shall have three days to prove yourself. Here in Bristol.

"Do so and I will personally take your case to my father. Anointed by God, he will have authority to question our Bishop. But fail and I'll have no qualms in submitting you to the Bishop's justice. Bishop Godfrey, can you agree to these terms? For the sake of justice, it means only a three-day delay."

The Bishop trembled with fury before storming from the hall without a word. Matilda knew she wouldn't get any better offer and gave a humble bow.

"You will stay here," Earl Robert announced to the hall. "Locked in a cell until you prove your innocence. Guards, take her away!"

The Earl stood and strode from the hall, a train of guards and servants in tow. The hall burst into frantic discussion, the other nobles' own petitions completely forgotten.

Walter and William walked over to Matilda.

"I thought I told you to…" Walter started angrily.

"I wasn't leaving my life to your bumbling!" Matilda snapped.

Walter paused and looked sheepish.

Matilda turned to William. "I need you to get back to Holford. Fast. Get everything you can from the mill, from Matthew. The wire, the books. Some lights. Bring it all here so I can show off some of our actual work."

"I can help you here!" William protested.

Matilda gave a gentle smile.

"I appreciate the offer but I'm afraid this is up to me now. Run along, you might make it in time if you're quick. Oh, and let me know what damage was done to the mill!"

William nodded and ran from the hall. Sir Phillip followed, promising to find him a good horse.

The Earl's guards came to take Matilda and Walter made them wait.

"I'll make sure you're properly cared for," he said. "And I'll see what I can arrange from out here."

The guards warily took Matilda by the arms and led her from the hall through an inconspicuous door and down a dusty spiral staircase.

Matilda's anxiety rose with each step that she descended, reaching its crescendo as the iron latch to her cell slammed shut.

No, she told herself. *She had planning to do.*

CHAPTER THIRTY-EIGHT
25 September 1124

John felt guilty. A year of servitude under Godfrey had robbed him of his tongue.

He'd spent an entire day in the cart with the Book's author but hadn't spoken a word, her young companion's protective glare stilling words within his throat.

John had listened to her valiantly defend herself against the Bishop before Bristol's nobles yet his voice never came to her defence. A single word in that crowded hall and Godfrey would've skinned him alive.

Yet John loathed himself for his silence. For missing a chance to call out Godfrey's hypocrisy and defend the damsel. Not that she needed it.

John was eager to see what the Redhead planned to reveal. She was just as magnificent as he'd imagined the author of the Book to be, poised and prideful. He was still astounded that the author was a woman. He had never met a female scholar. The memory of her glib smile, despite the looming threat from a hall full of nobles, taunted John late into the night. He regretted his priestly vows.

He and Peter had been accommodated at a local monastery, though Godfrey's peevish assistant had quickly disappeared to keep watch over the woman which left John to endure a morning of probing questions from the annoyingly insistent monks.

"Is she truly wicked?"

"How did she come to Somerset?"

"What efforts has our blessed Bishop taken to purge her corruption?"

John couldn't leave soon enough.

Bristol was abuzz when he finally departed for the castle. Crowds thronged along the tall streets towards the monolithic castle walls. The scale of both the town and the castle amazed him, all so much larger than the insignificant backwater where he'd been raised. With a pang of loss and amusement, John wondered what his family would make of his involvement in the current predicament.

John enjoyed stretching his legs after days cramped in the wagon but the crowd made him uncomfortable. News of the peculiar events at the castle had spread like wildfire, fanned by a handful of zealous priests who roamed the streets decrying Matilda's depravity and declaring her either a sorceress or devil worshiper. John was promptly recognised as a member of the previous day's procession and unwanted interrogation quickly resumed as he walked to the castle.

Complete strangers nipped at his heels, yapping their endless questions despite his refusal to answer. The crowd grew denser as he neared the castle wall and people stood shoulder to shoulder at the castle gates.

John elbowed his way to the front of the crowd, his most insistent questioners following in his wake. Their tenaciousness finally proved valuable when their jabbering drew the attention of the guards. A captain recalled that John had ridden in Matilda's cart and let him through, prompting cries of protest from the restless crowd.

Their cries faded as John crossed the castle lawn. He reached the keep and re-entered the Earl's vaulted hall. The room bubbled with excitement and it too was packed to capacity. None of Bristol's elite dared to miss the unique proceedings.

The Earl and his wife were already seated at the front dais, with the Bishop and Baron waiting impatiently on either side. Godfrey and Peter stood with their heads together, scheming potential strategies for the days ahead.

John didn't have to wait long before a small door opened behind the dais and the Prisoner was led into the hall by a pair of guards. Pockets of the crowd met her arrival with angry jeers and Godfrey sneered triumphantly as she was escorted before the Earl. The Redhead looked exhausted. Her hair was dishevelled and eyes bloodshot, as though she hadn't slept a wink the previous night.

The Earl agreed.

"You look weary," he said as she stood before him. The crowd became deathly quiet. "I confess that I feel much the same. My wife and I debated your preposterous claim late into the night. Coming from the future, ha! How could such a thing be true? And yet, if not, how can you speak with such conviction about events yet to come?"

"My apologies for disturbing your sleep Earl Robert," Matilda replied reverently. "I hope to enlighten you over the coming days, first to prove that I am from the future and then that my actions were for humanity's benefit rather than an affront to God. I spent the evening planning some activities…"

"I think not!" Godfrey objected. "Robert, the accused cannot dictate her own trial."

The Bishop had a point and John heard many in the crowd agreed.

The Earl called for silence with a raised hand and looked at Matilda thoughtfully. "I would normally agree Godfrey, but this is no trial. I am not qualified to judge her innocence, you have made clear that is a matter for the Church. I merely seek to understand the validity of the various claims and to determine whether this needs consideration by higher authorities. And as such, we will hear her proposal."

The Redhead made to start but was interrupted by the steward.

"My lord, before you begin. The guards are reporting scuffles outside the walls and property is being destroyed. The crowd is baying for swift justice. It might be wise to send men beyond the walls to disperse them."

The Earl considered the news with concern but Matilda spoke up.

"Earl Robert, if I may? They're here because of me. The gossip that inevitably leaks from this hall will only further inflame their passions. Perhaps you could let them watch firsthand? I'm sure the entertainment provided by Godfrey's interrogations will distract from further destruction."

The Earl raised an eyebrow at the Bishop who merely shrugged. There was no denying that a frenzied crowd would support his case.

"Very well," Earl Robert announced. "Everyone outside!"

John raced from the hall and nestled himself amongst Bristol's elites as a makeshift stage was hastily constructed in the shadow of the keep. The Earl's throne was placed in the centre with a short bench on either side. Several ranks of guards took position around the platform before the gates were opened to a loud cheer and the rowdy commoners flooded in.

A hush fell over the crowd when the keep doors opened and a procession of nobles made their way onto the stage. The Bishop, the

Baron and their most trusted advisors settled onto the benches while the Earl's wife claimed her throne. Earl Robert stepped forward and addressed the crowd.

"My dear subjects, you have been permitted here today to witness a truly unusual event. Word reached me some days past of a quarrel. But this was no ordinary squabble, it was between a bishop and a baron. The cause of their debate was a singularly strange woman. One who reportedly creates sunlight in the depths of night and claims to come from the future."

A wave of concern swept through the crowd.

"I agree," the Earl declared with a nervous laugh. "I too was shaken by the talk of her powers. But we have men of God with us and they have assured me that the Lord will protect us."

John noticed a few nearby people glance toward him and his priestly attire. Some even shuffled closer.

"Bishop Godfrey, have you anything to say?"

"Just get this farce over with," Godfrey snarled.

The Earl gestured for the Redhead to be brought onto the stage. The crowd burst to life as soon as she emerged from the keep, arms bound and flanked by a pair of guards on either side. Some expressed shock at the mere sight of the woman while others hurled abuse. Godfrey seemed to feed upon their spite.

She let their anger flow past her like a stone in a stream. John admired her composure.

"Despite the Bishop's claims," Earl Robert continued, "this woman has provided innovations that stand to benefit Bristol, the Kingdom and perhaps all of Christendom. To squander such potential talents without proper consideration would be a sin. As such, I have granted her a chance to explain herself. So, please tell us who you are and where you come from."

The Earl took his seat and Matilda walked to the centre of the stage, guards in tow.

"My name is Matilda," she told the crowd, "and as Earl Robert has told, I come from the future."

There was a confused rumble from the crowd.

"I grew up in these lands," Matilda continued, "on the outskirts of Bridgwater. Though things there were very different many years in the future."

Godfrey scoffed but the Earl stared on intently. "How so?" he asked. "How is it different?"

"There are many more people. Many more dwellings. Cities sprawl for miles and buildings tower up into the sky. Almost every road is paved and they are dominated by horseless carts which transport heavy loads over great distances. One can wake in Bristol and be in London well before midday."

John's mind reeled at her description, trying to fathom how such things could be. The crowd also grew animated, chattering away to one another. Some unruly pockets hurled abuse and called Matilda a liar.

"A most fanciful account," Godfrey interrupted. "She's deluded but I grant that she has quite an imagination."

There were scattered laughs from the crowd.

"The entire claim is absurd," he continued. "I can get to tomorrow. A short nap and there I am. I can get to next week or next year, albeit with a few more grey hairs. But I cannot return to yesterday, no matter how much I try. And one can't know what will happen next week, yet alone years from now. This is merely an elaborate lie to distract from your sins."

The crowd erupted in laughter at the Bishop's words. Matilda ignored their taunts.

"Well, Bishop. I'd wager that the improvements you witnessed in Holford were unlike anything these lands have ever seen before. So perhaps there is more that you don't yet know. And I can in fact prove that I come from the future. But to understand the future, it helps to understand what can be known about the past."

She paused to ensure she had the crowd's attention. John saw little reason to worry.

"The Bishop is right. Yesterday has been. Last week was longer ago and last year even further again. I came to you from about *one thousand* years in the future. It was almost as far for me to see you here today as it would be for you to see Jesus Christ. So I'll start with a question. If he was so far in the past, how do we know that Jesus truly existed?"

"Heresy!" Godfrey cried, prompting cries of outrage from the most devout pockets of the crowd. John felt the commoners surge toward the stage and saw the guards strain to keep them back.

"Order!" the Earl cried, before turning to Matilda with a stern warning. "You be careful now."

"It is but a question," Matilda appealed. "There is much evidence, beyond just the Bishop's word."

The crowd calmed. Godfrey pouted but kept silent.

"The Bible!" came a sudden cry from the masses.

"Yes," Matilda chimed. "Textual evidence tells us stories of his deeds. But there are also texts concerning dragons and pagan gods. So how do we know this period actually existed?"

The crowd was silent.

"Relics!" came another cry.

"Now you're getting closer. Actual objects from the time. Evidence we can hold. But how can we be sure that they are from the time in question and not planted by some malicious fraud? How do we know that the relics are what people claim them to be?"

The crowd was entranced, rooted in thought. Godfrey was seething.

"Let's try something different," Matilda suggested. "What evidence proves that the Roman's ever existed?"

The crowd was more comfortable with that.

"The aqueducts!"

"Baths!"

"Roads!"

"Coins!" came another cry.

"Very good!" Matilda exclaimed. "All examples of things, tangible things, that the Romans left behind which prove that they existed. And coins are a particularly interesting example, as they bear unique markings that show precisely when they were made. I trust you've seen a Roman coin, Earl Robert?"

"Indeed, in the royal treasury," the Earl responded.

"Very good, so you'll know some of their unique features? Inclusion of the emperor's head for instance."

The Earl nodded.

"Well, I propose that we unearth a hoard of previously undiscovered Roman coins to undeniably demonstrate my knowledge from the future. They were discovered in my time, after lying undisturbed for almost two thousand years."

"That proves nothing!" Godfrey protested. "You could get lucky. Or have them planted in anticipation of such a test!"

"I thought you might say that," Matilda grumbled at him before addressing her broader audience. "If Holford's villagers were here they could testify that I've not left the region since I arrived last year. But unfortunately, they are not. So, those of you present yesterday heard from the Bishop's own mouth that he has sought news of my movements since we first met at Baron Walter's castle almost a year ago. Would it be fair to assume that he would've heard of a strange red-haired woman moving around his own town?"

The crowd murmured their unconvinced agreement.

"Do you think that the Bishop would've heard word of this red-haired stranger digging holes in a public place at the centre of his town?"

There was stronger agreement from the crowd.

Matilda turned to the Earl.

"My lord. I know you are a busy man and don't wish to traipse all over the countryside. As your prisoner I have poor grounds to ask, but might you consider undertaking a short expedition to the town of Bath to unearth a vast haul of Roman silver? Over seventeen thousand coins. You can keep whatever we find," she added cheekily.

The Earl considered the proposal, looking thoughtfully to Godfrey before the spirit of adventure overcame him and he beamed like a child.

"Prepare the horses!" he commanded.

The castle courtyard burst into a flurry of activity as attendees raced to prepare for Matilda's treasure hunt and the crowd excitedly vacated the castle. Some enterprising townsfolk departed immediately in the direction of Bath, keen to get a head start on the other treasure hunters.

"But Robert," Godfrey feebly protested amongst the commotion, "this really won't do. There is nowhere to adequately imprison the girl. And... There aren't sufficient sleeping quarters for a man of your nobility."

The Earl gave a hearty laugh. "You'll have to do better than that Bishop. You forget that I've just returned from campaigning in Normandy. Months of tents and campfires. Any English soil will surely be superior to the mud I endured on the European mainland.

Plus," he added with a wry smile, "surely a bishop has sufficient quarters to offer a man of my station?"

Godfrey smouldered.

"Your prisoner will be watched over at all times until this is over," Robert continued. "You have my word. Now come, let us depart!"

It took time to prepare horses for the journey but eventually the group departed. The Baron and the Earl rode ahead of the convoy, merrily chatting away as if merely out on a leisurely hunt. They were followed by a steady stream of Bristol's aristocracy, none wanting to miss out on gossip that would be talk of the town for years to come.

Godfrey ordered John to keep an eye on Matilda in the cart while he rode ahead with Peter to resume his scheming. Without complaint, John clambered into the wagon to sit opposite her. A pair of the Earl's guards piled in behind him and they departed.

They reached Bristol's outskirts and overtook straggling townsfolk making for Bath. John couldn't hold his tongue any longer. "From the future?" he blurted. "Surely you're not serious?"

Matilda glared at him. "You won't get anything from me, priest. I won't give Godfrey extra rope to hang me with."

"You're mistaken," John replied earnestly. "The Bishop is no friend of mine. I too was abducted and he reneged on his promise of a fine education. Giving me your Book was as close as he came to delivering on that pledge and even then, I understood little. But I take your point and will press no further."

The pair rode in silence as the countryside slipped by.

"You've read my bible?" Matilda eventually asked, her bizarre accent tinged with intrigue. "You can read modern English?"

"I speak English better than I can read. My father always said that we should use the language of our people and that talk of Norman superiority was rubbish. But yes, I've read your Book. Tried to at least. Several times."

Matilda gave him an appraising look.

"I guess the Book does support your claims of being from the future," John mused. "Even Adelard hadn't seen some of the ideas in his many travels. But he had seen enough to know it was true."

"Adelard? Of Bath?" Matilda noted excitedly. "The monk!? *He's* read my Book?"

John nodded.

Matilda maintained her silence but John felt the mood in the back of the cart warm slightly. It made the rest of the journey to Bath more bearable, though he cringed when they passed the fields where Godfrey's men had thwarted his escape attempt.

The group arrived in Bath a little after midday. The Earl reined in as the town came into view and drew his horse up alongside the cart.

"Well then. Where does our alleged time traveller claim this treasure lies?"

Matilda responded to him with calm confidence.

"In a garden. Near the Roman baths in the centre of the town. We'll need a few things. Shovels, a barrel of water with a pail and some coarse brushes. I'd recommend breaking for a midday meal while you wait for them to be gathered. I can't help because Godfrey burned my hand, so you lads will need your energy. It'll be heavy work. Once we get to the cathedral, shall I show you the way?"

The Earl's men were taken aback by Matilda's frankness but Earl Robert just laughed.

"You're a plucky young woman. Very well, you lead the way."

Hands still bound, Matilda eventually led the party to a small courtyard practically in the shadow of Godfrey's new cathedral. John enjoyed watching the Bishop squirm as they drew closer to the area he knew so well. The Bishop whispered waspishly to his assistant and Peter ran off towards Godfrey's palace.

Matilda made several more requests as food was distributed amongst the nobles.

"Could you please summon the neighbours of this property? And some of the eldest residents of the town?"

Matilda's requests slowly started to arrive, as did a crowd of Bath townsfolk intrigued to see so many nobles. John waved when he spotted Adelard in the crowd. His stablemaster nemesis was there too. Earl Robert let the food disappear before calling the assembled crowd to attention.

"Greetings to our new arrivals. For those of you that don't know, we have journeyed here today from Bristol to hunt for Roman treasure."

There was a stir of excitement among the crowd. He motioned for Matilda to begin.

"You will all be familiar with the Roman baths that gave this town its name," Matilda started. "But what you don't know is that on this very spot there lay another bath. A thousand years ago, around the time of Jesus," she added, prompting another wave of excitement. "Hidden inside a secret compartment within this bath is a hoard of seventeen thousand coins, some as old as Christ himself."

This prompted the biggest bristle from the crowd yet.

"So?" Matilda asked with a pause. "Are there any volunteers to start digging?"

There was an enthusiastic rush of willing participants but Matilda picked up the first shovel and offered it to the Earl, earning a collective gasp from the crowd.

"Would you like to lead our expedition?" Matilda asked with a cheeky grin.

"Sure," the Earl replied, grabbing the filthy shovel and beckoning for more men to join in.

The yard was soon a frenzy of men tearing up soil as Matilda directed their efforts. The elderly owner watched on unimpressed, though he luckily had more sense than to question the Earl who had miraculously appeared at his doorstep.

Adelard strolled over to John. "You made it back! I was worried when you disappeared from the Mass. What's all this? Who's the Redhead?"

"The author of our Book, would you believe? The genius we so longed to meet," John replied excitedly. "Godfrey arrested her in some tiny village. She claims to be from the future and is trying to prove it."

"You don't say?" Adelard noted with accepting intrigue.

The crowd continued to swell as travellers arrived from Bristol and an excited cry eventually sounded over the worksite.

"Lady! A wall!" a knight called out from a waist-deep hole.

"Very good!" Matilda encouraged. "The treasure lies along the western wall of the structure. Focus your efforts on uncovering the wall and then look for a stone chamber."

The digging resumed in the area around the wall, though fewer men could participate due to the tight quarters. The Earl led the charge, his expensive leather boots caked in mud. John found himself longing to participate.

"Oh how it hurts to tear up such an archaeological marvel," Matilda lamented to no one in particular.

The group had uncovered several meters of wall when cries of excitement once more erupted from the diggers.

"We found it!" the Earl cried, dropping to his knees and scraping dirt away with his hands. "Matilda! A stone casket!"

Matilda and John rushed over as the men expanded the hole around the casket and scraped off more dirt. Even Godfrey came to investigate, accompanied by a recently returned Peter who seemed more interested in the ruined courtyard.

"Careful now," Matilda warned as she directed the men from above. "Pry the lid open but don't let it fall on the coins."

They levered the lid and there was a press of people trying to catch a glimpse of what lay inside. Matilda leapt into the hole herself and urged everyone to take a step back.

John saw only a muddy mass of flat stones within the pit.

"The pail and brush!" Matilda requested.

She dropped to a knee and delicately used her bound hands to lever a chunk of the mass from the hole. Someone handed her the pail of water and a brush. Using her good hand, she dunked the chunk in the water before delicately brushing away some of the grime.

The crowd held its breath until, with a flash of silver, one of the coins came loose and fell into the bucket. Quick as a fox, Matilda scooped it up and wiped it on her skirt before handing it to the Earl.

"Does this look like a Roman coin to you?" she asked with a smile.

Earl Robert was struck speechless as he rubbed the muddy coin with his fingers. When he finally spoke, it was a reverent whisper.

"It truly does."

A crush of people surged forward to see the coin. The Earl ordered everyone back several yards before passing the coin to one of his knights to show to the assembled crowd. The knight handled the silver coin as delicately as a baby bird.

Matilda meanwhile brushed away the mud surrounding the other coins, eventually revealing a giant glimmering mass of silver.

"I'm going to need some help to get this out," she said feebly.

She stood aside as the Earl ordered his knights to lift the valuable bulk out of the hole. It came away in large chunks as they heaved it from the casket and John saw Matilda cringe at their rough handling.

"Gently, please! These coins are worth so much more than the weight of their silver. This is a treasure so precious that it will be admired for centuries."

The knights proceeded with greater care and Earl Robert called for a chest in which to place the newfound treasure. The crowd babbled away excitedly as more and more silver was extracted.

The crowd spread out when the knights had withdrawn the last of the silver and scraped every corner of the casket. Matilda took the opportunity to call upon the assembled villagers.

"Bishop Godfrey said back at Bristol that I had planted the coins here to prove my innocence." She pointed at the massive hole. "You've seen the scale of the digging. Is this something a single woman could achieve by herself? Without being noticed?"

The crowd murmured their disapproval.

"I ask the Bath elders," Matilda continued. "Has there ever been another building in this place?"

"Always just a garden," an elderly man chimed. "Since I was a boy."

"And to the neighbours, the owner and the townsfolk. Have any of you seen this land so disturbed? Ever?"

There were scattered cries of no from throughout the crowd.

Matilda looked around the crowd, pausing at Godfrey before turning to Earl Robert with a twinkle in her eye.

"So?" she asked. "Do you believe me now?"

Before the Earl could answer, John saw a flurry of movement from a building above. Matilda grunted and dropped to the ground, a feathered shaft protruding from her chest.

Screams filled the yard.

CHAPTER THIRTY-NINE
26 September 1124

Matilda was soaking in her victory when a sharp pain suddenly exploded in her chest. She was flung from her feet and quickly lost amongst the ensuing chaos. Knights streamed towards the Earl who barked commands over the screaming onlookers, ordering his men to find the bowman.

Earl Robert cleared a space around Matilda and propped her up, revealing an arrow jutting out from her dress and a small pool of blood. The Earl, Baron and Bishop gathered around her, their faces etched with concern. Wasting no time, Sir Phillip ripped his knife through her dress with a practiced hand to examine the wound.

"Oh!" they all exclaimed in unison when greeted by the sight of Matilda's chainmail. Even as she struggled to breath, her ribs almost certainly broken, Matilda knew that the Institute's parting gift had saved her life. The shirt had split under the force of the assassin's shot but it had prevented the arrowhead from tearing deeper into her skin. She pulled the arrow from the remnants of her dress, hands shaking as she registered her own blood upon the tip.

"There's more to this woman than meets the eye," Sir Phillip noted with admiration. "That's one mighty fine suit of mail you've got there!"

Matilda gave a meek smile before passing out from the shock.

+++

The sky was dark when Matilda woke. She found herself inside a tiny square cell, barely wide enough for her to lie across. She was still in the tattered rags of her dress, though someone had kindly left a change of clothes by the heavy oak door. She sat up gingerly and also saw some mouldy bread with cheese beside a goblet of wine. Matilda could guess which of her hosts had provided each element.

Matilda shrugged off her rags and struggled out of her chainmail, wincing at the combined pain of her small cut and at least one broken rib from the arrow's impact. She examined the wound by the moonlight that streamed through a small barred window. It was the width of her smallest finger but deep enough that she would have liked to stitch it. Taking her wine, she cleaned the wound before draining the rest of the goblet. She passed on the bread.

Matilda mournfully fingered the small tear in her chainmail, wishing she had the means to repair it. Knowing it still offered protection even in its flawed state, she donned both the mail and her new dress before examining her surroundings.

A quartet of guards were stationed outside her door, two from Bishop Godfrey and two from Baron Walter. Matilda heard them bickering but they ignored her calls.

"Shut up woman," Godfrey's guard eventually called out. "You might've impressed the Earl but the Bishop says you're still his until the third day. Even if you are from the future, it's just not natural."

Even Walter's guards grunted their agreement.

Matilda returned to her blanket and pondered her predicament, wondering what more she could possibly show the following day.

Her elation at uncovering the Roman coins had been short-lived. The discovery of the Beau Street Hoard had fascinated her as a child and she had visited the coins on display in the Bath museum each summer. Her Institute friends had often joked that they were certain to be rich as there were treasure-troves to be found no matter where they were sent. Matilda was glad that such special coins could serve a more noble purpose, demonstrating knowledge that could only come from another time. She hoped that the stunt would convince people to at least consider her claims.

But she had no clue how to surpass the coin discovery. Without William's reinforcements or her tools, every idea paled in comparison. She slumped down against the wall, lost in thought. Each breath brought a distracting stab of pain and Matilda was still without answers when sleep finally claimed her.

+++

Matilda woke to thundering knocks upon the heavy cell door early the next morning. She barely had time to sit up before the door crashed open and Godfrey's rat-faced assistant strode into the cell.

"I beg your pardon!" Matilda exclaimed, suddenly fully awake.

"Get up," Peter ordered. "Quickly now!"

"Settle down. Why the rush?"

"The Earl is eager to show your treasure to his wife. And the Bishop wants you away from here without delay, before your corruption has time to spread. So move along!"

Matilda propped herself up and glared at the Assistant. "I'd have thought a priest would know to give a woman some privacy? Wouldn't want to risk corruption would you?"

"Be quick or I'll have the guards drag you out in whatever state they find you," he called as he left.

A guard sniggered from the doorway but abruptly stopped when he saw Matilda's slightly cocked head and deadpan stare. He reluctantly closed the door.

Matilda dragged herself from the floor, wincing from her broken ribs. She felt surprisingly refreshed, despite her total lack of a plan. Her hands were bound once more and she was led to the now familiar cart. It was empty besides the heavy chest of coins.

"You take good care of that for me," the Earl said with a smile as he rode past the cart. "Though I'm sure you could just find more. You had me worried after last night's antics but I hear you're relatively unscathed. I look forward to seeing whatever you have in store for us back in Bristol."

Matilda's stomach dropped.

They were just about to depart when the Young Priest vaulted into the back of the cart, a heavy sack slung over his shoulder.

"Sorry!" he apologised to the driver, who grunted and whipped the cart into motion. "Godfrey asked me to watch over the troublemaker."

He sat opposite Matilda and gave her a warm smile but gratefully didn't force conversation. Matilda settled in for another long ride, wincing in pain as the cart went over each bump, and started concocting a plan to fill the afternoon. She hoped that William would be waiting for her at the Earl's castle but knew she needed a contingency.

She was deep in thought when the priest piped up.

"Having the Earl take up a shovel was truly inspired."

Matilda stared at him vacantly, her mind still busy searching for a plan.

"What have you got planned next?" he asked cheerfully, reading her mind.

"I honestly don't know," Matilda admitted despairingly. "Nothing seems good enough. It seems my only hope is William waiting for me at the castle."

The priest gave a thoughtful look. "You just need to outmanoeuvre Godfrey. It shouldn't be too difficult, he's not exactly dynamic. The Earl is furious with him after the foolish attempt on your life. The archer was found dead before anyone could question him but it doesn't take a genius to guess who put him up to it."

The casual discussion of the attempt on her life sent a chill down Matilda's spine.

"Godfrey claimed ignorance," the priest continued. "Said any number of God-fearing townsfolk could've hired the man. He knows the Earl can't touch him, there's already talk of unrest from Godfrey's most loyal followers. So perhaps this might help with your idea?"

Matilda was puzzled as he reached into his sack and started to remove clothes. And then, a very familiar bag.

"Consider it an apology for doubting your outlandish claims."

Matilda wasn't even listening. Her eyes were fixed upon her satchel.

"I'd appreciate if you kept this from my colleagues," the priest said in a hushed voice as he handed the bag to Matilda. "I'm sure things are missing, Godfrey tends to take whatever he wants."

"Th…Thank you, so much," Matilda stammered. "Thank you…gosh, I don't even know your name!"

"I'm John," he said with a smile.

Matilda instinctively peered over her shoulder to confirm Godfrey was far away before ripping open her satchel.

Nothing was in its right place but simply seeing her familiar belongings was comforting. Her valuable metals and spices were missing but the first item Matilda withdrew was much more precious. The second half of her bible. She picked up the torn tome and, unable to help herself, gave it a kiss.

"Godfrey will be furious when he returns to Bath and finds that missing. I'd end up in chains with you. Probably worse."

Matilda felt a pang of concern. "True! How will you ever go back to living with the Bishop?"

"I'm not going back," John said with conviction. "Hostage life never suited me. I intend to witness the rest of your spectacle and then slip away into the night. So please make it worth it."

Matilda nodded and resumed pawing through her possessions. Everything was broken or covered in dried mud. Her grandmother's engagement ring was missing, the emerald no doubt a magnet for Godfrey's greedy eyes. Matilda withdrew Richie's toy soldier, smiling at the memory of painting with him while belting out their favourite songs.

At the very bottom of the bag was a crumpled piece of paper and tears welled in Matilda's eyes before she had even unfolded it. It had been a year since she'd laid eyes on her family. The photo of them all eating ice-cream by the coast was the next best thing. Her only proof that they had ever existed. It was a fond memory – little Richie had more ice cream on his face than in his cone – though now bittersweet. Tears streamed down Matilda's face but it was exactly the motivation she needed.

She spent the following hours planning her approach, one that would undercut Godfrey's best efforts to vilify her. She flipped through her ruined bible for inspiration but each idea felt underwhelming or incomplete. The Book continually opened to her annotated anatomy diagrams, which John said had particularly fascinated the Bishop. The seed of an idea started to form.

The sun had just begun its descent when they arrived back to Bristol. John motioned for Matilda to return the satchel.

"Don't worry," he said after seeing the scandal in Matilda's eyes. "You'll get it back. I promise."

Matilda reluctantly handed the bag to John, though she hid the photo of her family in her boot. Merely knowing that they were close filled her with energy.

She needed the extra motivation as there was no sign of William or anyone from Holford when the cart finally arrived at Bristol castle. To make matters worse, the local townsfolk had erected both gallows and a pyre while they were away.

Giving Godfrey options, no doubt.

The Bishop rode directly to the keep but the Earl and Baron pulled up to supervise as attendants unloaded the treasure from the wagon. With everyone focused on Matilda and the chest, John and his illicit cargo slipped away without notice.

"I hope today is as stirring as yesterday's exploits," Earl Robert said excitedly.

"There will be less treasure, unfortunately," Matilda replied.

"Never mind that, just prove Godfrey wrong. I want the viper gone from my castle."

The Earl's men hauled the chest down from the cart and lugged it into the keep. The nobles retired indoors to show off the treasure but Matilda remained in the cart, surrounded by guards and wondering if her half-baked plan would be enough to keep her audience engaged.

The nobles dallied indoors, no doubt enjoying a leisurely meal. Matilda's stomach grumbled – Godfrey's mouldy bread a cruel memory – and after a long while, a guard delivered her some fresh crusty bread. Matilda was absentmindedly gnawing on it when she heard a commotion at the castle gate. She stood in the cart and peered towards the gatehouse, hoping against hope that William had finally arrived.

"Get the Earl!" a gatekeeper cried as he ran towards the keep. "There's a mob from Bath demanding to see the time nomad! Whatever the blazes that is."

Earl Robert and his guests emerged from the keep and marched to the walls above the castle gate. Matilda couldn't hear what was said but saw sweeping gestures followed by strong protest from Godfrey. After a short consultation with his steward, Robert descended the steps and marched towards Matilda and her cart.

"It appears yesterday's exploits have earned you quite the following," the Earl told her. "Half of Bath followed us here to see what you'll do next. They've inflamed my own townsfolk too, the streets were full for as far as I could see!"

"Goodness," was all Matilda could manage.

"They're on the verge of rioting but setting my guards upon them would be a terrible look, no matter what the Bishop might say. He's concerned the crowd might side with you."

A sudden idea struck Matilda.

"Let them in, like yesterday. And, give them some food."

Robert looked perplexed. Matilda forgot that feeding peasants wasn't second nature for an Earl.

"Nothing extravagant, just bread and water. They've travelled far and will love you for it all the same. It will calm them down and give us time to set up my next demonstration. You've still got the stage in front of the keep but I'll need a long table and three pigs."

"Not that fable with the wolf I hope. Or is it possible to blow down a stone structure with nothing but wind in the future?"

"It is actually," Matilda said absentmindedly. "But no, nothing like that. I promise it's relevant."

The Earl looked at Matilda quizzically. "Madness. And pigs aren't cheap."

"Do you think seventeen thousand silver coins might buy me a few pigs?" Matilda shot back with a cheeky smile.

Unable to argue with that, the Earl gave the order. He returned to the gatehouse and addressed the crowd directly, prompting a loud cheer.

"You'd better have something good planned," Baron Walter warned, making Matilda doubt herself once more.

The castle yard filled with servants carrying loaves of bread and rolling barrels for the townsfolk. The crowd was let in and they collected food before assembling to watch the final preparations. Three pigs were brought to the stage and slaughtered with brutal efficiency. Matilda grimaced but the crowd watched the purposeful violence completely nonplussed. A long trestle table was placed on the stage and the pigs were unceremoniously distributed along it. Blood pooled on the freshly laid planks.

The nobles took their seats and Matilda moved to stand beside the freshly killed pigs. She was surprised by the size of the crowd. There were easily over a thousand in attendance, with more collecting food from hastily erected stalls and a steady dribble continuing to arrive through the castle gate.

"Good afternoon everyone," the Earl began. "This is the second day of our hearing for Miss Matilda…" Matilda waved to the crowd. "…who was arrested by Bishop Godfrey several days ago on charges of heresy and behaviour most unnatural. Matilda argues that her actions are perfectly explainable and none can deny that she has brought prosperity to the regions she's touched. In the name of justice, I have granted Matilda three days to explain herself.

"Yesterday was truly extraordinary. Claiming to be from another time, Matilda dragged us to Bath in search of long-lost Roman treasure. From the time of Christ. As those of you from Bath can attest, she delivered exactly as promised."

There were excited whispers from the Bristol crowd.

"Her argument, while supremely irregular, is quite convincing. Even Bishop Godfrey has conceded that our visitor could be from another time, though his charges of heresy and unnatural behaviour remain.

"Today Matilda has promised a second demonstration to prove her innocence. How she plans to do that with three butchered swine is beyond me so I too will wait in anticipation. Godfrey, anything you wish to say before she begins?"

The Bishop angrily dismissed Robert with a wave.

"Very well. Matilda, if you will?"

Hands still shackled, Matilda strode to the centre of the stage. She was bemused to still feel a familiar pit in her stomach at presenting before such a large crowd. Thinking of Harry, she elected for a charismatic approach.

"Thank you Earl Robert. I see some familiar faces from the dig. Didn't we work you hard enough yesterday?"

There was some scattered laughter from the crowd.

"As the Earl said, Bishop Godfrey accuses me of unnatural behaviour. But what he failed to mention was that the Bishop arrested me in the act of cutting up a recently deceased man. One of my good friends."

There were gasps from the crowd. The Earl looked shocked that Matilda would incriminate herself. Godfrey beamed with glee.

"I understand your horror," Matilda continued, "but please, allow me to explain."

Matilda knew she walked a dangerous line and risked losing the crowd. It was time for some audience participation.

"Are there any barbers here today?"

There were a pair of wary cries from the crowd and Matilda invited the two barbers up on stage. One had recently arrived from Bath.

"I'll need a third assistant for this demonstration," Matilda called out. "If there are no more barbers, then perhaps someone that has experience with battlefield wounds?"

"I'll help." Matilda jumped as a call came from directly behind her and Sir Phillip stepped forward.

"Thank you Sir," Matilda said, regaining her composure and asking him to stand beside the other two volunteers.

"Everyone knows that barbers provide vital services, beyond just trimming beards. Tooth extraction. Sewing a wound. Amputations. These are common procedures, no?" Matilda asked the barbers, prompting an enthusiastic nod and a nonchalant shrug.

"These valuable services reduce suffering for sick family members or save the lives of injured neighbours. Bishop, have you never had a tooth removed by a hasty visit from a barber surgeon?"

Godfrey mumbled something unintelligible.

"So there is nothing unnatural or heretical about these valuable services. I ask you all, is amputation not a form of dissection?"

The crowd's murmurs were unsure.

"Understanding how the body works is key to saving countless lives. Today I hope to show you the lessons I sought to teach my village before the Bishop's interruption."

Godfrey leapt up in protest. "You cannot teach these people your filth!"

"No, Bishop!" Matilda said firmly, the nerve of her assertiveness sending a disapproving ripple through the crowd. "I won't let you deprive the world of an ability to save lives. Today's work is butchery at worst. There are no human bodies so there can be no claims of desecration. Swine are not ideal but they will suffice. So let us begin."

Unable to find an appropriate rebuttal, Godfrey sat down in defeat.

Matilda set each of her volunteers behind a pig and talked them through the first steps of the dissections, using each beast to highlight a different system within the body. The volunteers handled their tasks with grit and determination, unfazed by the gory work and eager to demonstrate their surgical abilities for the assembled crowd. Matilda was holding up a pair of lungs to describe the circulatory system when she was interrupted mid-sentence.

A guard elbowed his way through the crowd and ran onto the stage to whisper in the Earl's ear. Behind him, the trickle of townsfolk entering the castle had become a flood, complete with carts and beasts of burden. Familiar faces led the swell. At its head was William.

Matilda yelped in excitement and vaulted off the stage, weaving her shackled wrists through the crowd before the guards could apprehend her. She sprinted across the castle courtyard and ploughed into William, navigating her bindings to draw him into a bear hug so tight that her broken ribs screamed.

"You made it! You came!"

William grinned sheepishly, embarrassed at Matilda's affection.

"Of course I did. You didn't think I'd abandon you?"

"I was so worried," Matilda confessed. "I took everyone to Bath to find Roman coins so they'd believe I'm actually from the future. And I got shot with an arrow. But when we arrived back today and there was no sign of you…I thought I'd have to do this alone."

"Never!" William replied, looking genuinely scandalised. "It took some time to convince everyone what had happened, and given you'd told the Earl, to persuade them that you were from the future. Then when they finally understood, *everyone* insisted on coming along to help which took even more time! Well, almost everyone. The Brewers and their lot stayed behind. I really hope there aren't bandits in the Quantock hills because there's barely a soul left to protect Holford!"

Matilda looked over William's shoulder and saw that he was right. They were all there, each person bearing the fruits of their year's labour and looking weary from the hard walk. Luke Ploughman's cart carried her metallic pod and a collection of Elizabeth's plants. Even Father Thomas had journeyed from Nether Stowey, accompanied by the repentant large thug who'd restrained Matilda behind the ruined hut at Godfrey's command. His weasely friend was nowhere to be seen.

Seeing the villagers with all of their projects, an ingenious plan instantly formed in Matilda's mind. She was saved!

"We're going to need more pigs…" Matilda said airily.

The guards finally caught up to her and grabbed Matilda's shackles. Ignoring them, she greeted her fellow villagers. Even Rachel had made the journey. Heavily pregnant, she had ridden with the recovering Roger beside Matilda's plough in the back of Luke Ploughman's cart.

"We had to stop to rest overnight," William told her, "and some of the older villagers had to take a slower pace but they should arrive by tomorrow morning. We somehow collected extra people along the way. They insisted on coming along when they heard what was happening."

Matilda couldn't believe her eyes. Matthew and Ralph followed behind the convoy, large saw blades swinging wildly from their own overstocked cart. Matilda welcomed them all, urging them to grab food and to settle in with the rest of the crowd. Only then did she remember the audience that she had left waiting. She urged her guards back towards the stage, making a beeline for the Baron and the Earl.

Matilda took great pains to explain the significance of the new arrivals. She outlined her plans for the next day and breathed a huge sigh of relief when Earl Robert approved. She turned to address the crowd waiting before her.

"Everyone, your attention please! Apologies for dashing off but some very distinguished guests have arrived. We're joined by the inhabitants of Holford, a village in the shadow of the Quantock Hills. The village I have been honoured to call my home for the past year.

"These amazing people have journeyed far to show you the wonders that can be achieved by ordinary folk possessing the knowledge of the future. And show you they will, for tomorrow we will hold a festival, the likes of which you have never seen. There will be food and fighting. Dancing and handicrafts. I promise it will be a festival to remember."

The crowd thronged with excitement and the newly arrived Holford villagers were warmly welcomed. They were instant celebrities and locals rushed to befriend a Holfordian.

"But before tomorrow," Matilda continued, "let me finish the demonstration I so rudely disrupted. Rest assured that these beautiful beasts won't go to waste. At the conclusion of the demonstration, there will be a feast."

The crowd met this news with an almighty cheer.

Matilda resumed her demonstration with renewed energy, calling upon Astrid to help show how to cut out specific organs from the circulatory, respiratory, nervous, digestive and reproductive systems. The crowd correctly named most of the organs as the barbers removed them, getting particular bawdy with the reproductive system. Some more outgoing folk hazarded guesses at the organs' functions before Matilda described their true role, associated diseases and how to fix them.

The crowd was divided between those fully enthralled in Matilda's work and others more preoccupied with socialising. Matilda completed her demonstration as the sun started to set and the Earl ordered that several spits be erected over Matilda's pyre for roasting the pigs. The Earl supplemented Matilda's contribution with additional pigs and even some barrels of ale. By the time the sun had fully set, the castle courtyard was full of singing and food and music.

The Archer family were permitted to bring food to Matilda and they sat together to plan logistics for the following day's activities. Ever the killjoy, Godfrey insisted to Earl Robert that Matilda remained his prisoner and that she should be locked away once more. The crowd let Godfrey know what they thought of his decision, pelting pork scraps in his direction.

Matilda didn't care. She was elated by the arrival of her dear friends and the joy that her more recent acquaintances were taking from the spontaneous party. William, Elizabeth, Margery and John insisted on escorting her to the dungeon to spend the night together but were all shooed away at the jail entrance.

Godfrey followed Matilda all the way to her cell, lingering by her door's iron bars as the jailor retreated to his post.

"You've done well," the Bishop conceded. "You have the crowd eating from the palm of your hand and Earl Robert fawns over you. Enjoy it while you can. I'll find a way to have your head. I promise."

His utter determination sent a shiver down Matilda's spine.

"I pity you Godfrey," she called as the old man began to slowly ascend the spiral stairs. He turned to face her. "Your lonely bishop life, with its incense, cathedrals and gold crosses. It has sapped all of the imagination and wonder from your mind. You poor little man."

Godfrey looked at her with a vacant stare before leaving the dungeon without a word. Matilda couldn't know for sure but she felt that she had finally found a chink in the Bishop's armour of arrogance.

She turned to her familiar cell with its cold stone walls and old rushes scattered across the floor. It reminded Matilda of her cave.

Matilda savoured going to sleep without the pressure of finding a new idea. She was excited for the festival. A chance to show off Holford's hard work and allow others to participate in the spectacle. Matilda took Godfrey's threat seriously but couldn't help smiling. There would be no closing Pandora's box, even if he somehow managed to take her life. Word of Matilda's teachings would be out in the world.

One way or another, her mission would be a success.

CHAPTER FORTY
27 September 1124

Bristol was abuzz the next morning. Fuelled by free food and drink, the revelry had carried on late into the night and many people were undeniably worse for wear. Yet even they were up and about, bleary-eyed and grumpy but driven by the same expectant excitement.

John was baffled at how quickly news of the festivities had travelled. Even before sunrise, a flood of people began to arrive from the surrounding villages, lured by the promised festival and a chance to glimpse the mysterious red-haired woman rumoured to be from another time.

So great was the influx that John and Adelard struggled to move along the bustling streets leading into the castle. After passing through the large gatehouse, they escaped the crush by climbing the castle walls to watch the festival take shape.

"They've been busy," Adelard noted as Matilda's villagers darted around below. The villagers had spent the previous evening planning a meticulous layout for their displays. Fire pits were dug, tents erected and long tables set up to display the villagers' wares. The aroma of exotic foods filled the air and bolts of colourful fabric were hung around as makeshift banners, adding even more life to the bustling festival.

Eager to capitalise on the swell of potential customers, Bristol's townsfolk also set up stalls in the castle courtyard. There were so many that the Earl's steward opened up the outer courtyard for additional stalls. It was the biggest festival John had ever seen.

The Holford villagers were in their element, each knowing the specific role they had to play.

"That's Matilda's protégé," John told Adelard, pointing out the shaggy-haired boy who ran around in a frenzy, shouting orders to ensure that everything was just right.

"Amazing to see such respect for one so young."

Adelard was right. William was obeyed instantly, mixing Holford and Bristol stalls to create specific zones dedicated to particular crafts and increase the transfer of knowledge.

An enormous crowd had gathered in the castle courtyards by the time Matilda was finally escorted from the dungeon. Guilty or not, she was responsible for the spontaneous festival which awarded her instant celebrity. She was greeted with ear-splitting yells from the crowd as she was marched onto the makeshift stage, a conflicting mix of mocking jeers and adoring cheers. The guards elected to leave Matilda's arms and feet shackled, though it didn't seem to bother her in the slightest. She just stood on the stage soaking in the crowd's mixed energy while waiting for the nobles to arrive.

The doors of the castle keep finally opened, prompting even more noise from the crowd. The Earl and his wife led the way. They were dressed in surprisingly simple clothes which looked just like those of their subjects, though each garment was crafted with incredible care and still using the finest materials. Behind them came the Baron and the Bishop. Baron Walter revelled at the size of the crowd and the good favour of his Earl. Godfrey was the complete opposite, surly and withdrawn. His eyes widened as the full scale of the audience became apparent.

The nobles made their way back onto the stage and settled on their bench while the Earl called the crowd to silence.

"Good morning and welcome!" The crowd erupted. "I can already tell that today promises to be a most interesting affair. But first, a reminder of the serious reason for today's proceedings. Bishop Godfrey?"

Godfrey sprang up enthusiastically.

"My dear flock, I am burdened to reiterate the charges faced by this woman that stands before us." Elements of the crowd booed and one particularly bold man yelled at Godfrey to get on with the festival. "She showed extreme luck in unearthing her treasure and her anatomy lessons were filled with dubious contradictions of the widely accepted medical humours."

"Rich coming from the walking contradiction himself," Adelard muttered to John.

"Do not let her silver and feasts blind you to her wickedness. She is a dangerous woman and wishes to guide you down a treacherous path. A path of sin. Toying with an animal as you butcher it could be called excessive or wasteful. But to do the same with the still-warm corpse of a fellow human is a crime against God himself."

With that Godfrey finally succeeded in sobering the crowd. A small number of particularly pious quietly exited the castle as Godfrey took his seat.

"Matilda? Anything to say?" Earl Robert asked.

Matilda walked slowly to the front of the stage. Some onlookers hurled abuse but most of the crowd stood deathly silent, ready to hang off her every word.

"There is always something scary about the unknown, the new or the unusual. We've all felt it as children, scared of the depths of an unexplored forest or the flame of a blacksmith's forge. Only as we grew did we discover paths to beautiful forest glades or appreciate the awe-inspiring utility of the forge's fire.

"The Bishop has made serious allegations but you saw yesterday how I only wish to heal. Today you will see firsthand that my gifts have nothing to do with sorcery or wickedness. Is the blacksmith a sorcerer for hardening metal by quenching with oil? Is the brewer a warlock for turning barley into beer or a midwife a witch for guiding new life safely into the world? I think not.

"You will see that there is nothing special about the knowledge I have gifted. Anyone can do it. Many of you have already seen the scale of what is on display today. Surely keeping track of every single project would be too much for any one mind to follow, even for the most powerful of sorcerers. I assure you that I won't be in a dark corner whispering incantations or casting spells."

This earnt scattered laughter from the crowd.

"I intend to spend the day in the company of our esteemed hosts, explaining how each innovation works. I'm sure that the holy presence of the Bishop will only further reduce any chance of wickedness.

"Which leaves the rest of you to enjoy the day free from their supervision. Embrace the unknown and try to learn something new. But most of all, enjoy!"

There was a rush as villagers raced back to their stalls and others dashed off to see what was on offer. The festival was suddenly in full swing. The air came alive with unusual music and the cries of excited children.

John and Adelard pushed against the streaming crowd and back towards the stage.

"What are you doing here?" Godfrey snarled.

"I wanted to introduce Adelard to Matilda," John said with more confidence than he felt.

"Why would she want to meet some lousy monk?" Godfrey sniped, only to be cut off by Matilda.

"Adelard!? This is *the* Adelard of Bath?"

Everyone but John was surprised by her enthusiasm.

"Yes, my lady," Adelard replied with a bemused smile.

"As salam alaykum," Matilda said with a bow. "It's an honour to meet you. You'll be pleased to know that your work on Arabic numbers greatly influenced English science and your translation of Euclid's Elements was the oldest to survive to my time."

Adelard looked genuinely touched.

"I didn't realise we had such notable thinkers in our midst," Earl Robert said. "Please brother Adelard, you and your friend must join us."

"Well," Matilda said excitedly, "what would you like to see first?"

The Redhead led the Earl, his wife, the Baron, Godfrey and Peter around the stalls. Everyone hung off her every word. Eager to get the same experience of the festivities as his subjects, the Earl ordered his knights and retainers to follow behind at a specified distance. They were visibly uncomfortable at keeping so far from those they were sworn to protect.

It turned out that the Earl wanted to understand everything and had a flood of questions for both Matilda and his subjects. John found it comical to see the Earl, dressed in his peasant clothes, comparing the size of local pumpkins to the larger ones grown in Holford. The commonfolk shared his amusement but, despite stifled giggles, John marvelled that they all left with an increased respect for their relatable leader.

The Bishop was furious that the Earl was so engaged and that the event was going so well. And yet he too couldn't resist being drawn in by what Matilda was saying. John and Adelard shared the sentiment. A chance to finally understand the Book's contents, directly from the source.

Matilda led them around the yard, introducing villagers and their projects. Matilda humanised each of the stallholders, emphasising the sheer effort that went into each project and the unique contributions that each person had made. She served as a bridge between the vastly different worlds of the Earl and the commoners, drawing the conversation along and making the commonfolk feel comfortable talking in his presence. A masterful decision, this only further emphasised that the villagers had done the work themselves and that Matilda was merely a guiding hand.

Matilda was a gracious host, taking the time to answer all questions, even if they had already been asked before. She also engaged with stallholders from beyond her village, praising their own craftsmanship and telling the nobles the natural philosophies behind how a particular bread was made or why a wooden axe handle returned less shock when shaped a certain way. She tactfully explained what could be done to improve various wares and there wasn't a single stall that didn't buzz with excitement as the group left for the next tantalising display.

At midday the party returned to the stage where a long table had been prepared for the nobles. A decadent array of dishes was spread along the table, a combination of Matilda's culinary introductions and the finest local fares. Matilda called upon William's youngest sister to exhibit the exotic uncooked plants used to make each dish. Matilda described the distant lands of their origin before getting each cook to personally introduce their dishes.

The nobles gushed praise, declaring each delicacy more marvellous than the one before. Some lit the tongue on fire while others made it sing.

"No more!" Earl Robert cried in mock distress. "I cannot take another bite. This food is more than fit for a king. I swear, my father will have my head if he learns that he missed such brilliance!"

Matilda complied and instead summoned some Holford performers onto the stage to perform music for the assembled crowd using their strange instruments. John marvelled at their playing. The instruments looked familiar but the sounds were completely ethereal.

At the insistence of her villagers, Matilda herself took up an instrument and, despite her shackles and burned hand, joined in a handful of songs. She started with a traditional piece that transported John back to the fireplace in his parents' hall before transitioning to an energetic number that invoked images of running through a forest. The music was so eclectic and unusual that members of the crowd gasped at its quick twists and turns, bursting into cheers when it came to an abrupt end.

"And on that note," Matilda called over the applause, "I think it's time we returned to the festivities."

She urged the crowd away and directed her fellow performers to play another lively jig to reenergise the nobles, who still looked comatose from their meal.

Fortunately, the afternoon proved to be even more interactive.

Matilda first took them to a makeshift archery range where attendees compared traditional longbows to the strangest bow John had ever seen.

"It's called a recurve bow," Matilda explained. "Easier to transport than a longbow and the power can be adjusted with different limbs."

She made each noble have a shot. Earl Robert and Baron Walter proved the most competent, though Adelard was surprisingly close. John's first attempt missed altogether but Godfrey's frail arms struggled to draw the bow at all.

The group followed Matilda to a giant metal sphere which looked to John like the eye of some enormous cyclops. They each clambered inside as Matilda told them how she had journeyed from the future and lost her partner.

Next, Matilda led them to a large loom, more complicated than any John had ever seen before.

"Come my lady," Matilda urged the Earl's wife, who had kept to herself all day despite showing keen interest in the developments. "Feel this cloth. Have you ever seen a weave so fine?"

"Goodness no," she said in awe as she marvelled at the patterns William's mother had managed to create. "It's so delicate. And woven directly into the fabric."

"Come," Matilda prompted. "Have Emma show you how it works."

William's mother led the Earl's wife around to the loom and in no time, she was creating her own brilliantly coloured patterns.

"Good lord Matilda," Earl Robert remarked. "She's a natural. And I've never seen her engage so quickly. You have a real talent."

"It's no talent my lord, merely courteous treatment. I've been watching as we traipse from stall to stall, she's much shrewder than she's given credit."

Earl Robert was pleased with Matilda's appraisal of his wife, looking at her in a new light before walking to the blacksmith stall next door. Baron Walter gave her a wordless nod of approval.

As the day progressed, it became clear that the Earl clearly saw the economic and societal benefit of Matilda's inventions. Still, Godfrey tried at every turn to convince Earl Robert that the tools and techniques weren't sanctioned by the Church and wove all sorts of fanciful stories about how the creations could corrupt.

"Who knows what evil could be concocted with this device," he said as Holford's priest demonstrated his printing press. "Giving commoners access to the written word is a recipe for depravity."

"Come now Godfrey," Matilda said, as though she were talking to a petulant child. "Even you can't deny the marvel of a device that could print hundreds of bibles in only a handful of years. Surely that is a machine that can do the Lord's work?"

Godfrey reluctantly approached the press and the Holford priest delicately showed his superior how the device worked.

"Just rearrange the letters, like so. Then turn that wheel."

Godfrey spun the press down, giving it an extra squeeze for good measure.

"There you have it," Matilda said as she handed the page to the Bishop. "Page one of the Godfrey Bible."

Godfrey beamed despite himself and rushed to show Peter.

"A little smeared," Matilda whispered to Adelard as they moved on. "Amateur!"

John marvelled at her bravado.

Dusk had just started to fall when Matilda called the group to a halt. They were all weary but the Earl's enthusiasm remained.

"My lord," their red-haired guide said. "I think it would be wise if we considered calling the festivities to a close soon."

"But there's still at least a quarter of the stalls left to go."

"I know, but your party looks exhausted. There is only so much a mind can absorb in a single day."

"Very well," the Earl said begrudgingly.

"We could," Matilda continued immediately, "resume the last of the tour tomorrow, before you announce your verdict."

"That would be good…"

"And although it has been a big day of revelry, why not treat your subjects to another feast. There's already plenty of food."

Earl Robert paused in thought.

"Bah, why not?!" he cried, summoning his steward. "Bring more ale and pigs, the crowd is even larger than yesterday."

Hearing of another free feed breathed a second wind into the crowd and they swarmed in to help set up. Matilda's musicians mounted the stage once more and the party was soon back in full swing. Matilda sat on the stage with the nobles, discussing the day's events and answering their many questions.

When darkness had fully settled in she surprised them all by withdrawing one final wonder.

"It's called a telescope. A pair of lenses that bend light to make distant objects look much closer. Here, look at the moon."

"Amazing," the Earl whispered. "Truly amazing! Look at all of those pockmarks! What I would've given for one of these on the battlefield."

"That's one use for them. But look, we can find the planets. Mars. Saturn. The same principle can be used to make impossibly small objects appear bigger. To learn about the body and disease."

"I need one," the Earl insisted as he peered into the device once more. "Why haven't I met the craftsman responsible for *this* marvel?"

"He's unfortunately no longer with us," Matilda replied mournfully. "It was his body that I was dissecting the night Godfrey abducted me. This is the problem with my knowledge being held by so few."

Earl Robert dolefully handed the telescope to the next in line.

Adelard, always obsessed with the night sky, was similarly amazed by the device.

"You were right about the world being round," Matilda whispered to him.

When Adelard was finally done, Matilda invited the crowd to follow the nobles. One by one they came onto the stage to peer up at planets in the clear night sky. John savoured the unique sight of the commoners joining the rich, all having eaten their fill and enjoyed the same entertainment.

The music eventually stopped and the musicians summoned Matilda. Everyone expected her to pick up an instrument once again but this time she merely stood in the centre of the stage. She nodded to her musicians and they started a haunting tune that sent a shiver down John's spine. And then Matilda started to sing.

The lyrics were foreign but the raw emotion of the song wasn't lost on a single member of the crowd. Matilda sang like a wounded swan, every word dripping with sorrow. There wasn't a dry eye in sight by the time the last note quivered from her mouth. Not even Matilda's.

A deathly silence fell over the crowd as they processed the emotion of her song. With the same tact he had shown since his raid on Matilda's mill, Godfrey chose that moment to remind the Earl that he had promised three nights of imprisonment.

"Very well," he said heavily as he stood to address his people. "My loyal subjects, today has been a day of wonders. Truly. But a young woman's life hangs in the balance. Matilda will return to the dungeon for the night and I will weigh the evidence I have seen. Tomorrow morning, I will share my judgement."

The Earl's words cut through Matilda's trance and incensed the crowd. In an instant, the good will of the food and drink was shattered and the crowd erupted into boos and profanity.

Godfrey tried to order silence which only increased the heckling. Fights broke out among the crowd.

"If I may?" Matilda asked gently.

The Earl gestured her forward.

"My friends. Please, be calm." The crowd stilled. "I thank you all for being here today. For your open minds and, especially my neighbours from Holford, for your open hearts. Savour today, for we can never truly know what will come tomorrow. Enjoy the music, company and plentiful food while you can. I will see you all in the morning."

With that, Matilda allowed herself to be led away by the guards. With Adelard's encouragement, John insisted on following and was joined by William. Godfrey voiced his protests once more though the Earl peevishly waved him away.

"I thought you priests believed in compassion. Let them accompany her on this final night."

The Bishop stormed off and Robert continued quietly, "Keep a close eye on her. I don't trust that man, he's not finished yet."

The pair followed Matilda into the dungeon, standing guard outside her door and listening as the merriment continued outside.

Yet another gift from the future.

CHAPTER FORTY-ONE
28 September 1124

William was woken by a commotion outside the dungeon. The Earl's jailor grumbled as he trudged up the tight spiral staircase, flicking through his ring of heavy iron keys as he went. Having enjoyed the previous evening's festivities a little too much, each clang reverberated through William's head.

"Some guards we are," the Young Priest noted sleepily, pushing himself up from the floor to stretch his stiff legs. He held out a hand to assist William. "What's all the racket?"

William flinched at the priest's offhand comment. It wasn't the first time he'd let Matilda down by falling asleep.

"I'm not sure," William replied as he accepted the outstretched hand. "Perhaps the crowd didn't get enough of Matilda last night?"

Upstairs, the screech of rusty hinges signalled that the jailor had found the right key and a flurry of footsteps echoed down the stairs. Anticipating trouble from the Bishop, William was looking around for a weapon when Elizabeth burst into the dungeon.

"Willy! You missed such an amazing party! It was better than Matilda's mill. And Rachel's wedding. No offence," she called over her shoulder.

Margery burst into the hallway, followed by a waddling Rachel.

"None taken," Rachel said as she manoeuvred her stomach around the tight staircase.

"The whole family's here?" William asked incredulously.

"We sure are," Elizabeth replied. "Baron Walter said the Earl has practically sided with Matilda and we can take her up to the castle walls to celebrate. He even sent along a breakfast basket. It's upstairs with Ma."

"The Bishop's men will be watching," Margery added, "but at least we'll get some time away from the masses. A little more like being back at Holford."

"Yeah, but on top of a castle!" Elizabeth exclaimed. "When have we ever done that before?"

The jailor shuffled back down the stairs and clanked through his keys to open Matilda's cell. Elizabeth barged in and tackled the Foreigner, prompting a stream of sleepy obscenities.

"Come on Tilda!" Elizabeth cried, dragging the bleary-eyed time traveller out and up the spiral staircase. Rachel groaned at the prospect of climbing back up the stairs.

They all rushed outside where Ma and Pa waited patiently. The Young Priest led them above the castle gate which was flanked by a pair of towers. They climbed another spiral staircase and exited onto the ramparts where they could watch Bristol wake. The Baron had provided an assortment of leftovers from the previous day's feast and a bottle of fine wine.

William sensed that Matilda was nervous. She picked at her food and a slightly vacant look betrayed that her mind was elsewhere.

Matilda's ears pricked up when Margery recounted William's frantic return to Holford.

"I was finally asleep after tidying the mill all day when suddenly William's back and calling for help at the top of his lungs. He didn't care who he asked, he just ran from house to house beating on doors and calling for assistance."

"Seriously?" Matilda asked.

"Bloody William," Elizabeth chimed in, "who we hadn't seen since the fire, running through Holford like some crazed demon."

"Hey!" William protested. "Watch it! They'll put me on trial too."

Margery continued, "The whole village gathered in the square and tried to calm our poor brother. He'd travelled throughout the night and was absolutely haggard but blurted out his story. Following the Bishop, the Baron's intervention, the Earl's summons. The excitement sent a buzz through Holford but everyone was weary after yet another mill fire…"

"It is becoming a bit of a habit," Matilda admitted.

"…so we agreed to get a few extra hours of rest before coming to your rescue. It took both Ralph *and* Matthew to convince William that he needed sleep. Even then, he was one of the first people up.

"Everyone got involved the next morning, packing anything we could to aid your rescue. Well, almost everyone. Martin's grudge is still pretty strong."

"He loathes you," Rachel interjected softly.

"That's right!" Matilda cried. "Rachel! What are you doing here? Where's Alan?"

Rachel looked down at her hands.

"I missed William's entire return. I was awake, the baby had been kicking my bladder all night. But Alan insisted that there'd been enough evening excitement in Holford and locked me indoors. I was relieved that my brother was alright, as surprising as that might seem. But I obeyed my husband and went back to bed.

"The whole village was abuzz in the morning but I was trapped, not even allowed outside to gather vegetables. Alan made me sit inside, the windows shuttered and door barred. I realised that I couldn't take it. That I shouldn't take it. I strode to the door and wrenched it open.

"I've never seen Alan so mad. It was scary. He commanded that I return to my place by the fire. He looked so serious. Too serious. I couldn't help it. I laughed.

"It was uncontrollable. The final step to breaking Alan's spell over me. I felt free. So I left. I just got up and left. Something inside me snapped and I just didn't care anymore. It was worth it just to see his face. That instant when he tried to fathom what was going on. How anyone could dare to defy him. Oh that was sweet."

"Didn't he try to stop you?" Matilda asked.

"He didn't really have time. I just closed the door and left. Didn't even bother to take clothes. By the time he came outside I was already next to Pa in the wagon and we were on our way. I did risk a glance over my shoulder. Alan stood there yelling until he realised we weren't coming back. He looked like an abandoned puppy. It was so sweet."

"Good for you!" Matilda applauded. "It's not easy to leave."

"It's really not. But for that I should thank you. And apologise. You opened my eyes, that night at the mill. I didn't want to admit it but, ever since, I saw Alan's bullying for what it truly was. I got there eventually."

Matilda got up and gave Rachel a warm hug. Seeing the former enemies embrace felt odd to William. But nice.

The family enjoyed some lighter conversation but were eventually interrupted by the Baron and Sir Phillip.

"It looks like you're all having fun," Baron Walter called up from the castle gate. "May we join you?"

The pair clambered up the gate tower and joined the family's meal.

Baron Walter was in a particularly good mood. "I knew you'd worked wonders Matilda but I never thought you'd achieved so much. The Earl is most pleased. He's all but guaranteed to bring your case to the King. Godfrey's seething!"

The Baron did a little jig.

"Patience," Sir Phillip advised. "Don't count your chicks before they've hatched."

"Bah! You heard Robert. We're going to London!"

Sir Phillip shook his head and laughed, helping himself to dried fruit and shifting the conversation to Holford's future.

Baron Walter was on his third mug of wine when they heard a commotion coming from the town. They peered through the crenellations and saw a large crowd thronging towards the castle. Godfrey strode at its head.

As they drew nearer, William saw a scattering of priests and monks in the vanguard, mingled amongst commoners carrying prayer beads and crosses. Further back, several townsfolk carried torches and a group of men bore the deconstructed components for a second pyre.

Seeing Matilda on the wall, Godfrey called his mob to a halt.

"Ho, Bishop!" the Baron cried out jovially. "You're a little early. The Earl is still resting."

The Bishop wasn't amused. "We're here for the Foreigner. Hand her over to me, you oafish boar."

"You're getting a little ahead of yourself Godfrey. The Earl has yet to pass his judgement."

"Bring her down to me. At once!"

"I won't be doing that. We agreed that Robert would decide whether she sees the King. You can't rescind now."

"Who are you to obstruct the Church!?" Godfrey shrieked. "Bring her to me!"

The Bishop's final refrain was directed at his mob of followers. Led by the youngest priests, the fervent crowd heeded their Bishop's command and streamed into the castle.

Hesitant to lay hands on clergymen, the stunned gatehouse guards let the mob in unimpeded.

Sir Phillip swore. "They'll crucify her. Block the doors!"

He and Baron Walter each ran to a gatehouse tower and barricaded the doors. The family stood rooted in disbelief but Matilda summoned them and spoke urgently.

"This seems unlikely to end well. I don't know who but someone is going to get hurt. Just do what they say and keep each other safe."

Elizabeth trembled.

"William, you've been with me every step of the way. My right-hand man. You know my mission better than anyone. Promise that you'll make sure Holford keeps going. No matter what."

"But…" William tried to object.

"No matter what," Matilda insisted.

William gave a solemn nod.

"And John. We've only recently met but you've shown kindness, compassion and an awareness of *why* I'm trying to teach. Can you work with William to ensure the lessons are put to sound use? To prevent corruption and ensure they're shared for the benefit of *all*?"

"I will," John promised.

"Great. Everyone else, keep up the hard work and make sure word spreads. None of this will be worth it if it remains in the hands of the few. Whatever happens, know that I am truly grateful. You've been my family and have shown greater kindness than I ever deserved. I love you all."

The family mumbled their own thanks but Sir Phillip yelled out as the crowd pushed against the gatehouse door. William and Pa darted over to assist while John ran to help the Baron.

The door lurched as the crowd crashed against the other side. Sir Phillip fought like a demon.

In support from the ground, Godfrey's vile assistant led the mob in a crusader hymn.

"Amarae morti ne tradas nos."

The eerie chant empowered the crowd and their efforts against the door intensified. Godfrey's shrill shrieks cut a sharp soprano over the base of the mob's chanting to create an utterly unique war song.

Their melody was punctuated by a crash. Looking back to the other gate tower, William saw John and the Baron overrun. John lay curled on the ground being kicked by priests while others flooded towards Matilda. Pa rushed to protect Rachel but was clubbed over the head by a cross-wielding commoner. William cried out but his door also breached and he was shoved hard against the ramparts.

William caught glimpses of red hair in the chaos that followed, watching in horror as Matilda successfully downed several assailants before being overcome. Godfrey's mob let out an almighty cheer as Matilda was baled up and dragged back down the gate tower.

It was William's turn to have his hands bound. His family and Sir Phillip received the same treatment before being marched down to the castle courtyard. Only Baron Walter's hands remained free, though he too received an unfriendly escort.

The new pyre was already being assembled beside the stage when they were jostled into place and a gagged Matilda was quickly tied to its central beam. Her wrists were rubbed raw from her determined struggle for freedom.

A large crowd formed around the stage and a ring of priests served the role of guards. People streamed in from Bristol as word of the Bishop's intervention spread. William's neighbours shouted their protests, prompting scuffles with Godfrey's devout followers.

A hush fell over the crowd as Earl Robert and his wife emerged from the keep, dressed in their finest clothes and accompanied by a retinue of knights in similarly resplendent garb. Large flowing cloaks made of the finest fabric and trimmed with rare furs. Expensive leather boots. Exceptionally well-crafted swords. Such finery normally commanded respect and William's hopes rose.

"Godfrey!" the Earl bellowed as he marched towards the pyre. "What is the meaning of this!?"

"This woman is evil!" Godfrey answered. "A threat to Christianity itself. You have entertained her wickedness long enough!"

"This wasn't our deal, Bishop," the Earl shot with venom. "This is not your decision to make."

"On the contrary, Robert. I discussed the matter throughout the night with holy men from here in Bristol and further afield. We concluded that this woman has used sorcery to manipulate the world around her. To beguile a hapless village after a boy stumbled upon her lair. The crowd before us too. Only through prayer and the cleansing power of flame can her wickedness truly be purged."

Godfrey's mob continued to build the pyre around Matilda as their superiors debated.

"Stop!" the Earl ordered desperately to both Godfrey and his minions. He drew his sword and his knights followed suit.

"Earl Robert," Godfrey chided, "you'd dare to bear arms against the Church? See sense, I implore you. Consider the costs. If we are wrong, a single innocent soul will be sent to the Maker, who would surely understand our position and grant her mercy. But if we are right, how many must go to the Devil before our mistake is rectified?"

The crowd gave a collective shiver. Even the Earl looked troubled.

"What makes you think you can just do this?" he asked. "In the heart of my own castle?"

"You need to relearn your place, Bastard," Godfrey spat. "Religion transcends royalty."

That angered the Earl.

"My father is King Henry, anointed by God. You can debate whether he lies beneath the Holy Father but he certainly outranks you."

Godfrey's smirk disappeared.

"Look around you, stupid man," the Earl continued, waving his sword at the festival stalls. "Everything we've seen over the past days. Surely that demonstrates her utility. Her value to the common good."

"There is more to life than copper, pumpkins and pretty cloth. Such petty things are worthless in the Lord's eyes. A waste of our time."

"Hypocrite!" came a call from over William's shoulder. He was further shocked when John continued. "If they're so worthless, then why did you waste so much time trying to decipher the Foreigner's Book!?"

"I never," Godfrey denied unconvincingly.

"Yes you did," Adelard confirmed as John pointed to his confiscated bag and a nearby priest withdrew the tattered second half of Matilda's tome. "Plate armour with the blacksmith and countless days in your library. Every soul in Bath has heard whispers of your ungodly experiments on rats in your chambers."

The Earl took the offensive. "Look Bishop, not even your holy brothers agree with you."

"Fools!" Godfrey cried. "This is the Lord's way. It's what he would want!"

"No it's not," the blue-eyed priest from Nether Stowey cried. "The Lord I know teaches of compassion and mercy. Of care for thy neighbour and forgiveness. Not murder."

Father Daniel agreed too, adding his voice to those condemning the Bishop.

Seeing the priests divided confused the crowd. Even clergymen in Godfrey's protective ring looked puzzled. Holford villagers led other members of the crowd to add their calls for justice and grace.

The tide turned, drowning out the cries of Godfrey's followers and the Bishop found himself at the centre of a hostile baying mob once again. He spun around searching for support but found only his Assistant and a handful of devout faithful.

He stopped spinning and looked at the Earl. "You'll regret this Robert," he snarled. "You dabble in arenas you cannot even begin to comprehend and set your father's kingdom on a dangerous path. The Pope has shown little patience for the petty politics of Man. He castrated the Holy Roman Emperor with the Concordat of Worms. Now that is your future too."

With a malicious smirk, Godfrey tossed his torch onto the pyre before pushing his way through the crowd. Flames sprung up instantly.

William yanked himself away from the priest restraining him and urged anyone nearby to free his wrists. The Earl and his men barged through the crowd and rushed towards Matilda but the flames were already at shoulder height when they arrived. The Earl tore off his expensive cloak and beat at the fire while others hauled heavy timbers out of the way.

William watched Matilda's struggle intensify, her gagged cries muffled but eyes screaming with desperation. He couldn't look away and sprinted towards her the instant a monk finally severed his ropes. He hurled himself into the fire, coughing amongst the smoke and burning his hands as he heaved at large logs with the Earl's knights. Matilda also suffered from the smoke and, through weeping eyes, William saw her consciousness slowly slip away.

Time lost all meaning as he fought towards her. Eventually the smoke cleared and the flames shrunk. William felt helpless as he watched a pair of knights cut Matilda down from the beam and gently lay her beside the stage.

Her wrists bled from rope burn and her dress was singed but she was surprisingly untouched by the fire. William remained concerned, for Matilda's medical lessons taught that smoke and heat could cause serious internal damage.

"Careful," he warned as Astrid emerged from the crowd but her knowing nod reassured him.

William hovered as the Midwife tended to their dear mentor, begrudgingly accepting a bucket from Ma for his own injured hands.

The mob crowded in, holding its breath until Matilda gave a ragged cough and pulled herself upright. She wordlessly fought for space but Astrid insistently pushed a cup of water upon her. Matilda coughed and spluttered but consumed increasingly more with each sip.

A wave of relief flowed over William and he looked around at the crowd. Godfrey's fervent followers had been overtaken by concerned onlookers and were nowhere to be seen.

"Where's the Bishop?" William asked the Earl bluntly.

"There's no sign of him. Nor his aide. Their horses are missing so he's undoubtedly bound for London. We'll need to make pursuit."

Taking several deep breaths, Matilda pushed herself to her feet. William and the Earl rushed over to assist.

"Stage," she croaked. "Secure the crowd."

They escorted her onto the Earl's throne, seating her beside his wife. John handed her Astrid's cup of water. The Baron had already assumed his normal perch so William and John took the Bishop's seat while the Earl turned to the crowd.

"Bishop Godfrey has fled and surrendered his prisoner to my custody. I see no arguing that Matilda is a blessing. A gift to the English people. She has demonstrated her ability to dramatically improve the lives of people around her. As such, I declare Matilda a free woman!"

The crowd erupted, ecstatic for a woman that most had only just met. Any opposition was drowned out by cheers and shouts, screams and whistles. It was so loud that William couldn't hear his own cheering.

Tears of relief streamed down Matilda's face and she took a moment to compose herself before gingerly rising to address the crowd. Their cheers stilled instantly as they strained to hear her raspy voice.

"I understand your hesitance in accepting me and my teachings. Change evokes fear. And so, I forgive those involved in this morning's insurrection and ask that they see sense.

"I cannot prove my innocence any more than Godfrey can prove the appearance of angels. However, you've all replicated my lessons which should show there is no need for supernatural powers. Even the Bishop sought to use them for his own gain. What does his hypocrisy say of my innocence? Either my gifts are harmless and to be used to enrich the world. Or they're evil sorcery, making all who seek to use them, including the fallen Bishop, evil dabblers in the arcane arts. It cannot be both.

"No. The true magic is the power of the mind. Man or woman, adult or child. You've all shown the remarkable ability to learn. Harness this and you will achieve acts that can truly be described as magic."

The crowd stared up at the woman in awe. And yet she spoke once more.

"Enough seriousness. Resume the festival!" she added simply, gesturing to the tables and tents that remained from the previous day's festivities.

The crowd erupted and music played. The mob streamed away, many back to the stalls, some towards the stage. The energy of their revelry was even greater than the day before.

"Enjoy this," William heard the Earl say to Matilda, who was rubbing her tender wrists. "Godfrey is a bulldog and I'd bet my castle that he's already planning his audiences in London. So rest and enjoy your victory, you deserve it. But we leave for my father in the morning."

Matilda gave a simple nod. "Let the next step begin."

CHAPTER FORTY-TWO
29 September 1124

Matilda dreamt she was up in the clouds. White and fluffy. Surprisingly dry. Sunlight streamed through gaps between the clouds and wind whipped her hair around as she raced through the air, chasing little Richie and Harry who darted along in front of her. But how were they flying?

Suddenly she was dropping. Trapped in an iron ball that plummeted toward the ground, heating up as it fell and burning her hand. It burst through the sunny clouds and the world went grey and drab. The ground and trees rushed towards her. She ploughed through the branches, bouncing around like a pinball. But she was going too fast…

Matilda jolted awake in a comfortable four-poster bed, surrounded by a mass of pillows. Sunlight streamed through an arrow-slit in the keep wall, illuminating the Earl's guest room with its luxurious carpets and tapestries.

It took a moment to realise where she was and recall everything that had happened over the previous days. She'd been clubbed, burnt, shot and burnt again. A lifetime of injuries, all in a matter of days. It took even longer to accept that she had made it through the whole ordeal. Timothy's death felt like a lifetime ago.

The trauma of the previous day was still painfully fresh. Tied to the pyre, she'd been completely powerless and left to the whims of others. It strangely mirrored her mission which, at the end of the day, also relied on others. Matilda could never stop a solar flare by herself. Not even with Harry's help. It was the people she touched along the way that would make the real difference.

Matilda hadn't slept so well for an entire year. She was surprised to have slept at all. Feeling a stab of pain from her ribs, Matilda thought she could've really used more time in the comfy bed to rest and recover. But time pressure once again threatened her mission. There could be no two weeks of recovery, this time.

The bright beam of sunlight heralded a beautiful day for beginning the next phase of her journey. The journey to London. A step that should've started a whole year earlier.

Better late than never.

Noises outside the door told her that the castle was already awake and in full preparation for the trip. Knowing that her travel companions would be eager to catch up to Godfrey, Matilda tore her pus-crusted wrists from the Earl's crisp sheets and begrudgingly rose from the comfortable bed.

She strolled to the arrow-slit and peered into the courtyard below. Her room faced away from the stage but she heard shouts as an army of workers dismantled her festival. Matilda was relieved that the ordeal was over but already missed the energetic festival atmosphere. With a sigh, she washed her face and collected her satchel before departing to see how she could help.

Matilda wandered through the keep, appreciating the building's militaristic practicality but admiring the minor artistic touches that indicated it housed nobility. It felt strange being suddenly free within her former prison but that didn't prevent her from stopping by the keep's kitchen for a bite to eat. It hurt to swallow with her scorched throat but the kitchen hands fawned over her, insisting that she try their festival-inspired experiments.

The castle courtyard was a hive of activity when Matilda finally emerged from the keep. Bristol townsfolk hurriedly packed up tents and tables. The Holford villagers had already loaded their few remaining goods into the carts and milled around to say their farewells.

An army of attendants fussed over a pack of horses, making sure that they were equipped with everything that their lords might need for the journey to London. Seeing Matilda, an attendant ran over and indicated the horse assigned to her. He offered to load her satchel into the saddlebags but Matilda politely declined. She would be needing it.

Matilda made straight for the Holford villagers who quickly gathered around her, making space at the front for William and his family.

"Good morning!" she called, her voice still hoarse. "I can't thank you all enough for coming to my rescue. I wouldn't be here today if not for your valiant efforts."

The ashes of the pyre smouldered behind them.

"More than that, thanks for your hospitality. For welcoming me into your lives. It has been an absurd year. Busy beyond belief. But you've taken everything in your stride and shown amazing perseverance, adaptability and sense of community. I'll remember it for the rest of my days.

"This isn't goodbye. I will return to Holford and continue what we started. The village has truly become my home and you," she said looking at Ma and Pa, "have become my family. I must pursue the Bishop, to ensure he cannot slander our hard work. I'll seek the King's blessing, along with extra resources for Holford's continued growth. The Council will continue their guidance but keep reminding them that they serve the whole village.

"Please return home and, after a well-deserved rest, dive into your work with even greater energy than before. You've seen the impact your projects can have on your neighbours. And on the world. So keep up the good work and I look forward to seeing how far you have progressed when I return."

Matthew Smith led the villagers in three cheers for Matilda and they swarmed around her to say their farewells. The Council members filed through first. Walt wrung good her hand with his gnarled paws before giving her a rib-crushing hug. Matthew and Ralph complained that they would have too much spare time given the departure of their biggest customer and quiet Astrid gifted Matilda a woven bracelet.

The Holford villagers came next, filing through one by one to say their farewells before joining the convoy for the journey home. Matilda was amazed at how many people she'd gotten to know. It felt so quick but she remembered touching the lives of all but the newest of newcomers. And they hers. She had finally found a place she belonged.

Soon only the family remained. Matilda felt herself getting emotional already.

"Guys, I…just…thank you all so much."

They piled in and gently embraced Matilda as a group.

"Don't you go getting soppy on us now young lady," Ma said with a tearful smile as they broke away. "Don't think there won't be a mountain of chores waiting when you finally return from galivanting around the kingdom."

"Of course," Matilda replied. "I'd be offended by anything less."

"We need to thank you too, dear Matilda," Pa said gruffly. "You've done so much for us. The family. The village. The region.

Words can't express the depths of our gratitude, but you're a smart girl so I'm sure you understand."

Matilda gave a wordless nod.

"How was it sleeping in the keep last night?" Elizabeth asked excitedly. "You're pretty much royalty now right?"

"Not quite," Matilda laughed. "I'll keep an eye out for any eligible princes for you while I'm in London."

Elizabeth melted into a fit of giggles.

Matilda turned to Margery and Rachel.

"I'm sorry for all the disruptions I've caused…"

"Are you kidding?" Margery answered first. "If not for you I would never have met my friends. I would've never learnt how to read. I'd still be a timid little girl, moping around and feeling sorry for myself. If anything, I should apologise to you. I still feel terrible for blabbing to the deaf priest and leading the Bishop to Holford."

"Not at all," Matilda replied with a reassuring smile. "You weren't to know and no *real* harm done in the end. As for your reading, I think it would be best if you looked after this for me. To make sure it re-joins its other half."

Matilda reached into her satchel and withdrew the tattered second half of her bible. She handed it to Margery who stared in awe at the treasure Matilda had just bestowed upon her. And then Matilda was surprised by a sudden embrace from Rachel. The bulge of her belly pushed into Matilda's hip.

"I need to apologise and thank you too," Rachel said emphatically. "We had a rough start and I regret not getting to know you better. But without you I'd still be stuck in a loveless marriage, fearing for myself and my child. Ignore everything I've previously said, I am so glad that you came to our village. Things are headed in a much better direction now."

Matilda didn't know what to say so she just returned the eldest sister's hug. The genuine warmth made her heart sing.

She eventually disengaged and turned to face William. The boy who had started her journey. Who had saved her from the depths of despair. He was no longer a boy, she noted as she saw the man he had become. The events of the previous days looked to have aged him by several years.

"William. I can't even think where to begin."

She paused awkwardly and turned to Ma and Pa.

"I've already caused great disruption to your family and deprived you of so much time with your children, so it hurts me to ask. But I really must."

She took a deep breath.

"Would it be alright if William joined me in London?"

Ma and Pa considered her question and looked at each other before bursting into laughter.

"So formal dear Matilda!" Pa said, clutching his sides. "Of course he's going with you. I don't think anyone could stop him. He's already packed his bag!"

Only then did Matilda notice the bag slung across William's shoulder. She smiled in spite of herself.

"I'll admit that I'm not thrilled to see another child venturing away from the nest," Ma said. "But they've all come back so far, better than when they left. Just promise to take care of him while you're gone. And William, you take care of her too, ok?"

The pair gave Ma sincere nods before exchanging an excited glance.

"Well then," Matilda said, "we should find you a ride."

She spotted the steward and approached him to ask for a spare horse for William.

"I really ought to ask Earl Robert but you need to depart soon… Fine, but it won't be the finest mount."

He strode off toward the stables.

"Does he realise there isn't a single horse in Holford?" William asked.

The family were still laughing when Earl Robert emerged from the keep, deep in discussion with John. Baron Walter and the Earl's wife followed behind. Seeing Matilda, the Earl led them over to her.

"John here has provided invaluable insights into the Bishop and his network of allies in London which should help us navigate any potential schemes. I'd have preferred that John join us in London but he says he's had enough of politics, the Church and the Bishop to last a lifetime. He even went so far to say that he'd prefer a stint in my dungeon than another audience with Godfrey. Point made."

John looked quite proud of himself.

"I'd like to go to Holford, if they'll have me." John told them. "I thought about the promises you asked of William and I yesterday and I would love to start up a school. Godfrey left without saying goodbye so it's fair to say I'm free of any obligations to him. I renounced my vows to the Earl's chaplain this morning."

"A time of big changes," Matilda said. "I've gifted my bible to Margery but I'm sure she would welcome another scholar to help interpret its contents. As for the village's willingness to take you in, do you see any issues Pa?"

"None at all," Pa said with a smile. "A friend of Matilda's is a friend of Holford."

"Very well," the Earl said impatiently. "We'd best be off. There's no telling how quickly the Bishop will arrive in London and I'm loathe to give him time to turn the court against us. Mount up!"

The party of knights and nobles mounted their horses and, juggling broken ribs and burns, Matilda gingerly climbed up into her saddle as well. William struggled with his own burned hands and Elizabeth had to hold onto the reins while Pa boosted him onto the saddle, much to the family's amusement. But in no time, he too sat atop his mount and the party was ready to depart. The family gathered closely around Ma and Pa as they said their final farewell.

"Thanks again, for everything," Matilda called as the party started moving. "Goodbye!"

William's horse had a mind of its own but Matilda rode alongside him and helped keep control. Matilda looked over her shoulder and saw the family standing alone in the castle courtyard. An unfathomable sight only a year earlier. She gave one last wave as she exited the castle gates.

Outside the castle, Bristol's inhabitants lined the streets to catch one final glimpse of the red-haired time traveller. Their cheers started as soon as the procession emerged and continued until they had reached the town's outer limits. Even then, some of Bristol's younger inhabitants ran alongside to keep up with the horses. Matilda flushed with pride.

It wasn't until they were clear of the town and had settled into a steady pace that the magnitude of the departure struck Matilda.

At long last, her mission was underway.

EPILOGUE

3 July 2025

"…And that, Your Excellency, is how the Chronomad finally embarked upon her mission to see the King."

Ris fell silent and watched her rotund host process the conclusion to her tale about the distant past. The rest of his entourage looked bored and disengaged, working away on their computers as they humoured their superior's play at being an amateur historian. Ris felt insignificant in a room full of such powerful people. Standing before the starship's viewport, with the big blue planet as her backdrop, didn't help.

"Wonderful! Truly marvellous!" her host proclaimed with solitary applause. "I've never heard Matilda's arrival told in such detail. With such perspective. And finished just in time for the Chancellor's address. You must promise to finish the rest of the Chronomad's story when we return."

His entourage came to attention and hurriedly prepared for the flight down to Earth's surface. Ignoring Ris, they bundled up the priceless torn Book on display and followed their enormous superior to the landing craft. Powerful people had gathered from across the Galaxy to watch the event responsible for catapulting Humanity into the stars.

The Dawn of The Long Day.

They would gather on Earth's surface and enjoy the solar spectacle amidst an orgy of pomp and gluttony, protected from the charged ionosphere by rudimentary technology that was far beyond anything Matilda could've imagined.

But not Ris. She was a scholar, not a businessman or bureaucrat. She would remain on the starship and watch from space. Not that she minded. It meant more time to admire the planet and would allow her to witness the full magnitude of The Long Day.

Ris stared out from the starship's viewport and into the depths of space. The stars of the Milky Way were denser than she'd expected of the outer galaxy but augmented annotations from her Eyepiece revealed that many of the dotted lights were actually other orbiting spacecraft also awaiting the historical event. The closest star was much bigger than the rest, a particularly bright yellowish-white dwarf. Sol, the source of the event they were all there to see.

Ris was amongst the lucky few selected from the galactic colonies to witness the Event in person. She'd become a leading historian on the period that followed Matilda's arrival, yet it was her first time visiting the Sol system and she'd still never set foot on Earth. She hailed from the inner galactic colonies and the prohibitive costs of the long journey to Sol had always obstructed firsthand studies. She'd hoped that her expertise might one day merit funding to see the Cradle of Humanity and had been pleasantly surprised as the Long Day approached.

Ulrichs from across the Galaxy had flocked back to Earth and each sought a noteworthy historian for their pilgrimage. The Ultra-Rich were akin to the feudal lords that Matilda had tried to topple on her journey back in time. They terraformed planets and owned entire solar systems. It was their actions that now filled the history books and their existence proved the inevitability of human greed and oppression. Power breeds power, plus ever-increasing thirst.

Their mere existence was an insult to Matilda's memory. Yet when an Ulrich had invited Ris to witness the Long Day, she'd found herself unable to decline. She earned her passage by answering the Ulrich's many questions as the multi-day journey unfolded. Her benefactor could have easily achieved the same result with artificial intelligence or using comms arrays but the physical presence of a notable scholar was an antiquated symbol of prestige. Ris found the level of wealth in her lavish quarters aboard the Ulrich's starship to be morally repugnant but who was she to turn down the opportunity? Her host did have a passion for historical truth so surely he couldn't be completely bad.

Looking down at the planet, Ris knew that Earth's Chancellor would be lecturing his wealthy guests on the important role his planet had played as the origin of humanity's spacefaring civilisation, undoubtedly ignorant to the irony of his planet's current dearth of technology. Earth was the capital of a fallen empire but desperately clung to the myth of its glory days. The days of Galileo and Newton. Einstein and Sam. Matilda and William.

Matilda had been Ris' childhood hero, a fellow red-haired woman-born who'd dared to jump into the unknown. Ris confidently argued that no single person had played a larger role in shaping humanity. With the help of William the Explorer and at great personal cost, she'd initiated a chain of events that catapulted civilisation forward.

Beyond only technical gifts from the future, Matilda had unknowingly established the Seeker philosophy. A school of thought that morphed into a quasi-religion, it promoted the pursuit of understanding and personal growth to enhance the freedoms of others. The Seekers directly contradicted the Ulrich way of life and had been persecuted for centuries as a result. But like many other philosophies over humanity's history, suppression had only fuelled its growth and pockets of resistance continued Matilda's benevolent fight across the galaxy. Ris' parents were ardent believers and had taught their daughter in secret. Its illicit nature only increased Ris' excitement to learn more about the time traveller.

And it all began on this pale blue dot.

Ris' Eyepiece flashed a warning that the coronal mass ejection had commenced, meaning that the Long Day would begin in approximately eight minutes. The starship's other lowly inhabitants – crew, assistants, droids – poured into the viewing room and claimed seats around the vacated amphitheatre. Ris tried to claim a seat of her own but familiar faces urged her back to the front.

"Oh great Historian," an engineer mocked, "pray tell, what are we seeing?"

Ris cringed at the sarcastic tone but other cries of genuine interest convinced her back to the front to explain.

"Um, ok. You will all be aware of Matilda, humanity's first Chronomad. She used primitive technology to make the first journey back through time, seeking to advance humanity into a new era. It is common knowledge that a great calamity was the catalyst for her voyage and her goal was to prematurely inject science in the hope that future generations would avoid The Long Day. That is the Event we are about to witness."

Everyone knew what was coming but there was still a swell of excitement from the crowd.

"Matilda's premature demise robbed us of many gifts, but a wisened William took up her torch and illuminated a path out of the Dark Ages. A path to the stars.

"We are left wondering what could have been. How much *more* advanced would we be today if she had managed to impart all that she knew? She didn't share with us the secret to time travel, that is for sure. Deliberately, most scholars agree. While we eventually discovered it ourselves, it was left to us to learn the dangers of manipulating space-time. The Chronomad has left a permanent mark on our time. Literally. Our calendar was defined by the Chronomad's arrival. To her, the Event we'll see today occurred in 2025 rather than 0902.

"We may never know just how much more Matilda may have offered but the fact that we can safely watch the Event proves that her mission was a success. I think she would be ecstatic to see all that we have learnt."

There were murmurs of agreement from the crowd and Ris's Eyepiece went off again.

"It's about to begin," she announced.

A hush fell over the crowd as the amphitheatre lights dimmed. Auroras appeared in the sky around them, surrounding the magnetic shields of the spectating spacecraft and darting across the surface of the blue planet below. Ribbons of light rippled across the planet, first around the poles and then over the entire surface with ever greater intensity.

"The Chronomad was only ten years old when this took place," Ris noted. "See the magnitude of the excitations. Such intensity hadn't been seen for over a century and the magnetic forces wreaked havoc on the simple electronic systems of the Chronomad's time. Evidence suggests that corruption also played a role, with contemporary leaders funnelling funds into endless wars and corporate sponsors rather than essential infrastructure and environmental protection.

"Rudimentary shielding capable of guarding against the Long Day was developed only a century after Matilda's arrival from The World That Was. Additional development in the eight hundred years since guarantees that there won't be a single loss of critical infrastructure today. Instead, the Event can even be harvested as a source of power."

Ris drew her eyes away from the planet and looked up at the other spacecraft, the slipstream of their own magnetic shielding making them look like an array of stationary comets.

"Of course, the other spacecraft watching with us today would've been astounding to Matilda. Even the most basic of them contains technology beyond her wildest dreams."

Ris looked around the room and found her audience enamoured by the spectacle before them. Deciding to enjoy the sight for herself, she wondered what her hero would say if she could see it.

The planet. The starships. The auroras.

A single thought reverberated through her mind.

It was glorious.

Matilda's adventure is just getting started and there are more Chronomads to come...

Reader feedback helps shape my future works and is vital to spreading word about self–published books.

If you've enjoyed Matilda's journey so far (or even if you didn't!), please take a minute to **leave a review online** or **tell a friend.**

For more information about future books, sign up to the mailing list at

www.the-world-that-was.com

THANKS FOR READING!

Fun Facts

I had years of enjoyment researching and writing **The World That Was**. I climbed castle ruins and clambered down Somerset caves. I toured medieval towns and nuclear reactors. I quizzed museum curators and archaeologists. All in the hope of creating a realistic portrayal of 12th Century England.

I scattered historical tidbits throughout the novel, as well as a few pop culture and personal easter eggs. I will leave it to others to identify exactly how many improvements Matilda managed to bring back from the future but here is a list of interesting tidbits hinted at in TWTW.

1. The 1859 Carrington Event is the most intense recorded solar flare to have struck modern society, though it fortunately struck before humanity had become overly reliant on electrical devices. The miners referred to in the novel were working in Rokewood, Australia (mere kilometres away from my childhood home) when the Carrington flare convinced them it was time to resume work despite being the middle of the night.

2. Travelling back in time is theoretically possible under Einstein's theory of general relativity. A wormhole can be created by deforming space-time to enable the travel from one time or place to another, though in the theory it appears only possible to travel back to the time the wormhole was first created.

3. Matilda's cave is real and known as Howell Cavern. There are very few caves around the Quantock hills but I selected this one for its close proximity to other key locations. I ended up consulting with a pair of local spelunkers – thanks Nick and Peter! – who had mapped out the cave system over years of exploring. The owner of the farm where the cave is located kindly let my brother and I venture underground to explore and even joined us!

4. The disruptive succession crisis caused by King Henry I's death was called The Anarchy. Matilda could've been sent back earlier to prevent Henry's son from dying in the White Ship accident in 1120 but the Anarchy opened people's minds, albeit temporarily, to the leadership of

Henry's daughter Maude (also known as Matilda). Chronomad Matilda hoped to kindle this fleeting empowerment of women to build a lasting period of gender equality.

5. King Henry really did depart the British Isles to quash a rebellion in Normandy in late 1123. His bastard son Robert, Earl of Bristol, also travelled with him.

6. Holford is a quaint village nestled in the foothills of the Quantock hills. It was originally a Roman settlement and by the time of the Domesday Book had grown to include around 35 inhabitants, three plough-teams (two belonged to the lord) and a mill. Holford eventually grew to have two mills and was well known for its pottery.

7. Bishop Godfrey is a real historical figure! He was probably born around 1060 and was consecrated as Bishop of Bath on 26 August 1123 after accompanying King Henry's new wife to London from Leuven in Belgium. Relatively little is known about Godfrey, though it is written that he had land disputes with King Henry. Godfrey died on 16 August 1135 and was buried in the Bath Cathedral. I visited the cathedral in 2022 to offer an apology for casting Godfrey as my book's antagonist but centuries of reconstruction meant that the precise location of Godfrey's tomb had been lost.

8. Stowey Castle was a motte and bailey-style castle in Nether Stowey, Somerset. A stone keep had been constructed not long before Matilda's arrival but only the foundations remain today after the keep was reportedly dismantled as punishment for an uprising in the 1400s. My brother and I clambered over the castle's remaining mottes to get a feel for the scale and location of the castle. I later engaged with an archaeologist from the University of Bristol as I tried to accurately recreate the castle for inclusion on an early iteration of TWTW's cover design.

9. Baron Walter de Candos was the lord of Stowey Castle at the time of Matilda's visit. He was born in 1085, so was 38 when Matilda helped remove his ring. His mother Isabel had inherited Stowey Castle from her father Alfred, who was named as the lord of Nether Stowey in the Domesday book. Also, Matilda's trick for removing stuck rings works for real!

10. John's family hail from the village of Babcary in southeast Somerset. It is unclear if the mound of Wimble Toot was a burial mound or an old castle motte so I decided to interpret it as a simple castle with a small wooden keep that would've completely decayed by our time.

11. Silk existed in Europe around the time of Matilda's visit but was very rare and expensive. Mama would've obtained her small handkerchief when her husband was still working as Holford's miller.

12. The construction of Bath Cathedral was started by Godfrey's predecessor, Bishop John of Tours. Bishop John was originally based in Wells but moved his diocese to Bath and started construction of the new cathedral. He was known as "a very skilled doctor, not in theoretical knowledge, but in practice," and was the personal physician to William the Conqueror. John died suddenly when the cathedral was only partially constructed, leaving Godfrey to complete the construction after taking over as Bishop of Bath.

13. Plate armour was not widely used in Europe until the late 13th Century. In Godfrey's time, chainmail remained the predominant form of armour so the promise of more protective plate would've proven tempting for the Bishop.

14. Adelard of Bath is another historical personality. He was a widely travelled monk, noted to have journeyed across Europe and to the Holy Land. Adelard was a natural philosopher (a name for early scientists), writing early works on astronomy and alchemy. He is credited as one of the first people to introduce Arabic numerals to Europe and translated important scientific texts from Arabic to Latin, including Euclid's Elements.

15. There were Jewish communities across medieval England, with Somerset's larger communities being in Bristol and Wells. With usury – the charging of interest on financial loans – being considered a Christian sin at the time, it is plausible that Godfrey and his predecessor would have turned to Jewish lenders to help finance the Bath cathedral.

16. Though buttons had been used decoratively for millennia, fastening applications were limited until the introduction of buttonholes in Germany around the 13th Century.

17. Medieval Bath used to be surrounded by a city wall with four gates. When I toured the city with local historian Steve Pratt, he had copies of the oldest available maps and pointed out that John would've needed to escape from a different gate in order to subsequently flee towards Bristol. This really highlighted the benefits of seeing a place in the flesh, with an expert, rather than just relying on Google Maps!

18. Edric's copper mine is the Buckingham Mine in Doddington. It is unclear when the mine started but it was sometime before 1712. The same spelunkers who helped me discover Matilda's cave had also explored the Doddington mine and shared both their insights and their photos of its water-logged adits.

19. Earl Robert was the bastard son of King Henry and would've been around 34 at the time of Matilda's arrival. Despite his illegitimacy, he remained in his father's good graces and was made the first Earl of Gloucester after the death of his cousin, sometime around 1121. He was reportedly praised for his wisdom and, after his father died, he supported his sister's claim to the throne rather than seeking to rule himself.

20. The Beau Street Hoard was discovered in Bath in 2007 during the construction of a new pool for a Bath hotel. It has been estimated to contain 17,500 silver roman coins, fused together into a large block. The hoard is on display in the Roman Baths museum.

21. Little remains of Bristol castle but there are several maps and illustrations of its design, which hugged the River Avon. When I visited the site in 2022, the remnants of the castle's great hall had been converted into a café (which conveniently let me in to take photos despite having closed for the day!).

ACKNOWLEDGEMENTS

This book was in development for over a decade, my pen first hitting paper as I sailed down the Mekong on a rickety boat propelled by a truck engine roaring away in the background. It would not have been possible without the help of a few very special people, to who I give my sincerest thanks. They include:

- ∞ **Mum and Dad,** you've patiently listened since the very first plot outline
- ∞ **My dear Jubles**, you lost your partner for many a weekend. May this all prove to be worth it!
- ∞ **Mat and Phil**, for an inspiring weekend in Stockholm that catapulted this story to completion
- ∞ **Matt**, you helped tame the hummingbird
- ∞ **My dear test readers (Dan, Luke, Sue, Ben, Sam, Clancy, Dani, Timmy, Sara, Em, Matt, Oma and those already thanked)**, your feedback has been invaluable! You each provided some unique insight that helped reshape the book, from highlighting annoying character quirks to suggesting major plot revisions. I truly can't thank you enough!
- ∞ **Nick and Peter**, for helping me to vicariously explore Matilda's cave and the Doddington mine
- ∞ **Steve Pratt,** for a most memorable tour around Bath's remaining medieval wonders
- ∞ **Brian,** your emails over the years have provided great motivation. I will never misuse the word 'voyage' again
- ∞ **Hari,** your enthusiastic engagement alone made the whole writing process worthwhile

Jay Pelchen started his working life in a chocolate shop.

At university he studied engineering and physics, though friends always said he liked reading too much to be a 'real' engineer.

He has spent his professional career working to stop the proliferation of nuclear weapons, first as an analyst for Australia's Department of Defence and then at the global nuclear watchdog.

The World That Was is his first novel.

Jay lives in Vienna, Austria with his wife Joti.

Thanks for reading right to the end!